BELOVED
ENEMY

Katherine Sinclair

BELOVED ENEMY

PIATKUS

Copyright © 1978 by Amanda York

This edition first published in
Great Britain in 1994 by
Judy Piatkus (Publishers) Ltd of
5 Windmill Street, London W1

**The moral right of the author
has been asserted**

*A catalogue record for this book is available
from the British Library*

ISBN 0-7499-0237-X

Printed and bound in Great Britain by
Bookcraft Ltd, Midsomer Norton, Avon

PROLOGUE

Kingsburch, 1793

The towers of Kingsburch seemed to be waiting, hovering on the edge of the bleak cliff above the restless sea. A fortress that had waited in vain for invaders from across the water, musty rooms that had never become a royal residence. The tenant farmers had long ago forgotten that Kingsburch was owned by the Crown and servants did not linger for long within those desolate walls.

To be summoned to Kingsburch by royal command and find oneself the only guest, attended by an ancient caretaker and his half-witted son, was a trial lesser men would have found harrowing. Jared Malford, however, had other things on his mind.

The wind howled mournfully in the chimney, sending sparks dancing across soot-laden brick, and a gust of smoke into his face as he stared impassively into the flames. Above the mahogany mantelpiece the clock ticked away the minutes. Long past midnight, it would soon be over. The first chimes of the new hour were beginning to ring out as there was an urgent tapping on the door, and almost immediately the caretaker's son entered the room, clearing his throat nervously.

"Milord . . . he's here. The royal personage . . ." The boy wore a leather apron which he kneaded between his fingers. His mouth hung open and his eyes were slightly vacant. Geordie was unaccustomed to dealing with guests and there was no point in explaining to him the incongruity of addressing a young Admiralty clerk as "milord."

Jared Malford turned slowly, his face silhouetted in the

1

firelight. The pointed chin, aquiline nose and heavy eyebrows were thrown into sharp relief in the flickering light, but the piercingly blue eyes were veiled, diminishing the hauteur of the profile. When he spoke, Jared Malford's voice, like his thin features, was spare—a flat, emotionless voice that seemed incapable of expressing surprise. "Where is he?"

"The Cromwell retreat, milord. I am to conduct you . . . there be only me and my dad know of it. My dad fetched him from a boat 'cross the bay. T'other servants and steward mustn't know he came tonight. Nobody to see him come and go that way. Up through the cliff from the beach and only us knows how to get in and out at low tide."

The boy hovered between the threshold of the room and the stone-flagged hall beyond, holding the door ajar to admit icy drafts.

Curious, Jared Malford reflected. A secret room and only the caretaker and his idiot son to know of the visit. One would imagine the Duke had something to hide, rather than . . . but it would be better not to think about that. Coincidence only, that an obscure Admiralty clerk had been summoned here at this particular time. Yet the scandal at the Admiralty and the events that followed must have some bearing on the matter. The royal family was aware that Jared Malford had married into an aristocratic family linked to their own bloodline. Perhaps they were concerned on that account? Surely they could not know. . . .

Jared Malford arose, unhurried, kicking aside the footstool, and moved with the precision of a fencing master between the shrouded furniture.

The hollow echo of their footsteps followed past the suits of armor and crossed broadswords, beside shadowed alcoves housing dusty tapestries and busts of forgotten ancestors. The boy stopped before an iron-studded door and opened it to reveal a deep cupboard lined with shelves. At the touch of his hand the shelves revolved and a small room built during the time of Oliver Cromwell as a refuge for fugitive Royalists came into view. The boy withdrew silently as Jared Malford stepped through the aperture.

A lantern, wick burning low, barely illuminated the leather armchair and its occupant, a man whose face was hidden under a wide-brimmed hat, his body enveloped in a Garrick coat thrown carelessly across his shoulders.

2

"No doubt you are wondering why you were invited to Kingsburch at this particular time," the man said softly. A faint trace of a stammer was carefully controlled by slow and precise speech. "Especially as you are the only guest."

"I do not question royal invitations, Your Grace," Jared Malford said.

"Not even when they happen to coincide with . . . uh . . . plans of your own of a . . . uh . . . secret nature?"

Jared Malford waited, not rising to the bait. The royal personage had come alone. There were no soldiers or runners to take anyone into custody; therefore, there was no reason to panic.

"We know what you planned for the unfortunate wretch in the Tower. The guards you bribed to allow the escape have confessed to everything."

The silence hung threateningly in the air between them, but Jared Malford made no response. His passion for fencing had taught him that there were times when it was advantageous to let one's opponent make all the moves.

"You went to sea at an early age, did you not? Midshipman Malford rose quickly to the rank of lieutenant, but was then shuffled from ship to ship because various captains felt the lieutenant interpreted their orders somewhat more harshly than they intended. At length you were sent to the Admiralty, where, I believe, you were extremely unhappy. . . ."

"I believe I performed my duties adequately, Your Grace."

"Until the unfortunate incident . . . yes, well, we live in strange times. The upheaval in France, the troubles with Spain and others . . . perhaps the whole thing was a storm in a teacup? The fact that a young Admiralty clerk gave certain information regarding the movement of our ships of the line to a young man who is supposedly a fugitive from the French mob, and then the Spanish fleet later lay in wait . . ."

Even if he knows, Malford was thinking, he will not let the scandal become public because of my wife's connection to the royal family. His voice was calm: "Richard Trelayne, the prisoner in the Tower, was accused of the leakage."

"Yes. Quite. And how fortunate all the clues were there, pointing to the guilty party, what?"

"I don't believe any real harm was done. I understand our ships were more than a match for the Spaniards."

3

"But that isn't the point, is it, old chap? The point is that selling secret information to the enemies of one's country is treason. Of course, I can understand the temptation of a young man . . . third son of a poor family, no means, his career going nowhere after a brilliant start, suddenly enamored of a beautiful, but expensive, woman."

Jared Malford shifted his weight from one foot to the other. There was no chair for him to sit on in the cramped room.

"Supposing," the man in the Garrick coat said, "that the escape took place and the poor fellow was killed during the attempt . . . conveniently before he stands trial for treason and has the opportunity to shift the blame elsewhere. A fine solution for all concerned, wouldn't you say? Especially for the real culprit."

"But you are not aware of the identity of the real culprit, and the prisoner in the Tower has no proof of any allegations he may have made; otherwise, he would not be where he is," Malford said smoothly.

"But is it not a coincidence that the man accused by the prisoner Trelayne and the man who the guards say bribed them to let the prisoner escape are one and the same?"

"Perhaps he was merely trying to help the prisoner."

"I think not. I think he wanted to seal the prisoner's lips forever. The guards say they were to be waiting outside the Tower walls to thwart the escape by killing the prisoner."

"It is one thing to make accusations, and quite another matter to prove them," Malford said. "It is also a simple matter to shift blame for a guard's carelessness by fabricating a plot involving other parties."

"Indeed, yes. Now, suppose the entire matter was simply hushed up. Naturally, we would like to keep your wife's family out of the scandal entirely. A certain young Admiralty clerk could return to sea duty . . . possibly be given command of his own ship later on, in return for a favor."

"A favor?"

"You are acquainted with Madam Digby?"

"Of course. Is there anyone in London who does not know that notorious lady?"

"Notorious . . . yes, but so beautiful . . . and with the knowledge that can drive a man . . . even a . . . but let me

4

not wax too eloquent about the lady's charms. She is expecting a child."

"That will cramp her style somewhat."

"Quite so. We want you to, take the child when it is born. You have a childless wife and, after we have made certain arrangements, the aura of respectability we want for Madame Digby's child."

Actually, the Duke cared little about Madam Digby's forthcoming child, but he cared a great deal about Madam Digby herself. And she had been adamant. She wanted a name, a home and respectability for her child or else further favors and a closed mouth would no longer be provided to the Duke.

"The child is yours, Your Grace?"

"It is not necessary for you to know who the father is."

"But *you* invited me to Kingsburch and you came to see me secretly."

"Just as *you* arranged for the escape of Richard Trelayne."

"Am I to pass the child off as my own?"

"Yes. Birth certificate . . . everything. . . . There is to be no way the child cannot be proved to be yours. The families of all the persons involved must never know. And that brings me to the reason you were invited to Kingsburch. The estate will be settled on the child when he or she reaches the age of twenty-one. Meantime, you will be custodian. The child is to be brought up here—far from London and Madam Digby."

"I know nothing about caring for an estate. I would prefer to return to sea."

"So you shall, a command, as I promised. You need return here only occasionally. A competent steward can run the estate. We have never used the place as a royal residence, although we have allowed various favored subjects to live here from time to time. The tenant farms look after themselves."

In actual fact, Kingsburch and its tenant farms had been a royal headache for generations. The place was simply too remote. Responsibility for its upkeep had fallen upon the Duke's shoulders, and he had soon learned that few estate stewards could stand its loneliness and isolation. It would certainly be a relief to plague someone else with this white elephant. In a way, a fitting punishment for a man who was about to escape responsibility for a crime because of his wife's lineage. And then Madam Digby's son and

5

heir would dispose of Kingsburch himself when he came of age. All in all, a neat way to solve several problems at once.

"When does madam expect the child?"

"A few months . . . four or five. What will you tell your wife?"

"My wife, Your Grace, is dying of consumption. It will not be necessary to tell her anything. I will have the physician certify that she died in childbirth . . . if she lasts that long."

"Someone will be sent to care for the infant. By the way, speaking of children, I understand Trelayne had a son."

"Had? You use the past tense, Your Grace?"

"Your planned escape took place, Malford—two days earlier than you expected. Unfortunately, Trelayne's wife was waiting in the carriage and was killed with him."

Jared Malford did not speak. He stood motionless, staring at the floor as the seconds passed, and at last swore softly under his breath. "And the boy?"

"There was a French maid—Claudine St. Clair. She and the boy have disappeared. They are not at the Trelayne house, nor is the boy in school. We sent runners to both places. We thought you might know where they went. And . . . uh . . . be concerned about it."

"I have no idea. Possibly she took him back to France. An eight-year-old boy is hardly an adversary I shall lose sleep over."

The man in the Garrick coat stood up, turning his back to Jared Malford. "We understand each other, then. You shall have your command, and everything said in this room tonight will be forgotten."

"Agreed," Malford said quickly. "It would appear I have drawn a stern sentence—twenty-one years of caring for a bastard not my own."

He was gratified when he heard the swift intake of breath that was not followed by a remonstration. Jared Malford was satisfied that his last parry had proclaimed him victor in a verbal match over a powerful opponent. It was necessary to him to feel the last verbal thrust had been his; it helped staunch the bleeding of that other wound. . . . After all, he must be practical. His own command and an occasional visit to this drafty old fortress was actually a small price to pay for a command, and for the knowledge that he was safe from the fate that had befallen the late prisoner in the Tower.

6

CHAPTER 1

London, 1811

The caped figure hiding in the shadows where the London road dipped into the moonless hollow was unaware that he was being watched. The two men caught a glimpse of him as they reined their mounts at the top of the rise, keeping the ribbon of road in view.

Just before the moon slipped behind a cloud the pale light caught the face of one of the pair, handsome features alive with excitement as he clutched the arm of his companion and pointed.

"You were right, Damon," he whispered, "the man is a highwayman. He's waiting for the London coach to leave the inn. What an opportunity! If I didn't know better, I'd swear you arranged this."

"Get back into the trees. The coach will pass us first. There'll be time to ride down there after he stops it." Damon St. Clair's voice betrayed no excitement. His movements, as he slid from his horse, were smooth and unhurried.

His companion jumped down from his mount and pushed his hat back from a mane of deep bronze hair. He was the younger of the two, and he wore an expression that plainly said he was ready for any adventure the night might have to offer.

"Why didn't you speak to the lady back at the inn, Damon? Introduce yourself there? What if providence hadn't provided the highwayman?"

"Keep your voice down, my impetuous young friend, or

I'll be sorry I allowed you to accompany me," Damon St. Clair said. "For one thing, the lady's companion was certainly no lady. Did you hear that accent?"

"A maid, perhaps? Ah, but Damon . . . the girl . . . I've never seen anyone as beautiful. When are you going to tell me who she is and why you came all the way to England seeking her?"

"It is not she I seek, but her father. Now, if you don't hold your tongue, Rafe, the highwayman will hear you." Damon had already regretted allowing Rafe Danvers to accompany him. He had done so merely to have a messenger should Damon decide to remain in the village across the bay from Kingsburch. Rafe would have been dispatched back to the ship to advise the captain to sail without his supercargo.

The rattle of the coach wheels echoed through the quiet of the English countryside, and they could see the black outline of horses, coach, and driver silhouetted against the moonlit sky as they rolled past and down into the dark hollow.

Damon and Rafe were remounting, eyes fixed on the shadowed stretch of highway concealing the bandit. "All right, now," Damon said, "circle to the left and come up behind him while I take the road."

They did not hear the cry of "Stand and deliver!" but the pistol shot that rang out reverberated through the night. Damon, cantering down the center of the highway, saw that the coach driver was attempting to make a run for it, whipping the horses until their hooves slid and their backs glistened with sweat. The coach leaned dangerously as it rounded the curve, and a second shot caught the driver full in the back, sending him sprawling between the thrashing hooves. Now the horses bolted, running blindly down the hill, the coach swaying violently from side to side.

The highwayman was remounting when Damon drew alongside and flung himself from his mount. He caught the man around the shoulders and the two of them fell to the ground, rolling between the whinnying horses. The bandit had dropped one of his pistols, but he raised the other like a club as Damon lunged for it. Seizing the pistol, Damon pressed it back into the man's belly, then swung his fist into the masked face.

Rafe went galloping by, in pursuit of the coach with its

dead driver and bolting horses, as Damon stood up over the inert body of the highwayman.

At the bottom of the hill Rafe spurred his mount and caught the lead horses a second before a wheel went flying from the side of the coach.

The coach went over onto its side with a scraping thud. From inside came a babble of frightened voices and then a head appeared through the window. The head was crowned with impossibly red hair and a hat rakishly askew. "Cor!" a ripe Cockney voice said. "We don't 'alf owe you something, laddie. 'elp us out, there's a dear."

Despite her flamboyant clothes and hennaed hair, the woman was attractive. In her late thirties, Rafe guessed, with a pretty pink-and-white face. His gaze quickly moved to her companion and remained there even as he helped the other passengers from the fallen coach.

The girl was perhaps seventeen or eighteen, with pale gold hair and the largest, bluest eyes Rafe had ever seen. Her eyes glistened like two jewels set in the fairest of faces. He had been intrigued back at the inn to learn that Damon's mysterious journey to this remote stretch of coast had been to inquire about Sir Jared Malford, owner of Kingsburch. The innkeeper, surprised, had informed them that Sir Jared was out of the country, but did they not know that the lady awaiting the arrival of the London coach was Sir Jared's daughter? The innkeeper did not know who the red-haired woman was. She, too, had come to the inn asking directions to Kingsburch and had reappeared a couple of days later with Miss Malford to await the London coach.

When all of the passengers were out of the coach, Rafe turned to the red-haired woman. "Rafe Danvers, at your service, ma'am."

"Edwina Digby. Miss Digby. And this is Miss Malford. We are ever so grateful to you, Mr. Danvers."

Rafe did not hear the comments of the other passengers. His eyes were still locked with the dark blue eyes, and a peculiar weakness was overcoming him.

"I'm afraid your driver is dead," he said at length, "and your coach will have to be repaired. We can unhitch the horses so that you gentlemen can ride back to the inn. My friend and I will take care of the ladies. If you don't mind sharing my horse, Miss Malford?" Rafe wanted to get the girl onto his mount while Damon was still taking care of the highwayman.

She smiled up at him, the smile transforming the cool beauty of her features into a radiance that stopped his breath in his throat.

Placing his hands around a tiny waist, he lifted her to the saddle just as Damon St. Clair came down the road, pressing a pistol into the back of the stumbling highwayman.

The English spoken in America had not changed significantly from that spoken in the mother country in the thirty-five years that had gone by since America won independence, and Rafe Danvers' voice carried a hint of the Irish lilt of his ancestors. He was as accomplished with a compliment or a dash of blarney as any of his relatives in the old country. With his arms around the slim waist of the girl from Kingsburch, however, all of his wit and practiced repartee seemed to desert him.

She had remained remarkably calm, in view of the circumstances, but her arms trembled as he reached around her to hold the reins.

"You will go on with your journey to London?" he asked.

"I hope so. I've never been there and I was so looking forward to the visit."

Rafe was surprised. It seemed strange that the daughter of Sir Jared Malford had never visited London, especially in view of the isolation of Kingsburch and the inevitable lack of social life there for a girl of marriageable age.

"Miss Digby is an old friend of the family and came to invite me for a short season in London. And you, Mr. Danvers, are you journeying somewhere? We don't get many visitors in the village, and none, I'm afraid, at Kingsburch."

"I'm on my 'grand tour,' as we call it," Rafe said. "My father owns a rice plantation in the Carolinas and he wanted me to see Ireland . . . and England, of course. Our friend Damon St. Clair, who has custody of the highwayman, owns a ship presently docked in the port of London. I sailed here with him. Would it be impertinent, Miss Malford, if I were to ask your first name?"

"Leona Anne . . . but I've always been known as Lanna, a corruption I believe I made up myself as a small child." Odd, she thought, that she should say that. She had told Teddie Digby the same thing. Whenever Leona Anne had been accused of any improprieties by her stern governess,

10

she had attempted to avoid a caning by explaining that a very naughty little girl named Lanna was actually responsible. Now twice in as many days, the wicked Lanna had been invoked.

"Lanna . . ." Rafe repeated softly, his tongue lingering over the word lovingly. "The ship will only be here a short time, so I can't wait to broach the subject like a gentleman, but I must see you again. May I call on you when we get to London?"

She turned to look over her shoulder, eyes wide. Then realizing how close his face was to hers, she turned back quickly. "Why, Mr. Danvers . . . yes, I'd like that."

Rafe dug his knees into the flanks of his horse, resisting the urge to give an exuberant yell. He was anxious to begin his courtship of the beautiful golden-haired girl who was already enclosed by his arms.

Although it was the black-haired American, Damon St. Clair, who had actually caught the highwayman, it was the auburn-haired young Rafe Danvers who received most of the admiration of the passengers and villagers. Rafe Danvers was handsome, with a cheeky sort of recklessness about him that appealed to the people of the small fishing village that profited more from smuggled goods from France than from the harvest of the sea.

The other American, they noted, was dark and morose and not inclined to accept thanks or be drawn into conversation. Damon St. Clair had an inscrutable expression and faintly mocking eyes that discouraged questions. Rafe, on the other hand, had an easygoing charm and was properly modest about saving the coach from the highwayman who was now locked up and awaiting the hangman's rope. The barmaids at the inn simpered and giggled as they set up the tankards of ale the coach passengers insisted on buying for the Americans.

Damon St. Clair soon retired to his room for the night, leaving Rafe to hold court, and Rafe became more charmingly attentive to Lanna Malford as the ale disappeared. At length Edwina Digby insisted they must return to Kingsburch until the wheel was repaired and the coach was ready to resume the journey to London.

Lanna had agreed at once and Rafe wondered again at the relationship between the two. The girl was so obviously a lady and a sheltered one at that, whereas to describe

11

Edwina Digby as a woman-of-the-world would have been putting it kindly.

As soon as Lanna and Miss Digby had departed, Rafe smiled engagingly at the nearest barmaid and pulled her down onto his lap. She giggled and snuggled closer to his ruffled shirt, her mop cap slipping sideways over unruly curls.

"I shall need a warming pan for my bed," Rafe whispered in her ear. "I'm not accustomed to your chill English nights. It's hot where I come from."

The girl giggled again, squirming on his lap and pressing her ample bosom against the linen of his shirt. The hot scent of her assailed his nostrils and the memory of Lanna Malford's liquid blue eyes and tiny waist stirred his blood. Rafe stood up, tankard in hand and one arm about the barmaid.

"Gentlemen," he said, "my thanks for your hospitality, but my encounter with your road agent has wearied me."

There was a shout of laughter from the assembled men as Rafe lurched away, the barmaid still glued to his side.

"S'truth, guv'nor," she said as they negotiated the narrow stairs of the inn, "you'll not need a warming pan, as hot-blooded as you are!" And she shrieked with laughter as her hand darted out to touch the hard bulge in his breeches.

When the wheel of the coach was repaired, Damon sold their horses so that he and Rafe could travel to London by coach, an arrangement that was much to Rafe's liking. Before they reached the city, Rafe had discovered that Lanna Malford would not be staying with Edwina Digby while in London. He had also contrived to be invited to a ball being given by Lord Dunstan, who was, surprisingly, a friend of Miss Digby. The ball was to be the main event of the season and Lanna Malford was to be Lord Dunstan's guest.

After learning from Lanna that her father, Sir Jared Malford, was presently the captain of a frigate based in the Indies, Damon St. Clair showed no further interest in conversation with anyone.

Rafe regaled the coach travelers with humorous accounts of their voyage from America and drew a raised eyebrow or two when he casually mentioned that Damon's ship was named the *Wayward Woman*. He received more laughter

12

when he described the skipper of the *Wayward Woman* as being actually a trained gorilla.

"I swear!" he said, light green eyes crinkling with mirth. "The man has arms that are longer than his legs . . . but strong, powerfully strong. He could probably hoist all the sails singlehanded. Oddly enough, despite his grotesque body, he has the face of a saint. A Frenchman—L'Herreaux. But to see him standing on the bridge, barely tall enough to reach the wheel, with arms that . . ."

"Rafe," Damon interrupted, "Alain L'Herreaux is my friend." There was no emotion in the statement.

"Of course, Damon," Rafe said easily. "I mean no disrespect. But to see him climb the rigging, one is reminded of a monkey scurrying up a tree. I hasten to add that as captain of the ship, it is not necessary for him to do so, but the man has a dedication to his ship, and a common seaman's duties are not beneath his dignity."

"You had no trouble, then," one of the passengers asked, "during your voyage? You say your captain is French, and we are, of course, at war with that country."

"American-French," Rafe corrected, "what we call Creole. He has lived most of his life in America, as has Damon . . ."

"Rafe"—Damon's voice cut off his countryman smoothly —"since you were merely a passenger on our ship, you were unaware that we beat a hasty retreat several times to avoid ships of the Royal Navy and the French Navy." Damon turned his black eyes to the passenger who had spoken. "The Anglo-French blockades are strangling our ports and commerce, sir, and the stopping of our ships by your navy and impressment of our seamen will surely have disastrous consequences before long."

There was an awkward silence and Rafe moved quickly to bridge it. "Before you tire the ladies with your talk of the Orders in Council, Damon, let me ask Miss Malford if that finger of land across the bay is the same one that leads to her home, Kingsburch."

Their coach was above the village, and the grey sweep of the bay came into view, the tall masts of several oceangoing vessels visible amid the profusion of fishing boats.

"Yes. Kingsburch is built at the point, almost overhanging the sea," Lanna said, and for a moment her eyes clouded as she looked across the bay and down the corridor of lonely years she had spent behind those grey stone walls.

13

Teddie Digby began to chatter about forthcoming events in London and no one noticed that Damon St. Clair had effectively steered the conversation away from himself, his ship and his friend, Alain L'Herreaux.

The early spring garden parties in London and the late suppers after the theater were soon buzzing with news of the two most interesting new arrivals in town. One was a girl of extraordinary beauty who gave the impression that she had suddenly arrived in the world from some distant planet. She was innocent, shy and, despite her looks, totally without coquetry. Indeed, she appeared to be entirely unaware of the effect she was having on a society jaded by exhibitionism and scandalous behavior. Regency London was a strange place to find someone like Leona Anne Malford. There were even those who whispered the girl must surely be an actress. . . . No one could actually be that naïve.

Almost at the same time as Lanna arrived in London, a young American burst upon the scene with the impact of a whirlwind. Tall, handsome, with dark bronze hair and a skin turned golden by the sun, his good looks and devastating charm were making feminine hearts flutter, while his quick wit, easy conversation and good sportsmanship at the gaming tables equally endeared him to the men.

His dark-haired companion, the enigmatic Damon St. Clair, returned to his ship and did his gambling in private. Waterfront men of every class found their way aboard the *Wayward Woman* and left it considerably lighter in the pocket. Few returned. St. Clair was a professional gambler, they decided, despite his claim to be owner of the ship.

Rafe used the ship as a hotel, returning to sleep in his cabin after taking Lanna back to whichever of Teddie Digby's society friends the girl happened to be staying with at the time.

"You should stay aboard and play cards with me and my friends," Damon said to him on the afternoon before Lord Dunstan's ball.

"No, thanks. I've seen some of the cutthroats you play with," Rafe answered.

"I hear you've been seen frequently in the company of the Malford girl," Damon said, not looking up from the entry he was making in the ship's log.

"Alain tells me you have a cargo for the return voyage,"

14

Rafe said, not wishing to discuss Lanna. "I'm glad. But I'd hoped we wouldn't have to sail quite so soon."

Damon looked up, his eyes calculating. "I take it the conquest of Miss Malford is not yet complete?"

Rafe flushed slightly. Damon St. Clair always made him feel like a schoolboy. "I'd prefer it if you didn't speak of her like that. I am going to ask her to return to America with me."

"That would be foolish," Damon said. "She doesn't belong in your world, nor you in hers. Besides, wouldn't her arrival be difficult to explain to your family?"

"Leave my family out of it, Damon, damn it. You act like you were part of the family. You may own part of the plantation, but you don't own me. I'll do as I please," Rafe said angrily.

"I believe I'll accompany you to the ball tonight, after all," Damon said as Rafe turned to leave. "By the way, we sail in two days."

Something spellbinding happened every time they were together—a quickening of the senses, a keener perception of all that was beautiful in the world. They came from opposite sides of the world, and yet it was as though they were two halves united to become whole at last. When Rafe Danvers looked into the smoky-blue eyes of Lanna Malford, he forgot who he was and did not consider the hopelessness of loving her.

He knew her self-appointed mentor, Teddie Digby, arranged for Lanna to attend all of the social functions designed to bring together young ladies and gentlemen of marriageable age. Many titled and wealthy young men tried to attract Lanna's attention, but she had eyes for no one but the handsome young American who had saved her from the highwayman.

In his cabin, Rafe sat on his bunk and pulled off his boots savagely. He did not want Damon to accompany him to the ball. Rafe would have enough trouble with the young Lord Dunstan without having to worry about what Damon might say to Lanna. Lord Dunstan had been trying to see Lanna alone since they arrived in London. Dunstan had recently returned to England from a sugar plantation in Jamaica, having inherited his title. He now had a seat in the House of Lords and strong political ambitions. He needed a wife, and Teddie Digby had hinted that Rafe was spoiling Lanna's chances for an excellent match.

15

Now Damon's announcement that they were to sail in two days . . .

The ball was being held at Almack's and the guest list was as exclusive as those six female tyrants on the committee could make it. Teddie Digby, however, had connections which had guaranteed that Lanna would be a guest before Lord Dunstan had ever laid eyes on her. Unfortunately, in a surge of gratitude at being saved from the highwayman, Teddie had also extended invitations to the Americans—a gesture she would live to regret.

Rafe gloomily considered not attending, but he could not miss a whole evening in Lanna's company with time so short. He was sorry now he had told Damon of his intention to ask Lanna to return to America with him. No doubt that was why Damon insisted upon accompanying him.

There was an immediate ripple of interest among the guests, particularly the women, when Rafe and Damon arrived. Both wore impeccably tailored evening clothes and were taller than most men present, with the exception of their host, Lord Dunstan. After the similarities of height and dress were noted, the difference between the two Americans quickly became apparent. Rafe's handsome features were constantly animated and his pale green eyes danced with devilment—except when they looked at Lanna, and then they were filled with boyish longing. Damon, on the other hand, had the expressionless face of the soldier of fortune, and a pair of black eyes that made women uneasy and made men wonder if they would be called out at dawn with their seconds.

Rafe searched the room for Lanna and quickly saw she was dancing with Lord Dunstan. Her eyes met Rafe's and lit up with happiness.

The moment Rafe took Lanna in his arms to dance with her, he forgot Damon, Lord Dunstan and everyone else. The assembled guests were going to waltz tonight. Rafe and Lanna had slipped away among the trees in Hyde Park the previous day to practice the new dance when they were supposed to be attending a concert. They had laughed and stumbled, hidden from view by a copse of trees, trying to waltz to the somber strains of the music of a brass band drifting from the pavilion.

"One-two-three," Rafe whispered now, smiling down at her and closing one eye in an elaborate wink.

"Oh, Rafe, with you leading we shall be the most ac-

16

complished couple on the floor," Lanna said, smiling her slow smile, her eyes wide with delight.

"I hope I can remember how to lead you into the reverse turns . . . when I look into your eyes I tend to lose control of my entire body." She always seemed to him to be like Cinderella transformed from kitchen maid to princess, so great was her wonder in all she did. It was, he supposed, because she had led a lonely life at the isolated Kingsburch and this was her first season in London.

"Can we slip away—and be alone?" Rafe asked, his hand tightening about her waist. "There is something I must ask you."

"Yes . . . when the refreshments are served—we won't be missed then." He knew from the sudden light in her eyes what her answer to his question would be.

They went into the anteroom where buffet tables were set up for a late supper, and Rafe dispatched a footman to find a hansom. While waiting for the footman's return, Rafe was confronted by Lord Dunstan, who was flushed from an excess of champagne.

"Understand you're from the Carolinas, old chap," he said. "Visited your country while I lived in the Indies. Some years ago . . . little better than a wilderness, what? Expect you have considerable trouble getting white women to stay in that miserable climate?" He turned to Lanna. "A stinkin' swamp, m'dear. Full of alligators and insects that bite. White man's grave. The country would not exist without the black slaves."

Rafe drew in his breath sharply, stifling his first impulse to reply in the same tone. With Lanna at his side he was more concerned about her feelings than his own desire to parry the attack. "Then you cannot have stayed in Charleston, Lord Dunstan. It is as gracious a city as any in Europe," Rafe said.

"Ah, yes. Charleston. That is what you now call Charles Town, is it not?"

Neither man was aware that Damon had joined them until he spoke softly from behind Rafe.

"For someone who has lived as a planter in the Indies to speak disparagingly of the use of black slaves seems strange."

Dunstan turned to look into Damon's dark stare. "Ah, but in the Indies most planters leave a steward in charge and live in England. The sons of planters spend time there learning about the running of the plantation, as I did. But we keep our wives and families here. In your American planter society, you leave a handful of whites at the mercy of vast numbers of slaves. Certainly no place for a decent woman, as I said." He looked pointedly at Lanna.

"Perhaps that would be for the woman to decide," Rafe said, his voice still pleasantly soft despite the flash of yellow fire that had appeared in his green eyes. He took Lanna's hand and drew it through his arm.

"Then too," Lord Dunstan said as though Rafe had not spoken, "I believe the only truly happy unions are those of kindred souls. Do you not agree with me, Miss Malford?"

"Absolutely, Lord Dunstan," Lanna replied quietly, her eyes fixed on Rafe.

"Which would, of course, include nationality," Lord Dunstan added. "Especially in these perilous times. But apart from the chance of war splitting one's loyalties, there is the problem of different customs, different backgrounds. Would you not say, Miss Malford, that marriage is a risky enough business without adding all of these problems? Blood will tell, in the end. Breeding is everything. Those of us who are your friends, Miss Malford, hope you will marry an Englishman."

"You may have made it necessary for me to call you out, sir," Rafe said, unable to hold his temper any longer.

"Just a moment, Rafe," Damon interrupted. "I believe you are taking offense where none is intended."

Rafe turned to Damon in astonishment but Damon went on, "For what, after all, is an Englishman? If I may quote your own Defoe: 'A true-born Englishman's a contradiction. In speech an irony, in fact, a fiction.' And in case Defoe's meaning escapes you, Lord Dunstan, he was referring to the fact that Englishmen are mongrels . . . the blending of many races. Angles, Saxons, Normans, Vikings . . ."

Lord Dunstan had not heard anything after Damon had said "mongrels" and his face was livid. "It is not my practice to challenge one of my guests, sir, therefore I shall merely ask you to leave."

Out of the corner of his eye, Rafe could see the footman trying to catch his attention. The hansom he had ordered was waiting and this was not the moment for him and Damon to be thrown out of the club.

"Of course," Damon said smoothly. "Would you be so kind as to show me the way, Lord Dunstan?"

Lord Dunstan hesitated for a second, his eyes still fixed

18

on Lanna, but he had no choice but to lead Damon toward the exit. Moments later, when he returned, the beautiful Miss Malford and the bronze-haired American had disappeared.

"Would you be afraid to live on a plantation, Lanna?" Rafe whispered as they slipped out of the club.

"I wouldn't be afraid of anything if I were with you, Rafe," she said softly.

In the hansom his arms went about her and he spoke into the satiny folds of her hair. "It's true the country is still young and wild. Perhaps the same could be said of me, but I love you, Lanna. I know we've only just met . . . but I can't bear to go away and leave you. Will you marry me? Come back to America with me?"

"Oh, Rafe . . . oh, yes. Yes."

"Lanna, my darling. We can be married at sea, by Captain L'Herreaux. I must return with them . . . my father needs me to take over Clearview, our plantation, because of his failing health. Can you be ready to sail the day after tomorrow?"

"Yes, I think so. I can pack tomorrow. I shall be ready."

"Good. Come to the pier as early as you can. I shall be waiting for you. Shall I send a carriage for you?"

"No. I'll hire one. I'm not sure where I shall spend the night. I would like to see Teddie before I go but she insists her flat is not the place for me because of some of her eccentric friends . . . so unless I can persuade her to let me stay . . . Rafe, we mustn't stay away from the ball too long, we shall be missed."

Rafe called to the driver to take them into Hyde Park and a little while later they left the cab and walked beneath the trees, losing themselves in the shadowy stillness.

The evening was warm and the air heavy with the scent of blossoms, the paths overgrown with flowers. A nightingale was singing and the stirring of the branches of the trees whispered a muted accompaniment. There was no need for words. They paused in a grassy hollow surrounded by trees and banks of shrubbery. Rafe took her in his arms and drew her down on the soft grass amid the fallen blossoms.

Her lips were as tantalizing as a first sip of wine, and he followed the cool column of her throat until his mouth came to rest on the soft swelling of her breast. His ears pounded and his loins ached with longing and she was clinging to him, whispering her love and breathing his name. He knew his caresses were leading them both dangerously near the brink, but his lips and hands would not heed his mind's warning. The thin material of her dress was pushed aside and his lips found skin as delicate as silk. Scarcely knowing what he was doing, he found her skirts inching up her thighs and his own buttons unfastened.

She felt his hand moving gently beneath her skirt, the hard maleness of him touch her and then his weight as he lowered himself down upon her. There was a sudden sharp pain. She gasped, rigid with fright and the knowledge of what they were doing.

"Rafe, no . . . please, not yet," she begged, and the pain between her legs was unbearable. There was a terrible sense of loss as he pulled away from her.

"Lanna . . . I'm sorry, I couldn't stop myself. Please forgive me. I should have waited, but oh, God, you're so beautiful."

"Rafe, my darling, it's all right. I love you and in just two days we shall be together for always," she whispered, feeling her tears slip down her cheeks.

"How can I bear to take you back to the ball . . . how can I bear not to see you all day tomorrow?" he murmured, stroking her hair, kissing her eyes.

"I must pack . . . buy some things. I shall come to the ship as soon as I can. Just a day, my darling—only one more day to wait."

Neither of them saw the horseman who had followed their hansom into the park, and who now followed through the silent streets of the city back to St. James', always keeping enough distance between himself and the hansom so he would not be seen.

CHAPTER 2

From the bridge of the *Wayward Woman*, Captain Alain L'Herreaux watched with interest the arrival of the carriage on the pier below. The coachman handed down a slender girl, and the morning sunlight glistened on the wheat-gold hair which whipped from her hat in the fresh westerly breeze.

She was dressed in a blue pelisse trimmed with swansdown over a matching walking dress. Large dark blue eyes widened as the panorama of the river unfolded before her and a lusty shanty sung by sailors on a weatherbeaten homeward-bounder assailed her ears. Their ship was preparing to dock, sails neatly stowed, red ensign at the peak. The sailors hung over the rail, yelling exuberantly as they caught sight of the girl, and she lowered her eyes to concentrate on the luggage the coachman was placing at her feet.

At Alain's side a voice said quietly, "Let her decorate the dock for a while and then send a man to bring her to my cabin."

"*Mon ami,* you are a hard man. Have you no pity?" Alain asked.

"She is my enemy, Alain, and you have no love for her breed yourself," Damon St. Clair replied.

"Ah, but she is so young, so fair." Alain sighed. "I cannot see her as an enemy."

"Then see her as the key to my plans, my friend."

Alain shrugged his great shoulders, arms and hands ex-

21

pressing what his English could not. A squat, powerfully built man, it appeared his long arms and muscular torso had been mismatched with his short bowed legs. "And our outward-bound passenger, M'sieur Danvers. What of him?" Alain asked as Damon turned to leave the bridge.

"Safe. Where no one will find him." Damon's teeth flashed in a grin that made unexpected changes in his rugged features. "For five or six weeks, anyway, depending on the wind and currents in the North Atlantic."

"Sacré bleu! You had him shanghaied?"

"He'll survive. Now you'd better prepare to be under way, the tide will soon be in the flood."

The raucous sounds of the river and dock filled the air— from the cry of "Stern eas-eee!" to the curses of the watermen forced to tack out of the way of drifting barges. From a nearby taphouse came the screech of a fiddle and drunken laughter.

Dark blue eyes squinted anxiously about the pier as the girl searched for the man who had promised to be waiting. The name of the ship seemed to be emblazoned in giant letters, the *Wayward Woman*. It seemed to be an accusation. She could feel a pulse beating in her throat and she stared at the confusion of vessels in the water. Schooners, ketches, barges, and dodging in and out of the assorted craft were the busy tug boats.

Aboard the *Wayward Woman* there was a flurry of activity as swarthy men in red and blue shirts, sheathed knives hanging from their belts, began preparing to cast off. One of them swung down the gangway toward her.

"Welcome, Miss Malford. I'm to take you aboard." He hauled the largest trunk up onto his shoulder.

"Rafe . . . Mr. Danvers? Where is he?" Lanna asked, but the sailor was already moving up the gangway. Uncertainly, Lanna picked up a portmanteau and followed.

She waited on deck as the sailor returned for the remainder of her luggage, uncomfortably aware of the bold stares of the crew. Where was Rafe? Why had he not come to her? The sailor had all of her luggage aboard now and there was still no sign of Rafe.

Some of the ships were being towed by tugs. The larger vessels were in command of both pilots and watermen, and she marveled that they all managed to avoid collision.

"We'll be under way in a minute, ma'am," the sailor said. "You want to stay on deck and watch afore I take you down to him? He's waiting in the cabin."

22

Lanna opened her mouth to say, "No . . . take me to him," but the words were drowned as a shout like a clarion call rang out. "Stand clear the checks there . . ."

The tide was in the flood and the ship was taken into the river stern foremost, then allowed to drift upstream to be checked on the knuckle of the landing stage. As the *Wayward Woman* was dragged from the lock, the pilot kept her to windward to clear the pier, watching closely to see she did not run too far into the tideway. The men onboard waited to play out the hawser when the waterman in his boat passed the line to the tug. The ship straightened up, proud as a swan, the pilot blew his whistle, the rope settled on the bitts and the check ropes were cast off. The tug took the strain and the *Wayward Woman* sheered away.

"Too late for you to make the pier head jump now, ma'am," the sailor said laughingly. "Come on, I'll take you below."

Lanna glanced back toward the bustle of the port of London and then followed the sailor along the damp deck, down the narrow stairway and along a cramped passageway to a cabin door. He knocked once, pushed open the door and held it for her to pass through.

Seated with his back to her at a small desk beneath a porthole was a man whose shoulders were too broad and whose hair was black, not deep bronze as it should have been. Lanna's breath escaped in an audible gasp as the man turned to face her. It was not her beloved Rafe, but his sinister traveling companion, Damon St. Clair.

She swayed backward, her hand to her mouth. He was beside her in an instant, his fingers cupping her elbow. At the same time he kicked forward a chair which was attached to the deck by a chain.

"Sit down, Miss Malford," Damon St. Clair said. "We'd better talk."

"What . . . where is Rafe? What have you done with him?"

"No hysterics, please. Or swooning. Danvers isn't here."

She looked into that face of chiseled stone and remembered with a shudder what Rafe had said about this man. *His name is Damon . . . but there are those who say it should be Demon.* The sunlight slanting in through the porthole seemed to make the black eyes glow as they went over her slim figure with an insolent scrutiny.

"Do you have to get married?" he asked as matter-of-factly as if he were inquiring if she had to attend a ball.

23

She looked away from the penetrating stare. "Where is Rafe?" she asked again.

"He can't marry you. He already has a wife."

Lanna sat quite still, but it seemed the cabin was rushing about her in a dizzying circle and all that she could see and be sure existed was that pair of black eyes glowing like the stare of a hungry wolf. I must keep control of myself, I must not panic. "I take it he is not here to tell me this himself?"

"No. He isn't here. You didn't answer my question about whether it is necessary for you to get married."

Necessary! She loved Rafe, and apart from the impossibility of ever returning to the hated Kingsburch, she feared that there might be another equal urgency. Her mind went back fleetingly to the warm, sweetly scented moment in the park when it seemed all the night birds were singing and all the flowers in the world were blooming . . . Oh my God, she thought, what if . . . and now . . .

She had never before experienced such joy as she found in Rafe's embrace, but with it had come an abandonment of reason. They had been swept away on some dizzying tide, and although it seemed that their bodies had never achieved a complete union, the sharp pain she had experienced must have meant he had penetrated her. . . . Even Lanna Malford, who knew nothing of men and very little about her own body, realized that what she and Rafe had done could produce a baby. And if there was a baby . . . and no husband . . . she might as well be dead.

"I take it from your silence that it may well be necessary for you to find a husband quickly," Damon St. Clair said. "In which event, I will marry you."

Lanna thought at first she had not heard him correctly, but he was saying in a disinterested voice, "We can be married at sea, by Captain L'Herreaux."

"But I don't understand," she found her voice at last. "Why you should do this . . . why you would want to."

"You haven't exactly been charming to me, have you, my dear Lady Malford?" he asked mockingly.

"I'm not a lady. My father was knighted by the king, but that does not make me a lady."

"I shall never accuse you of being one again," he said, "and as to why I am offering you my name . . . well, I'm a gambler. And you are the only daughter of an extremely wealthy man. I believe it is a fair bargain. I shall save you from disgrace and humiliation and in return have access to

your fortune. Besides, you aren't a bad-looking wench . . .
I'm not surprised Rafe Danvers was overcome by your
charms."

Disgrace and humiliation. Lanna had not heard anything
he said after those two words echoed through her mind. If
she were *enceinte* as a result of that stolen moment, her
father would kill her. And she couldn't take the risk of
waiting to find out. But to marry this man, to live with
such a hateful man . . .

"After all," he added, his voice still coldly impersonal,
"we might find we like one another in time."

"You are . . . not a gentleman, sir."

"Granted. And since you are not a lady, we should make
a fine pair. Besides, I am something Rafe Danvers is not. I
am available for matrimony."

"Do I take it we would be man and wife in name
only?" Lanna did not dare look at him. *An annulment,
later . . . if I'm not with child . . .*

"I am offering you my name. No other promises, for
my part of the bargain. However, it may interest you to
know you could be a widow as quickly as a wife, my life-
style being what it is."

Lanna looked miserably at the deck. Oh, Rafe, how
could you have done this? Yet how could she go back
now; how could she face her father's wrath? Kingsburch
had been a prison before . . . she shivered. What if she
sent word from the Carolinas to her father that she had
been tricked into marriage with a fortune hunter? That
would be better than going back now, unmarried and possibly pregnant.

Damon was watching her closely and she was afraid
he could read her thoughts, so she said quickly, "You
haven't told me where Rafe is. I can't believe that he
would let me sail on your ship without even telling
me . . ." She looked at the floor again.

"He is already on his way back to America. He sailed
yesterday on a ship bound for New York."

"And he did not even leave me a note?"

"Face it, milady. You have been used and cast aside.
You aren't the first woman to be jilted and you won't be
the last. You, at least, have an alternative to disgrace not
offered to most women in your circumstances."

Lanna looked up at him now: "And what if I decline
your offer?"

White teeth flashed in the swarthy face. His shirt was

25

carelessly open half way down his chest, revealing a mat of black hair. A broad leather belt separated shirt from tight-fitting breeches which disappeared into hessian boots.

"Then you can go ashore with the pilot. There is still time to go back and tell everyone you have not eloped after all . . . that Rafe Danvers jilted you, toyed with your affections when he already had a wife. It's immaterial to me, as I said. All I am interested in is your fortune. As you well know, English law makes you my chattel . . . I will have complete control of your wealth. But it's a small price to pay for your honor, is it not?"

Lanna looked down quickly so he would not see the tears that sprang to her eyes. It had occurred to her that this man was Rafe's friend. What if—what if the two of them had hatched the whole plot to secure a rich wife for Damon? Her pulse quickened at this terrible idea.

"But surely I am not the only rich woman you know? Why do you choose me?"

"Because you are available without the necessity of the chase. It wearies me to court a woman. Now will you make up your mind, before we lose our pilot?"

Americans! Sir Jared had said they were not civilized . . . they were barbarians. "If I agree . . . will you promise to send me back to England as soon as possible? If we reach the Carolinas and I am not . . . not . . ."

"Pregnant?" he suggested.

Lanna blushed, feeling the hot stain travel swiftly upward from her neck. "I mean . . . a short-term marriage will gain you your ends, will it not? My father would probably pay you to agree to an annulment."

Damon laughed a short laugh that was without mirth. "I repeat that I make no promises. I will marry you as soon as we are in the open sea. Beyond that I cannot say what will happen."

Suddenly Damon reached out and drew her to her feet, pulling her close to him in a breath-stopping embrace. Before she realized what he was going to do, his lips found hers and it was like being drawn into the mouth of hell itself; a hot, burning kiss that seemed to drain her veins of their lifeblood. Rafe had never kissed her so, and neither had anyone else in her sheltered life. This was the kiss of a man who was not used to stopping with just a kiss . . . it was almost . . . the thought raced through her mind . . . as though their bodies were coupled in a much more intimate way.

26

She struggled feebly, raising her hands to push him away, and her fingers touched the coarse black hair where his shirt was unbuttoned. She could feel the hard muscles of his chest and, even as she touched him, his hand slid from her back around her waist and came to rest in the hollow between her breasts. She raised her hand and slapped him across the cheek, a stinging slap that snapped her fingers backward.

He laughed softly and released her. "I felt it only fair to give you a sample of what you can expect . . . before you accept my proposal."

Supposing she did . . . naughty little Lanna whispered to the terrified Leona Anne . . . supposing the captain married them and then she pretended seasickness . . . she could be prostrate with *mal de mer* all the way across the ocean . . . and on the other side of that ocean was Rafe . . .

In her confusion and misery there remained the one small hope that Rafe had really loved her . . . even if he already had a wife. If she could be near him, see him occasionally . . . what else did life have to offer? Her father's terrible wrath and perpetual imprisonment at Kingsburch —no man would marry a woman with a bastard child. Marriage to Damon St. Clair would at least give her child a name and allow her to see her beloved Rafe once in a while . . . it seemed the lesser of two evils in that shocking moment of absolute panic.

"I will marry you, Damon St. Clair," she said in a very low voice.

She caught the triumphant gleam in his eye just before he bowed mockingly over her hand, planting one of his searing kisses on her palm.

In her elegantly appointed flat in the heart of London, Teddie Digby had just found Lanna's note and was waiting impatiently for her maid to respond to the bell. Edwina Digby had never learned to read or write. She knew, however, what the note was bound to say.

Teddie was almost forty, and with that mellow age looming before her she had been overwhelmed with longing to meet the child who had been raised at Kingsburch. *He* was dead these many years and the guardian was out of the country for long periods of time. What harm would it do to bring the girl forth from her cocoon of virtual imprisonment? Just a short season in London, so the girl

27

could choose her own husband instead of some oaf Sir Jared found for her.

It had been easy. Teddie was an old hand at getting her way. The sour housekeeper at Kingsburch was quickly bamboozled and the lonely Lanna easily convinced that Teddie was an old friend of the family come to take her for a short holiday in London.

If only that blasted highwayman had not been waiting . . . or the Americans to catch him. Teddie's flat was the gathering place for many of London's influential men and, despite her lack of formal education, she was knowledgeable about current events from overheard conversations. She knew, therefore, that there were disturbing rumors of unrest in the former colony, having to do with the boarding of American ships by the Royal Navy.

The war with Napoleon dragged on and the naval blockades continued. It was feared the Americans might seize the opportunity to tweak the lion's tail while England was engaged in the life and death struggle with the French tyrant.

No, an American husband was not at all what Teddie had in mind for Lanna. With the right guidance, Lanna could make a fine match.

"You rang for me, mum?" The maid spoke from the doorway, startling Teddie, who jumped up from her satin-cushioned chaise and thrust Lanna's note at the girl.

"What does it say? Quick, read it."

The maid slowly mouthed the words before saying them aloud. "Dear Teddie . . ."

"Hurry up, for Gawd's sake," Teddie said, exasperated.

How can I thank you for your kindness to me? I have been so happy these past weeks. I know you do not approve of Rafe . . .

Teddie groaned, her hand going to her temple where the violently red curls escaped from a jeweled headband.

. . . but we have fallen in love and we are eloping. By the time you read this, we will have been married at sea. I have sent word to Kingsburch. Oh, Teddie, I could not go back there . . . these past weeks have been so exciting and it's all your doing. I loved every minute, especially having friends my own age at last . . . I shall miss them all. But Rafe is so wonderful . . .

28

like Prince Charming in the fairy story, I know we
shall be happy. Please be happy for us.

Your devoted friend,
Leona Anne

Teddie paced back and forth across her white-carpeted floor, tiny slippers trimmed with ostrich feathers flashing beneath the swishing negligee. "Send Harry to the dock to see what time that ship is sailing . . . if it hasn't gone tell him to get her off and bring her back here. I don't care how he does it."

"What if it's already sailed, mum?"

"You'll have to write a letter for me to the Indies . . . I can't wait for *him* to go home to Kingsburch and find her gone . . . but don't just stand there, girl . . . go!"

The maid scurried away and Teddie kicked at the sheepskin rug lying in front of the fireplace.

"Blasted Americans," she said.

CHAPTER 3

The *Wayward Woman* was a cargo vessel, but it was equipped to carry two or three passengers in austere accommodations. An elderly couple named Verity were returning to their home in the Carolinas after having visited relatives in England, and they were happy to stand up for the young couple about to be married by Captain L'Her reaux.

Lanna stood beside Damon on the gently heaving deck, a fresh breeze whipping her hair about her face. Hair the color of a wheat field at sunrise, Rafe had said . . . eyes like a mountain lake in the morning . . . oh, why couldn't it have been Rafe who stood there, answering the age-old questions?

"Do you, Leona Anne, take this man, Damon . . ." The English coast was slipping away on the horizon, and old Mrs. Verity held tightly to her husband's arm.

The beautiful ivory lace wedding gown still lay packed in Lanna's trunk. The dress had been purchased, along with its fourteen-foot veil and headdress of tiny pearls set in silver filigree, only the day before. Lanna could not bear to wear it and instead she wore a plain afternoon dress of muted blue with a matching fichu.

She was aware of the captain's accented but musical voice stumbling over the words that tied two people together, and of Mrs. Verity crying into a lace handkerchief.

Lanna did not look at the man beside her, but she felt the invisible aura of him. Like Rafe, he was tall and mus-

cular. She wondered if that was the first thing she had
noticed about the Americans, how very tall they both
were. And their bold eyes . . . why, she wondered, as she
heard Damon give his responses in a steady voice, was she
thinking of them together, as though they were a pair? No
two men could be less alike, apart from the similarities of
nationality and height. Rafe was a happy summer day, and
Damon was thunder clouds lashing a night sky.

She shivered suddenly and then realized that Damon
was slipping a heavy gold band onto the third finger of
her left hand. Where did he get the ring, she wondered
vaguely.

". . . now pronounce you man and wife . . ." the captain
said with a sigh of relief, and Damon turned, cupped her
chin in his hand and kissed her so lightly and casually that
it might have been only a breath of warm air across her
lips.

The sun was dipping low to the horizon now, and the
last smudge of land was gone from sight as the ship
glided into the vastness of the Atlantic.

Alain L'Herreaux had arranged a special wedding dinner
and he even produced a bottle of champagne to toast the
bride and groom, who were both strangely silent. Lanna
had always been a good sailor and the fresh salt air had
sharpened her appetite. Time enough, she decided, to feign
seasickness *after* dinner. Besides, the ship's supplies of
fresh food would quickly become depleted. Best to enjoy
them while she could.

At length Damon rose and extended his hand to her.
"Come, my dear, let us look at the moon as husband and
wife for the first time," he said, his mouth twisted at one
corner in a mocking smile.

The men at the table exchanged knowing glances and
old Mrs. Verity, who had hardly touched her food, dabbed
her eyes again with her sodden handkerchief.

Eyes demurely downcast, Lanna placed her hand in
Damon's warm grip and they went out on deck where a
crescent moon was floating in a cerulean sky. An errant
breeze sighed in the rigging. They stood at the rail, looking
out over the silvered water. Lanna gripped the wooden
rail tightly, acutely aware of the man at her side. He was
so overwhelmingly masculine, she thought, as though he
wanted to emphasize the fact with every gesture, every
movement of his muscled body. The only defense a woman
would have against such a man would be her wits.

31

"If you will excuse me, I think I should like to retire to my cabin."

"*Our* cabin," he corrected.

"I won't share a cabin with you. You promised . . ."

"I promised nothing," he said, "except that I was marrying you for your money."

She would have remained at the rail all night, but two sailors appeared from the fo'c'sle on their way to stand watch and she had no choice but to allow Damon to slip his arm about her waist as they walked back along the deck.

At least they would not have to share a bed, she thought as he pushed open the cabin door, remembering with relief that there were two bunks, one above the other. But the idea of sleeping in the same cabin . . . she must develop seasickness quickly. She stepped uncertainly through the doorway and the door closed behind her. Surprised, she realized she was alone.

Quickly she drew the long bolt across the lock. She listened for a moment, but heard no sound from the other side of the door. She unpinned her hair, undressed, and washed hurriedly in the tepid water that had been placed in a pitcher for her use. The yellow bar of soap made no lather and the water scratched her skin. Salt water, of course. She turned down the lantern and climbed to the upper bunk, feeling it somehow offered more sanctity than the lower one.

For a long time she lay in the semidarkness listening to the creaking of the ship's timbers, the song of the wind in the rigging and the slapping of the sea against the hull. The soothing motion of the ship was lulling her to sleep when she heard the sound.

Someone was trying to open the cabin door.

She sat up so suddenly she bumped her head. The door rattled again against the lock and then there was a loud knock. He was out there. Trying to get in. She heard his voice, thick with wine.

"Open the door, damn you."

Then there were other sounds, crashes and oaths. She sat frozen with fear, clutching the rough blanket to her body.

Moments passed. The door was splintering against the lock. The next second he was in the cabin, staggering slightly as he reached for the lantern and turned up the wick.

32

The dark eyes were bloodshot and his face was contorted with rage. In a flash he was beside her and the blanket was snatched from her hands. Then her nightgown was rent from neck to hem. She cowered away from him, trying to cover herself with her hands, but he caught her wrists and held both of them in one of his hands as easily as if they were broken twigs.

"There are no locks to keep me out, madam," he said savagely, "and you will do well to remember that a locked door enrages me. But fear not, sweet wife, it is not your body I crave, but my bunk so I may sleep. There will be no consummation of this marriage until I am sure you are not carrying Rafe Danvers' child."

She awoke to find the rolling of the ship more pronounced. Through the porthole the grey skies were filled with ominous black clouds. She lay still, remembering the previous night, not daring to look to see if Damon still slept in the bunk beneath her. There was no sound apart from the rising wind and distant voices muffled by the blanket he had hung over the shattered cabin door.

Cautiously she leaned over the edge of her bunk and saw with relief that his bunk was empty. She felt the blood rush to her face as she realized that everyone on board would know about the broken cabin door. That nice old couple, the sailors, the captain with his sad, all-knowing eyes. Quickly she dressed and went up on deck.

Sailors were busy tying lines to and from strategic points in preparation for the heavy seas they were expecting. Angry white-topped waves were already breaking over the bow of the ship as she moved slowly, her trimmed sails ready for the expected wind.

Old Mr. Verity stood at the rail, watching the rise and fall of the giant swells, and he turned as Lanna approached.

"My wife is a little under the weather," he said. "We've been married forty years and she still will not allow me near her when she feels she is not looking her best."

At least with the rising storm everyone would have other things on their mind than the strange wedding night of the St. Clairs, Lanna thought. Aloud she said, "Is she alone? Perhaps I should go to her?"

"That would be kind of you, my dear. But perhaps your husband . . . ?"

"He's busy," Lanna said quickly. She paused for a moment, feeling the deck leap beneath her feet and the sting of salt spray. The impending storm brought a sense of exhilaration, and she was loath to leave for the confined cabin below.

"You must be a good sailor, Mrs. St. Clair, to have such a healthy glow in your cheeks." Old Mr. Verity's eyes watered in the wind.

Lanna smiled. "I've always loved sailing. We lived near the sea."

"Then you certainly chose wisely in selecting a sailor for a husband. I only hope you won't find your loyalty divided in the event of . . ." He stopped himself quickly. How foolish to frighten the poor young thing. She appeared frightened enough of that morose-looking bridegroom who had to batter his way into their cabin.

"In the event of what, Mr. Verity?"

"Nothing, my dear. I'm an old man, inclined to wander in my thoughts." Mr. Verity looked embarrassed.

"No . . . please. Perhaps if I understood more about your country I would be a better wife."

"I shall have your husband after my hide, but doubtless you will hear talk of action being taken against England . . . because of the impressment of our sailors into the British Navy. The hotheads in our government are already talking of a 'second war of independence.' "

"Do you really think America will declare war against England?" Lanna asked in alarm. "I mean, surely not while England is fighting Napoleon?"

"Of course not," Mr. Verity said. "I'm sure an honorable solution will be found."

"I'll go to your wife," Lanna said. As she walked away, she thought how wonderful it would be if the Royal Navy would impress Damon St. Clair into service. But that would not happen because the Royal Navy did not take American citizens. Her father had told her so. Sometimes English deserters hid aboard American ships and that was what necessitated the searches and seizures.

Lanna made her way below as the ship headed toward a smoky bank of cloud ablaze with lightning bolts. She averted her eyes as she went past the ship's carpenter, who was hammering nails into the new plank he had inserted into her cabin door.

The ship struggled onward through the stormy seas of the Bay of Biscay, and Lanna saw little of her new husband. Damon and the captain appeared to work as hard as the crew: she had seen both of them climb aloft to reef sail. When they sailed at last into the placid waters of the South Atlantic Damon continued to ignore her, coming to their cabin only to snatch a few hours' sleep. It seemed to Lanna that they changed course several times and that they would quickly veer off if they sighted another sail.

Lanna saw Damon occasionally at mealtimes, but usually she and the Veritys ate alone or with Captain L'Herreaux, a strange little man who seemed genuinely concerned with her welfare. He was, Lanna thought, part gargoyle and part god . . . his body was like that of a gnome, but when one looked into his even features and bottomless eyes, one realized he had been blessed with a face both arresting and sensual. She began to like and trust Alain L'Herreaux.

They had been at sea six weeks when they were becalmed. The ship floated listlessly beneath limp sail and the air was as wet as the sea. Lanna went down to their cabin after dinner one debilitatingly hot night and stripped down to her shift to try to find some relief from the heat. She drenched a handkerchief with the coolest water she could find, then lay down and placed it over her eyes.

She had begun to doze when she felt a hand slide under her shift and close over her breast. She sat up so quickly that her face touched his. Damon was looking at her with a speculative expression as his hands explored her body slowly and deliberately.

"What are you doing?" she gasped, her heart beginning to hammer.

"What did you think, my dear, when you learned that you need not have married me after all?" he asked.

So he knew! She had tried to hide the evidence that her fears of being pregnant were groundless, but they shared a small, cramped cabin and menstrual towels had to be washed and dried.

"Leave me alone . . . go away," she whispered, frightened out of her wits.

For answer his hands slid under her and she was borne from the bunk and placed on her feet, her body pressed so tightly against his that she could hardly breathe. He was naked to the waist and she tried to twist away as he pulled her shift down so that her breasts pressed against his warm flesh.

"You are my wife. Had you forgotten?" His voice came from the depths of her hair as she turned her face to escape his mouth. She felt his lips move to the hollow of her throat and then downward to her breast. Panting, struggling, she tried to push him away but she soon found herself flung to the deck, the length of his body upon her. His hands pinioned her arms to her sides.

She was sobbing and trying to scream at the same time, but his mouth closed over hers and the only sound she could make was a choking in the back of her throat. His knee was forcing her legs apart and she tried desperately to keep her thighs together, but he was too strong. His tongue was in her mouth and that other part of him thrust into her with a violence that made her body arch in rebellion.

For a moment she felt a tearing pain between her legs, and as her body jerked in reaction her head slammed against the deck, sending a shower of flashing lights exploding in her brain.

Suddenly it was all over and he was slinging her back up onto her bunk like a sack of potatoes and plunging out of the heat of the cabin to leave her crying into her pillow, dry wracking sobs that made her feel worse instead of better.

Rafe Danvers stood at the ship's rail, looking unseeingly into the black mass of ocean and sky that should yield the first glimpse of land when dawn broke. Newfoundland . . . a long way from his home in the Carolinas, and just as far from Lanna and England.

The weeks had slipped away and he had had little time to agonize over his predicament. Now, as the voyage was coming to an end, he relived every moment in his mind . . .

When he had first awakened, there was a dull throbbing in his head, a sour taste in his mouth, and his arm dangled limply from a hammock. Someone was shaking him and he opened his eyes to look into a windburned face and a mouth full of uneven teeth.

"Come on, mate, the skipper wants to see you."

Rafe slid from the hammock, not fully awake. A ship . . . he was on a ship. Hammocks all around him, some occupied by snoring men. The forecastle? This was not the *Wayward Woman*. He stumbled to the porthole and looked out. There was no sign of land.

"What ship is this?" he asked hoarsely as the sailor's

face went out of focus. "Where are we bound?" He had no recollection of having come aboard.

"Newfoundland, mate. This is the brig *Sarah Jane*. Come on now, skipper don't like to be kept waiting."

The brig *Sarah Jane*, Rafe thought dazedly as he followed the sailor. There was a slight swell and plenty of wind in the square-rigged sail. The fresh air cleared his head as they made their way to the captain's quarters. Lanna! Rafe stopped dead in his tracks. She would be waiting aboard the *Wayward Woman*.

"Wait!" he called to the sailor, "What day is this?"

"Friday, mate. And the month's July and the year is 1811. Now come on, will you?"

Friday. The *Wayward Woman* was due to sail today . . . Lanna would be waiting for him now, at this minute.

"When did we sail?" He caught up with the sailor, who moved with ease across the heaving deck.

"Yesterday forenoon. They brought you aboard just before we cast off. You've been out ever since. Here's the skipper's cabin." He knocked loudly on the cabin door and called out, "The American is here, Captain McLeod."

The captain was a wiry Scot, dressed in bell bottoms and a woolen jersey. He was bending over his chart table, sextant busy. He did not turn to greet Rafe.

"I assume I've been shanghaied," Rafe said to the back of the captain's head. "Although I can't recall exactly what happened." Damon, he was thinking, Damon will tell Lanna . . . what? That I've simply disappeared? He struggled to remember why he did not want Damon to talk to Lanna alone . . . Damon knew Lanna's father, had gone to England to seek him. There had been whispered conversations with Alain about Malford, conversations that ended when Rafe appeared.

The skipper of the *Sarah Jane* turned faded blue eyes to examine Rafe's broadcloth coat, linen shirt and well-fitted breeches, all somewhat the worse for having been slept in. The pale eyes flickered over the remnants of a shine on Rafe's boots.

"I wouldna say ye've been shanghaied, lad. Still, this is a cargo vessel, although it will eventually take ye where ye want to go. We'd cross the Atlantic faster with a full crew. But full crews are hard to come by."

"I have no useful knowledge of sailing, I'm afraid."

"Ye speak like a gentleman. An educated one," Captain McLeod observed. "I've no love of writing, so ye could

37

keep my log. And I've twelve-year-old boys who soon learn to climb aloft. You will too."

"I suppose there's no way I could persuade you to return to port?" Rafe asked. "I would pay handsomely."

"Not as much as the owner is paying me to get his cargo to Newfoundland. Besides, it's unlucky to turn back."

"Then I suppose I'd better make myself useful. I'll be happy to keep your log, if you tell me what to write. As for climbing aloft . . . I suppose I have little choice. Can you supply me with some suitable clothes?"

"Aye. I'll have the Mate fetch some." The faded blue eyes turned back to the chart. A large crew was needed aboard a square rigger to climb out on each yard to shorten or let out sail. There was no need, the captain decided, to let young Mr. Danvers know that his passage had been paid to New York. An extra hand was always useful. An educated sailor was a rarity and would be doubly useful. The gentleman who had brought Mr. Danvers aboard had merely requested he be put off in New York. The gentleman had not bothered to inquire whether they were bound directly for New York. They were not. New York would be their last port of call.

Rafe was given a duffel bag to stow his clothes in. He would not find the letter Damon had stuffed into the inside breast pocket of his coat until he disembarked from the *Sarah Jane*.

After the first climb aloft and horrified glance downward at the small, swaying, distant deck, Rafe learned to concentrate on hoisting canvas and not think about the possibility of a sudden gust of wind plucking him from his precarious perch. His hands began to callus and his skin became ruddy with wind and sun. He spent hours with the taciturn skipper, keeping the log, watching him plot their course, talking, learning.

Inevitably, Rafe's keen interest in everything about him endeared him to the dour Scot, whose knowledge of wind and wave was considerable. The captain, for his part, soon discovered that the young American also knew some facts that were new to him. There was, evidently, some merit in spending more years in school than had previously seemed necessary to the simple man of the sea.

When the captain spoke of the great storms of the Atlantic, of the Northeast trade winds and the Southeasterlies below the equator, or of the sudden terrible storms of the Caribbean the natives called *hurucano,* the young American would surprise him by telling him he had read in books of a dreaded wind of the China seas called the *taifung,* of other winds called monsoon, and of yet another that blew off the Argentine plains with awe-inspiring violence and which was called the *pampero.*

As the ship plied the relatively calm midsummer waters of the Atlantic, Captain McLeod began to realize he had a born sailor aboard. Rafe Danvers learned quickly and brought to every task an enthusiasm that soon made him friends in the forecastle.

Since the ship was of British registry and a merchantman, they had no fear when a Royal Navy frigate bore down on them the second week out of port. The Navy would want to be sure they flew their true colors and that there were no deserters from the King's service aboard. Still, to a man, the crew of the *Sarah Jane* decided the American should be hidden from the Navy boarding party who came to check their manifest. It was well known that the Royal Navy, when short-handed, sometimes liked to assert that Americans were actually English deserters and impress them forthwith into service.

Watching the sails of the frigate disappear over the horizon, Captain McLeod had said grimly to Rafe, "A different life they lead, lad, on that kind of ship. A Navy captain has the power of life and death over his crew. Never let one of their press gangs get a hold of ye."

"I'll avoid it at all costs," Rafe said with a grin. "But perhaps you'd better continue my lessons in navigation. Just in case . . ."

By the time they docked at New York the summer had passed, and so too had most of Rafe's misery at leaving Lanna behind. He would simply take the first ship back to England and claim her. She would be waiting for him, he was sure. The *Sarah Jane* was temporarily without a cargo and there was no telling where her next port of call would be. Merchant vessels were tramps, picking up cargoes wherever they could find them.

Rafe shook out his broadcloth jacket and linen shirt, the tailored breeches and fine leather boots, in readiness to go ashore. The letter slipped from the inside pocket and Rafe opened it and read it slowly, disbelief spreading across his handsome features, pale green eyes beginning to flash angrily.

39

Rafe,

I have a responsibility to your father and to Clearview, therefore I believe it best to send you home before you make a grave mistake.

One other thing I forgot to tell you. I shall be marrying Miss Malford myself. Alain will perform the wedding at sea as soon as we sail. See you in Charleston.

Damon

Rafe's Irish temper erupted in a molten flood. He flung the letter to the deck, smashed his fist futilely into the bulkhead and bellowed like a wounded bull. Then he swallowed all the grog the captain could be persuaded to part with and staggered to the nearest brothel. There he slammed a startled prostitute against the bed with a violence that brought a wary look to her jaded eyes. But since his endowments were considerable, the prostitute found herself responding to the act for the first time in years. Inexplicably, when he was done, he suddenly buried his face in her battered pillow. Great sobs shook his body.

The next day he signed on the *Sarah Jane* for a voyage to Portugal.

CHAPTER 4

It was an exotic, foreign world. The *Wayward Woman* sailed into Charleston harbor, past tiny islands crouched like animals frozen in stone, and the city on the narrow peninsula lay basking in a late summer sun that made Lanna wilt before she ever set foot ashore.

Images blurred and ran together . . . she was being whisked by landau beneath swishing palmettos lining the avenues, past tall houses of stuccoed brick with steep slate roofs. Wrought-iron gateways set in high walls gave glimpses of lush gardens sleeping in the sun. Fig trees curving over walls dropped ripe fruit on the street outside. Some of the houses were turned sideways to the street, and many had open galleries. Flowers and flowering shrubs unknown to Lanna were everywhere, and the air was heavy with their scent.

Damon had told her briefly that he owned a house "on the Battery," and that it would be reasonably cool for her English blood, since the rear lawns reached the seawall. They stopped in front of a handsome iron fence which enclosed a small flagstoned front courtyard. The house was surprisingly grand, with a stately two-story portico flanked by Ionic columns. When a black servant opened the doors to admit them, Lanna was immediately aware of a magnificent crystal chandelier in a wide hall that led to a broad staircase.

Black servants, the women with their hair wrapped and their white aprons bristling with starch, hovered excitedly

41

about the hall as Damon, Lanna and their luggage were ushered into the house. Lanna looked with amazement at all of the black faces and wondered if they were slaves. There did not appear to be any white servants at all.

She felt faint from the unexpected heat and the excitement of disembarkation, and she had difficulty understanding the dialect of the black servants. They were all smiling broadly and chattering, and out of the confusion Damon managed to convey the butler's name: Joshua. Joshua clasped the hand of a very young black girl and brought her forward. Lanna smiled at the girl she gathered was to be her personal maid.

"Myrtle has been trained by Indigo herself and you will find her invaluable," Damon was saying. "By the way, Joshua, where is Indigo?"

There was a sudden hush among the servants and the shiny face of the butler, under his grizzled hair, looked perplexed. What a wonderfully expressive face, Lanna thought.

"Ah specks Miss Indigo will be along direckly, suh." Joshua said. Even Lanna, who knew nothing of the household or the servants, could tell that he was not at all convinced of the truth of this statement.

"Indigo runs my house," Damon said briefly to Lanna. "I suppose you would call her a housekeeper. Myrtle, take Miss Lanna up to her room."

The voices were buzzing again and Lanna, following the young black girl up the stairs, wondered why the mention of the housekeeper's name had caused the abrupt silence. She was remembering, too, that she had not eaten that morning and that part of her faintness was probably due to that fact.

Myrtle threw open the door to an airy room that was beautifully furnished—and, joy of joys, the French windows opened to a wrought-iron balcony that caught the faintest stirring of a breeze. Myrtle was still chattering unintelligibly.

"Myrtle," Lanna said, "you are going to have to speak very slowly for me. You see, I am a foreigner and not used to your way of expressing yourself. Could you bring some water for a bath and perhaps some fruit? I'm quite hungry."

When dinner was served early, she was sorry she had consumed so much of the fruit. Despite her great interest in the exotic dishes that lined the table, Lanna had little appetite. Something called "Calapash," which Damon said was turtle cooked in the shell and which, Joshua added proudly, had come from their own "cooter pond," was the pièce de résistance. In addition there was a variety of shellfish, vegetables and delicately flavored rice bread, as well as another rosy, spicy dish they called "jambalaya." Lanna tasted everything she possibly could until her corset became a whalebone prison and, sighing, she had to give up.

She had dressed formally for dinner because the house seemed to demand it. Her dress was a frosty blue, woven through with silver threads, and a silver rose nestled in the low décolletage.

Damon sat at the head of the table and Lanna felt his eyes on her, but she did not look up. In the warm dusk of the evening she was remembering what had happened between them in the hot cabin of the *Wayward Woman*. It did not seem possible that that savage beast and this elegantly dressed man with the impeccable table manners were one and the same.

In the silence left by the departing servants Lanna felt ill at ease. As she sipped her wine she glanced about the room, noting the tasteful furniture, much of it of French origin. Feeling Damon's relentless gaze, she was sorry she had dressed so elaborately and allowed Myrtle to wrap her long hair in a swathed style caught by a fresh flower. When at last the silence became unbearable, she looked up into his dark stare and said, "Your home is lovely. Not at all what I was expecting."

"Of course not," he drawled, "you thought we lived in log cabins."

"Not at all," she said quickly. "Just as you did not believe all English people lived in thatched cottages."

"*Touché.*"

So much for her attempt at conversation. She put down her wine glass and stood up.

"Before you deprive me of your scintillating company," Damon said, "I must tell you about Beth Grenville. I understand she and her grandfather are in Charleston and I expect she will be calling on you."

"Oh? And why would she want to do that? Whoever she is . . ." There was something in his eyes that made her fearful, and it was more Lanna who spoke than Leona Anne.

"She is Rafe Danvers' fiancée."

43

Lanna sat down abruptly. "Fiancée . . . you said he was *married!*" Her voice dropped to a horrified whisper.

"I lied," he said calmly.

Lanna wanted to stand up and charge toward him, to scratch at his face. Leona Anne and reason prevailed as it occurred to her that if Rafe were free, she would be able to have her marriage to Damon annulled and . . .

"How very transparent you are," Damon said. "I can almost see your scheming little mind at work. It will do you no good. Rafe Danvers will no longer want you, you'll find."

Under the linen tablecloth Lanna's fingers slowly pleated the material of her dress. "None of this makes sense," she said. Her voice almost broke. "Why have you done this? Committed yourself to a mockery of a marriage with me . . . why?"

"I told you why. I married you for your money."

"Then you will be disappointed. I have no money. And Rafe . . . what of him? I thought he was your friend."

"He was never my friend. Merely a paying passenger on my ship. Since I own a share of his father's plantation and that plantation is in serious financial trouble . . . well, it is to our mutual benefit that young Rafe marry Beth Grenville, whose grandfather owns the neighboring plantation. Combined, the two plantations will be worth a great deal more."

Rafe didn't jilt me, Lanna was thinking. He isn't married, he loves me, nothing else matters. Damon tricked both of us. When I see Rafe I can tell him everything, get my marriage annulled and marry him. She was not listening to what Damon was saying.

"As far as your own wealth is concerned, I have made a careful study of your father's assets . . . long before I laid eyes on his beautiful daughter. Apart from Sir Jared's career as commander of a frigate, he also owns two merchantmen and various sugar and rum interests in the Indies . . . the merchant ships inherited from your late mother's family, I believe, and the other interests acquired over the years he spent in the Caribbean. Then there is Kingsburch and its tenant farms back in England. And you are his only living relative. You are not listening to me, madam."

Lanna looked at him, her eyes still registering shock.

"If I am not present when Beth Grenville calls on you, I want you to be polite and friendly, do you understand?"

44

Lanna's agony was reflected in the tears filling her eyes as she continued to stare at him in disbelief.

"She is the only true lady I have ever met," Damon continued. "Completely honest and without guile. Defenseless against your wiles, madam. Therefore, I am warning you that I will not allow you to vent your jealousy on her innocent head."

"I would like you to arrange an annulment of our marriage as soon as possible." Her voice was little more than a whisper.

"Oh no, my dear, not I. If you wish to write to your father and beg him to come rescue you, by all means do so. But I must remind you that you are in this country at my expense—and until your father comes for you, you would do well to behave yourself. After all, you left home and country with nothing more than a few clothes. You will have to have food and shelter until help arrives." He was smiling faintly, and he casually lit a long black cigar without asking her permission.

Lanna went up to her room, sat at her desk and began to write a letter to Teddie in London, pouring out her entire misadventure, but then she stopped and tore up the paper. Teddie had been a dear, but what right did Lanna have to burden her with problems for which she was neither responsible nor able to provide a solution? She began another letter to let Teddie know of the safe arrival of the ship. She would have to await Rafe's return. He would help her get an annulment. She was halfway through the letter when the door burst open and Damon stood on the threshold, reeling slightly from an excess of brandy.

"I forgot to add, my dear, that I don't keep useless pets about the house," he said, his voice slurred and husky as he approached her.

Lanna picked up the inkwell from her desk and flung it at him. He sidestepped as the heavy glass crashed into the wall behind him. The black liquid dripped down the delicately embossed wallpaper to stain the carpet below.

He caught her wrist as she tried to slash at him with the quill snatched from the desk. He held her hands above her head and ripped the bodice of her grown, exposing the thin chemise beneath. She turned her face away, but his hand went around her neck, pulling her toward him, and then his mouth was on hers and she could neither breathe nor struggle. When he released her to tear at her chemise,

45

she broke away and ran, but he caught her and pushed her down on the bed, cursing under his breath as he fumbled with her skirts.

Lanna cried out and clawed helplessly at those insistent seeking hands. At last she lay naked in the moonlight that streamed in through the French windows. He ran his dark hands down the length of her squirming body. He seized her wrists, twisting her arms behind her back, and lowered his body over hers. His knee forced her thighs apart and she cried out in pain as he thrust into her and his mouth closed over hers again.

Closing her eyes, she tried to clench her teeth, but his tongue forced her lips apart and that other part of him was penetrating ever deeper as her own muscles relaxed in swift betrayal. She did not know when he stopped holding her wrists and she let her hands cling to that lithe back, nor when his hands closed over her breasts, moving the nipples in slow circles until she gasped and heard a faint whimpering noise that surely was not coming from deep inside her . . .

She was rushing toward some dizzying pinnacle of exquisite sensation and he was part of it and they were joined in a sweet, fierce explosion of mind and body that left them suddenly limp.

He lay beside her, his arms still holding her close, and she buried her face in the black hair of his chest, smelling the slightly musky scent of him. She should be angry, berating him, she knew . . . but a delicious sense of euphoria had robbed her limbs of any desire to move. Ridiculously, she wanted to sleep . . .

Sometime in the night she came drowsily to consciousness and found he was kissing her breasts, slowly, tantalizingly, his tongue tracing the outline of the nipples that hardened under his lips. Then his mouth was moving down, lower and lower, and she clutched at his head in alarm. But it was too late to stop his lips from touching the soft mound above her thighs, and his tongue was seeking and finding a quivering response as she moaned and gripped his head with feverish fingers.

Then he was kissing her mouth again, and this time when he entered her she lifted her hips toward him eagerly, moving to meet each thrust of his pulsating member with her own wildly wanton undulations. Somewhere in some distant corner of her mind a small voice was telling her

46

that no lady ever acted this way, but it was quickly stilled as she lost herself in the magic of being one with him.

He was gone when she awoke in the morning. The bedroom was flooded with sunlight, and Myrtle was offering her a breakfast tray because "Miss Indigo done come back and Miss Beth is waiting on y'all in the drawing room."

Lanna smiled as she looked at the bedsheets, wrinkled and tossed in a heap. There was an indentation in his pillow where his head had lain beside her. She sat up slowly, smiling at his pillow, at Myrtle, at the world.

The breakfast tray contained surprises. Boiled rice with thick gravy, and delicately flavored breast of chicken. Some kind of corn flour made into cakes, with ginger preserves and freshly churned butter. She was hungry and the food was delicious.

"You'd better stay and help me dress if I have visitors," she told Myrtle. And then she remembered who Beth was and that Rafe was still free.

Her unfinished letter to Teddie still lay on the desk. She tucked it under the blotter as she went by to her dressing room.

As Myrtle helped her dress, Lanna found herself thinking not about Beth and Rafe, but about Damon, and the unwilling response of her own flesh to the animal lust of him. She was sorry she had slept so late and had not had the opportunity to observe Damon this morning. Yet it seemed every secret part of her body remembered him and trembled at the memory. Oh, how was it possible to hate a man and want his caress at the same time? Could it be . . . perish the thought . . . that under Leona Anne's ladylike demeanor, there lurked a loose woman? Quickly she snatched back her hair, twisting it into a bun at the nape of her neck, and put on a high-necked gown that immediately made her feel uncomfortably hot.

Two women awaited her in the drawing room, and Lanna's eyes went first to the exquisite mulatto who was pouring tea from a silver pot. Indigo . . . the housekeeper, it had to be, but someone should have mentioned she was breathtakingly beautiful. Lanna almost felt a physical jolt as she looked at the woman.

Her skin was the color of creamy coffee, and her hair, not wooly or crisply curled like the other slaves', hung silken as a raven's wing almost to her waist. Nor was she dressed in the calico and starched aprons of the other

47

servants: her morning gown was of well-cut pearl grey merino. Enormous honey gold eyes observed Lanna from beneath curling black eyelashes. Flaring nostrils and full sensual lips completed the strikingly lovely face.

Reluctantly Lanna dragged her eyes from Indigo to the girl who stood up shyly and came toward her. "Why, she's plain!" Lanna thought with relief. The girl was slender and frail-looking, with camelia pale skin and a mass of light brown hair that seemed too heavy for her small features and slim neck. She had soft brown eyes that sought Lanna's eagerly, and her tiny hands were outstretched in greeting.

"Welcome, oh, welcome, Lanna . . . may I call you that?" Her voice was slightly breathless and she smiled a shy smile that transformed her face miraculously.

"She isn't quite so plain when she smiles," Lanna thought, offering her hand. She noted too that Beth Grenville moved with an almost ethereal grace, her morning frock swaying like billowing sails beneath her childishly flat bosom and thin waist.

"How do you do, Miss Grenville?"

"Beth . . . please call me Beth. Damon called early this morning and we are so excited and happy for you both. Oh, it's so romantic . . . being married at sea, and—oh, Lanna, you are so beautiful!" Her words tripped over each other impulsively, and she was asking about the voyage and chatting as though they were old friends.

When at last Beth broke off, looking embarrassed as she realized she was monopolizing the conversation, Indigo looked at Lanna and said, "Welcome, milady. I am Indigo." Her voice was a surprise. There was no trace of the Negro accent of the other servants. It was a husky, feminine version of Damon's accent. Indigo's eyes held for a second longer than necessary and Lanna again felt the full power of her beauty. There was an uncomfortable silence for a moment as Lanna tried to imagine what she should say as mistress of the house.

Finally she gained control of herself and said, "I'm very glad to meet you, Indigo. And thank you for entertaining Miss Grenville. I would like very much to talk to you about running the house sometime today. For now, I can manage the tea by myself. Perhaps you'll send in another cup and saucer for me on your way out?"

Indigo paused for a moment, her eyes still locked with

48

Lanna's, and then she turned and left the room, moving swiftly and sinuously as a cat.

"She has been Damon's housekeeper for quite some time," Beth said after the door closed behind Indigo. "I suppose she may feel a little threatened having a new mistress in the house. But you will be patient with her, I know. Lanna dear, tell me, how is my beloved Rafe? Damon tells me Rafe wanted to see New York before he returned. He won't be home for a couple more weeks, and I do miss him."

Lanna looked into the other girl's shining eyes and felt a stab of pain. But Rafe doesn't love her, he loves me.

"He was well, when I saw him last. Are you staying in town long?" Her voice sounded stilted and unnatural but Beth did not appear to notice.

"Until the weather cools. We spend the summers here because it's too hot at Oakside . . . that's our plantation. Grandfather is getting on in years and he gets the malaria. Not too many white folks stay during the summer, it just isn't healthy. The past two seasons Rafe's parents have stayed and I do worry about them. They have Clearview, you know, and are our neighbors. Rafe's father isn't too active nowadays, he was injured in an accident . . ."

Lanna sipped her tea. Rafe had told her little about his family except that he was an only child and his parents were anxious for him to marry and take over the plantation. He had neglected to mention he was expected to marry their neighbor.

"But I chatter too much. I have the carriage outside and as soon as you've finished your tea I would like to take you for a drive and show you our lovely city."

Lanna hoped that Damon would have returned when Beth's carriage at last returned her to the house in the late afternoon, but he had not. She caught a glimpse of Indigo setting the table in the dining room, her hair a blue-black curtain over her face as she bent to place a floral centerpiece on the white cloth. She had changed into a brilliant red silk gown. Lanna paused in the doorway and tried to sound casual as she said, "After today I would like to supervise the table arrangements, Indigo."

The amber eyes met hers. "Of course, Mrs. St. Clair. And I will help you. I know what the master likes."

Lanna turned around slowly and went upstairs. She felt angry, without really knowing why. She poured almost

49

a whole bottle of cologne into her bath water and tried and discarded several dresses before choosing one of pure white, embroidered with a gold thread that picked up the color of her hair. She brushed her hair until it shone and left it hanging loosely, in much the same way Indigo wore hers. Lanna was glad she had resisted Teddie's urging to cut her hair in a short style. Her hair was too straight to be attractive cut short and, besides, Damon must approve of the style, Lanna's intuition told her.

Damon . . . Lanna's heart was beating excitedly as she went downstairs to dinner. Damon would be home soon and after dinner . . .

She ate dinner alone, served by Joshua. When she inquired about Indigo the expressive black face crumpled and the eyes rolled skyward and he said she had been called away for the evening and no, ma'am, Mr. Damon has not come home either.

Sometime in the early morning hours she awoke to find herself still alone in the bed. The air was a sultry, smothering cloud. She arose and went through the French windows to her balcony, standing in the warm darkness for a moment before she heard the soft murmur of voices below and then, distinctly, a woman's laugh, vibrant and full of unspoken invitation. Indigo . . . it had to be she. How dare she entertain someone at this late hour? A man?

Then she heard his voice, clearly. "Come here, you bitch," and it was low and husky with passion. Damon's voice.

CHAPTER 5

She had been named for the plant that had brought riches to the early plantations of the Carolinas, but the indigo crops had been ruined by disease and caterpillar infestation, and now the rice crops that had replaced the indigo were in turn giving way to cotton.

Indigo's mother had been a slave and her father a planter of mixed Irish/Scots blood. He had sold her when she was five years old because her skin was too fair, her hair too straight, and this offended the planter's wife and his family.

Indigo had been lucky. She was bought by a man who had a daughter almost her age, an only child named Cindy Sue who was pampered and indulged even to the point of having her favorite slave share the schoolroom with her. Moreover, Indigo lived in the "big house" all of her life and by the time she was sixteen was more beautiful, more willful and infinitely more desirable than the planter's own daughter. That was when Indigo learned about white people, for when her companion of the illegal schoolroom days realized that the beaux who called were more interested in Indigo than in the daughter of a wealthy planter, Cindy Sue's attitude began to change. She complained to her parents that Indigo was much too uppity for a slave, that she borrowed possessions and did not return them, that the black bucks among the house servants became impossible in Indigo's presence, that the slave women disliked her. Cindy Sue's parents made soothing

51

noises and did their best to mollify their spoiled daughter. They had both grown fond of Indigo over the years.

Inevitably, there came the day when Cindy Sue fell in love with a neighboring planter's son who spent a great deal of time visiting the girls. Unfortunately, when he came to ask for a hand in marriage, it was not Cindy Sue's but rather Indigo's he asked for.

Cindy Sue insisted her father had to sell Indigo or his own beloved daughter would kill herself. Besides, the law clearly stated slaves could neither learn to read, nor marry whites . . .

Indigo was sold to friends of the planter who lived in Georgia, but on the eve of her departure she had run away.

She went to Charleston and hid among the Negroes who lived in the maze of narrow alleys there. Half-starved, she had been caught by Claudine L'Herreaux in the act of stealing a freshly baked loaf of bread that was cooling on Claudine's window ledge. Claudine had married a widowed sailor named Pierre L'Herreaux. They had a son named Alain, and they had also adopted an English orphan, Damon. Now Claudine persuaded her husband to accept the lovely young Indigo too, because three men made for a great deal of work.

Indigo had fallen in love with Damon almost the moment she first saw him. He was two or three years her senior, and he had fixed his careless black-eyed glance on her indifferently when she was presented to him.

Damon St. Clair had already discovered the thrill of gambling, of suddenly setting off on a journey with no particular destination in mind, of being answerable to no one. Claudine had always been a servant to him; her Frenchman and his bowlegged son were not related to him. None of them could tell Damon what to do or what not to do. Damon took women casually, as merely another of the body's appetites to be appeased. On his travels about the young country, to New Orleans, to any Gulf town where gamblers gathered, he found plenty of beautiful women.

When Claudine threatened him with slow death if he laid a hand on her protégée, he shrugged and told her he wasn't interested in mulattoes anyway. Nevertheless, when Indigo looked up at him from under lustrous black lashes, her amber eyes pools of sparkling light, her golden skin glowing and her silken mane of hair falling softly about

52

rounded shoulders . . . Damon St. Clair's glance would begin to smoulder.

The men were glad to have Indigo in their household, especially after Claudine died. Then, Pierre stayed away at sea for longer periods, and Alain followed his father into the merchant marine.

"You take care of the restless one, nightflower . . ." Alain had told Indigo, "he is too lucky at cards to live long."

Indigo smiled at Alain. They had been at ease with each other from the first, almost as though they had been brother and sister from birth. Alain was thoughtful and gentle, treating her as an equal. It was always Alain who leaped up to relieve her of a heavy shopping basket, or lingered to help her clear the remnants of a meal, despite Damon's taunts at him for doing so. It was to Alain she turned for advice, for sympathy, for news of the world beyond the square mile in which she lived.

"I wish you weren't going away to sea, Alain," Indigo said. "I shall miss you, but I suppose the sea is in your blood and you are happier on a ship."

"I believe my short legs were meant for the deck of a ship," Alain said with a grin, "and my long arms for climbing the rigging. A special animal, you see, how you say . . . an aquatic animal. Not bred for the land." His sensitive dark eyes smiled sadly.

"Don't speak so of yourself," Indigo said sharply. She wanted to tell him how he appeared to her, but the words would not come, and he was already lifting his duffel bag to his shoulder and stepping through the door. She did not have time to tell him that there was a grace to his facial features and an inner strength that eventually made those around him forget the peculiarities of his body. Nor would she have been able to express the thought if there had been time.

She was surprised and vaguely disturbed to discover how much she missed Alain. She found herself storing up little stories and questions for his return. It was, she supposed, because she had grown accustomed to having him around.

Damon came and went as swiftly and surely as night followed day, and he oi   ignored her completely when he was home. She spent nours thinking of ways to make him fall in love with her. In Damon's presence she was

53

Eve, Cleopatra, the mythical sirens of the seven seas; forever inviting, always beguiling.

Yet it was Alain who left the great gaping hole in her life with his departure. There had never been anyone she had trusted so completely. She knew beyond a shadow of a doubt that he would never hurt her, would always protect her . . . as indeed, so often he had . . . from the unwelcome advances of both blacks and whites in the crowded alleys and back streets of Charleston—those places that the white aristocrats hardly knew existed.

If Indigo had not fallen madly, passionately in love with Damon at first sight, she would have been well content to serve Alain in any way he desired. Her love for Damon was a flame that was fed by unfulfilled desire. No man had ever looked upon the beautiful Indigo with indifference, and it was unthinkable that the one man she wanted so desperately should do so. In her obsession to overcome Damon's lack of interest, to make him aware of her, to make him love her, she did not realize that for all her passion for Damon, she was actually happier in Alain's company.

Alain talked to her, made her laugh, sympathized with her problems. She wanted Alain to remain near her always. With Alain there, she did not worry about the white planters and the Cindy Sues of the world. Alain was her father, her brother, her friend, and so much more. There was a mystical bond between them that transcended any earthly union. It was so much a part of her life that she took it for granted. Alain would always be there when she needed him.

She counted the days until Alain's ship returned and flung herself joyously into those comforting long arms when his voyage at last brought him back to Charleston.

Solemnly and shyly, he presented her with a filigree brooch and a sinuous she-lion, carved from a piece of ivory. "I see so many strange lands, Indigo," he told her, "but none to compare to this land of ours, and no woman in all the world as lovely as you. Ah, nightflower, you should be queen of us all, and we your humble subjects . . ."

Indigo laughed delightedly and served him the elegant feast she had prepared for his homecoming.

"Fit for a prodigal's return!" he gasped when he could eat no more. "But where is our other prodigal son? Damon is not here?"

"He's been gone for months this time. He never lets me know where he is or when he will return. It wasn't so bad while Claudine and your father were here . . ."

"Ah, *ma petite,* you have been lonely. We should not both go away at the same time . . ." He struck his forehead with his palm in a gesture that expressed his disgust with his own thoughtlessness. "I shall not leave until he returns . . . and then I shall sail only short voyages. And when our time of mourning for Claudine is over . . ." He broke off, afraid to say what was in his heart. Besides, he must make many voyages before he would have enough money to even hope . . .

Indigo had her back to him, carrying the dishes from the table, moving in her effortlessly graceful way, humming softly to herself. She was so happy to have Alain back to feed and pamper and talk to . . . Then she straightened up abruptly, her head inclined to the side as though listening.

"What is it, fair one? What do you hear?" Alain asked.

"Damon . . ." she breathed. "He's coming home . . . he'll be here tonight." She did not know how she knew this. She knew it in the same way she knew exactly what time it was when she opened her eyes in the morning, or when the last day of summer was upon them, or when a rainstorm was approaching.

When Damon appeared late that evening, Alain felt a sinking premonition as he watched the two of them. Damon stayed only long enough to eat and change clothes, but the light in Indigo's eyes remained even after Damon had gone out to find a poker game.

The next day, when Damon, bleary-eyed and considerably richer, staggered into the house, Alain told him sternly that they must make better arrangements for Indigo. She should not be left alone and unprotected.

Damon had looked at him in surprise and then had glanced carelessly at Indigo. "You're right, Alain, as always. Go ahead and sign on for a voyage, I'll stay around Charleston for a while," he said.

Alain signed on for a voyage up the coast, reluctant to be gone for long despite Damon's promise.

Indigo waited and hoped. She was on the point of asking one of the old women for a potion to slip into his drink when he came home one night in a rage because he had lost a great deal of money in a card game. Indigo was sitting outside their tiny house, enjoying the cool air. Suddenly, Damon seized her by the arm and dragged her in-

55

side to his bed. He deflowered her with little preparation and no tenderness, falling asleep immediately afterward.

She lay in his arms all night, cradling the dark head to her breast, thinking of him, and not of the pain he had inflicted.

The next morning Alain returned from his voyage to find the two of them in each other's arms. Silently he took his belongings from the house to a permanent home on his ship.

Damon awakened and looked up at her for a moment. Then he pulled her to him. "I was angry last night. It was not the time to make love to you. But you know I can't share a house with you and not take you to my bed . . ."

"Damon, it's all right," she whispered, running her hand down his chiseled face, tracing the outline of the stubbornly set mouth. He needed a shave and his beard was rough against her skin as he began to kiss her breasts. She lay back and watched him explore her golden body with his hands and his mouth. This time when he entered her there was no pain and her hips moved wildly with his until she clutched his body and gasped her fulfillment.

They stayed in bed all that day. She brought wine and fruit from the kitchen, a bowl of warm water to bathe away their sweat. She begged him to tell her what she must do to please him, that she would be his slave forever.

Their fortunes changed in the following years as Damon traveled the young country, returning each time with more money. He was acquiring the toughness and chillingly calm exterior of the professional gambler. His clothes were fancier and his expression more inscrutable.

But he always came back to Indigo, bringing gifts. Fancy dresses, jewelry. Whether he had been gone a week or six months their reunion was always the same. Always there was a gift, and then he spent the day and often the night as well making love to her. The lovemaking became more professional as time went by. The fancy ladies of New Orleans and the sophisticated gambling queens across the South taught Damon there was more to making love to a woman than thrusting himself inside her.

Indigo never questioned where he had been, or what he did. She came alive when he returned to her, and she died a little when he left.

He returned from one of his trips and, instead of the customary lovemaking, he produced a bottle of champagne

56

and seated her ceremoniously at the head of the table. "Indigo, my high priestess of desire," he announced, "I have news for you. I sought out your former owners and have legally bought your freedom."

"Damon . . . my love . . . oh, thank you, thank you!" It was as though she had let out her breath after holding it for a long time. The terrible fear that had always haunted her had been lifted from her shoulders. Damon did not know that when she slept alone she was tormented by frightening dreams, nightmares in which she was again at the mercy of Cindy Sue and a white master.

"And I might as well tell you," he continued, popping the champagne cork, "that I promptly won back all I paid for you . . . which was a considerable amount . . . in a card game with your ex-owner. His Cindy Sue, by the way, is not yet married. Simpering little idiot. I can see why she wanted to get rid of you." His dark eyes were veiled for a moment and then he threw back his head and laughed at some memory he did not share with her.

Later, when Indigo lay in his arms and he was a part of her and she wanted him to stay there, inside her, always, she realized she was still a slave . . . a slave to her love for Damon.

Alain did not share Damon's hunger for wealth, nor his love for gambling. Alain loved the sea, his ship, and the fair warm winds that carried him to distant shores. Alain also loved Indigo. He loved her worshipfully, hopelessly, agonizingly. He adored her silently from afar, and he suffered the tortures of the damned when Damon casually made her his mistress.

Long voyages could not erase the vision of the amber-eyed beauty from his mind, and he embarked on a reckless series of adventures in his effort to forget.

He had the courage and foresight to remain on board a ship that went aground on a Caribbean reef. He stayed aboard to prevent plundering and to secure the salvage rights for the owners, but as luck would have it, the weather improved and the ship floated again at high tide and was saved.

The grateful owners made Alain captain and gave him a share of the profit on the cargo. They also agreed to allow him a portion of the hold space for cargoes of his own on future voyages.

Damon would join him sometimes on a short voyage,

when his restless soul craved new vistas, having purchased a young black girl to keep Indigo company when they were away. And it was Damon who urged Alain to buy high-profit cargoes. They found at last the one cargo that brought nothing but profit. The slaves of the Indies were very partial to banjo music. Fiddlestrings were hard to come by, in constant demand, and they took little space away from the owners' cargoes.

Eventually Damon had secured the *Wayward Woman* for them, in a poker game that had lasted three days and nights and had almost bankrupted the Clearview plantation, owned by Michael Danvers, a compulsive but unlucky gambler.

Alain still went straight to Indigo the moment his ship arrived in Charleston. One day, finding her alone, he asked, "He treat you all right, Indigo? He is kind to you?"

Indigo sighed contentedly and a sensuous ripple passed through her slim body. It expressed her feelings for Damon more clearly than any words. "Did he not buy my freedom?" she asked with profound gratitude in her voice. She did not know that it had been Alain who had traced her former owners and made all the arrangements by means of careful correspondence, before Damon had presented himself to consummate the transaction. Alain had felt that the gentleman planter would not want to deal with a rough seaman.

When the *Wayward Woman* next put to sea, Alain left Damon behind and deliberately sought out-of-the-way ports for his cargoes, not returning to Charleston for many months.

At length, in New Orleans, Alain had met a delicate Creole girl and, on the rebound from Indigo, had fallen passionately in love with her. When he declared himself to the girl his happiness shattered into shards of pure horror. The girl laughed at him, laughed at the thought that any woman could love or marry a man who looked like Alain L'Herreaux.

"You little monkey!" she had taunted. "I let you court me only to amuse my friends. How dare you say you love me, you with your ape legs and gorilla arms. You should be in a zoo . . . you little freak." She had laughed so hard the tears ran down her cheeks and, blinded by his own tears, Alain had stumbled out of her life.

He had never learned that she was dying of consumption and had had only a few more months to live.

Alain told himself sternly that he would never again forget that the tenderness of his heart, the yearning of his soul and the hot surging of his passionate blood were trapped forever in a misshapen body. No other woman would ever be given the opportunity to laugh at Alain L'Herreaux or make a mockery of his love.

Arriving back in Charleston, Alain found Damon had steadily been amassing a great deal of money. Indigo wore silks and jewels. Imported furniture crowded their tiny house and they had two black maids. Indigo glowed with happiness and Alain's misery was lessened when he realized that Damon was making her happy.

Ironically, it was Indigo herself who destroyed the idyll. Damon was well aware his method of making a living excluded him from Charleston society, or from acceptance into the planters' social circles. After he became part-owner of the Clearview plantation, he was determined to break into the exclusive ranks of Charleston society. Therefore, he bought a house on the Battery and slaves to run it. When they moved into their new home, Indigo found an old trunk that Claudine had brought with her from England all those years before. Sorting through the musty contents, Indigo found the leather case which contained several yellowing documents. Damon's birth certificate . . . Damon *Trelayne* . . . marriage lines, a diary and several letters.

Damon became very drunk after reading all of the documents several times. He staggered about the house, speaking his thoughts aloud in anguish.

"She told me they had been killed in an accident . . . she never told me he had them murdered. I'll find him . . . kill him . . ." and, over and over again, he repeated the name of Jared Malford.

CHAPTER 6

By the time the *Sarah Jane* reached Portugal, Rafe was as
sure-footed on the yards as any member of the crew, although Captain McLeod preferred to keep him on the
bridge or at the chart table. A quiet companionship had
sprung up between the old Scot and the handsome young
American. Captain McLeod was disappointed when Rafe
announced he must find a ship for the Carolinas so that he
could return to his home and his duty there.

"My father almost lost his leg some years ago. It was
crushed by a falling tree," Rafe told him. "And our plantation has been in dire straits ever since." He did not add
that this was due more to his father's luck at cards than to
his shattered leg. "My parents sent me to university and
then on my grand tour, but it's time I returned to ease my
father's burden."

"Aye, lad. I understand," Captain McLeod said. "We'll
find ye a ship for the Carolinas. But it's a mistake ye make.
Ye'll not be happy as a lubber . . . not now ye know the
ways of the wind and waves."

Rafe gazed at the sun-splashed walls of the Portuguese
village, and then back at the endless mass of the sea. It was
not only the thrill of feeling a ship respond to the right
handling. There was also the excitement of setting foot in a
strange port. The camaraderie of shipmates.

He thought of Clearview with its dull toil and its sea of
black faces. It had been a relief to go North to university.
He had dreaded returning in the summer to the inevitable

60

spell of duty with the Patrol—the "patterolers" who hunted down runaway slaves. All planters' sons were expected to serve, although many preferred to pay a substitute, or even the stiff fine imposed for shirking the duty. In Rafe's case, he felt guilty enough at the financial hardship his college tuition had caused, without asking for money to avoid having to serve on the Patrol. So he rode out after runaways and was sickened by the punishment inflicted on the unfortunate wretches they caught.

His father's only joy came from a bottle, and his mother lived in some grand place in her imagination. Neither of them seemed to understand that the prosperous plantation built by his grandparents, the grand-scale entertaining and lavish living, were gone forever.

Then there was Beth . . . sweet little Beth, an angel who never should have been allowed to leave heaven. They had known each other all of their lives, and no one knew better than Rafe that Beth was good and pure as few mortals can ever hope to be. Perhaps that was why he flinched inwardly at the thought of marriage to her. How did a man make love to a saint?

The distant sweep of blue sea made him think of Lanna's liquid blue eyes and the difference in his feelings toward her. Outwardly her demeanor was as ladylike as Beth's, yet an unseen force passed between them whenever they were together. Lanna's cool beauty was merely a thin veneer over a deeply passionate nature, Rafe knew. The slightest touch of her fingertips set his blood on fire.

He looked down again at the village and the olive-skinned women who wound their stately way up the steep streets.

"I'm going ashore, skipper," he said.

Captain McLeod's faded blue eyes crinkled at the corners. "Aye, take your time, lad. I'll find a ship for the Carolinas for ye." The young American had a healthy appetite for women as well as an exuberant zest for all of the other pleasures life offered. Just being with him made McLeod feel young again. Rafe Danvers would be sorely missed aboard the *Sarah Jane*.

Lanna finally wrote to Teddie, asking her to send word to Sir Jared that she had made a terrible mistake and wanted to go home. Perhaps if Teddie interceded for her . . . Teddie had such a way about her, she could persuade Sir Jared if anyone could.

61

Damon was eating breakfast on the piazza and Lanna dropped the letter on the table. "Will you have this posted for me?"

His dark eyes flickered over her briefly. "You haven't written to your father, I see."

"An old friend . . . she will help me to get an annulment."

"Unfortunately, my dear, an annulment is no longer possible. You will have to face the stigma of a divorce," he said coolly.

"Divorce!" Lanna gasped, all the horror and disgrace of the word overwhelming her. Why, that would brand her for life . . . she would be shunned by decent people.

"Yes. You see, an annulment is only possible when a marriage has not been consummated." His eyes slipped down the length of her body, pausing suggestively in the region near the top of her legs.

All this time, in her naïveté, she had been counting on an annulment, a means of escape from this dreadful situation. And all this time, *he* had known, known it was not possible. She sat down limply and stared at him. "Why . . . why?"

"Contrary to what you may believe, my lady wife, I want you to stay here. Be mistress of my house. A woman of your breeding, to say nothing of your fortune and looks, is an asset to a man. Particularly a man like me, whose own breeding is suspect by the old line aristocrats here."

"I suppose you feel having a wife will give you respectability and hide from the world your . . . your low animalistic vices." The thought was Leona Anne's, but it was Lanna who spoke the words.

"Oh, I seem to recall a mutual sharing of . . . animalistic vices." He laughed softly, his eyes mocking her, and she rose and sped into the house, her cheeks flaming.

She had barely reached the top of the stairs when Damon appeared beside her. She jumped back, startled.

"I just came to say goodbye," he said. "I shall be gone for a while, so you won't have to worry about my 'animal lust.' Beth will invite you to stay with her. I suggest you accept. She will be better company for you than Indigo."

"I suppose that means you will be taking Indigo with you?"

His eyes narrowed. "What is that supposed to imply?"

"Nothing . . . I'll stay with Beth." She was thinking that

62

Beth's companionship would be better than living under the same roof as Indigo. At least until Rafe arrived.

Damon's arm snaked out and caught her about the waist, spun her around and crushed her to him. Then he kissed her slowly and deliberately, with a seeking, pulsating kiss that was almost an act of love in itself. For a second she responded before pushing him away.

He laughed again and bowed his head before turning on his heel and running down the stairs. It was only then that Lanna saw Indigo standing silently in the hall below, watching them, her sinuous body poised like a cat about to spring.

Sir Jared Malford stood at the window of the villa overlooking the bay, his eyes on the ship that swayed at anchor beyond the reef. The silence between master and servant lengthened as the white-jacketed houseboy waited for instructions regarding the unexpected visitor.

"The name is meaningless to me. He is the master of the vessel at anchor?" Sir Jared asked.

"The ship's captain is one Alain L'Herreaux," the servant answered in his precise, slightly sing-song English. "This gent who awaits my master's pleasure is, I believe, the supercargo of the *Wayward Woman*."

"And you are sure he said his name was St. Clair?" There was something oddly familiar about the name.

"Oh, yes, master. St. Clair . . . but he is not French, master, he speak English like an American."

"Very well, show him in. And tell Lucas I will see him as soon as I have found out what the American wants."

"Master Bassey come to see you about sailing away again, master?"

"No, Samuel. My ship will need extensive repairs. I shall be in residence for some weeks."

Sir Jared poured himself a glass of rum from the decanter that rested on the intricately carved table in front of him. Both table and rum were products of native craftsmen. The decanter was poised over a second glass when the American entered the room, walking with a sailor's roll. His dark eyes swept over the room and came to rest on Sir Jared.

Tall, well-muscled, with the expressionless face of a gambler or one of those bandits who roamed the wild American continent, Sir Jared noted. The black hair and swarthy skin made him look as French as his name.

63

For Damon's part, he looked at a man who was now a little younger than Damon's father would have been had he lived. A man still in his prime, despite the lines of dissipation beginning to show on the thinly aristocratic features. Sir Jared's hair was iron grey, his eyes a piercing blue. Damon could see no resemblance to Lanna other than the color of the eyes. She must have favored her mother.

They stared at each other for a long moment, and at last Sir Jared filled the glass with rum and placed it on the table, gesturing toward a chair. "Sit down, my young friend. Have a glass of rum and tell me your business. If you are looking for a cargo for your ship you've come to the wrong man. I have my own merchantmen to carry our excellent local rum for sale to the navy. A stalwart custom, that of splicing the mainbrace . . . I understand it is not followed on American ships?"

Damon ignored both the rum and the question. "My father was Richard Trelayne."

Sir Jared's expression did not change. "So?"

"He was killed eighteen years ago . . . while attempting to escape from the Tower, where he was awaiting trial for treason."

"A serious offense." Sir Jared's eyebrows lifted slightly. "But you must admire his daring to even attempt such an escape."

"Escape from the Tower was . . . is . . . virtually impossible. Someone had to arrange it on the outside, bribe guards . . . that someone was you."

"And you've come to thank me, after all these years?"

"I've come to destroy you. After my father's name has been cleared."

"Most interesting, but I haven't the vaguest idea what you are talking about. I remember your father, of course. His death was tragic, but perhaps merciful in sparing your family the disgrace of a trial? It was all a long time ago."

"I would have come sooner, had I known. I only learned the whole story after our servant died. She kept certain documents and facts hidden from me . . . perhaps waiting for the right time to tell me. Who knows? She died without telling me, and we only found the documents and diaries a few months ago. I realize the trail is cold, but I will clear his name and see you hang. Meantime, I have made my start on my plan for revenge. You have already paid the first installment."

Sir Jared leaned back and regarded Damon for a long moment. "And what is that?"

"You took from me the two people I loved most in the world. I have taken from you the only person you have."

Damon watched closely for Sir Jared's reaction. Years of gambling had made him sensitive to even the slightest change in an opponent's expression. He was unprepared to see the thin lips curl into a smile.

"I have your daughter," Damon said, believing he had not been understood. "I made her my wife. She is in America at this moment. If you don't believe me, here is a letter she wrote to an old friend in London, begging her to intercede with you and rescue her from the clutches of the demon who married her . . . myself."

Sir Jared was not a man given to laughter. The mouth smiled while the eyes did not, but the smile was the closest he came to registering humor, and Damon saw that his father-in-law was truly amused. It was not feigned.

"I'm delighted to hear it, St. Clair. By the way, I notice that you do not use your father's name, which is interesting. As for Leona, she's been nothing but a drain on my resources and a nuisance that required frequent trips to England, taking me away from my interests here. Naturally, I shan't be providing a dowry since you present me with the marriage as a *fait accompli*. Perhaps I can at least offer a piece of advice. Keep a tight rein on her. She may look like a lady but she had a slut for a mother and the mother's blood seems stronger than her . . . aristocratic paternal strain."

"I believe . . ." Damon said slowly, "I shall worry more about her coldblooded strain. Are you telling me you don't care what happens to her? Your only child? Do you realize how I can use her, if I wish? I can make her life a living hell."

Sir Jared shrugged. "She married you of her own free will, I take it?"

"Read her letter. You will see that she tells her friend I tricked her and married her only for her fortune . . . the fortune she will inherit from you one day. It's all true."

"I repeat, Mr. St. Clair . . . you have relieved me of a burden. I am indebted to you."

Damon stood up, still not quite believing. "Then I will proceed with the second installment, sir. Just remember, any time you want to stop making payments, what my price

65

is: a full confession that it was you and not my father who sold naval secrets."

The smile faded from Sir Jared's gaunt features as he picked up a bell to ring for the manservant. "This interview is at an end, Mr. St. Clair. I never expect to see you or your wife again."

Damon stared into the cold eyes. There was no doubt that Malford was not bluffing.

"Show Mr. St. Clair out, Samuel," Sir Jared said, "and send in my other visitor. If Mr. St. Clair ever comes here again, set the dogs on him."

Samuel's expression did not change as he gestured for Damon to precede him to the front door. Sir Jared, meanwhile, walked across the room to the Spanish credenza that dominated one wall and picked up a foil and fencing mask, tapping the latter impatiently.

"Mr. St. Clair is gone and here is Mr. Bassey," Samuel announced. "Master would like to fence later, yes?"

"When Mr. Bassey leaves, Samuel. Outside on the lawn. I want to be able to see that ship while we duel. Everything in order aboard our ship, Lucas?"

Lucas Bassey eased his bulk slowly into a chair. "Two more deserters, sir. We caught one of them."

"I shall be onboard tomorrow. We'll deal with him then. I am going to sail back to England eventually to exchange the ship for a new one." The average life of a warship was only seven years, due to the green oak from royal English forests that was used in the building, made necessary by the long war with the French. "Meanwhile, Lucas, I want you to take the fastest ship you can find for the Carolinas." He tossed Lanna's letter onto the table. "There will be an address in there. My daughter married an American."

Lucas Bassey picked up the letter. "We'll be at war with them before long. You want me to bring her back here?"

Sir Jared looked at his boatswain, the man who inspired terror aboard any ship and with whom Sir Jared had long ago formed an unholy alliance. Sir Jared had the power, and Lucas Bassey the physical strength and blind loyalty, to enforce the harsh rules of discipline that had made the Royal Navy rulers of the waves for a hundred years.

"No. I don't want her back. But we must learn all we can about her new husband and decide how we will use the knowledge. Come, Lucas, walk with me outside while I tell you what I want you to do."

66

CHAPTER 7

As Damon had predicted, Beth invited Lanna to stay at the Grenville townhouse while he was away.

Beth's grandfather was a lively old man with white whiskers, ruddy cheeks and a great booming laugh that rang forth constantly. He obviously adored his granddaughter.

Grandpa Grenville's house was constantly thronged with visitors. It seemed everyone in Charleston knew and loved the old man and his granddaughter. Beth presided over dinners and musical evenings with grace and dignity, while the old man and his friends argued politics, laughed uproariously and generally enjoyed each other's company.

The women, Lanna noted, were all like Beth. Sweet, soft-spoken, content to fade into the background and serve their men. In return they were rewarded with extravagant gallantry.

Lanna was quickly drawn into Beth's circle of friends, and they did their best to make the newcomer feel at home. The men retired nightly to Grandfather Grenville's study for rousing conversation and free-flowing cognac. During heated discussions about British naval arrogance, the phrase "Orders in Council" drifted from the smoke-filled room. Lanna waited and worried that war would come and she would be trapped in an enemy land.

In spite of her feelings for Rafe, she was drawn to Beth, who she learned had been orphaned as a baby when her parents were felled by yellow fever. Besides, Beth was so sweet and friendly, so solicitous of Lanna, that it was impossible not to respond. Beth saw only goodness and kindly motives in everyone around her. She had never suffered betrayal nor been led to believe that those dear to her were anything less than what she believed them to be.

When Damon had not returned and the Grenvilles were ready to close the townhouse for their winter sojourn at the plantation, Lanna accepted the invitation to go with them.

The evening before they were to depart by river for the plantation, the Grenvilles' house was, as usual, filled with guests. No one was ever turned away from their doors and on this night there seemed to be more guests than ever milling about the gracious drawing room and spilling out onto the piazza.

Lanna slipped away to sit by herself on the garden seat on the cool lawn. A feeling of uneasiness had been with her all day. While everyone had been busy packing and preparing to close the house, Lanna had sensed, rather than seen, eyes seeking her out as she moved about the house. Now in the cool dimness of the garden, she leaned back against the wrought-iron seat and wondered why she had been so jumpy all day.

"Leona . . . don't move or call out," a man's voice said. "Want to speak to you in private." The voice was rough, more waterfront English than cultured Charlestonian. A dark figure emerged from the shadow of the fig tree. "I've come from your father. Name's Lucas Bassey."

Lanna slid to one side of the seat as he sat down beside her. He was a huge man, with a small head set upon massive shoulders that gave him a reptilian look. This impression was further emphasized when he removed his hat and exposed a head that was totally bald. He peered at her in the dim light with pale, beady eyes.

"Thank goodness you're here," Lanna whispered. "But why the secrecy? My husband is away on a voyage. When can I go home?"

"We can't talk here. We must go somewhere and talk privately."

Looking into those odd eyes, Lanna was suddenly afraid. "How do I know you are from my father?"

"You wrote a letter to Teddie Digby in London. Asked her to get your father to help you." He patted his jacket pocket as though to indicate the presence of the letter. "There's a coffee house we can go to. I have a carriage waiting."

The coffee house was crowded with people, and Lucas Bassey led her through the tightly packed tables to a door in the rear. Beyond lay several private rooms. Lanna reluctantly followed him into one of them.

"They say more intrigue goes on here than in Boney's court," Bassey said, throwing his coat across the back of a chair.

"Intrigue . . ." Lanna repeated.

"You know there's a chance of war? The hawks are beating the drums here. Think they have a chance while we're saving the world from Napoleon. Bloody jackals."

"I've heard that the Royal Navy is blockading the ports and boards American ships at will. They say American seamen as well as English deserters are being impressed into British service."

"Whose side are you on? I thought you wanted to go back to England."

"I do. When can I leave?"

"Soon. We have to be careful. Tell me about your husband. From what I've heard, the toffs in these parts aren't happy about him moving in on 'em. Some kind of gambler, isn't he?"

"Yes. And part-owner of a ship, the *Wayward Woman*. He is away at sea at the moment. He owns a house here and a share of a rice plantation up the river. He did tell me once he has enemies. I suppose the men who lost money to him. What will happen to me if war comes?"

"We shall have you on a ship before then. There are plenty of Englishmen moving in and out of Charleston. We're sending agents into the interior to make treaties with the Indians. Maybe we'll stir up the slaves on the plantations a bit too, if the Americans declare war. We can't afford to withdraw our armies from the peninsula, see. Victory over Napoleon comes first. The ship I came on was full of Englishmen coming to see the lay of the land."

"Indians . . . slaves . . ." Lanna repeated. "You mean to organize a massacre?"

"Only if there's war. Now, you're going upriver to visit a plantation, and you can do me a favor while I see about making arrangements to send you home. I'd like you to take an extra trunk with you and keep it hidden away until I come for it."

"No . . . no, I can't. The Grenvilles are my friends. I can't be a part of anything that might harm them."

"You are an Englishwoman, with a duty to your country."

"I am married to an American . . ."

"A marriage you beg us to end. Once a subject, always a subject, remember that. It's something the sniveling cowards who desert and hide on American ships forget. You can't just say you're not English anymore and make it so."

The room was beginning to swim dizzily and Lanna put her hand to her brow. Lucas Bassey's eyes seemed to have a hypnotic effect; she found herself held by their gaze, and she grew uncomfortable as the pause in the conversation lengthened.

"Has my father made my return to England dependent upon my cooperation with you?"

"He'll be disappointed if you won't help your country."

"Perhaps there won't be a war?"

"It won't be of England's making. But the hotheads I've heard about here . . . Calhoun and Cheves, Williams and Lowndes . . . they won't rest until they've started another war with us."

"I can't believe that England would wage war by causing the uprising of Indians and slaves. It isn't honorable. Innocent people would be killed."

"You think it's honorable for America to make war while England is already fighting the worst tyrant the world has ever known?"

"I'm sorry. I won't be a part of it. If my father won't help me to return to England, I shall have to help myself. Would you be kind enough to take me back to the Grenvilles?"

Lanna felt rising nausea as Bassey placed his hand under her elbow to guide her through the crowded rooms. Faces blurred and lights flickered. She wondered vaguely if she were coming down with the grippe. Concentrating on getting out into the open air, she did not see the narrowed eyes that followed her progress, nor the woman with the curtain of blue-black hair who rose to swiftly follow them into the night.

Lanna still felt ill the next morning, and she refused breakfast. Beth fluttered about her worriedly, but wouldn't leave her behind, despite Lanna's pleas that they go on without her.

"I can't leave you here, dear. Damon's servants are somewhat notorious for their . . . lack of discipline. He is away at sea so much, it's understandable. Indigo, especially,

70

comes and goes as she pleases. I should worry about leaving you with them. You might not get the proper care." Beth was too well bred to add that Damon St. Clair had few friends in Charleston society because of his life-style.

Lanna felt too lethargic to argue. Later, she would worry about Rafe's delayed arrival . . . about her marriage . . . about Lucas Bassey who said he would be staying in Charleston for a while, awaiting instructions from her father. Then there was the possibility of war to worry about . . . But none of these things was as frightening as the biggest worry of all: the absence of her monthly cycle since her arrival in Charleston.

She was only remotely aware of the journey to Oakside, the Grenvilles' plantation. The river trip was soothing and she slept most of the way, but bouncing over rough dirt roads in the carriage brought back the nausea. Everywhere there were black slaves working in the flooded fields, and it seemed there were hundreds of them. Lanna thought that it would be easy for them to overcome so few whites.

"Over there is the beginning of the Clearview plantation. That's Rafe's home." Beth pointed and Lanna roused herself briefly to look over fields of black workers. They didn't seem any different from those they had already passed.

"Rafe said he would explain everything when he gets here," Beth was saying. "As to why he came back to New York instead of Charleston. He is going to take a ship down the coast as soon as he can. Apparently it's quite difficult because of the English blockade of our ports. But I gather Rafe has developed a fascination for the ocean . . . he loved the voyages across the Atlantic. Isn't it odd that men fall in love with the sea? I've always been a little afraid of it . . . of storms and great fish."

The climate seemed hotter and more humid than on the coast, and Lanna wondered if they had perhaps left Charleston too soon. She was conscious only of the misery the heat and the movement of the carriage were causing, and she barely realized that Beth was telling her she had received a letter from Rafe.

"Oh, my dear . . . you are looking so pale. Would you like me to stop the carriage for a while?" Beth asked.

"No—please. I shall be all right." Lanna felt that if she were to get out of the bouncing carriage no power on earth could persuade her to get back into it.

"Lanna, I know it isn't polite to ask . . . but . . . do you

71

think you might be . . ." Beth crimsoned with embarrassment.

"I don't know," Lanna said weakly.

"Damon would be so happy . . . he would love to have a son, I'm sure . . . those very masculine men always do. And perhaps it would help him to settle down." Beth gave Lanna a little squeeze of encouragement.

At last the carriage was swaying around the gentle curve of a wide gravel drive lined by live oaks. Ahead was Oakside, a handsome colonial house with wide steps leading to a terrace behind stately columns.

Beth and her personal maid, a girl named Zenobia, soon whisked Lanna away to her room and put her to bed. Lanna was glad to find that Zenobia had come from the Indies and that her English was easier to follow than that of some of the other slaves, who spoke in a dialect Beth called "Gullah." She brought Lanna a cool drink with a slightly bitter flavor.

"Good for missy. Make baby stop deviling her," Zenobia said.

"Baby . . . no . . . no baby," Lanna tried to protest, but her aching body sank gratefully back onto the soft pillows, and Zenobia's voice receded into the distance.

Lanna found that she was tired all the time and for the next several weeks she did little but lie on a chaise longue on the terrace or in her room. She rarely joined Beth and her grandfather for meals and was not pressed to do so. She told herself that she ought not go into a decline, but it was always easier to put off doing anything until tomorrow. Waiting . . . waiting for Rafe to come . . . waiting for Damon to return . . . to hear from Teddie, or her father . . . everything was out of her hands.

Two months had already slipped away when, sitting in her room one afternoon, she heard excited shouts from outside. Surely that could not be Beth who squealed with such excitement?

Lanna went to the window, trying to close her dressing gown before stepping out onto the balcony. None of her clothes seemed to fit properly, her bosom had become so full. Probably as a result of the way Damon had handled her, she thought resentfully.

The balcony swept around the entire upper story and since the rooms on either side of Lanna's bedroom were unused, she was able to wander the length of the balcony

72

on her side of the house without being seen. Through the treetops, she could catch a glimpse of the front terrace.

The sunlight filtering through the branches shone on the dark bronze hair of the man who had alighted from the carriage and was leaping up the terrace steps. Lanna's breath stopped.

Rafe . . . he was here at last. But Beth was hurling herself into his arms and he had placed his hands about her waist and lifted her up to meet his kiss. Lanna turned away, feeling as if a knife had been pressed under her ribs. She went back to the dressing table and peered anxiously at her reflection. What she saw was puffiness . . . pallor . . . dull eyes. "A pretty dress," she thought. She must dress in her best. The gowns Teddie had bought in London were so much more fashionable than those the American women wore . . . also a lot more daring. It was almost evening, she would wear one of the delicate gauze dresses. She had already tried and discarded three when there was a knock on her door.

"Lanna . . . may I come in?" It was Beth's voice, excited.

Lanna hastily pulled her dressing gown on as Beth came bursting into the room.

"Lanna . . . he's home! Oh, my darling is home again. You must come down to dinner tonight, please. I know he is anxious to see you again; he's already asked about you."

"Oh? He knows I'm here then?" Lanna avoided meeting Beth's shining eyes.

"He found out in Charleston . . . that you and Damon were married. What will you wear? I'll help you dress. Oh, Lanna, I'm so happy!"

They were able to find a walking dress that Lanna could fit into. She had not worn it since she left Kingsburch as it had been made by the local seamstress and was not only too large, but also of a drab charcoal color that made Lanna look paler than ever.

"We shall have to have some dresses made for you. You will be needing a new wardrobe to accommodate the little St. Clair," Beth said, oblivious to the dismayed expression on Lanna's face when the subject of the baby was mentioned. Since Beth believed that every woman must be ecstatic to be married and expecting a child, it did not occur to her that Lanna was not.

Looking at her somber reflection in the mirror, Lanna

would gladly have killed Damon had he been there. There was no doubt she was pregnant. She was ugly . . . and the grey dress emphasized it. Plain little Beth, on the other hand, had suddenly been transformed into a beauty. Her eyes shone, her cheeks were pink and she was wearing a gorgeous dress of deep green, embroidered with gold thread. The green and gold combs in her upswept hair gave her features a classical serenity. She was the perfect picture of a woman in love.

They went downstairs together, down the endless curved staircase to where Rafe lounged against the balustrade watching their progress. Looking into his eyes, eyes that were as green as the Irish hills from whence his ancestors had sprung, Lanna could have wept with anguish. His greeting was polite and noncommittal. He took her hand and bent forward to lightly kiss her wrist.

"I must wish you every happiness . . . Mrs. St. Chair." Lanna's eyes filled with tears. "I trust your husband will be joining us soon? There is much I must congratulate him about." The green eyes were opaque, but there was hurt in them.

"He is away on a voyage," Lanna said in a small voice, feeling the twisting pain again as Beth slipped her arm through Rafe's and looked up at him.

They went into the elegant drawing room where a silver-haired gentleman and a beautiful woman with hair the same color as Rafe's were rising to be introduced to her. They were his parents, Michael and Kathleen Danvers. The elder Danvers walked with a cane, and his handsome features creased with pain when he moved. Lanna remembered that Rafe's father had almost lost a leg in an accident. His wife was much younger. She must have been a slip of a girl when she gave birth to Rafe, Lanna thought.

"Lanna, we have another surprise for you," Beth burst out. "We have another unexpected guest. We are going to delay dinner for just a little while so that he may change clothes. I was just afraid to spring too many surprises on you all at once, first with Rafe coming home . . ."

"Settle down, honey," Grandfather Grenville said indulgently, "the gentleman will be down directly. I for one want to hear the rest of Rafe's adventures at sea. If that doesn't beat all . . . shanghaied!"

Lanna sat down. The conversation droned in her ears,

74

but she was unaware of anything but Rafe sitting across the room.

Rafe was talking about his voyages. Foolishly, he explained, he had allowed himself to be shanghaied. Still, it hadn't been so bad. An adventure really. Their ship had been stopped by an English man o'war, but since he was on an English merchantman they had merely checked the ship's documents to be sure she was flying her true colors. In fact, he'd liked it so much that he'd made the crossing again.

Lanna listened silently, her eyes fixed on his handsome face. All the feelings she'd had for him in England came back to overwhelm her senses.

As Beth had indicated, there was no doubt that Rafe had found life at sea exciting, and Lanna wondered if he too had been bitten by the wanderlust that evidently controlled her husband's life. She sensed an undercurrent of outrage about American shipping being harrassed by the Royal Navy, but Rafe was too polite to speak out about it in her presence. An uneasy question formed in the back of her mind. Was it possible that Rafe might choose a love affair with the sea over either Beth or herself?

"Ah, here comes our other guest now," Grandfather Grenville interrupted.

"Lanna dear," Beth said, "your father's dearest friend has come to visit you."

Lanna turned her head to see a huge man with a small bald head coming into the room. She looked into the beady eyes of Lucas Bassey.

CHAPTER 8

Somehow she got through the meal, never aware of what she ate, acutely conscious of Bassey's crude table manners and the polite but puzzled way everyone regarded them.

Several times Rafe's eyes would seek hers, but he never addressed any remarks to her directly. His mother watched Lanna covertly and more than once let her gaze drift from her son to Lanna in a speculative way.

He was different from the happy-go-lucky young man she had met in England, Lanna decided. More reserved, less inclined to make the joking remarks she had found so irresistible. The only time his conversation really came to life was when he spoke of ships and the sea.

Sleep was a long time coming that night. Lanna tossed restlessly beneath the mosquito net over her bed. At last she sat up, pushing the damp hair from her forehead. She slipped out of bed, padding across the floor with bare feet. Moonlight spilled into the room through the French windows along the balcony. She stepped outside. Lingering for a moment, she was glad the rooms on her floor were unoccupied and that there was no one to see her.

One of the huge old trees at the corner of the house grew close to the wrought-iron rail. A beckoning staircase of gnarled limbs led to the shadowy ground below. For a moment Lanna had a wild urge to climb down and flee into the night. Away from the distant look in Rafe's eyes, away from everyone ... but most of all from the terrible mistake she had made in marrying Damon.

Surprisingly, she awoke the next morning feeling well, and she had an appetite that Beth said, laughingly, would have done justice to a field hand. Lanna ate large quantities of hashed turkey with boiled rice, half a broiled quail and several slices of rice bread.

Grandfather Grenville watched approvingly and said, "Got to take good care of you now, especially since you aren't used to our climate. Now don't blush, my dear, I'm an old man. And I'll tell you this, that little St. Clair you are carrying is going to make a difference in how folks feel about your husband. Lot of 'em didn't take kindly to Damon moving onto the Battery and being accepted by the Danvers up here ... and I was one of them. Figured he wasn't fit to associate with decent folks, begging your pardon for saying so, Lanna. But I've changed my mind about him since I met you. He must have some good qualities to get a woman like you to marry him."

Lanna was not blushing with embarrassment, she was coloring with the resentment she felt whenever she remembered she was carrying Damon's child.

"Rafe will be over soon to take me riding. You won't mind, will you, Lanna?" Beth said. "I would ask you to go with us, but of course you really shouldn't in your condition."

In the days that followed, Lanna would hear those words until she was ready to scream with frustration. Although she was only a little over three months pregnant, she was not allowed to ride or to exert herself in any way.

Lucas Bassey had returned to Charleston after announcing that Lanna's father would be dispatching wedding presents for the newlyweds. He repeated this to everyone so many times that Lanna, remembering his having asked her to deliver a trunk to the plantation, and his talk about the insurrection of slaves and Indians, felt a chill. Would they send arms in the guise of wedding presents? She must leave Oakside before they had time to do so. Yet how could she leave when Damon had not returned and when she had never had a moment to speak to Rafe alone?

Rafe called to take Beth out riding, and he came to dinner frequently, but Lanna always saw him with a group of people or with Beth alone. His eyes seemed to

look through Lanna and by contrast his tender glances at
Beth seemed deliberately intended to hurt. A forthcoming
party about which Beth talked excitedly was to be a combination welcome home and engagement party.

"I hope you will have a wonderful time at the Danvers'
party," Lanna said forlornly. They were sitting in Beth's
bedroom.

"Oh, but you are coming too!" Beth cried. "I know you
won't be able to dance . . . but you can come and listen
to the music and enjoy the refreshments and the company.
And I have a surprise for you . . . look . . ."

Beth pulled a bolt of cloth from beneath her bed. It was
white muslin with tiny blue daisies embroidered here and
there. "It's for a new dress for you. Zenobia is going to
start cutting it out right away. She is quite an accomplished
seamstress."

Lanna allowed herself to be measured and fitted, and
though she was grateful, she wasn't really thinking about
the dress. She had to find a way to see Rafe alone, to tell
him what had really happened. But what could they do?
Now . . . now there was a baby on the way. If only it
had been Rafe's child she had conceived . . .

The day of the Danvers' party the house was filled with
scurrying servants and an air of anticipation. Some of the
Oakside slaves were going over to Clearview as there was
to be a separate barbecue for the servants. Two carriages
and a curricle would make several trips back and forth.

Beth and Lanna were about to climb into the landau,
party dresses packed in boxes, when Zenobia came running after them.

"Miss Beth . . . yo' grandfather done lost his tobacco
pouch again and he won't go till he find it."

Lanna was already seated and Beth closed the door after
her. "You go on, dear, I'll be along as soon as I've found
it for him. You know what an old bear he will be if he
doesn't have his favorite tobacco along," she laughed.

Lanna smiled and nodded. She would have a chance to
see Rafe alone before Beth arrived.

The landau rolled into a heavily wooded area and the
countryside seemed wilder than that surrounding Oakside.
Trees hung heavily with Spanish moss created the feeling
of ghostly apparitions creeping toward the narrowing road.

What had once been a pair of handsome wrought iron
gates stood before a driveway still in need of weeding,

78

although it was evident some attempt had been made to clear it before the guests arrived.

Lanna was shocked. She had expected the same grandeur as at Oakside. The fields they had passed appeared to be as well cared for as the Grenvilles', but the house itself was much smaller. Although built of handsome red brick, it was little more than a large farm house with several outbuildings and a single row of slave huts set well away from the main house. It occurred to Lanna that the money the Danvers were spending on this party, including the orchestra from Charleston, could better have been spent on renovation of their house and grounds. A very old Negro with bent shoulders and tired eyes held the horses when they stopped in front of the house, and a second slave came hurrying down the cracked steps to greet her. She followed him into the gloom of a sparsely furnished entry hall.

Mrs. Danvers came through a door to one side of the hall, followed by a very young black girl.

"My dear Mrs. St. Clair, how nice that you could come. But where is Beth? Did she not accompany you?" The older woman gave Lanna a perfunctory embrace and gestured toward the open door. "We shall have some tea and then you can go upstairs to rest."

"Beth will be along shortly," Lanna said, following her hostess.

"Rafe will be so disappointed. He's waiting for her so eagerly." Kathleen Danvers seemed to emphasize every word, as though Lanna were slightly deaf. "Just between two old married ladies, my dear, I believe we shall hear an important announcement about those two tonight."

Lanna bit her lip to avoid saying anything that might give her away. The date of their wedding mustn't be announced tonight. She must see Rafe alone.

She stepped into a room that would have been called a morning room or solarium in England. A wall of windows flooded the room with sunlight. Lanna blinked in the brightness and would have stumbled had not a strong hand been placed firmly under her elbow. She looked around to see Rafe at her side. He smiled at her with a hurt look in his eyes that tore at her heart.

"Welcome to my home, Lanna," he said softly. "Come, sit over here out of the sunlight."

Lanna sat down on a wicker loveseat and felt her heart

79

begin to hammer as Rafe sat next to her. Like his mother's, his hair was fiery red in the sunlight.

"Mrs. St. Clair tells me that your beloved will be along any moment, Rafe dear," Mrs. Danvers said, handing Lanna a china cup and saucer. There was no one else present, Lanna realized, except for the little black girl who stood waving a palmetto frond to keep the air moving.

"When you've had your tea, perhaps I could show you around?" Rafe asked.

"Oh, mercy me, Rafe, no!" Kathleen Danvers said at once. "Mrs. St. Clair wants to rest, so she'll be fresh for tonight, don't you, my dear? You know, ladies in her . . ."

She's going to say "delicate condition," Lanna thought, horrified, and blurted out, "Oh, no, I'm not the least bit tired. I'd love to see your home. Everything is so different here. I'm really quite fascinated."

"Then I shall take you around myself," Mrs. Danvers said smiling sweetly, "and Rafe can wait for Beth."

Rafe ignored her and turned to Lanna. "I was sorry I was not able to visit your ancestral home in England."

"Oh, Kingsburch is a dreary old place. Drafty and cold and constantly lashed by winds that come screaming in from the sea. Father spends as little time as possible there. It was given to us by the royal family—'burch' means 'fort' in old English, so it was, literally, the king's fort—built for defense against attack rather than for comfort." Lanna could not stop gazing into Rafe's eyes, every nerve in her body responding to his nearness.

"How very interesting," Mrs. Danvers' voice cut in. "I suppose you and your husband will be spending some time there in the future. Mrs. St. Clair? I said, I suppose you will be . . ."

"What? Oh, yes. My husband. Rafe, would it be possible to go for a short walk around the grounds before I see the house? I am quite interested in all the different kinds of trees you have . . . just for a few minutes? We . . . could watch for Beth's carriage."

"Of course. Come along, I'd enjoy a walk myself," Rafe said.

Lanna avoided looking at Mrs. Danvers as they went through the French doors of the room to an untidy garden, but she felt the cold stare that followed their progress.

They walked in silence until they were away from the house, then Rafe said heavily, "My marriage to Beth will be announced tonight. It will take place in a few weeks."

"You never told me about Beth," Lanna said.

"And you did not tell me you were being courted by Damon St. Clair."

"I wasn't being courted by him. I believed I was being courted by you."

"Yet you married him."

"You might have had the decency to tell me you had changed your mind . . . it was cruel to let me leave home and go to the ship to meet you when you had already left."

"Cruel of me!" Rafe stopped dead in his tracks and turned to face her, anger mingling with the torment in his eyes. "I awoke with a cracked skull to find myself on an English ship heading into the North Atlantic . . . going home by way of Newfoundland. I was forced to work for my passage. With a note in my pocket casually informing me that you and Damon were getting married."

"Damon!" She made the word sound like a curse. "Oh, Rafe, he tricked both of us. He told me you were already married to Beth."

"But why would you marry him? You didn't even like him."

"Oh, Rafe, Rafe . . ." How could she find the words to tell him she had been afraid she was pregnant with his child, had been terrified of what her father would do if she were? It seemed so cowardly now. But she had been so petrified, so alone, in the moment she had faced Damon aboard the *Wayward Woman*. If only she had been more worldly, perhaps she would have known that not every intimacy produced a child . . . or that Rafe had not actually consummated the act. But she had not known. She swayed toward him now. The need to be enclosed in his arms was too strong to resist. It was going to be all right, she would find a way to explain.

Rafe hesitated for a second, then pulled her gently to him. While his hand tenderly stroked her hair, he kissed her slowly.

"Rafe!" The voice separated them like the crack of a whip. They jerked apart and turned to see Kathleen Danvers standing behind them, her face livid.

"How could you? How could you cavort with that . . . that woman . . ."

"Mother, please. Let's go back to the house and I'll explain," Rafe said.

"There is no need. I heard everything. I wondered why

you'd been acting like a sick calf since you returned from your Grand Tour. Rafe, don't you see . . . you've been blinded by a woman of low morals. It's well known how decadent London society is . . . with their mad king and womanizing Prince Regent. They are all immoral . . ."

"Mother, please. That's enough. Lanna, go back to the house, I'll join you there," Rafe said.

Lanna hesitated, looking from Kathleen Danvers' blazing stare to Rafe's flushed, embarrassed face.

"And to think she had the effrontery to accept the Grenvilles' hospitality . . . while scheming all the time . . . don't you see, she wants you *and* Damon St. Clair . . . one man is not enough for a woman like her." There was a note of rising hysteria in her voice.

"Please, Lanna, go back to the house. Rooms have been prepared . . . go to the right at the top of the stairs. Wait there," Rafe said, tight-lipped.

Lanna made a wide detour around Mrs. Danvers and sped back to the house, her cheeks flaming.

CHAPTER 9

Lanna lay on the bed in her shift. The young black girl had brought her a cool drink, closed the curtains and had withdrawn to leave Lanna in the semidarkness.

Her thoughts were a wild jumble of hope and despair. Hope that Rafe would somehow make everything right . . . despair that Damon, for whatever devious reason, had planned to marry her all along.

Her short season in London and Teddie's blunt advice on how to avoid acquiring a "reputation" confirmed what Mrs. Danvers had said about the morals of London society. But Lanna had spent her entire life in a lonely fortress, and she had had only a scant month in London. The parties, the dancing at Almack's, the pretty clothes were all so new to her. She had been convinced that Rafe, and the other young men who called to take her riding in the park, had all been dazzled by her surroundings and her clothes. Why else would they have been attracted to a country bumpkin, lacking in sophistication and unable to engage in the flirtatious repartee the other girls found so easy? Now she wished desperately for a way to convince Mrs. Danvers that she was not a scarlet woman.

An hour passed before there was a light tap on the bedroom door. In response to her eager, "Come in," a sheet of paper was pushed slowly into the room. Lanna was out of bed in an instant and opening the door, but when she looked up and down the landing there was no one there.

She picked up the sheet of paper, her heart leaping. It

was from Rafe, but his words immediately crushed her hopes. There was no salutation and the message was brief.

There is no use dwelling on what might have been, we have to accept what is. I cannot hurt Beth and, for better or worse, you are Damon St. Clair's wife and the mother of his child. I hope we can both conduct ourselves with dignity.

Blinded by tears, Lanna went back to the bed and sat down. Oh, for a magic carpet to transport her back to England . . . away from humiliation and heartbreak. She had to get away; she had to go home.

The orchestra had arrived and was tuning up, the guests were sated with food and wine, and the ladies were upstairs changing into ball gowns. In the drawing room the men drank cognac, smoked cigars and discussed the news from Europe.

Valencia was about to fall. It was certain that before the winter ended Napoleon Bonaparte would have conquered all of the continent. It was time, the men agreed, to fight a second war of independence with Britain. The Orders in Council with their sweeping regulation of trade with the continent of Europe, the blockades, the British ships violating the sovereignty of American territorial waters, to say nothing of the impressment of Americans into the Royal Navy: all made war the only course of action. It was a pity that America would have to align herself with the dictator Bonaparte and his dreams of world conquest. Even now it was rumored he was amassing his troops for an attack upon Russia. But the fact remained, the last time England faced a united Europe and a hostile America, she had given way. "Free Trade and Sailors' Rights" was the slogan that echoed about the room.

"We'd better change the subject before we join the ladies," Mr. Danvers said, placing his weight on his cane and easing himself out of his chair. "One of our guests is an Englishwoman."

"Damon St. Clair's aristocratic looking bride," one of the other guests, Jonathan Mallory, put in. "I saw her briefly, looking very ill at ease during dinner. Where is her husband? Away on some brigand's errand, I'll be bound."

"Ask me no questions . . ." Grandfather Grenville quoted laughingly.

"A handsome girl. Looks cold as ice though," another guest said.

"She's in a strange country, away from home for the first time in her life and not used to our ways, that's all," Rafe said. His voice was slightly slurred and his father glanced at him sharply.

"Well, we are gentlemen, we don't wage war against women," Mallory said. "But she's an odd choice for a man like St. Clair . . . I'd have thought he'd want a woman of more passion."

"You're forgetting . . . he's an Englishman himself, by birth at least," Grandfather Grenville said. "And I for one like the girl. I think there are hidden depths there."

"Like an iceberg?" someone suggested, and there was a ripple of laughter.

Rafe rose unsteadily to his feet and was about to speak when his father said abruptly, "I believe the orchestra is ready. It won't do for the ladies to come down and find themselves without partners."

As the men moved slowly out to the improvised outdoor ballroom, Jonathan's Mallory's son, Jon, whispered to his companion, "From what I saw of wicked old London on my Grand Tour, I doubt there's a virgin left in the whole city." His companion poked him in the ribs and chuckled.

When Lanna, at the insistence of the young black girl, had come downstairs for the barbecue, she had found Rafe with Beth on his arm. There was a hard, blank look in his eyes as they looked through Lanna. Beth was radiant and noticed nothing, but Mrs. Danvers flitted about like a watchful moth in a gown of ecru lace. Now that the dancing was about to begin, Lanna found a secluded seat amidst a group of oleanders, well back from the taut canvas floor. She longed for the evening to be over so that she could escape the watchful eyes of Kathleen Danvers and the curious glances of the other guests, who no doubt were wondering why Lanna had attended the party while her husband was away at sea.

She watched, silent and alone, as Mr. Danvers got up to make an announcement.

"Ladies and gentlemen," he began and motioned for Beth and Rafe to come forward. "You all know that my son and Miss Beth Grenville have been promised to each other almost from the minute our sweet Beth was born

. . . so it's no surprise to any of you that now that Rafe has returned from his Grand Tour, the two of them will be settling down . . ." He paused. An excited murmur ran through the guests and several of the girls impulsively clapped their hands. ". . . so all that remains is for me to announce the date, which will be Christmas Eve. And now, at the insistence of my wife and all you other ladies who have been clamoring to do the new European dances . . . the orchestra is going to play our very first waltz. My son, who learned the dance while in England, is going to lead off with his bride-to-be."

Lanna could not bear it. She remembered waltzing with Rafe in London, the two of them in the center of the universe. She stood up quickly and stumbled away from the sight of Rafe leading the diminutive Beth into the center of the circle of approving friends.

Unconscious of direction, Lanna moved away from the strains of the waltz. It was some time before she realized that she was walking toward music of a different kind. Gay, lighthearted, made up of many different sounds but led by . . . a violin?

An old Negro was playing the fiddle and at his side a boy strummed a banjo. The other sounds were made by bare feet stamping the hardpacked earth, hands clapping, the snap of whirling calico and laughter.

Spellbound, Lanna watched the black dancers silhouetted against the leaping flames from the fire pit. To one side of the clearing a table had been set up, and several of the older women were clearing away the remains of a meal, while children darted about between dancers. One small boy came upon Lanna.

She felt the small hand tug her skirts and looked down to see the grave face regarding her.

"Hello . . ." she whispered, "I'm lost."

The small face broke into a smile, and the boy ran off with an effortless loping stride. Watching him go, Lanna did not notice the tall, powerfully proportioned black who detached himself from the dancers and approached her.

"Yo' looking for me, Mizz St. Clair?" It was Florian, the Grenvilles' butler.

Embarrassed at being caught at what must have looked like spying, Lanna spoke without thinking.

"Oh, no, Florian. I heard your music . . . everyone seems to be so happy, enjoying themselves . . . I didn't think slaves . . . I mean . . . do you hate being a slave?"

"A slave can git in plenty of trouble if he don't mind what he says and who he says it to," Florian said cautiously.

"Would you . . . fight for your freedom . . . if there was a war and the English came and gave you guns?" It was suddenly important for Lanna to know.

Florian stepped back in alarm. "If I was free . . . where would I go? I was born here."

"But . . . well, you work in the house. What about the field hands . . . it can't be all dancing and happy times for them. Are they never mistreated?"

"Overseers come and overseers go." Florian shrugged. "You should go back now. You get us in plenty trouble."

The dancers had stopped and were watching her uneasily, but the fiddle and banjo played on.

Still mesmerized by the music, Lanna reluctantly retraced her footsteps. There had been one wild moment when she wished she had been one of them, able to dance so freely, without shame. At least two or three of the women dancers had been visibly pregnant.

Beth was looking for her and came swiftly to her side as she emerged from the shadows. "Lanna dear, I was so worried when I couldn't find you. Are you all right? How thoughtless of me to have neglected you so."

Beth's concern was too much to bear. A tear slipped down Lanna's cheek and, before she could stop herself, she was sobbing in Beth's arms.

"There, there, dear . . . it's all right. It's quite normal, you know, to want to cry a little in your condition . . ."

There they were again, those awful words. Lanna straightened up and choked back her tears. Suddenly, unreasonably, she wanted to take out her disappointment on Beth. "It has nothing to do with my condition," she moaned. "I'm young and healthy and . . . lonely. I want to dance like everyone else." As soon as the words were out she regretted them.

Beth's anxious concern was replaced by a smile. "Oh, how thoughtless of me," she said again. "Of course you do . . . and why shouldn't you? Why, you hardly show at all, and you're past the early weeks when it would be dangerous for you. It always did seem unfair that the mother has to give up so much . . . hide herself away for months. Come along, we are going to do something about it right now."

Before Lanna realized what Beth was doing, she had

87

seized her hand and dragged her toward the dance floor to where Rafe was waiting.

"Rafe dear," Beth said, "you must dance with Lanna. No! I won't hear another word until you've danced with her. Really now, one little waltz is not going to hurt her a bit and I declare I shall never speak to you again unless you do!"

Thankful that the dim light concealed her flaming cheeks, Lanna found herself in Rafe's arms. His fingers seemed to burn through her gloves, as the orchestra struck up a waltz.

She did not dare look up into his face as they began to turn, slowly at first, then with gathering momentum. The lanterns flickering among the trees went out of focus and the shadows of the other whirling couples flitted rapidly by. Then suddenly, out of nowhere, a voice cut in on her consciousness like the slash of a rapier.

"I'll take my wife now, Rafe. Thank you for keeping her entertained."

Rafe's hand was dragged from hers and a viselike grip replaced it as she was crushed against the chest of Damon St. Clair.

CHAPTER 10

Afterward, she wondered how she had been able to stay on her feet. Damon whirled her in fast circles, covering the perimeter of the makeshift dance floor in dizzying spins and abrupt reverse turns. He was an accomplished, if aggressive, dancer. Vaguely Lanna was aware of other couples falling back to let them through. He never spoke to her, or even looked into her face, and she bit her lip to keep from crying out.

At last he led her from the floor. After murmuring politely to their hosts what a wonderful party it had been, he said that his wife was tired and that they would be retiring now.

Lanna caught a quick glimpse of Rafe and Beth. Rafe avoided her eyes and Beth looked at her anxiously. In the shadows Alain L'Herreaux also watched, shaking his head and sighing deeply.

When the sounds of the music and voices began to fade, Lanna realized that Damon was leading her into the house.

"Where are you taking me?" Lanna asked, breathing heavily in the effort to match his steps. "I had planned to return with Beth . . ."

"You will stay here with me tonight and tomorrow we shall return to Charleston."

They went quickly up the stairs to a room where Damon had apparently already been. She recognized several items of his clothing folded neatly on a chest of drawers, and there was a pair of his boots on the floor.

"Why are you so angry . . . is it because I was dancing with Rafe?" Lanna asked. Her heart was beating painfully from exertion and fright. He had the same hard, contemptuous look on his face that he had worn the night he took her so brutally on the ship.

"I warned you not to hurt Beth," he said shortly, kicking off his shoes and unfastening his belt.

"But she . . ." Lanna was going to say that Beth was the one who had insisted she dance with Rafe, but before she had a chance he had flung himself upon her and the words were lost under the assault of his mouth on hers.

She struggled, trying to turn her head, but he caught her hair and forced his tongue into her mouth. She froze with pain as he tore at her dress. Her lovely new dress . . .

Her words came from behind clenched teeth, chokingly, "If you rape me . . . I swear I will . . . punish you somehow . . . some day . . ."

"Why, I wouldn't dream of raping you, dear lady," he said mockingly. "In a moment there will be no need. You will be begging me to take you. Oh, perhaps not in words . . . but . . ." His hands closed over her breasts, then slid downward. As his lips closed her eyelids, she no longer saw his wolf's eyes glowing in the darkness.

She was aware of a red haze and exploding pinpoints of light. She tried to detach her mind from what was happening to her body but his caresses were becoming more intimate and his lips and tongue were sending ripples of sensation all through her body. Her breath was coming rapidly now and she was having trouble lying still. Unwillingly, her hips reached upward toward him.

"Did you know," he whispered, his breath as labored as her own, "that there are primitive tribes who believe dark gods lurk in our loins . . ."

She moaned softly as his organ pressed tantalizingly close to the throbbing center of her being.

"And that once awakened, the dark gods must be appeased."

She cried out as the hard column of his flesh found its mark and became part of her and her wanton hips joined his in a mad wonderful whirling dance of worship.

Indigo paced back and forth in her room, her hands to her head as though by pressing her temples she could make Myrtle's words fade from her mind.

The young black girl who was Lanna St. Clair's maid

had announced their return from upriver and with a sly smile, had described the new Mrs. St. Clair's condition.

Indigo moved to the window, and gripped the ledge so hard that one of her fingernails broke off. All this time . . . all those many nights of lying in his arms, and Indigo had not conceived a child.

Yet she, the pale Englishwoman with the colorless hair and cold eyes . . . she was with child. Perhaps, the thought rose unbidden, she was not carrying Damon's child? Indigo thought of the night she had seen the Englishwoman in the coffee house with Lucas Bassey . . . an evil one he was, but surely not somebody that Lanna St. Clair would have an affair with? Her friends in town would keep watch on Bassey and let her know what he was about. Indigo had many friends among the black servants and plantation hands. It was only a question of time before she learned all there was to know about the pale-haired usurper who had moved into Damon's life.

She had not gone downstairs to greet them upon their return from the plantation. Joshua was ordered to send dinner to her room, and she had barely finished eating when Damon pushed open her door.

"No greeting for me, Indigo? And sulking up here all alone? Come, tell me what ails you," he said, dropping back onto her bed.

Indigo closed her eyes, did not look at him. "I begged you . . . sell me to someone far from here. Send me away from my torment. I can't bear to stay any longer."

"You are free, Indigo . . . you've been free since I sought out your last owner and settled with him. Besides, I don't want you to go. Nothing has changed between us."

"Give me a paper that says I am free then, so I can travel far from here. Nothing is the same. You have a wife now."

"Come now, you know I'm man enough for both of you," Damon said lazily, reaching to catch her by the wrist and pull her down onto the bed with him. Indigo tensed for a second, but as always his nearness melted her anger and sadness. All she could feel was the hot surging of her blood as it churned with need for him.

He pushed the soft hair back from her face and kissed her slowly. His hands slipped her dress down from her shoulders and found her breasts, cupping the firm honey-colored flesh, while his index fingers circled her nipples until they were as hard as the bulge in his breeches. Her

91

lips parted and her tongue went hungrily into his mouth. Then she was unbuttoning his shirt, and following her fingers with her mouth. He unfastened his belt and slid out of the breeches. Her lips found his erect member. Her tongue darted, teased. Her fingers slid downward, encircling, squeezing gently. He pulled her dress from her body as she brought up her legs, felt his fingers trace the outline of the mons and part the lips to make way for his tongue.

She broke away suddenly, sitting up and placing her hands on his face to disengage him. "No . . . I want all of your seed inside me tonight," she whispered huskily. She lay back, spreading her legs, her hips moving invitingly. He rolled over to mount her, smiling as he entered her with a quick thrust.

"My little Indigo is still afraid I'm not man enough . . ." he began, but she reached up to pull his face toward her and silence him with her kisses. *Give me a child, oh, give me a child,* she thought desperately.

When at last they lay in each other's arms, their bodies sated with the pleasures of the senses, he said softly, "Tell me again that you want to leave me . . . tell me that, Indigo. You can never leave me, you are a part of me."

She sat up, trying to shake off the drowsiness and contentment. "She will send me away . . . sooner or later she will find out and send me away."

"No one can send you away but me."

"In time . . . you will feel differently. She means nothing to you now, but in time . . . when the child comes."

Now he was alert, sitting up beside her abruptly. "Child?"

"She hasn't told you she is with child?"

Indigo could not read the expression on his face in the candlelit room. She saw the flash in his eyes and felt the muscles of his body contract, heard the suppressed exclamation.

He lay down, again slowly, pulling her into his arms. For a little while longer, he stayed with her, not speaking. Then he rose and dressed, kissed her lightly on the mouth and left. Indigo turned her face into her pillow and cried silently, the sobs shaking her body, until at last sleep came.

Lanna was asleep when Damon burst into the bedroom and lit the lamp on the bedside table. The flickering light and his hand closing around her arm awakened her.

"Is it true?" he asked harshly. "Are you pregnant?"

Lanna winced beneath the pressure of his fingers and tried to sit up.

"Answer me, are you with child?" he said again, shaking her slightly.

"Yes. Damn you. Yes," she cried.

The grip on her arm relaxed and he stood back from the bed, looking down at her. Neither of them spoke for a moment and Lanna struggled into a sitting position, pulling the sheet up to her chin as she did so.

"Why didn't you tell me?" he asked at last.

"You didn't give me a chance. First you appear at the Danvers' party and waltz me around like a madman, then you rape me. I find myself and my luggage placed on the river boat and learn from a servant girl that you are on the same boat, although you don't take the trouble to come to see me. Then we are in a carriage and you glare out of the window and tell me that you are leaving again almost immediately on a voyage."

"Well, at least I found out in time to do something about the situation before I go," he said ominously.

Fear rose in Lanna's throat as she looked into his hard eyes. "What do you mean?"

"You don't want the child, obviously. Well, neither do I. The thought of my blood mingling with . . ." He drew in his breath sharply and looked away from her as though she were repugnant. "I know of a doctor who will take care of the situation. I'll make the necessary arrangements."

"No!" Lanna screamed the word. "No . . ." She was so afraid she could not speak. She began to cry, burying her face in the sheet. It was true she did not want his child, but what he was suggesting was worse than bearing an unwanted child.

"Look . . . I'm sorry. If it's any consolation to you, I'm sorry I married you and brought you here. I was wrong. I was trying to punish someone else. The doctor is reliable. After it's over, I promise you can have your freedom. No doubt Rafe will break his engagement and go back to you; there's no doubt he still wants you. Or, if you prefer, I'll take you home to England."

"I don't understand. Why are you suddenly concerned about me? And who were you trying to punish by marrying me?"

"Your father."

"My father . . . but . . ." Lanna stopped herself in time. She had not mentioned to anyone the letter that Lucas Bassey had delivered to her at Oakside. She had not even wanted to think about it herself. Perhaps she should keep the contents secret for a while longer.

"He was responsible for the death of my parents. Your father is a traitor who sold naval secrets to the French and Spaniards. Then he had my father imprisoned for the crime. But he arranged for an escape . . . of a sort.

"Almost nineteen years ago, before you were born. I myself was a child of eight, away in boarding school. I was not told of my father's arrest. One day my old nurse appeared at the school and told me she was talking me away to America. She told me she had a friend, a sailor, who would help us. She said my parents had been killed when their carriage overturned. I was to use her name—St. Clair—rather than my own, because she would raise me as her son. I didn't question it. When she died a year ago, I finally learned the truth. I have sworn vengeance on your father and you were to be the first installment of it. But I won't father a child with Malford's tainted blood."

"I don't want your child either," Lanna said, "but I won't risk my life to get rid of it. Neither of you is worth it."

He looked at her with a faint gleam of respect. "What do you propose then? There isn't anything we can do if you bear my child, unless, of course, you can convince Rafe that it is his."

The color rose to her cheeks and her quick downward glance revealed that the thought had crossed her mind.

"So . . ." he said, his voice edged with flint, "you had actually considered passing it off as his . . . in which case I feel bound to point out that while Rafe Danvers is a self-centered and indolent charmer, he is not a complete fool. He can add, and I doubt you can convince him an extended gestation period is normal."

"If I could return to England . . ." Lanna said, not raising her eyes to meet that cold stare.

"And then?"

"I don't know. I would have to ask you to support me and the child for a little while—until I could find a way to support myself."

"You wouldn't return to your father?"

"He won't have me back," Lanna said shortly. The letter . . . she could show him the letter and change his

94

opinion of her, but why should she? What was the point of it? As for the child, it was as much his as hers. He could take some responsibility for it, if only financial.

"How do you know your father won't take you back? Have you heard from him?"

"Yes. My father hates Americans. His father was killed in the revolution in '75. His death left the family in reduced circumstances."

"Your grandfather died in America? That's interesting. But your father is an extremely wealthy man."

"My father married into a wealthy family who had property in the Indies and several ships. He acquired Kingsburch for himself later. It will come to me when I am twenty-one . . . but that's almost three years away."

"So your father has disowned you, but given you Kingsburch. Curious." Damon sat down on the edge of the bed. Instinctively Lanna drew back from him.

"There's no need to cringe," he said sharply, "I'm not going to touch you. There's no need any longer." He stood up again in a swift and angry gesture.

"Perhaps you're right," he said over his shoulder as he strode toward the door. "If he doesn't care for his daughter, perhaps a grandson will provide a bargaining point. You'll stay here until the child is born."

When the door closed behind him, Lanna slipped out of bed and went to her dressing table. She pulled the single sheet of parchment from beneath the crystal tray which held her hairbrushes and slowly read the words again.

Leona,

In regard to the predicament of your marriage, this is entirely your own doing and how you extricate yourself from it is no concern of mine. You have, by this deed, absolved me of all responsibility for you.

I can now tell you that you are not my daughter, nor the daughter of my deceased wife. You were brought up at Kingsburch under my protection as a favor to your natural father. Kingsburch and its holdings will legally become yours on your twenty-first birthday, at which time I would have withdrawn from your life in any event. Your marriage has merely hastened that event.

95

Should you decide to return to your inheritance when you are twenty-one the solicitors who can advise you are Maccleson and Hewitt in London.

Lanna slowly tore the letter into small shreds.

CHAPTER 11

The following morning when Myrtle announced that she had a visitor, Lanna was surprised to see Captain L'Herreaux waiting for her in the hall.

"Bonjour, madame," he said in his oddly resonant voice.

"Hello, Captain L'Herreaux . . ." she began.

"Please, madame . . . Alain. L'Herreaux sounds delightful in your Anglo-Saxon accent, but I know it to be cumbersome for you." He smiled and Lanna thought again what extraordinarily handsome features he had. If only they were not set upon such an ill-proportioned body.

"Won't you please be seated . . . Alain," she said and then realized there was nowhere to sit in the hall. I must try not to be so conscious of his lack of height, she thought, and added quickly, "We can go out onto the piazza, it's rather pleasant out there."

He walked beside her, his dark eyes openly appreciating her. "You look very lovely this morning, Madame St. Clair. Your visit to the plantation agreed with you, no?"

"If I am to call you Alain, then you must call me Lanna. It is the name my friends use," Lanna said, more than a little pleased at his compliment. Between Rafe's rejection and Damon's contempt, she had forgotten how pleasant it was to have a man pay her a compliment.

"Would you like something to drink . . . or perhaps you have not yet breakfasted?" she asked when they were seated on the brick patio.

"Please, no." His eyes were still searching her face.

"Damon is not here," she said.

"I know. He is aboard the *Woman* . . . the ship. There are things to do before we sail. I came to see you, Lanna. Forgive me, but I must be blunt. I learned of your meeting with M'sieur Bassey . . . the private meeting you had with him. I come to warn you to be careful of that man."

Lanna glanced away from his searching eyes. "He is merely a messenger from my father. They serve aboard the same ship."

"Lanna . . . again, forgive me, but you were seen with him in the private room of a coffee house. And I hear bad things about him. He is known to be dealing with men who would sell guns to the Indians. You cannot know, but the Creek warriors are . . . The frontier is not so far away . . . and then too, there are unscrupulous . . . What I am trying to tell you is that these men, these gun-runners, want only fast profit. The plantation slaves are closer than the Creeks. Americans, even bad ones I think, would not deliver muskets to the slaves. But an Englishman . . ."

"Did my husband ask you to speak to me about this?" Lanna asked, carefully studying her hands that were folded tensely upon her lap.

"No! He knows nothing of this."

"You saw me in the coffee house?"

"No. Someone else saw you. I do not question you, Lanna, but there is much about this country that you do not know. It is a young, wild land."

"I thought Lucas Bassey might help me to return to England, Alain. I want to go home . . . I don't know why I am telling you this, you are my husband's closest friend. You see, my husband does not love me . . . we both entered into this marriage for the worst possible reasons. The only thing for me to do is to go home."

Alain drew in his breath sharply and impulsively leaned forward, catching her hands in his. It was as he suspected then, despite the coming child.

"Perhaps things will be better, if you give them time."

Lanna felt strangely comforted by the pressure of his warm hands and by his sympathetic eyes. She felt her own eyes fill with tears.

"Lanna, *ma belle fille* . . . *chérie*, hush, it is all right. Damon will not hurt you again, now that he knows about the child. But listen, the high seas they are no place for a woman who carries a child under her heart. This is not

98

the time to return to England. Wait, wait until after the child is born."

"I can't stay here . . . with that woman in the house. Sometimes she looks at me as though she would like to poison me," Lanna burst out.

From the quick recognition in his eyes, she knew she did not have to mention Indigo's name.

"Then we will make the arrangements to have her sent somewhere else. Leave it to me. But you will promise not to pursue any acquaintance with Lucas Bassey?"

Lanna nodded. She found him so comforting that she was loathe to have his visit end. If only Alain had been blessed with a body and legs like Damon. The thought brought a flush to her cheeks and she hated herself for thinking of Damon's body and of the feelings he had aroused in her. If only Damon could have the warmth and sympathy of this little man who held her hands and reassured her with his beautiful voice.

Alain was as good as his word. Before the *Wayward Woman* sailed, Indigo was on her way to the Clearview plantation where she would be Mrs. Danvers' housekeeper. Apparently all of the house servants had gradually been shifted to field work, or sold to defray gambling losses, and Indigo would not only assist in the running of the house but would also keep a watchful eye on Damon's interests at the plantation.

The doctor who visited Lanna was a kindly older man named Crawford. Despite the taunts of fellow physicians, who called him a male midwife, Crawford was concerned about improving the conditions of childbirth. He pronounced her in excellent health, but did not tell her that her hips were a little narrower than he would have liked for an easy birth.

Damon rarely came home, spending his days and many nights on the ship in preparation for the voyage. On the nights he did come ashore it was to visit his gambling friends.

Before Indigo left for Clearview, Lanna knew she had slipped out of the house on several evenings and did not return until dawn. On those nights Lanna paced her room restlessly and tried not to imagine Damon making love to the beautiful golden-skinned girl.

Lanna herself was feeling well physically, but she was lonely in the way she had been at Kingsburch. She tried to fill the hours with her embroidery and sewing, but she

99

wished her pregnancy did not keep her from more active pastimes. As a child, she had believed her parents had shut her away in a lonely old house because of some terrible deed she had committed but could not recall. For her, loneliness was punishment in its worst form.

The dour woman who was her nurse and tutor had pointed out to Lanna many times that there was an extremely unladylike streak in her nature and that she must constantly be on guard against it. The greatest crime a lady could commit was to lose her composure. A lady did not indulge in any show of either pleasure or displeasure. The expression of any form of raw emotion was for low-class women. Lanna thought that perhaps it was this character fault that had caused her parents to abandon her to the grey confines of Kingsburch. She had found it so difficult not to shout with joy when the new green buds miraculously appeared on bare branches.

Alain called to see her several times, usually in mid-morning. He kept her amused and intrigued with stories of the sea, of his father, of Claudine and Damon. Lanna appreciated Alain's brave heart, steadfast loyalty and integrity, and she grew more fond of him with each visit. It was with a pang of real regret that she bade him bon voyage on the day before the *Wayward Woman* was to sail.

That night Damon came home for dinner. Lanna had spent so many lonely evenings that she had not bothered to dress and had ordered a tray to be sent to her room. She was sitting on her balcony wearing a loose wrapper. There was now an unmistakable thickening of her waist and her breasts were so full she found it cooler and more comfortable to shed everything but the thin robe. She pulled it self-consciously up over her bosom as he entered her bedroom and came to join her on the balcony.

He stood looking at her for a moment, legs braced as though he were standing on the deck of a ship, and Lanna was acutely aware of the muscles of his thighs beneath the leather breeches. As usual, his shirt was carelessly open halfway down his chest. There was a dark shadow on his chin that plainly said he had not shaved. Lanna squirmed under his scrutiny. Would she ever become accustomed to the maleness of him, she wondered.

"The doctor came?" he asked.

"Yes."

"We shall sail on the morning tide."

"I know. Alain told me."

"He did? I had no idea you two were so friendly. I didn't think he was your type . . . no red hair and Irish charm. Funny how Englishwomen find Irishmen so irresistible. I've often thought it may be the reason Englishmen behave so abominably toward them."

"Who? The women or the Irish?" Lanna asked.

In spite of himself a grin plucked at his mouth. "I see you are feeling better. Good. I take it Indigo has already left for Clearview?" Alain had wanted him to buy a small house for Indigo, or allow Alain to do so, but Damon needed someone to watch over his interests at Clearview and Indigo would need some work to keep her out of mischief.

"I shall be back, I hope, before the baby is born," he continued. "Meantime Myrtle and Joshua will take care of you. I would ask you to remember that ladies in your condition do not show themselves in public, but if you wish to attend Beth's wedding I will have Joshua take you." His voice was expressionless.

The wedding . . . she would not be able to bear it. For once her condition would be a blessing. She would not have to go.

"You won't reconsider and let me sail back to England now?"

"Stay here, Lanna. It will be better for you and the child. Five months isn't such a long time."

Neither of them could know that by then their countries would be at war.

Kathleen Danvers was more than a little annoyed at having Indigo thrust so unceremoniously into her household. Not that Kathleen did not need the help, but she was well aware that Indigo had been Damon St. Clair's mistress. Charleston society was more broadminded than most in these matters, but slave concubinage was still an extremely delicate subject. Indigo was simply too beautiful for an isolated plantation. Every male on the premises, black and white, would be panting after her. Especially now that Damon had taken a wife and banished the girl.

A husband, that was it. Kathleen would have to find a husband for Indigo. Florian, perhaps, or his brother Nero who was the foreman of the field hands.

The important thing was to keep everything on an even keel until after the wedding. Kathleen shuddered when she thought of the drunken binge Rafe had indulged in

101

after the English girl had gone back to Charleston. Those damned Sassenach, they could always cause trouble just by their very presence. Rafe, of course, had been born in the Carolinas and did not know what it was like in the old country. But Kathleen had come to America as a child. Her parents knew the Sassenach well and told Kathleen how they had ravaged Ireland.

"We shall have to go over your wardrobe, Indigo, and choose something more suitable for your new position," Kathleen said, emphasizing the last words. The girl would have to know right from the start that no nonsense would be tolerated under Kathleen Danvers' roof. Not that Kathleen was worried about her husband. He drank himself to sleep every night to overcome the gnawing pain of his shattered leg, and it had been years since he'd approached her for more than an apologetic kiss.

Indigo glanced down at her demure brown day dress, trimmed with black ribbon. The dress was well cut, fashionable and in impeccable taste—it was not the coarse calico of a servant's attire.

"Whatever you say, Mrs. Danvers."

"And I shall expect you to perform cleaning chores in addition to your duties as housekeeper. We keep only one slave in the house on a full time basis, the others we bring in from the fields as we need them."

Indigo's expression did not change. She'd learned long ago to mask her feelings.

It was only after Kathleen Danvers had shown her to the tiny room above the kitchen and produced two faded calico dresses and several darned and patched aprons that Indigo closed the door and showed her true feelings by flinging the ugly slave clothes on the floor.

Claudine L'Herreaux had been the only white woman Indigo had ever truly liked, for Claudine came to the new world with a total lack of color consciousness. Indigo had loved the white girl with whom she had shared a nursery and schoolroom, but that love had been betrayed, and it had taken Claudine some time to heal the scars. Indigo's old mistrust and dislike of white women had flared anew when Damon had brought home his new bride. Yet Indigo loved him and could not stop loving him, even now when he had so callously sent her away. She had never had another lover, although she was well aware that Damon had had many women. Sometimes she wondered if that was the problem . . . all she knew about lovemaking she had

102

learned from Damon. Did those other women know something that she did not?

She had heard rumors among the slaves that Rafe Danvers was being forced into the marriage with Beth Grenville to save the Clearview plantation from bankruptcy, and that he had known the Englishwoman in England. It was suspected that he was still attracted to her. Could it be that the cold-looking Englishwoman knew more about handling men than she did?

There was a polite tap on her door. Opening it, she looked up to see a tall young man with dark skin, even features and a regal bearing. Indigo noted his expressionless face when he spoke.

"I am Florian," he said, "from Oakside. I brought Miss Beth here to visit, and Miss Danvers sent me to fetch you down to the kitchen to make 'freshments."

Indigo went downstairs in her brown day dress, but she did slip on an apron. Florian accompanied her to the kitchen and watched as she fumbled with unfamiliar cupboards and drawers.

"If you know where things are, why don't you help me? China and spoons, where are they? That is, if you are a house servant and not some field hand," Indigo said, becoming exasperated by his unwavering stare.

Silently he opened the right cupboard for her, noticing as she reached for the cups that her hair moved like dark windswept grass and smelled just as fragrant. Mrs. Danvers had hinted in her coy way that Florian should take note of her new housekeeper's beauty, because Mrs. Danvers liked to have all her female employees married and settled. She had spoken in the slow, careful way one addresses a child, repeating herself several times until she was sure Florian understood her meaning.

Florian was uneasy. Like everyone else, he knew Indigo belonged to Damon St. Clair . . . no matter what Mrs. Danvers might have in mind. Women . . . black, white and mixed . . . meant trouble.

Indigo glanced up at him and said sharply, "Will you please stop staring at me?" She spoke like a white, Florian noticed.

"Beg yo' pardon, ma'am . . . I cain't help it, you're the most beautiful thing I ever seen."

Indigo softened somewhat. She was going to need friends. "How do they treat their people here?" she asked.

"New steward and new overseer this year . . . both bad," Florian said gloomily. "Reckon they're getting ready to run the two plantations lahk one after the weddin' . . . ole Mist' Grenville he's going to live in Charleston all the year then. That Mist' Danvers is no account. Never sober seem lahk . . . and young Mist' Rafe a mite wild and not good enough for Miss Beth. Both those Danvers sneak down to the slave cabins at night."

They went on talking about blacks and whites on the two plantations, some of them known to Indigo because of the Grenvilles' custom of spending the heat of the summer in Charleston. The Danvers, however, remained on their plantation all year and it was a miracle, everyone agreed, that they managed to avoid the fever. Rafe, of course, had been sent away to school and had, in common with other planters' sons, gone to Europe for his "Grand Tour," although in his case it was the economy version: passage on the *Wayward Woman* and visits only to Ireland and England. Florian told her that the Danvers were flat broke, the plantation mortgaged to the hilt, and only the coming wedding and merging of the prosperous Oakside plantation could save them from certain disaster.

By the time Indigo retired to her small room that night she was more tired than she had ever been in her life. She was asleep almost the moment her head touched the bed. She dreamed Damon was standing over her, caressing her body, his hands hard on her breasts, sliding downward to slip between her thighs and penetrate roughly, before she was ready. She stirred and tried to protest that he was hurting her. Then the hardness was against her throat and she awakened, gasping, almost suffocating.

A wooden stick was pressed to her throat and, inches away, someone was breathing unevenly, deep rasping breaths. She looked into the face of Michael Danvers, perspiration dripping from his upper lip, his eyes dulled with brandy. The cane he used to walk with was pressed against her throat and his clothes were in a heap on the floor.

"Please . . ." she gasped out the word, "I can't breathe . . ."

The pressure against her neck eased slightly.

"You have to make me whole," he whispered in a strangled voice. "Make me whole and I won't hurt you. I . . . can't . . . do it the normal way any longer . . ."

She wanted to scream, but who would come to her aid?

During the miserable hours she tried to bring her new master to his zenith, she thought bitterly of the one who had brought her this misery.

CHAPTER 12

The *Wayward Woman* was under full sail before a brisk breeze, heading southward for the Caribbean. From a distance she appeared to be a merchantman, although of rakish lines and rigged for speed.

A transformation had taken place during her stay in Charleston, however. Carpenters had built a false poop deck at the stern. It covered four gun ports. And her hatches were empty of cargo, so she could run should she sight a British ship of the line with its double tier of guns. A ship like that would be capable of reducing the *Woman* to matchsticks with a single broadside.

"Sail ho!" The cry rang out from the masthead.

Alain handed the telescope to Damon. "A whaler, *mon ami*. She shows no colors. She could be out of Nantucket."

"It's too early for the rum ships out of Port of Spain," Damon answered. "I reckon we'll sight the first tomorrow."

They were rapidly overhauling the other vessel and, as the expanse between them lessened, Alain clutched Damon's arm and pointed. The whaler was running up British colors.

"We run up English colors also, no?" Alain suggested.

"Why not?" Damon grinned.

They waved to the English seamen as the *Wayward Woman* swooped alongside the slower vessel, passed her and quickly left her behind.

"She goes around the horn to the Pacific whaling grounds . . . ah, the stories I've heard of the islands there.

106

Maybe I sign on a whaler, *mon ami,* and avoid swinging from an English yardarm?" Alain suggested.

"You'll have to learn to play better poker first," Damon growled. "My share of the *Woman* is greater than yours now, but I'm not ready to buy you out. You know more about the sea than I do."

"I will gladly teach you all I know about the sea . . . if you will teach me about women."

Damon smiled. "Don't tell me . . . let me guess. You've fallen in love again with some little waterfront floozie who told you you have the face of a god and the voice of a saint."

Alain took the wheel roughly from Damon's hands. "You steer us off course, *mon ami.* You have more to learn than I think. And no, I am not in love again. But tell me about your love life, M'sieur St. Clair . . . what you propose to do about your wife and mistress?"

Damon could not see Alain's eyes, which were fixed on the far horizon, but there was something in his friend's voice that prompted an honest reply.

"You know why I married the Englishwoman. The child was conceived before I learned I could not use her against her father. I don't know . . . after the child is born I shall probably send her back to England."

"And the child?"

"My son stays with me. He will be born an American citizen, safe from his grandfather's clutches. At first I was appalled at the idea, Alain, I'll admit it. That my blood should mingle with Malford's and produce a child . . . it was something I hadn't considered when I married her. I suppose because Indigo . . ." he stopped, wondering if he would have married Indigo had she conceived his child, and, guiltily, he realized he would not have. That such a marriage was against the law, he did not consider.

"And you think Lanna will meekly give up her child and return to England alone? You think her father will allow this?"

"Hell, it's too far in the future. I'll worry about it when it happens. Who knows, I may not live another five months."

"Sad, but true, *mon ami.* But it's not too late to give up this harebrained plan."

Damon thumped Alain affectionately on the back, not thinking about the harebrained plan, but of Lanna and the child. He had not meant to lie with her, damn it, let alone give her a child. It had been that infuriatingly composed manner of hers, those cool blue eyes that regarded him with such contempt and loathing, her whole blasted aristocratic bearing. He had wanted to humiliate and degrade her, to wipe the composure from those lovely features. How could he have known that all the ice was on the surface? It was unfair of a woman to look and behave like some unapproachable goddess and then melt in his arms with a passion that rivaled his own. The same passion, he reminded himself, that she had shared with Rafe Danvers.

He turned to leave the bridge as Alain swung the wheel, eyes on the horizon where the deep blue of the sea met the lighter sky. The color reminded him, disturbingly, of the eyes of Damon's wife.

They sighted their prey the following afternoon.

"I can make out her name . . . it's the *Cardigan Castle*," Damon said excitedly. "Run up the English colors again so we can get in close enough before she gets suspicious."

The other vessel rode low in the water, her hatches heavy with cargo, moving at the sluggish pace of a merchantman whose only concern was an occasional squall. These waters were well patrolled by the Royal Navy and a merchant vessel flying English colors had nothing to fear.

Aboard the *Cardigan Castle*, the skipper watched, unconcerned, as the other English ship bore swiftly down upon him. No doubt the other captain had need of supplies that were depleted aboard his own ship. By the time the *Wayward Woman* had come about and put a warning shot across his bow it was too late to try to run, even if the *Castle* had been capable of outdistancing the *Wayward Woman*. Startled, the English skipper gave the order to heave to. The *Wayward Woman* came full speed, shaving the *Castle*'s bows so closely that her mizzen rigging barely cleared the bowsprit of the attacker.

With only a few feet of water between them, the crew of the English ship looked into a row of muskets pointed in their direction, as the grinning Americans hauled down their false English colors.

Damon swung aboard the *Cardigan Castle* with two sailors at his side and faced the open-mouthed English skipper.

"Your cargo, except what we shall take for our own needs, will be jettisoned," Damon informed the Englishman.

"This, sir, is an act of piracy. Are you mad?" the Englishman sputtered. "English gunboats will blow you out of the water for this."

"Ah, but there are no gunboats near. Come, captain, we have much to do. My men here will take a couple of kegs of your rum for our crew and we could use some meat and any other fresh food you might have."

"What do you propose to do with my ship and my men?" the English captain inquired stiffly.

"Nothing. So long as you behave yourselves and do as you are told, you will be free to return to the Indies. Your sister ship, I understand, is hard on your heels? You will have to take a roundabout route to avoid meeting her. When you return to Port of Spain you are to deliver a message to your owner, Sir Jared Malford. Tell him his precious rum has gone down under and that next time I will put your crew into the boats and sink the ship. By the way, if we meet again I doubt it will be at this longitude or latitude . . . so if he decides to give you an escort, it will be needed all the way to England . . . and back again. But on your next voyage you will lose your ship. Understand?"

The Englishman nodded grimly. "And may I know who makes these threats?"

"Tell Sir Jared that they are made by Richard Trelayne's son. The same Richard Trelayne who was murdered by him. Can you remember all that?"

"Aye. I doubt I shall forget."

Before the empty *Cardigan Castle* arrived back in Port of Spain, her sister ship, the *Canaerven Castle*, its crew removed, had been set afire and sunk. The *Wayward Woman* sailed swiftly for the African coast before the Royal Navy had time to send a frigate to search for the privateer.

Safe in an African bay, the *Woman*'s false poop-deck and guns were hauled ashore and hidden, the place carefully marked. The ship was repainted, the rigging changed and a cargo of coconuts and spices was stowed in the hatches. The first mate took command and Damon and Alain, resplendent in linen jackets and pith helmets, retired to the passengers' quarters for the return voyage.

The subterfuge, as it turned out, was unnecessary. They were not intercepted, although several times they beat a hasty retreat upon sighting sail. Alain's knowledge of the Indies, their every safe harbor and inlet, kept them hidden for the next two months until it was time to return to pick up their guns and lie in wait for the *Cardigan Castle* off the Azores. This time, the English crew was put into boats, the cargo removed and the ship set afire.

Damon was exultant, and he refused to consider the fact that since Sir Jared was well aware of the identity of the marauder, he was bound to try to get retribution sooner or later. The disguising of their ship. while sufficient at sea, would not bear close inspection. They did not dare return to Charleston, or to any American port, especially because of the blockading Royal Navy.

Alain began to realize that Damon had not planned beyond the sinking of Sir Jared's ships.

"Ah, *mon ami,* I shall miss the *Woman,*" Alain sighed.

"We'll get a second *Woman* . . . newer . . . faster. We have the money from the rum we sold and we can sell the ship . . ."

"Damon, no. I believe you are too . . . optimistic. We shall have to abandon her. If we try to sell her someone is certain to recognize her and you and me, *mon ami,* will hang."

It was true. They had broken all maritime law and the American authorities would deal with them as harshly as the British.

"Then, old friend, we shall have to continue our privateering a while longer and this time take prizes instead of sinking them."

"With only four guns? You think we will always be able to bluff the captains as we did with the *Castles?*"

"All right. I can't let you lose your ship. I'll return to America and you sail for the China seas. Lay low for a while. I'll get you another ship, one way or another."

Damon did not add that he was beginning to tire of living at sea surrounded by men. His need for a woman's comfort grew stronger each day. He thought longingly of the silken embrace of Indigo and, unwillingly, of the cool beauty of his wife.

Lanna had avoided looking into Beth's hurt eyes when, at the last minute, she had declined to attend the wedding. She pleaded ill health and complained about the bitingly cold weather. Beth was at once contrite that the wedding was to take place on the plantation, instead of in Charleston.

"The house is just too small here, you see, dear," she ex-

110

plained. "And after the . . . honeymoon," she blushed becomingly, "Rafe and I will spend several months visiting our various relatives. I'm afraid it will be spring before I see you again. Have you heard from Damon? Will you be all right?"

"Yes. He will be back very soon. Don't worry about me," Lanna lied.

Beth sent her a charming letter, describing her wedding in detail, which Lanna read with sadness. Beth had written to her *on her honeymoon*. Lanna thought forlornly that if she were on a honeymoon with Rafe she would not have taken the time to write to anyone.

The days passed slowly. Lanna saw Doctor Crawford occasionally, but no other visitors called upon her. Sometimes she wondered wearily what had happened to her husband, why he had not returned. Perhaps his ship was at the bottom of the sea, or maybe Damon had been impressed into the Royal Navy. She devoutly wished that it were so.

The days had grown warmer and the garden was a profusion of spring flowers when Myrtle came to her one day to announce she had a visitor. Lanna assumed it was Beth and went downstairs eagerly. She stopped short halfway down the stairs when she saw who was standing in the hall below, but it was too late. He had seen her.

" 'Morning, Mrs. St. Clair," Lucas Bassey said, removing his straw hat and handing it to Joshua. The sunlight slanted across his bald head and his eyes were almost transparent.

"What do you want, Mr. Bassey? As you can clearly see, I am in no condition to receive visitors," Lanna said, glancing balefully at Joshua, who wore a woebegone expression. Bassey had, of course, insisted upon seeing her.

"Wouldn't have come if it weren't urgent," Bassey said. "Come all the way from Trinidad, I have."

Lanna led the way to the piazza, dismissing Joshua, and turned to face Bassey. "What is so urgent?"

"You have to go to the Grenvilles' plantation. A trunk has been shipped to you there. From your father."

"But . . . I don't understand. Why did he not send it to me here? And what does it contain?"

"Wouldn't do nobody no good here," Bassey said laconically.

"But they will think it odd . . . that I should go to the plantation just as they will be preparing to come here for

111

the summer. And I am so close to my time . . . what in the name of God is in the trunk?"

"You can tell them you have come to say goodbye, that you're going home to England. Never mind what's in the trunk. Tell them it's wedding presents from Sir Jared."

"But they will think it strange I wouldn't go to their wedding, but travel upriver now. And they won't believe I am going to England when I am so near my time."

"They will believe you want to go before war is declared."

"War? Is it really going to happen?"

"Aye, within days. Madison has as good as said so to the Congress. If you want to get out in time, you will have to leave on the ship I came on. You won't be the first woman to give birth at sea, nor the last. Sir Jared might even accept a child born at sea. Being a navy man himself. Such children are lucky, they say."

"But why do I have to go upriver to claim the trunk?"

" 'Cause they won't be suspicious of it with you there. Give me time to get what's in it stowed away and make my arrangements with the buyers."

Lanna did not have to ask what was in it.

"Anyway, you don't have no choice," Bassey said. "You can't stay. Your husband won't be coming back to you. There'll be nobody to support you and the child. You're a widow."

Lanna clutched the back of a chair for support as cold chills swept through her body. She moved her lips, but no words came.

"Your husband sank both of your father's merchantmen —the first one months ago, and both of them during peacetime. Piracy it was. Your father caught up with him and sank his ship too. Now you're a widow in an enemy country with nobody to take care of you. Soon as I take care of the business upriver, we shall be on a ship. So no more arguments."

Lanna sank limply into the chair. The shock of the news he had so callously given made her head pound.

"W-w-what about the others?" Lanna stammered. "The . . . captain?"

Bassey shrugged. "All lost, I believe. If they didn't go down with the ship, they'd be hung as pirates. And I can tell you this, girlie, the people here won't help you. They didn't like St. Clair anyway, he was never one of 'em. This lot are more aristocratic than the toffs in London."

112

Lanna pressed her hand to her temple to ease the throbbing pain. He was right, she could not stay here now. She was an enemy. Besides, she realized for the first time, she had no proof that she was legally married to Damon St. Clair. There was the entry in the log of the *Wayward Woman*, but that was now at the bottom of the sea. She would hardly have any claim on his estate without some documentary proof that the marriage had taken place. She had to think of her child, but it was difficult because she was filled with a sense of total desolation. Almost as though she had loved the man her father had hunted down and killed.

CHAPTER 13

Beth and Rafe were too polite to show their surprise at Lanna's sudden appearance at Oakside. Beth welcomed Lanna warmly, apologizing for not having come to Charleston to see her. They had spent more time visiting relatives and friends than they had planned and were only now preparing to close the plantation house for the summer.

Beth's smile quickly faded, however, when she learned the reason for the unexpected visit, that Lanna intended to sail for England before war was declared because Damon and all hands aboard the *Wayward Woman* were lost. Beth's sympathy enveloped Lanna like a warm cloud.

"Oh, my poor dear friend," Beth exclaimed. "To lose your husband so tragically . . . oh, I cannot bear it."

She enclosed Lanna in a tearful embrace and over her shoulder Lanna's eyes met Rafe's.

Damon dead . . . she's a widow . . . and I'm married to Beth. Rafe wanted to tear his hair, smash the furniture, kill the already dead Damon.

"But you can't sail for England now, dear. You're much too close to your time," Beth continued. "Rafe, honey, you must convince Lanna to stay."

"Beth is right, Lanna," Rafe said. His voice sounded hollow, as though it did not belong to him. Lanna was carrying Damon's child . . . Damon St. Clair was not dead, he would live on in the child. Rafe felt as though he were drowning in the liquid blue eyes of the woman being embraced by his wife.

"You will be safe here," Rafe said. "No one will harm you. There are many new arrivals from England in our midst who are already loyal Americans, especially the fugitives from the Royal Navy." He was concentrating on keeping his voice impersonal and he was glad that Beth did not turn around to look at him.

"You are very kind, both of you," she murmured. "Could we talk about it later? I'm so tired." She was not merely evading the issue. She wanted to stay with Rafe and despised herself for it.

"You must be exhausted from the journey. Come, I'll help you up to your room," Beth said, taking her arm. "It will be at least another week before we can leave, and you will have to be very careful not to overtire yourself in the heat. We shall take you back to Charleston with us."

She wore her happiness like a great golden halo, Lanna thought enviously.

During the days that followed it became evident that Rafe was not as overjoyed as Beth was with their marriage. Lanna noted that he drank too much and that he appeared restless and ill at ease. Although he was charming and superficially attentive to his wife, he did not gaze at Beth in the same radiant manner with which she regarded him. Lanna was more than ever convinced that he had indeed married Beth for convenience. If only, Lanna thought, I didn't like Beth so much. If only I weren't so grotesquely pregnant. Little wonder Rafe looks at me in that strange way. He's probably thinking he's glad he didn't marry me.

He was drinking as much as his father. Rafe himself knew it, and he loathed himself for doing it. But the swelling of Lanna's body reminded him of how much he hated the dead Damon St. Clair.

The plantation, the house, his wife: they were his penance, his prison, his jailor . . . and Lanna was his torment. The moment he had always dreaded was upon him. It was time to take up the yoke of the plantation his grandfather had built and his father had neglected. Then there were the slaves. The sea of black faces that had always worried Rafe, even as a small boy.

Slaves on a rice plantation lived and toiled in the unhealthiest of all environments. They worked constantly, ankle-deep in muddy water, ditching, drawing, weeding, turning over the sodden ground. Many sickened and died and all were debilitated by summer's end. Yet it was impossible to run a plantation without slaves.

Impossible for old Grandfather Grenville and the crippled Michael Danvers to cope with the constant departures of white stewards and overseers. They were all looking to Rafe to take over their burdens. And now Damon was dead and he would be of no help either. Rafe felt like the last able-bodied white man left on earth.

At times he felt the trees were closing in on the house, that the great swamps were reclaiming what was rightfully theirs. He stared obsessively at the encroaching trees, thinking that he would keep them at bay. He knew that both Beth and Lanna watched him with worried eyes, and he filled his glass again and thought about the sea.

Halfway across an ocean a strange peace descends on a man. One shore left behind and the next still out of sight. The people, problems and fears of the land could not reach out to claim a man when he was safely under sail.

Rafe stayed up late at night with a bottle and, if Beth should be awake when at last he tiptoed into their room, he would turn and leave. All the way down the stairs, out into the night and down to the slave cabins he would tell himself that he would go back to Beth's bed. But on the rare occasions when he did, he would slip between the sheets and kiss her tenderly . . . and feel no desire . . . it was like kissing his mother . . . his sister . . . the alabaster saints in church . . . like trying to make love to his own conscience.

It did not matter which of the slave women he took. Old, young, ugly, willing, unwilling. In the dark they were Lanna, looking at him with liquid blue eyes, touching him with blue fire, sending his blood rushing in a great roaring torrent down into an endless sea.

One night the young girl beneath him began to sob uncontrollably. His besotted senses cleared for a moment and he looked down at her, at the thin body of a child-woman. Slowly he withdrew from her, shaking his head slightly as he saw her curl into a ball, clasping her knees to her thin chest and burying her face . . . returning to the womb.

Rafe reached for his clothes. Damon St. Clair's child would eventually be born. Lanna was a widow. St. Clair had had a wife and a mistress while he lived. Rafe Danvers would simply take his widow and make her his own mistress. She loved him, he knew that. But she was beginning

116

to love Beth too, although she probably didn't know it yet. She would no more want to hurt Beth than he would.

His loins still throbbed when he returned to the house, and his member refused to lie down and sleep. It became the pulsing focal point of his being, and he tried to turn his back to the frail body of his wife, to keep her from being touched by his grossness.

On their wedding night he had failed miserably and Beth, true to form, had believed he was being considerate of her shyness and fears. Their marriage had not been consummated until the night he had closed his eyes and lost himself in the memory of the night in the park in London . . . re-living the heady scent of blossoms, the heartbreakingly beautiful song of the nightingale. Lanna's lips parting sweetly, her body blending with his and every star in the fathomless ocean of the sky shining in her eyes.

When he opened his eyes and looked into Beth's face, her eyes squeezed shut and her lips bitten raw, looked down and saw that she was trembling violently, shaking from his assault upon her, it was as though she were a sacred vessel into which he had relieved himself.

The third day after her arrival, the trunk from the Indies was delivered to Lanna. Florian and his brother Nero brought it to her room and dropped it on the floor with a heavy thud. It was locked, and Lanna had not been given a key. She felt the ominous presence of the huge box all day, and that night she tossed in the grip of a nightmare in which the lid of the trunk slowly opened and hideous devils sprang out, brandishing guns that belched smoke.

Exhausted, she slept late next morning, waking to find the sun high in the sky and the sound of many voices drifting up to her room. Dressing quickly, she went downstairs to find Beth surrounded by visitors.

Michael and Kathleen Danvers, with Indigo standing subserviently behind them, and—Lanna stiffened—Lucas Bassey. She felt Indigo's eyes go over her swollen body, but she was much too aware of Lucas Bassey's transparent eyes to pay attention.

"Your father sent me to take you home," he said.

Immediately there was a murmur of protest from Beth and her grandfather.

Kathleen Danvers glanced at Indigo, who was still waiting, and said, "Indigo, why don't you go and visit with Florian in the kitchen. I'm sure he's anxious to see you

117

again." She did not notice her husband's eyes follow the girl as she went.

"Now, Mr. Bassey," Grandfather Grenville said, "we must sit down and discuss this situation sensibly. You can see for yourself that Mrs. St. Clair can't possibly travel."

Everyone but Bassey found chairs. Beth came protectively to Lanna's side, standing with her arm thrown across the back of the chair as though to ward off any attackers who might threaten her friend. Oh, Beth, Lanna thought miserably, if only you weren't so sweet and pure and loyal. If only Rafe was married to someone like Indigo, how easy it would be.

Bassey's huge frame dominated the room. He stood with his back to the window, casting a monstrous shadow.

"Her husband is dead and her father wants her home. I'm here to help her with her belongings," he said shortly. "There'll be a surgeon on the ship in case she needs him, but we'll only take her as far as the Bahamas for now. Send her home to England after the child is born. There's going to be war . . . you all know it. Your Mr. Madison made it pretty clear in that speech he gave, first of the month."

"It does seem," Kathleen Danvers put in, "that it would be a difficult situation for Mrs. St. Clair to be in . . . living in the land of her enemies and without a husband's protection. The penalty you pay, my dear, for being born an Englishwoman." Her voice faded, but the words seemed to hang in the air.

Beth said firmly, "But Lanna is an American now, by marriage. And she will have our protection."

Kathleen Danvers' green eyes flickered pityingly over her daughter-in-law, and Lanna suddenly had the urge to put her own arm around Beth's shoulders.

"I haven't decided yet whether I shall return to England, and I believe I am the only one who can make the decision," Lanna said, wondering why she felt so protective toward Beth.

"Beth is such an innocent," Kathleen said, "and, of course, we all love her for it. But the unpleasant facts of life must sometimes be faced. The newspapers are all clamoring for war with England and there are nasty stories about British plans to cause trouble with the Negroes and Indians. I should think a new arrival from England would definitely be suspect . . ."

"Oh, Mother Danvers," Beth said imploringly, "surely

118

not an expectant mother?" Her face was pink with concern.

"Will you excuse me?" Lanna said abruptly. "I really don't feel well this morning. I think I should return to my room and lie down." She stood up awkwardly, Beth's hand supporting her.

"You'll feel better when you're back in bed and have something to eat. I'll order some breakfast for you right away," Beth whispered.

Grandfather Grenville resumed his protests to Bassey as the two girls walked slowly up the stairs.

From the kitchen, Indigo watched their progress. She had hoped they would remain downstairs long enough for her to investigate the very large and heavy trunk Florian had told her about. The pieces were beginning to fit together . . . seeing the Englishwoman with Lucas Bassey in the coffee house, telling Alain about the meeting, Alain's distress that Bassey had been seen associating with known gun runners. When Alain had told her he would warn Damon's wife about the man, Indigo had been doubly resentful. It was bad enough to lose Damon. She would not share Alain with Lanna too. Indigo thought sometimes that since she had been banished to the plantation, she missed Alain's comradeship more than Damon's caresses. If Damon were really dead, then Indigo would have begged Alain to let her live with him. But Damon was not dead, no matter what they said about the sinking of the *Woman*. If he were dead she would feel it, in the same way she always knew when he was coming home. Why, he was on his way home this very minute. The tingling of her senses told her she would see him soon.

If only the Englishwoman could be exposed as an enemy, a British spy, before the child was born. She would be sent away, and Indigo could return to Damon's house. She could not go on living under the same roof as Michael Danvers, whose nightly visits were becomingly increasingly intolerable. Desperately she had tried to give him some satisfaction, so he would perhaps leave her alone for a while, but the more times he failed to achieve his purpose, the more he drank, and the more he drank, the worse became his feeling of failure.

Now he was beginning to blame Indigo for it, and his demands became ever more hellish as the unfulfilled nights passed. It was as though he turned into some depraved beast when darkness fell. By day he was at least an echo of the gentleman he had once been, although the shadow of pain never left his face.

Indigo had thought about running away, but she had no paper that said she was a free woman, despite what Damon had told her. Besides, Indigo did not want to leave when she was sure that Damon was so near. The large box in the Englishwoman's room, that was the answer. Whichever way she decided to play her hand, that box was her passport out of this nightmare.

The box, Florian had told her, was extraordinarily heavy. It was supposed to contain wedding presents from Mrs. St. Clair's father, but it felt more like a solid block of lead. Florian had been only too happy to tell the beautiful Indigo all she had wanted to know. He had been overwhelmed that she found him so interesting and he gladly answered all of her questions . . . he knew slave women were always interested in what the white women were about.

Florian was waiting for the right moment to ask Indigo to be his wife. Several times he had been on the point of bringing up the subject, but Indigo had always deftly steered him on to other matters. Unlike some plantations, both Oakside and Clearview arranged wedding ceremonies for their slaves and encouraged them to marry and produce children. Among the field hands, the "weddings" were of little consequence. That many of the couples soon changed their living arrangements and that the women bore children by men other than their "husbands" was overlooked by their white owners.

House servants were a different matter. Especially the ones who accompanied their owners to the coastal areas during the summer, as Florian did. Florian would be expected to choose a wife carefully and to be faithful to her.

"Have you ever thought about killing them all, Florian?" Indigo asked him.

Florian's eyes gleamed ferociously for a second, but he glanced over his shoulder before replying. "Sometimes I think I will fetch my brother Nero and we will lead all the slaves away to freedom. But then I stop and think . . . the field hands haven't got no gumption. All they want to do is sleep and lay about."

It was true the slaves who worked the flooded rice fields in the heat of summer had little energy left when their day's work was done. Many of them were ill when the fall came, and they spent the winter recovering from various sicknesses to which they fell prey.

" 'Sides," he continued, "where would we go if we ran away? To Africa? I don' speck we'd know how to live there anymore."

"You haven't talked about an uprising with anyone then? Besides your brother?" Indigo said. She moved closer to him, her voice low and her long black eyelashes curling softly around her brown velvet eyes. Indigo had occasionally felt a longing deep inside her to know how it would feel to lie in the arms of a black man. The other slave women claimed that black lovers were superior, but Indigo knew that the slave women could choose their black lovers, while their white masters took them brutally, usually against their will. That would make a difference. Indigo herself knew the joy of lying with Damon and the hell of Michael Danvers' ugly assaults. She did her utmost to stifle any longings that would plunge her completely into the world of black slaves. She was, after all, half white. As long as she stayed with white men she had some protection from being forced to live in the slave quarters and toil in the fields.

Florian was shaking his head to her question. "I never spoke of no uprisings. Nero, he ran off once . . . the overseer whipped him all afternoon. Said next time he run off he'd get gelded."

"That Englishman, Mr. Bassey. He say anything to you when he arrived with that heavy box?" Indigo said.

Florian grinned, his teeth white against his rich dark skin. "I couldn't understand a word that man said."

Indigo smiled too and turned back to her work. It was pleasant to have a man so obviously worship her again. Florian's devotion reminded her of Alain's gentle companionship, and she recalled longingly the lost days in the tiny house when she and Alain and Damon were a family.

She was little better than a maid at Clearview because of their lack of house servants. She missed being able to command servants and a butler, and she especially resented the way Myrtle and Zenobia and the other maids from Oakside and Charleston looked down on her reduced status. She spent her days and nights alternately hating Damon for sending her to Clearview, and longing for him to return.

Now Lucas Bassey had arrived. There was something he

knew about the Englishwoman that no one else knew, Indigo was sure of it. As she prepared a breakfast tray to take to Lanna, at Beth's instructions, she fingered the bread knife thoughtfully.

CHAPTER 14

The heat rose in shimmering waves from the flooded fields and smothered the sagging occupants of the house like a wet blanket. Insects hung lazily in the humid air and a lethargic hush fell upon the plantation.

Lanna knew she would have to decide what to do soon, but for the moment it was pleasant to lie in her room and pretend Lucas Bassey was not waiting downstairs, that the trunk did not exist . . . to pretend, in fact, that she was simply not here, but sleeping in the huge old fourposter bed at Kingsburch.

Her thoughts turned drowsily to Damon. She could not believe he was dead. Perhaps because his child moved restlessly within her, a small foot or fist occasionally punching at her. Besides, Damon was so vital, so virile . . . how could such a man be dead? She hated him, of course, but even hating him, she had to admit that Damon St. Clair was not easily dismissed to the forgotten world of spirits and ghosts.

Indigo had brought her a tray, and she inquired as to whether Lanna would like to have someone unpack her box of wedding presents.

Startled, Lanna had said, "Oh, it's stupid of me, but I seem to have misplaced the key to the trunk. I'll look for it later." Was it her imagination, or did Indigo's golden eyes look at her as though they saw through the lie?

"I'm sure Mr. Bassey has a spare key. If I can't find mine, I'll get his."

Late in the afternoon Lanna awoke and rang for Zenobia to help her dress for dinner. She had slept for hours but she was still tired. The weakness sapped both her body and her mind.

Zenobia told her that the Danvers had come for a final meeting about plantation business before Beth, Rafe and Grandfather Grenville left for their summer house. Both the Danvers and Lucas Bassey had been invited for dinner and no, Zenobia had not heard any further discussion about Lanna.

When she was dressed Lanna sat down heavily. "You may go, Zenobia," she said. "I need to rest for a moment before going downstairs. I feel so very tired today."

"It's near yo' time," Zenobia said knowingly, and she gave a happy grin.

Lanna smiled wanly and sat motionless for several minutes after the girl had left. She had to clear her head and think. What to do about the trunk . . . about returning to England with Bassey? Finally she dragged herself to her feet and stepped out onto the landing. She felt a wave of dizziness as she stood at the top of the stairs. She gripped the balustrade tightly, then sank down on the top stair until the feeling had passed. It was then she looked down and saw Bassey's great back propped against the half-open dining room door below. Almost simultaneously, she saw Indigo laying silverware on the table and smiling up at Bassey from beneath a flutter of charcoal eyelashes.

Lanna had never seen such a look on Indigo's face, and she thought with a pang of sorrow of how many times Damon must have seen it. But now Damon was dead and no doubt Indigo was looking for his successor.

She could not hear the conversation between the two of them, and the next moment she was startled by a footfall behind her.

"Lanna . . . are you all right?" It was Rafe, bending over her anxiously, drawing her to her feet. "Come, let me help you to a chair."

"Rafe . . . no, just let me step out onto the balcony for a moment for a breath of air."

He led her carefully through the unused bedroom that bordered her own, and out onto the balcony.

"Shall I bring you a chair? Lanna, you look so pale . . . oh, God, I hate to see you like this."

Somehow her head was against his shoulder and his

124

arms were holding her comfortingly in an embrace that was without passion.

Rafe, dear Rafe . . . their love could never be, but he would help her, she knew he would.

She looked up at him, at the concern creasing his forehead and the torment in his eyes. "Rafe . . . I've been so foolish . . . I—I—I . . ." the words were lost as she struggled with the river of tears that welled up and would not be stemmed.

"Hush, it's all right," he whispered against her hair. "As soon as you've had your baby . . . I'll slip away and see you as often as I can. I have to stay with Beth, because of the plantations . . . but now that Damon is gone, there's no reason—"

"No . . . Rafe, you don't understand . . ." Lanna raised a tear-stained face. She pulled away from him and stumbled back into the house, moving as quickly as she could to her own bedroom where she shut the door against his hoarsely whispered pleas. She could not ask Rafe for help; the price she would have to pay was too dear.

In the dining room, Lucas Bassey was congratulating himself on the progress he was making with the beautiful Indigo. Bassey had difficulty understanding the dialect of the other slaves and Indigo's flawless English was a boon.

The men who had sold him the muskets had assured him he would find ready buyers among the plantation slaves, but they had not warned him of the difficulty he would have in communicating with them. The slaves, he was told, usually were able to earn money from producing their own small crops in addition to those of the plantation. And the trusted house servants would know exactly where their owners' valuables were kept.

Bassey's unique opportunity was pointed out by the gun traders. He was English, and war was a certainty within a month. He could easily convince the slaves they would be supported by the British. A quick and handsome profit for Bassey, with very little risk. Since Bassey had been sent back to America to remove his captain's adopted daughter, he might as well make the trip worth while. Besides, Sir Jared had instructed him to gather any intelligence that might be useful in the event of war.

"And if Lanna refuses to leave, sir?" Bassey had asked.

"Tell her we sank her husband's ship and that she is a

widow," Sir Jared had answered. He did not see the need to explain to his boatswain the change of heart he had had in regard to Lanna. He had been unable to catch the *Wayward Woman,* and now Lanna was his only link to Damon Trelayne. Perhaps the girl would know something that would aid them in their search . . . perhaps, even, her husband would come looking for her.

And now, in the dining room at Oakside, Bassey was finding out that Indigo was more than willing to help him sell the muskets. Florian, she said, and his brother Nero, the tough Oakside driver, would certainly lead an uprising in order to gain their freedom. She suggested Bassey let her remove one of the muskets from the trunk in order to prove their existence to the brothers.

Bassey looked into the amber eyes and saw a spark of fire. This girl carried a grudge against whites. She could be trusted.

"And what of you, black beauty?" Bassey asked. "What will you do and where will you go?" He put out a great paw and touched the soft skin of her arm.

She looked up at him and smiled. "Anywhere . . . away from here. I never want to be at a white woman's beck and call again."

"You're light enough to pass for white yourself. In England now . . . they'd never know you wasn't white. They don't see too many mulattoes."

"Then perhaps I should go to England?" Indigo suggested, looking at him from beneath her eyelashes. At that moment she saw the Englishwoman, sitting on the top stair, watching them.

Dinner was strained and Lanna tried to detach herself from the conversation. Bassey stubbornly insisted her father would flay him alive if he returned without her. Kathleen Danvers said they surely could get to the Bahamas before the child was born. It would, after all, be an embarrassment for all of them to harbor an Englishwoman, an enemy of their country, at this particular time. While Michael and Rafe Danvers cast anguished glances at Kathleen and then at Lanna, Beth alone cried out against the folly of Lanna's departure.

"Please . . . all of you," Lanna said at last. "I really should not have placed you in this position. Mr. Bassey will accompany me back to Charleston in the morning.

When I arrive there I shall decide whether or not to go on to the Bahamas. That way the decision will be mine alone. I—I—I . . ." She was not sure what she was about to say. The childhood affliction she thought she had outgrown had returned again, and she found herself stammering helplessly. She clapped her serviette to her mouth, crimson with embarrassment.

When at last the meal was over, Lanna retired quickly to her room and, still fully dressed, lay on the bed to rest. Her eyes were fixed, as usual, on the menacing trunk. Something was different about it . . . a small piece of brightly colored silk was now showing beneath the lid.

Suddenly alert, Lanna got up and went over to the trunk. It was unlocked. Someone had come into the room while she was at dinner. Bassey was at dinner too, so it could not have been he. Slowly she raised the lid and looked at the bolt of silk. The metal barrel of a gun protruded from one of the folds of material.

She was still bending over the open trunk, staring in horrified fascination at the tightly packed guns, when they burst in upon her.

A still excitement had fallen upon the slave cabins.

Earlier, a young servant had slipped out of the house and taken the word to them. There was a white man . . . he had brought guns for the slaves. The whispered word traveled swiftly from cabin to cabin. Florian . . . we must wait for Florian to come and tell us what to do.

But Florian had not come to lead them to freedom. The field hands had to struggle to remain awake, forcing their exhausted bodies to forget the backbreaking toil of the day. Some of the men began to wonder if they would know how to make a musket shoot if they had it in their hands. Still, the beacon of freedom flickered in the distance, and long-dormant rage surged in their blood. Whispered threats and plans rustled through the crowded slave quarters like the stirring of wind through leaves.

The overseer would be killed first, then the white masters, the men decided. The slave women were already making plans to divide up the clothing owned by the white women. None of them, in their excited planning, thought about the housekeeper at Clearview, who had accompanied Mrs. Danvers to Oakside. They did not know that Indigo held everyone's fate in her slim fingers and that she had been

127

weighing carefully the advantages and disadvantages of a slave uprising.

Before dinner she had been poised on the brink of a fateful decision. She had the key to the trunk and had seen the contents. It would have been a simple matter to turn them over to Florian.

While the whites ate their leisurely dinner, Indigo stood in the kitchen and directed Florian and the other servants to carry the food into the dining room. She herself was imagining what would happen if she were to urge Florian to take the muskets and arm the slaves. All of the whites would be killed, of course. Including Damon's wife and unborn child. When Damon returned she would be protected. It would be Florian and the other slaves who would be blamed. Indigo herself could immediately leave for Charleston and wait there for Damon's ship to return.

The primitive part of her wanted to see white blood spilled, wanted to give the slave women knives and let them mutilate the white men who had used them. She herself would kill Michael Danvers. A heady excitement keener than any produced by wine sent Indigo's blood racing, and her heart pounded as she contemplated how it would feel to plunge a knife into Michael Danvers' pale flesh.

Then she considered the negative possibilities. First and foremost, she was not very popular with the other slave women. She did not look like them, for one thing. And until her arrival at Clearview, Indigo had held the exalted position of common-law wife to Damon St. Clair. Neither had she endeared herself to them by fluttering her eyes at Florian. Many of the women had hopes of marrying him. Supposing, she reflected, in the bloodletting of the uprising, some of the women decided that Indigo was more white than black? She would have to stay long enough to make sure that all the whites were dead. Would she be able to escape the slave women in time? Would they come after her?

After much thought, Indigo at last made up her mind. "Florian." She caught at the black butler's hand as he returned from serving the dessert. "Come into the pantry for a minute, I want to talk to you."

Indigo caught a quick glimpse of the expression on Myrtle's face as Florian followed her into the pantry, and she knew she was making the right decision. Myrtle had looked at her with open malice.

In the narrow pantry, Florian regarded her with hope and longing in his eyes, his ivory teeth flashing as he smiled.

"Florian, that man Bassey brought guns here," she whispered quickly. "He's offered to sell them to us, and I've been wondering what to do about it. I've decided that we must tell the whites." The "we" made them allies, she reasoned. Speaking of "the whites" reminded him that Indigo was black like him.

"The box . . ." Florian said. "He want to sell them to us? *That's* what he was tryin' to tell me."

"Listen, Florian, where would we go? They'd hunt us down with dogs and kill us. The field hands, they have everything to gain, but not us, Florian. We're house servants . . . we live like the whites . . . well, nearly. Mrs. Danvers told me if I were to marry . . . someone from Oakside . . . that she would buy that man to come and live with me at Clearview." Kathleen Danvers had said no such thing. She had merely intimated that Florian would have visiting privileges from time to time.

"If we could get away . . ." Florian said, "we could go somewhere, the two of us. I would work for you, Indigo, make a place for us . . ."

Indigo's hands swept upward like winged birds as she caught Florian's face and pulled him toward her, shutting off his words with her lips. She felt the momentary surprise, and then his lips responded to hers and his breath was hot in her throat. His arms went about her and she let herself go limp against his body, closing her eyes. For a second she clung to him, the thought flashing into her mind that she had never made love to a man other than Damon. There had been stolen kisses from Cindy Sue's beaux in those long-ago days before she ran away, but since then Indigo had only known the hunger of the flesh with Damon. And he had never shown her the reverence she could feel in Florian's embrace. But Indigo closed her mind to the thought. She was more white than black.

"No, Florian. There is nowhere for us to go," she whispered, pulling away from him. "We don't want to die, do we? Florian, stay here. We'll help the whites and they'll reward us. We don't want to die running away . . . torn to pieces by the hounds." Her hand ran over his chest, trailed down his arm. Their fingers intertwined. "I'm going to tell

Mrs. Danvers about the guns. And you must tell Mr. Rafe to take care of Bassey. Help him, Florian, and when it's all over I'll marry you. Promise me, Florian."

Florian looked into the golden eyes, at the parted lips, the swelling of her breasts. He heard a strangled sob in the back of his throat as he pulled her close again, burying his face in the curtain of black hair. He did not know that the sob was because he had lost an opportunity for freedom.

Why, he wondered, did the melancholy words of a Gullah song come suddenly into his mind:

I know moonrise, I know star-rise; lay dis body down;
I walk in de moonlight, I walk in de starlight,
    To lay dis body down.
I'll walk in de graveyard, I'll walk through de graveyard,
    To lay dis body down;
I'll lie in de grave and stretch out my arms;
    Lay dis body down;
I go to de judgment in de evenin of de day,
    When I lay dis body down;
And my soul and your soul will meet in de day
    When I lay dis body down.

Lanna was alone in her room for the first time since Kathleen Danvers and Indigo had burst in upon her. She had heard the click of the key in the lock after Florian and Nero had removed the trunk under the watchful eye of Rafe and the overseer, who kept their pistols tucked into their belts and their fingers nervously close to the triggers.

An atmosphere of fear prevailed throughout the house, and the night was filled with muffled voices and scurrying feet.

Lanna had tried to explain about the trunk and its awful contents, but she had begun to stammer and cry when she realized there was nothing she could say in her own defense. Nothing except that she had been frightened and indecisive—with no one to turn to.

Indigo had stood silently, triumphantly, while Kathleen Danvers screamed hysterically that Lanna could have had them all killed. At last a tight-lipped Rafe had stepped into the room and asked his mother to stand aside while the two slaves removed the trunk. Rafe had given Lanna an anguished, helpless look. Behind him stood the overseer, and at his side were Florian and Nero.

"Lanna, we shall have to ask you to remain in your

130

room," Rafe said as the slaves lifted the heavy trunk. "But don't worry, I'm sure as soon as Bassey has been questioned he will absolve you from any part in this. We've locked him in one of the slave cabins until morning. We'll send word to the militia in Charleston then."

"Absolve . . ." Kathleen Danvers screamed, "you fool, don't you see she was part of the plot? Why did she come here if she were not? In June—when she must have known you would be going to Charleston for the summer? And she about to drop her brat any minute . . ."

"Mother! Will you please go downstairs?"

Kathleen Danvers drew a deep breath. "A Sassenach, Rafe, and we'll be at war with them soon. Well, we shall see what the militia thinks of the whole affair. That is, if we've found all the weapons and are still alive when they get here."

Rafe went to his mother's side and took her firmly by the arm. "Come on, I'll go with you. Come, Indigo." He turned and looked at Lanna. "Ring if you want anything. Try to get some sleep." Despite his comforting words, the key had turned in the lock when they left.

Lanna sat on the bed. Her hands moved unconsciously to the great swelling of her belly where her baby was strangely still. She would have to face an inquiry about the guns and she did not know what Bassey would say of her part in the matter. How she wished she had taken Rafe into her confidence when the trunk had first arrived . . . now it was too late to claim innocence of the contents.

Her head ached with unanswered questions and awful possibilities. What would they do to her? Kathleen Danvers had said, in rising hysteria, that Lanna would surely bear her child in prison. Kathleen had been able to quote the law very explicitly. The penalty for "advising or conspiring with slaves to make insurrection" was death. Heavy fines were imposed for merely giving a slave an unauthorized pass, or teaching a slave to read.

Oh, why had she allowed everything to reach this state? How could she have been so unsure of what to do? She had felt so terribly tired the last few days; she had tried to tell Rafe and he had . . . misinterpreted. She had been so alone—and she had such little experience of the world. She wondered who had found out about the deadly contents of the trunk. Indigo . . . it had to be she. They must have surprised and overpowered Lucas Bassey right after dinner, just as they had surprised Lanna.

131

Her eyes drifted to the French windows opening onto the balcony. When everyone was asleep it would be easy enough to slip out there. If she were careful she could climb down the heavy branches of the tree at the corner of the house. They would not expect her to try to escape, in her condition. Even as the words formed in her mind, she thought bitterly that her condition had caused one disaster after another. But where would she go . . . and by what means? She had come here by river boat—there would be no boat during the night. A canoe or rowing boat would be out of the question; she would not be able to negotiate the river in darkness, even if she were physically capable of rowing. A horse then . . . she could perhaps sit a horse. There were several in the stables. If she could reach a safe haven until after her baby was born, she could perhaps leave the country then. She would not have her child in prison, it was unthinkable.

She watched the moon rise and the hands of the clock move inexorably toward dawn and still, when she ventured out onto the balcony, there were dark figures moving about the house and grounds below. The first light of dawn was slashing the sky when at last she clung to the rough bark of the ancient oak and eased herself out along the twisted limbs. Slowly, painfully slowly, she inched downward until the ground was beneath her feet. Panting, perspiring, fearful the summer sun would rise to reveal her at any second, she moved through the shadows in the direction of the stables, praying the Negro hands did not sleep there.

The door creaked open, dragging over the dirt, and a gentle-looking mare looked at her from the first stall. Heart thumping, Lanna reached for a saddle.

CHAPTER 15

In later years, Lanna would have a recurring nightmare that she was again fleeing through eerie cypress swamps, the trees with their protuberant roots and bulbous stumps creating the illusion of menacing figures, crouched ready to spring upon the unwary traveler.

Festoons of misty gray tylandria clothed the tree trunks like unkempt hair. Large black buzzards glided slowly over the treetops, and flocks of quail and larks rose with a startled whirring of wings at the approach of her horse.

Several times she splashed into water so deep the horse was almost swimming, and Lanna clung to the damp neck of her mount, blinded by the trailing vines, feeling the murky water dragging at her skirts. In the nightmares that came later, she never reached a safe haven, but rode endlessly through those ghostly trees.

The actual flight, she knew, would come to an end, one way or another. The first dull pain encircled her lower body, holding her for a second in a determined grip, then fading gradually. Minutes later the second contraction came.

She found a dry bank not too overgrown with creepers and crawled from the horse just as another intense pain wrapped itself about her. She clutched wildly at the heavy flanks of the horse as she slid from its back, and the frightened animal splashed away from her, quickly disappearing through the trees. She could hear the splash of the hooves and then, horror of all horrors, a roar of rage

... an animal of some kind ... The horse whinnied loudly in terror. She covered her ears to shut out the sound. It couldn't be happening, she couldn't be all alone in this dismal place and about to have her baby.

The next pain was beginning. She tensed, holding onto the base of the nearest tree, as she was engulfed again. How long had it been since the last pain? Somehow the frequency of the pains was significant. She did not know why she believed this to be so, but some instinct told her. Now she wished she had not run so blindly. Even giving birth in prison would be better than this. Perhaps someone would have believed that the muskets had been sent to her without her knowledge. After all, they were not at war yet ...

Word had not yet reached the plantations that on the previous day, June 18, 1812, war had formally been declared in accordance with Mr. Madison's message to Congress on June 1st.

Damon had heard the news that morning when he arrived back in Charleston, but even stranger news was awaiting him when he arrived at home. Miss Lanna had departed for the Grenvilles' plantation after hearing that the *Wayward Woman* had been lost with all hands.

So ... she believed herself to be a widow and had lost no time in rushing to be consoled by Rafe Danvers, he thought grimly.

And Indigo was working at Clearview. No wife, no mistress. He was tempted to stay in town and visit one of the bordellos, but he had seen a man in the advanced stages of the French disease once, and he had been wary of brothels ever since. He decided to take the news of the war to the two plantations upriver and bring back his wife and Indigo.

After everyone had recovered from their shock at Damon's return from the dead, Rafe led Damon outside just as the sun was setting. Briefly, he related what had happened.

"The box had been shipped from her father," Rafe said, avoiding Damon's eyes. "And Bassey apparently had been sent here by Sir Jared. All we can get out of him is that he served under Sir Jared as a boatswain, and that the guns were to be delivered to the Creeks ... in the event of war. He swears no slave uprising was planned. We sent two boys to fetch the army to take Bassey into custody, but

134

they haven't returned yet. And all the other slaves found out what's going on. It's been like a powder keg here all day."

"And where is my wife?" Damon asked.

"Mother and Indigo had found her bending over the trunk, examining the muskets. I tried to reassure her, but she must have been very frightened. She managed to slip out of the house, despite her pregnancy. She took one of the horses."

Damon swore and turned abruptly toward the barn.

"We have every field hand out looking for her . . . she can't get far," Rafe called after him.

Damon paused for a second and looked over his shoulder. "And how about you, my friend? Why aren't you out looking for her?"

Rafe flushed uncomfortably. He said quickly, "I had to stay here to protect Mother and Beth. We don't know that there won't be an uprising, or that the guns we found were the only ones smuggled in." Defensively, he patted the bulge of the pistol under his linen jacket.

Damon strode away, and a moment later Rafe saw him ride into the deepening dusk.

Indigo turned away from the window when Damon's horse disappeared from view. He had gone after his wife. He didn't care that Lanna was an enemy who had almost destroyed his friends. He had not even come to see her; he had not cared enough. Indigo felt a cold knot form in her throat, and rage welled up deep inside her. She wished passionately that she had let Florian and Nero have the guns and kill them all.

Savagely Indigo tore off the hated slave dress and flung it to the bedroom floor. She found the red silk gown Damon had brought her from France and she pulled it over her head. The whisper-soft material slid over her flesh as sensuously as the touch of a lover. She had known Damon was coming, had waited for him, longed for him. Damn him. Damn them all. Her flesh burned with need and hate. She wanted to lash out and hurt as she had been hurt.

She thought fleetingly of Florian, with his gentle strength and unconscious dignity. No, not Florian, what use was he? She did not want a black man, she wanted a white man who could take her away from servitude, who would make her forget Damon. She had heard Damon tell everyone that the *Wayward Woman* had not been sunk, that

135

Alain had taken the ship to the China seas. She had lost both of them. The only white men left were Grandfather Grenville, the newly married Rafe Danvers and—she shuddered, her arms crossing her body defensively—the crippled Michael Danvers. The overseer was little better than a slave himself. Then there was Lucas Bassey, locked up in a slave cabin with Florian guarding him.

The overseer had ridden out with a party of field hands, a rifle under his arm. Rafe and his father, pistols tucked in their belts, prowled the house restlessly. The two women were in Beth's room with their door locked from the inside, and two of the youngest slaves had been sent to Charleston to tell the militia of the plot that had been uncovered.

Indigo thought of Bassey, wondering if he would try to implicate her in the plot in return for her treachery. Bassey was an Englishman. The two countries were at war. In England . . . he had told her . . . you would pass as white.

No one noticed when she slipped out of the house and walked down to the slave quarters. It was time for the evening meal. Many of the hands had been dispatched into the swamp to search for the Englishwoman, and the others were concerned with the bubbling rice pots.

Florian looked at the lower class field hands, and wondered when he would be relieved of guarding Bassey so that he could return to the house to supervise dinner. He jumped as Indigo came up behind him and softly spoke his name.

"The army . . . are they here to take him?" Florian asked hopefully.

"No, not yet. But you can go and get something to eat. He can't get out, can he?"

"I reckon not." Florian nodded to indicate the wooden bolt on the outside of the cabin door.

"Go then . . . no, not back to the house. You can eat in the quarters tonight."

Florian looked at her incredulously.

"Just for tonight . . . so you will be nearby if I need you," Indigo said in a coaxing tone. "I shall stay here and watch the cabin. Go to Maybelle's cabin, she's the best cook . . . it's the last one down the row."

She waited impatiently as he strolled slowly down the row of cabins. As soon as he had gone into the last one, Indigo turned quickly and lifted the wooden bolt.

136

Lucas Bassey was tied to a chair, his hands behind him. His glassy eyes regarded her malevolently.

"Come to gloat, have you, girl?" he asked sourly. "They going to feed me too?"

He did not blink as she drew the knife from beneath the thin shawl that covered her shoulders, nor did he flinch when she placed the point beneath his chin.

"If I cut you loose . . . help you get away . . . will you take me with you?"

He nodded, holding his breath.

"Where will you go?" she asked, not moving yet to cut his bonds.

"Back to the islands . . . back to my ship."

"News just came that we are at war with England. How will you get out of the country?"

"I've got a 'protection' saying I'm American. I'll get us on a ship." Such documents were carried by most American seamen because of the Royal Navy's practice of stopping ships in mid-ocean to impress sailors. The certificates, which stated that a man was an American citizen, did not help much if a British ship was particularly short of a crew—especially since it was known that many British sailors had also acquired the "protections." It would, however, be honored while in America. Bassey quickly explained this to Indigo as she slipped the knife under his bonds.

The rope broke beneath the blade and Indigo turned her attention to his feet, also tied to the chair.

"All of the horses are being used to search for the Englishwoman. She ran off into the swamp," she said. "We shall have to take one of the small boats."

"I'm a sailor," Bassey replied, "and glad to be finished with a lubber's job."

Lanna wondered feebly how long it took to bring a baby into the world. Would she have the strength to labor further into the night? Hours had passed since the rhythmic pains had begun, and they had grown stronger and more frequent. What would happen when she could no longer stand it? Her fists were bitten raw from trying not to cry out. She feared the sound would attract some marauding animal.

Would they send searchers after her? She prayed they would. To have other human beings near, even if they took her to prison when it was all over . . .

137

Darkness came and she was more aware of the sounds of the swamp, the splashing of water, the stirring of night creatures. Between pains, she had cleared a small area of ground at the base of an old giant of a tree, and had wrapped one of the sturdier vines about the base so that she could hang on when the pain became unbearable. She had no idea of what to expect—no one had ever told her. Once, when she was very small, she had witnessed a cat giving birth to kittens. She remembered only that the mother cat had bitten through a cord that attached the mewling little creatures to her own body.

Now, as the pains came so close together she could only pant helplessly and strain downward trying to ease her torture, she no longer thought about the swamp, or the proximity of animals, or anything but the terrible tearing pain that had no end.

There was a sudden hot rush of fluid from between her legs and she cried out in fear, thrusting her hands between her thighs. The moon was rising, pale fingers of light probing the darkness about her, and she saw that it was not blood that had gushed from her body, but a clear, slippery liquid.

The long sigh that escaped her lips was echoed by another sound in the darkness. Someone was calling her name! Was she imagining it? No, there it was again: *Lanna! Lanna!* It couldn't be! He was dead! It was some terrible trick her imagination was playing on her. No, she didn't believe in ghosts! Unless she too was already dead? No, she was just delirious with fear and pain. That was all.

At that moment the worst pain of all began, making her whole body twist convulsively and bringing a scream to her lips. The scream died to a hoarse sob as she felt the baby's head begin to emerge and then, suddenly, she was no longer alone in the clammy night.

She saw only his shadow above her. She heard him tie the horse to a tree, and then he was on his knees beside her, his hands warm as he gently separated her thighs and placed his fingers at each side of the baby's head.

"Push, Lanna," he said calmly. "When the pain comes push as hard as you can . . . yes, that's right, it's almost over . . . breathe, don't forget to breathe . . . deeply, slowly, push . . . push . . ." Lanna did not know how long it was before he said, "He's born, Lanna. We have a son."

She lay back limply, seeing the flash of his knife in the moonlight and not worrying about it, because she remembered the kittens. She would not have to bite through that connecting cord. She tensed again as another pain ripped through her, unexpectedly, and he said quickly, "It's all right . . . that's the end of it."

He had removed his shirt and wrapped it around the baby, who gave a single cry as Damon placed him on Lanna's breast. Her arms closed about him.

"Are you cold?" Damon asked.

Lanna shook her head weakly.

"We shall have to stay here until morning. I can't risk taking you both back in the darkness. Sleep now, everything is going to be all right."

I'm dreaming, Lanna thought, and inside this dream is another dream. The nightmare is that I've just given birth to a son in a dark and dreary swamp. And within the nightmare is the dream that Damon is here taking care of me, speaking to me in a soft and tender voice.

Then she closed her eyes in exhaustion as Damon took the baby from her and lay down beside her to keep her warm.

"It isn't far back to Oakside," he told her in the morning. "You went around in circles, which is probably why they didn't find you. I want you to hold the baby and I am going to put you on the horse and lead her, very slowly and carefully. Can you stand it, do you think?"

"Damon . . . do you have to take us back there?" Lanna asked fearfully. She was stiff and sore and ravenously hungry. "They may have me arrested . . . there were some muskets in a trunk my father sent me. I didn't know what to do . . . Lucas Bassey . . ."

"I know. If I can't convince the army you had no part in the plot, then I'll get you out of the country. Alain will be bringing the *Woman* in now that . . ." he broke off. No need to tell her yet about the war.

"What shall we call our son?" Lanna asked shyly, feeling the wonderful weight of the babe in her arms.

"I'd like to name him Richard. It was my father's name."

"Yes. Richard is a good name," Lanna said. She paused. "I don't know what my father's name was."

Damon glanced at her, to see if she was delirious. Several times during the night she had murmured softly in her sleep.

139

"Lanna, your father's name is Jared Malford. You know my son will not be given that name."

"No, Damon. Sir Jared is not my father. I should have told you before . . . but . . . oh, what does it matter now?" She told him of the letter she had received.

Damon stared at her for a long moment, the silence broken only when the baby cried fretfully.

"He's wet," Lanna said, "we need to get something dry to wrap him in."

All the way back to Oakside Damon pondered the whimsical fates that had provided him with a wife and son. The child, his tiny face contorted with suppressed rage at his unceremonious arrival in the world, even looked like him.

And the woman . . . she sat white-lipped on the back of the horse, never crying out, although there was a ghastly pallor to her face and, despite the humid heat that came with the sunrise, the hands that held the baby were blue with cold. Her hair clung damply to her forehead and straggled over her shoulders, and her dress was torn, dirty and streaked with blood. In spite of it all, she sat with her back straight, her head high. With every step the horse took, Damon could almost feel the wave of pain pass through his wife's body. Her eyes were dark with it, yet she said nothing. She might have been a queen riding at the head of a royal parade, he thought, a grudging admiration for her stoicism creeping into his thoughts.

No, damn her, he told himself. Even if she isn't Jared Malford's flesh and blood, she was raised by him—and she's in love with Rafe Danvers. Remember that, Damon St. Clair, always remember that.

A little while later, they met a group of searchers led by Rafe.

"My God! The baby!" Rafe said. "Is she all right?" he asked, as though she were not there to answer for herself.

"Yes. Did the army come?" Damon asked.

"No. We think the two boys we sent for them may have run off. And Lucas Bassey has escaped."

"How the hell did that happen?" Damon asked.

Rafe glanced downward. "We believe . . . Indigo may have helped him. She's gone too." He leaped down from his horse as Lanna swayed unsteadily. "Let me take the baby," he said.

Lanna was barely aware of what was being said. She could feel her blood on the saddle beneath her. And the people around her seemed to be far away, as though she were looking at them through the wrong end of a telescope. Was that Rafe who took her son from her arms?

Who, then, caught her as she slid into oblivion?

CHAPTER 16

Voices reached her and there were vague images glimpsed from beneath half-closed eyelids. She was in bed and the room lay mistily beyond the gauze folds of a mosquito net.

". . . best for all concerned if I simply take them away." That was Damon, his voice low.

"And what about the British plot? Are you simply going to let her get away with everything? After she betrayed you? And not just with the plot . . . she tried to get Rafe . . ." An angry whisper, like escaping steam, suddenly muffled. Who was that? A woman . . . Lanna was too tired to concentrate.

"She is my wife. I will ask you to remember that. If you wish to discuss the matter further, I suggest we step outside, so we don't disturb her. She's been through enough."

"And what of us? We could all have been murdered in our beds."

"You weren't, though. And you let Bassey get away. What good will come of avenging yourself on a helpless woman?"

"Helpless . . . pah! She is a Sassenagh devil."

"You forget, I was too. By birth, if not by choice."

"Your loyalty is not in question, Damon, you know that."

"Besides, there is my son . . ."

Their voices drifted away. Lanna turned her head wearily and slept again. When she awakened it was mid-day. Damon sat at her bedside, watching her.

"Hungry?" he asked. She nodded.

He left the room. Her eyelids drooped heavily and she could feel perspiration between her breasts. Moments passed and then he was pushing aside the net. He placed a tray on her lap and she struggled to sit up.

"The baby . . . where is he?" she asked, picking up a glass of juice.

"He's asleep in the next room. Zenobia tells me he probably won't be hungry today, but you should nurse him anyway. If you want to, that is. If you don't, we'll have one of the women come up from the quarters—a couple of them have babies not yet weaned."

"No. I'll feed Richard myself." She paused, then asked, "What is going to happen to us?"

"I'm going to take you away, as soon as you're well enough. Don't worry about anything now."

"They won't arrest me?"

"No. The militia hasn't been notified. The boys who were sent with the message apparently ran off . . . Danvers is searching for them. But I believe we can keep you out of any inquiry. The guns in your trunk are Kentucky rifles, made right here—not the Brown Bess muskets the British army uses. And that trunk wasn't shipped from the Indies. No doubt Bassey bought the rifles here and shipped the trunk himself. But I believe it will still be best for us to leave, as soon as you're strong enough to travel."

Lanna let out a long sigh. Her eyes met Damon's and her heart leaped at the concern she saw in his glance. The intensity of his gaze and the lengthening silence made her cast about for something to say.

"Did I dream it, or did Bassey get away?"

"He's gone."

"And Indigo?"

"Gone too. I have to go now. Ring the bell on the table if there is anything you want. The baby will be brought to you shortly."

Feeling strengthened by the food and the calm presence of her husband, Lanna lay back in bed and ran her hand over her stomach. It wasn't exactly flat yet, but she felt as light as air.

Before bringing her the baby, Zenobia helped Lanna to bathe. She then produced a length of gauze which she wrapped so tightly about her middle that Lanna gasped.

"It's yo' binder, Mizz Lanna," Zenobia explained. "Make

143

all yo' insides go back in again. Tomorrow we pull it tighter. Now we fetch yo' baby." Her face broke into a wide grin. Evidently Lanna was not considered a pariah among the servants.

She learned a great deal from Zenobia, who had borne several children of her own. Her milk, Lanna was told, would not "come in" for a day or two, but she would suckle her infant to get both of them ready for this event. Meanwhile, he would receive another substance that nourished newborn babies. Lanna felt strangely at peace after the baby was laid to her breast, and she was sorry when Zenobia removed him with the admonishment that her nipples would be raw if she did not begin gradually.

A little while later there was a gentle tap on her bedroom door and Beth, eyes wide with concern, came cautiously into view.

"I'm not disturbing you, am I, Lanna? I'll only stay a moment."

"Oh, Beth!" Lanna wanted to cry when she saw the love and sympathy in Beth's face. They could all have been killed . . . and she, Lanna, would have been responsible. She had been so concerned with herself and her own predicament that she had not given any real thought to the catastrophe she had almost brought about.

Almost as though she had spoken her thoughts aloud, Beth said, "Hush, hush. It's all right. You know we don't believe you knew anything about those dreadful guns. Why, the fact that the trunk was sent here, instead of to your house in Charleston . . . now, now, dear, don't upset yourself. We are just so thankful that you and the baby are all right and that Damon is alive and with you . . . nothing else matters, nothing."

Lanna brushed a tear from the corner of her eye. Suddenly she felt weary again. The nightmare was over, she could rest now.

From Zenobia, Lanna learned that Kathleen Danvers had returned with her husband to Clearview and that Grandfather Grenville had also left for the house by the sea in Charleston. Beth and Rafe remained behind to wait until Lanna was ready to travel.

Damon was gentle and considerate, polite but not warm. In some way the new attitude disturbed Lanna more than his former hostility. She did not dare ask him what he planned to do with her once they left Oakside. She was too afraid he might say that she was to be put on a ship

144

for England as soon as possible. He was a dark, enigmatic stranger that she had married and whose child she had borne. She did not know him.

Doctor Crawford had been sent for, and he shook his head in disbelief upon learning the details of the birth. Privately he warned Damon and Beth to watch both mother and child for signs of fever or any other changes in their condition. Later he gently explained to Lanna that it would be necessary for him to take some stitches where she had torn the birth canal during delivery and afterward told Damon that he could be proud of his wife's courage.

During the ensuing days, Damon came to Lanna's room several times a day, bringing her delicacies to eat, or bearing the baby in his sun-brown arms. Lanna began to look forward to the visits eagerly. Each morning, she brushed her hair and arranged it carefully around her shoulders. She was astonished at the way he held the baby, looking down into the wrinkled little face of the child in wonder, and patiently allowing a tiny fist to close around his finger.

"The doctor said he is a fine healthy boy," Lanna told Damon shyly. "And Zenobia said she never heard such a cry from a newborn. 'Would do a Creek warrior proud,' she said. I explained that I didn't believe there was any chance our son had Indian blood . . . since we are both English."

"American, Lanna. And our son is American born."

Lanna was silent; she had no wish to quarrel. *Once a subject, always a subject,* Lucas Bassey had told her.

"By the way," Damon said, "you never told me about your parents . . . your real parents, that is. I don't mean to pry, but I wonder if you know who they were."

"No. Sir Jared merely told me that I was raised by him as a favor to my real father. When I look back on my childhood, I realize Sir Jared was never at home at Kingsburch. He would come for a few days, call the tenants in for a meeting, visit the village inn and then leave. I always thought he hated me because my mother died when I was born, but now I don't know if Sir Jared's wife was my mother or not. He says she was not."

"You told me Kingsburch will be yours when you are twenty-one. I would say that the answer to your parents' identity is there. No doubt the estate can be traced to your real father in some way. It doesn't matter, however. I will

145

provide for you and the child. You have no need of Sir Jared or Kingsburch."

"You mean . . ." Lanna took a deep breath, "that I can stay here in America?"

"If you want to." His tone was carefully light.

"But what about the muskets . . . the war . . . ?"

"I've persuaded everyone that Bassey is solely to blame. We sent word to Charleston to look for Bassey and Indigo. We are almost certain they have not left by ship. Since the war started the port authorities have been keeping close watch and Bassey should be fairly easy to spot."

"Do you want us to stay . . . the baby and me?" Lanna whispered the words. She raised her eyes to Damon's gaze and her heart leaped when she saw the bright flicker of interest.

His hand closed over hers on the bedsheet and he continued to look into her eyes. The spell was broken as the baby gurgled and cooed in his crib beside Lanna's bed.

"There is the child to consider," Damon said.

"Yes."

Damon's fingers ran caressingly up her arm and he said, "Do you believe that two people . . ."

Afterward Lanna agonized a thousand times over the whim of fate that had brought Beth to the door at that moment. How many times Lanna would later wonder if their lives might have taken a different course had Damon been able to finish what he started to say.

"Oh, do forgive me for disturbing you," Beth said in a flat, tight little voice. "But Rafe just arrived from Charleston and he wants to see you, Damon. And . . . oh, dear, what am I going to do?" She covered her face with her hands.

"Beth! What is it?" Damon went to her side quickly and drew her into the room.

Beth raised a tear-stained face. "Oh, I'm such a cry-baby. I'm so sorry . . . I didn't mean to upset Lanna."

"It's all right," Damon said. "Is it Bassey? Did Rafe bring back word about Bassey, is that what is upsetting you? What about Indigo?"

Beth shook her head miserably, accepting the handkerchief Damon offered and dabbing her eyes.

"Well, Bassey can't do any more harm here, so don't worry," Damon said.

Beth sniffed again. "It isn't that . . . it's Rafe . . . he's

146

going to leave me. He's joined the Navy and he's going to fight the British."

It was improper for any man other than the doctor or husband to visit the new mother, so Lanna was astonished when on the following afternoon Rafe walked hesitantly into the room.

"How are you, Lanna?" he asked, glancing about awkwardly.

"Much better, thank you. Where is Beth? Is everything all right?"

"Yes. Yes, of course. She's taking a nap . . . it's hot today."

"I'm sorry I'm the one who has kept you from moving to your summer quarters. I do wish you would take Beth—"

"I wanted to see you alone, Lanna. I waited until Beth took her nap and Damon rode out to look over the crop."

Lanna moved uncomfortably beneath the thin sheet. "Rafe . . . I never told you how sorry I am for making a fool of myself, the day of your party. Your mother was right. I behaved abominably."

"Lanna . . . listen to me, I'm going away. I've joined the Navy. I shall be leaving tomorrow and this is the last chance I shall have to talk to you alone."

"Rafe, there isn't anything we can say to each other, you know that. You were right when you told me that we must conduct ourselves with dignity."

Rafe's hand went up to his forehead. "Oh, God, don't taunt me with my own stupid words."

"Rafe, please go. I will pray that you come home safely to Beth."

"I loved you, Lanna." His eyes found hers and held them in an unwilling grip. "When we met in England . . . the magic happened for me, and I know it did for you too— the breathless excitement of just being near you. It had never been that way with Beth and me. We were kids who grew up together. She is more like a sister than a wife . . . oh, God, Lanna, I feel like a brute when I make love to her."

His hand reached for hers and she squirmed away to the other side of the bed.

"I would have defied my parents and married you, Lanna. When I arrived back in Charleston and found you were Damon's bride I could have killed him. I thought

147

about it. I would have, except you were carrying his child."

"Rafe, stop, please. It doesn't matter anymore. We are both married now and nothing is going to change that. You were right to marry Beth. Your parents are happy, Beth is happy, and you will be too, if you will let yourself. She is the dearest person I have ever known in my life. I didn't believe such goodness existed. She is an angel, Rafe. I am nothing but a sinner."

"Lanna, I am fond of her, I truly am . . . but . . ."

"No!" Lanna's voice rose to a shrill note. "Don't say it! Don't say anything we are going to regret later. It's only because you are going away to war and everything is suddenly . . . poignant is the only word I can think of. There is a sense of unreality . . . urgency . . . the drums beat and the bugles blow, and men begin to believe that making war is their only duty, their only honor. They cast aside human duties and human honor. Rafe, I know . . . my country has been fighting Napoleon and the French for so long. It's destroying our society . . . our families."

Rafe sat down heavily, arms stretched toward her. "Yes, I'm going off to war, but I shall come back, Lanna. I have to face death but I want to face life too. When I come back I shall come to see you, and we'll talk again. This isn't the time, I realize that now . . . so soon after your ordeal."

"Rafe, no!" Lanna said again. "Don't you see? It never would have worked, it's better this way. It's not only the two plantations, but your family is Irish and God knows I represent everything they hate in the world. Perhaps you were drawn to me for that reason, because I was the forbidden fruit. Knowing you had to come home to an arranged marriage, and knowing how your mother felt about the English . . . no, don't deny it. She has found several less-than-subtle ways to let me know, Rafe. Although I myself was not fully aware of how much England has ravaged Ireland until I came here . . ." She looked at him imploringly.

"English—Irish . . . what does it matter? We are both Americans now. Lanna, I still love you."

She felt hot and dizzy, his face had gone slightly out of focus and she was thinking, irrationally, that Rafe was Irish and Alain was French and Damon claimed to be American. England was an enemy to all of them.

"You must bid me goodbye and leave, I feel faint," she whispered weakly.

"Very well . . . but I will come back to you. Goodbye, my darling." He bent and brushed her cheek gently with his lips and she lay back on the pillow, grateful that he had gone. She was unaware that as Rafe emerged from her bedroom, Damon was coming up the stairs, bearing a large bouquet of flowers.

Nor did she know, as she slipped away into a feverish sleep, that Damon seized Rafe by the shirt and half-dragged, half-pushed him into the nearest room, closing the door behind them with a thud.

Looking into Damon's murderous stare, Rafe's chin jutted out defiantly, his fists automatically rising to a defensive position.

"All right, Damon. This talk is long overdue," Rafe said quietly. "Would you rather talk first and beat the hell out of each other afterward . . . or will it be the other way around?"

Damon was circling him, Indian-style, arms curved at his sides. He ignored the question and lunged, his hands finding Rafe's throat, slamming his body back against the wall. Rafe's fist came up, connected with Damon's jaw and broke his hold. A small table crashed to the floor.

Rafe had learned the rudiments of boxing while in college, but Damon had learned to defend himself in the alleys and waterfronts of many ports. As he reeled under the onslaught of a kidney blow quickly followed by a foot in his chest, Rafe realized this would not be a gentleman's fight. He fell back, gasping, as Damon's hand caught him in the back of his neck. Rafe swung wildly, sinking his fist into Damon's stomach. But in the next second a blinding blow to his head blocked out everything.

When he opened his eyes moments later, he was still sprawled on the floor. His jaw felt loose and made a snapping sound as he tried to open his mouth. Rolling on his back, he saw Damon looking down at him, his eyes black as a hound from hell.

"Stay away from my wife. You understand?" His voice was edged with flint.

"There is a parable . . ." Rafe said. His mouth was stiff and the words were difficult to get out. "About a dog in the manger . . . you don't want her yourself . . . yet you don't want anyone else to have her." He got up slowly, rubbing his jaw.

"You seem to have forgotten. You already have a wife."

"And I intend to keep her. But you aren't the only one

149

who can fight dirty. You married Lanna when you knew I wanted her. You tricked her into it by telling her I was already married to Beth. And you humiliated her by keeping your mistress in the same house. No, Damon, I don't feel bound by any rules of honor in regard to your marriage. I leave tomorrow to begin my service in the Navy, but I'll be back. I can't do anything about my marriage to Beth . . . but, by God, no power on earth can keep Lanna from my arms. You stopped me from being her husband, but you won't stop me from being her lover. You saw me come from her room? Well, next time you speak to your wife, remind her of my promise to her."

Damon stared at him with raw hatred.

Rafe's eyes gleamed. Damon might be able to beat him senseless, but he had the satisfaction of knowing that he was the real victor in the fight.

Damon turned without a word and strode from the room.

Lanna did not see Damon for several days. Beth had accompanied Rafe to Charleston and Lanna could not bring herself to question the servants about Damon's whereabouts.

Doctor Crawford had said Lanna could return to Charleston in about two weeks, and since the time was almost up she was sure that eventually Damon would come and tell her when they were leaving.

On the night before they left Oakside, he came to her room. His eyes were fathomless as he stood at the foot of her bed and told her all was in readiness for their departure. "The *Wayward Woman* will take out letters of marque, and we will fit her with more guns. I intend to fight the British by privateering. I shall put you on a ship for England as soon as I can get you to the Indies."

"But . . . I thought . . ." Lanna bit her lip. There was no doubt that he had decided she could not stay in Charleston. "Must I go back to England? Couldn't I stay in the Indies?" *If I go back to England, I shall never see you again!*

"And have my son die of yellow fever? No. You will take the child with you, and when the war is over . . . which it will be one day, I shall come to see my son."

To see my son, he'd said. He did not care if he never saw her again, Lanna thought, and she wondered why it hurt so much.

150

"I'm not being completely honest," Damon added. "I shall also come to England when the war is over because I still intend to make Sir Jared pay for the death of my parents. But that will have to be postponed for the time being. I don't know what the outcome of the war will be. If England finishes off Bonaparte and turns all her might against us . . . who knows what will happen?"

"You will privateer against us," Lanna said, "when you are English by birth."

"I am an American, Lanna. Don't ever forget it. This country has been my home since I was a child."

"But you are going to be a privateer . . . to reap personal profit from the war. You could have enlisted in the Navy, like Rafe." The moment she said it she wanted to bite back the words.

He gave her a long, hard, calculating look. "I don't take orders from other men," he said slowly, "therefore I will fight in my own way. And I don't give a damn how much you admire the heroic Rafe Danvers. Good night, madam, we will be on our way in the morning."

He turned and moved quickly, angrily, toward the door, slamming it behind him. Lanna, her head pounding, felt feverish and more alone than she ever had before.

CHAPTER 17

The war began badly for the Americans. Many distrusted Mr. Madison and his administration, and people were dismayed at the idea of being technically allied with the tyrant Napoleon Bonaparte.

It was rumored that British forces in Canada were being fed on supplies sent up from America, and that certain mercantile interests were continuing relations with Britain, despite the war.

Behind the scenes, however, a shipbuilding program was being implemented. Most American merchant ships took out letters of marque. If a ship met a British cruiser she and her cargo would be lost anyway, but if by good luck an unescorted British merchant ship was encountered, the letters of marque gave the Americans the right of capture.

The success of the privateers depended almost entirely on the skill of their captains. There was one skilled and daring captain who'd had considerable success even before the formal declaration of war: Alain L'Herreaux of the *Wayward Woman*.

Although Damon took command of boarding parties and supervised the guns and gun crews, it was Alain's skill in seeking prey, as well as his knowledge of the trade routes and ability to shadow a convoy, or cut out a prize from a protected anchorage, that made the *Woman* one of the most feared of the American privateers.

Upon rejoining the *Wayward Woman*, Damon had tersely answered Alain's questions about Lanna and the child.

As Alain had feared, there had been some kind of trouble involving Bassey. Alain was shocked to hear that Indigo had run off with the man. He feared for her safety and worried that he might never see her again. Indigo could never be his in the way he had dreamed when he was young. Still, while she had lived with Damon at least he could see her occasionally.

Believing Damon's black mood was the result of Indigo's defection, Alain did not question him further. But as time went by he wondered why Damon did not suggest they try to slip through the British blockade and return to their home port, and so he asked again about Lanna.

"As soon as she's well enough, we'll take her to the Indies and get her aboard an English ship somehow," Damon said, avoiding Alain's searching eyes.

"Wait . . . you say too much with too few words," Alain protested. "She is ill? *Mon ami,* you did not tell me. What is wrong? Why must she return to England? You said no charges were brought in regard to the guns."

"And you, old friend, ask too many questions," Damon replied. "There was some kind of complication following the birth. A fever caused by an infection. She will recover fully in time. And there are no charges against her."

"Then why? Why do you send her back to England? She is safe in Charleston. I thought you were happy about the birth of your son? Surely no man was more eager to see his son born?"

Damon turned his gaze toward the sea.

"The marriage was a mistake, Alain. Another of my blunders. She isn't even Malford's real daughter. And that cold old fish cares nothing about what happens to her. She serves no purpose in my plans any longer."

Alain gasped. His hands fell from the wheel and his long arms went around Damon's body. He spun him about so that he faced Alain's own blazing eyes.

"No! Don't speak so . . . cruelly. Cold fish! It is you who are the cold fish! *Mon Dieu . . . tu es sans cœur . . .* ah, you are . . . *je ne sais quoi.*"

Damon shook himself free. "Blast you, Alain. Mind your own business. Are you trying to humiliate me? I can't live with a woman who is pining after another man. *She loves Rafe Danvers!*" Damon turned and strode from the bridge.

And so the months slipped away. The *Wayward Woman* did not return to Charleston until the ship needed a dry dock for a complete overhaul. Alain also pointed out that

153

it was almost Christmastime, and said he had need of a church to reaffirm his faith. Damon raised a skeptical eyebrow at this last announcement, but he could not deny the *Woman* needed repairs. They sailed into Charleston, narrowly escaping the blockading British, one week before Christmas.

The baby was almost six months old—a healthy handful, already sitting up and taking notice of the world. Lanna had completely recovered from the infection that had weakened her following the birth. It was her fever that had forced Damon to allow her to remain in Charleston under Doctor Crawford's care.

Lanna had given herself to the joys of motherhood and, because of Beth Danvers, she never wanted for adult companionship. Most of the women she knew had husbands who were fighting the British, and while it was difficult for Lanna to rejoice in the American victories at sea, she shared everyone's concern at how badly the American armies were faring. Word of terrible defeats in the north and gruesome stories of Indian massacres added to the terror.

Lanna felt torn by old loyalties and new. Her feelings for this struggling young country were not yet defined. Perhaps, she told herself, it was her love for her son that made her uneasy when she heard the dreadful news from the north.

Her financial needs were taken care of by a local bank. All of Damon's servants had remained, with, of course, the exception of Indigo, who had not been seen since the night Lucas Bassey had escaped. It was assumed the two of them had managed either to slip out of the country, or to disappear in the vastness of the continent.

Life had become a pleasant routine, only occasionally marred by vague longings that Lanna pushed firmly to the back of her mind. She had accepted the hopelessness of her love for Rafe, and since he was at sea somewhere it was easy to think of him only as a lost first love. She was as proud as Beth that he was serving aboard the *Constitution*.

The *Constitution* had fought and beaten the dreaded H.M.S. *Guerriere*, writing the first glorious chapter in American naval history. As the word of Captain Isaac Hull's victory spread, America was jubilant. If England's superiority on the seas could be challenged, the war could be won, despite the disconcerting rumors that some cities

154

in the north had tried to surrender to the British before they were even under attack.

Rafe had written of the daring and bravery of the *Constitution*'s new crew. He had added in an amusing aside that Captain Hull had been so intent on yelling orders to the gunners as they poured broadsides into the *Guerriere* that he had leaned too far over the rail and split his breeches, thus exposing his derriere.

When the battle ended, Rafe said, the British flag was lowered from the stump of the *Guerriere*'s mainmast and she signaled surrender by a shot to leeward. All night long, and part of the next day, boats plied the water between the two ships, transferring the British crew to the *Constitution* until the last man was taken from the wallowing wreck. The hulk was then set ablaze, and within minutes explosions rent the air as the flames reached her powder magazines.

Rafe also added proudly that Captain Hull had received a gold medal from Congress for the action, and $50,000 had been distributed among the crew as prize money. It would have been theirs had the enemy ship not been shot to pieces.

Lanna had been thoughtful when she read this news. She had had no idea that the Navy received prize money, and she remembered how she had taunted Damon about privateering for profit.

Having successfully dealt with her feelings for Rafe, it was easy for Lanna to freely give her friendship and love to Beth. She had reached a point where she would have died rather than hurt the sweet and frail creature. Especially now, when Beth was heavy with Rafe's unborn child.

On the morning the *Wayward Woman* had sailed into the harbor, Joshua opened the front door to admit Damon. Swarthier than ever after months at sea, he moved toward Lanna like a predator stalking prey.

Lanna had just returned from an early morning ride, and her cheeks were flushed. Her new riding habit of black broadcloth emphasized the lithe lines of her body and softly feminine breasts. A white scarf was knotted at her throat, and her hair was tied back with a matching piece of silk, so that her face, with its delicately curved cheekbones and large eyes of deep blue, was unadorned and strikingly beautiful. Damon stopped in his tracks, and he held his breath for a split second as he looked at his wife. But

155

when she recognized him, her lower lip drooped in what seemed an unmistakable expression of dismay.

Damon's eyes hardened as he strode past her, dropping his duffel bags onto the floor.

"I'm hungry," he called over his shoulder as he went toward the kitchen. "I'll have news for you when I've eaten."

No greeting, no question as to her health or that of his son, Lanna thought miserably. When he had arrived so unexpectedly, her first thought had been that she was unprepared for his homecoming. Wearing a dreary black riding habit, her hair snatched back from her face—her skin would be shiny with perspiration from the ride. If only she had known he was coming, she could have worn one of her new dresses . . . her hair loose the way he liked it. She had tried not to think about him all those months, had absorbed herself in caring for her child. Now the leaping of her heart and the pounding in her ears told her that she had longed for his return.

No! she told herself wildly. I must not fall in love with him! I cannot bear to love in vain a second time. He hates me . . . hates Sir Jared so much. He married me only to punish Sir Jared.

She went up the stairs, calling for Myrtle to bring water for her bath. When she had bathed and dressed in a morning frock of navy blue merino, Lanna went downstairs again. She didn't want to receive her husband's "news" in her bedroom.

"He is with the baby," Myrtle told her happily, "in the nursery."

"I hope he didn't wake Richie from his nap," Lanna said shortly, and went out onto the piazza, ignoring Myrtle's puzzled expression.

Lanna sat in the winter sunlight, oblivious to the bone-chilling cold. Her eyes were fixed on the distant blue sweep of the sea. He would be sending them across that ocean to England. That would be his news. But at this time of year? She would have to insist they wait until spring before facing the rigors of the Atlantic.

Damon had made it very clear when he had brought her back to Charleston that her stay in his house would only be temporary. She had been too ill with the fever then to wonder at the savage hatred that seemed to have replaced Damon's former concern and gentleness. Later she thought that the hatred must have been what he truly felt toward her. The gentleness had merely been pity for the ordeal she'd suffered in bringing his child into the world.

Time and time again Lanna thanked heaven that Beth knew nothing of Rafe's visit to her before he had left to join the Navy. She believed that he'd been emotional because he was going away. Obviously, he'd felt sorry for her. When Rafe returned it would be to Beth and their child.

"That color is too somber for you," Damon said from behind her and she jumped, startled from her reverie. "It's an old woman's color. Did you choose that particular dress to repel boarders?"

Lanna ignored the sarcastic question and said, "I trust you did not waken the baby?"

"His sleep being more important than seeing his father again, of course," Damon said, sitting down opposite her and stretching out his long legs.

"In your present mood, perhaps I should worry more about your frightening him than awakening him," Lanna suggested, rising to her feet as though to rush to the nursery.

"Sit down, Lanna," Damon said quietly, "he's still asleep."

Feeling foolish, Lanna obeyed.

"You said you have some news for me?"

"Rafe Danvers will be coming home on leave. I heard the news through the grapevine."

Lanna flushed uncomfortably. "Surely that is news you should be relaying to Beth, his wife, rather than to me."

"He sent you a message. Reminding you of his promise. Of course, I'm not aware of what his promise is."

Lanna stared into the implacable dark eyes and the expressionless face, looking for some hint as to her husband's true feelings. She could find none.

"You once told me," she said, "that you did not want Beth to be hurt. Why are you, therefore, bringing such a message to me?"

"Because it will give me pleasure to see that you are far from here by the time Beth's husband returns. You are going back to England, my sweet."

"But . . . this time of year . . . the voyage could be dangerous for our son."

"I said nothing about our son. He stays here. It is you who will return to England."

Lanna clutched the edge of her chair for support, her

face white. "You wouldn't be so cruel . . ." she whispered. "I won't go without him . . . he's mine . . ."

"No, my dear, he is not. He is an American citizen, as I am. You have no rights where he is concerned and, as a rejected wife, I have every right to send you back to where you come from."

Lanna took several deep breaths. "Is this part of your revenge against Sir Jared? Is that why you are doing this? You promised that I could take our son with me when I returned to England."

"That was before I learned of your plans to break up Beth's marriage."

"I have no such plans. I don't know what Rafe told you . . ."

"Stop!" Damon's voice cracked like a whip, "before you lie to me. I hate lies even worse than I hate locked doors. You will have about two weeks to pack whatever you want to take back with you. By then the *Woman* should be ready to sail. We'll get you into a neutral port somehow, and then you can board a British ship." He rose and disappeared back into the house, leaving Lanna alone, frozen with fear.

"Did the master say he would be here for dinner?" Lanna asked Joshua a little while later.

"Yes'm, he did," Joshua nodded, smiling. "He say he and Mr. Alain be here 'bout seven."

"Thank you, Joshua," Lanna said. She went upstairs to the nursery and picked up her son, cradling him to her breast as she sat down in the rocking chair. She must think, make plans. She had two weeks. She must make Damon change his mind about separating her from her son. Crying and pleading would have no effect, she knew that. She must be more clever. No need to panic yet. There was Beth—and Alain—she could count on them for support. But what to do?

She spent the afternoon playing with the baby, making plans and rejecting them. At last, as the spicy aroma of jambalaya began to fill the house, Lanna called Myrtle to come in and care for the baby. Joshua was instructed to pile logs on the fire in her bedroom, and Lanna carefully washed her hair and dried it in front of the leaping flames. She had a new gown that had been intended for a party, a bold red velvet with a décolletage and the newest sleeves. Lanna had never worn such a bright shade before, but her

158

seamstress had insisted that it was made for someone with her coloring. She had worn safe blues and whites for too long. Now the red velvet dress was hanging in front of the fire. Lanna rang for Myrtle.

"Do something special with my hair, Myrtle, there's a dear . . . perhaps pile it up on my head? And I want a necklace and earrings . . ."

Myrtle beamed knowingly. An hour later Lanna descended the stairs and entered the dining room looking as ravishing as only a woman confident of her loveliness can.

Alain leaped to his feet and rushed to her side, encircling her in a hug of greeting. He held her at arm's length, admiration plainly written in his eyes and his smile.

"*Mon Dieu,* Lanna . . . you look . . . *magnifique* . . ."

Lanna looked over Alain's shoulder to where Damon sat at the head of the table, a half empty glass in his hand. He nodded slightly in her direction, but did not speak. Fortunately, Alain filled the void.

"I have met your son," Alain said, "a fine boy . . . but too bad he look more like his father than his mother, eh? Look, I bring you a present." He placed a gaily wrapped parcel in her hands. She tore off the paper and pulled out a handsomely carved music box.

Raising the lid, Lanna was enchanted to hear the strains of an old English ballad. She searched her memory for the words . . . "*On yonder hill there stands a lady, who she is I do not know . . .*"

"Oh, Alain, it's so beautiful. Thank you . . . thank you," she whispered, a tear slipping down her cheek.

"Eh, *chérie,* I did not mean to make you cry," Alain said. Inwardly he cursed the Latin blood that surged hotly in his veins. His appreciation for beauty and his capacity for caring deeply about a woman was a combination that would undo him one day. Of this he was convinced.

"Perhaps," Damon said, "it is just that the ditty makes my lady wife homesick. A situation we shall remedy before long."

Flushing, Lanna took her place at the table as Alain held her chair. She and Alain kept the conversation going through dinner, Alain telling her of the lighter moments of their life as privateers, and she telling him of the progress of the baby and news of various friends and acquaintances. One would have thought, she reflected later, that she and Alain were husband and wife. Damon ate and drank his way morosely through the meal, making

159

only an occasional sarcastic comment or issuing a brief order to the hovering Joshua.

Late that evening, while Alain and Damon were smoking cigars before the remains of the parlor fire, Lanna went up to her room and prepared for bed, leaving the door slightly ajar.

She bathed in scented water and put on her new white silk nightgown, spread her hair about her pillow and lay back to wait. At last she heard footsteps on the stairs. They proceeded unevenly along the landing, then stopped outside her door. Lanna could see his shadow in the moonlight.

She held her breath. Then he moved on toward the guest rooms. Swiftly, Lanna jumped out of bed and ran down the hall.

"Please, Damon. Could we talk for a moment?"

He turned and looked down at her. She shrank from the smell of brandy on his breath.

"So . . . first we present ourselves as the scarlet woman and now as the virginal bride all clad in white," he remarked, slurring his words slightly.

"Oh, damn you, you're drunk," Lanna said and turned to leave.

Before she had taken a step his arm went around her. She was swung off her feet and crushed against his chest. Then he was carrying her into the guest room and kicking the door closed behind him.

"Damon, please . . ." she whispered as he flung her down on the bed.

"Oh, come now, this is what you want, isn't it?" he asked, jerking the delicate silk from her shoulders. "Or shall I go and bring Alain to you? You seemed fascinated by him all evening." His hands closed roughly over her breasts.

It was no use fighting him, she knew that. She did not have the physical strength. Forcing herself to relax completely, she offered no resistance as his mouth came down on hers and his hands explored her body. He drew away after a moment, dark eyes burning in the half light.

"So . . . you've learned a new trick," he said, "and I assume I am to learn what it is like to make love to a cadaver."

"Damon . . . please, I'll do anything you ask, if only you won't take my son away from me. I swear . . ."

"But you see, my dear," he continued as though she had

160

not spoken, "I am a master in the art of resurrection. Let me show you how I raise a dead body . . ."

"Damon, please, will you listen to me for a moment? I want to tell you . . ."

"How my lips set you afire?" he asked. "Ah, yes, I believe once again we shall awaken the sleeping gods of the loins, Lanna . . . the dark gods who rule us."

His lips and tongue found her breasts and his hands made light fluttering movements on the inside of her thighs. He was no longer rough and when he swung his body in the other direction and was seeking that intimate place with his lips, she knew how she had been waiting for him to return. Her treacherous body had been longing for him all these months.

Sweet madness overcame her and she barely realized what she was about to do as her hands and lips reached for him. She felt him stiffen and groan softly as her tongue touched him gently, wonderingly.

Somewhere there was sound and movement, ancient words of love breathed against throbbing flesh, the ballet of the act of love when he entered her and she thrust her body upward to meet his. The exquisite sensation of feeling, of fulfilled longing, of breathless response. Was it still night? Or had the dawn broken? They were spinning, faster and faster, off the earth . . . she hated him, she loved him.

CHAPTER 18

Beth begged them to come to Oakside for Christmas. Well advanced into her pregnancy, her slight body seemed more frail than ever with its added burden, and she could no longer travel. Lanna had not been in the company of Michael and Kathleen Danvers since just after Richard's birth and, although she was not looking forward to meeting Kathleen's accusing stare, Beth's invitation could not be refused.

Damon had agreed readily. They spent their days being icily polite, their nights making wild love that was never mentioned in the cold light of day. It was almost as though they were possessed of other beings when night fell, Lanna thought. Little wonder those primitive people believed dark gods dwelt in their loins.

The only time she begged him again to let her stay had been early one morning while she still lay in his arms. Damon had looked at her with a harsh light in his eyes.

"No, my love. I won't keep you here for Rafe Danvers to find when he returns," he said, swinging his long legs over the edge of the bed. "He promised he'd come back for you. He swore it to me—and to you."

"Damon, that's over. Please believe me."

"You'd say anything I want to hear, wouldn't you, you lying little . . . And take my son away from me. Well, he is my son and I love him as much as you do. And I have every right to keep him with me. Legally as well as morally. How easy it would be for me to destroy you, Lanna.

Apart from the unpleasant incident of the gun running we concealed from the authorities . . . there is the question of the unfaithful wife. On either count the law would side with me in banishing you and keeping my son here."

"Unfaithful . . ." Lanna repeated. "I have never been unfaithful."

He was dressing quickly, angrily. "No? Tell me, then, how you've managed all these months . . . a woman with your . . . capacity for lovemaking."

Heedless of her nakedness, she leaped from the bed, scratching at him and screaming words she had not even realized she knew.

He caught her hands and held her as she struggled, turned her away from him as she tried to raise her knee. He held her close, and she panted with rage and frustration as he said softly in her ear, "How you do continue to surprise me, my lady wife. Besides your more obvious talents, I had no idea you were possessed of such a salty vocabulary."

He released her, pushing her forward on the bed, and she lay there, face buried in the sheets so he would not see her tears. She was appalled at the way she had lost control of herself, acting like a screaming, ill-bred virago. Only the lowest women of the streets made such spectacles of themselves. *Never make a scene, Leona Anne, no matter how great the provocation.*

The following day, Christmas Eve, they went upriver to Oakside. The plantation house was filled with the sights and sounds of Christmas and the atmosphere was one of love and gaiety, despite the war and Rafe's absence.

Lanna was shocked to see that Beth had a ghastly pallor about her. Her face was pinched and dark circles accentuated her eyes.

When they were shown to their room, Lanna turned angrily to Damon. "Why didn't you tell her you'd heard from Rafe?" she demanded. "She looks so terribly ill, and she didn't mention that she expects him to come home shortly. For heaven's sake, why didn't you tell her you'd seen him?"

"Because I haven't," Damon answered. "You assume I have seen him because I delivered his message to you."

"You . . . you liar! And you are the one who claims he hates lies."

"One always despises in others what is one's own worst trait, Lanna. However, it wasn't a lie. He did ask me to

163

tell you that he would be coming back to you . . . that message was to be given to you last June, before we left Oakside. And I did hear that the *Constitution* had suffered some damage in an engagement. Therefore, it was not purely conjecture that led me to believe its crew would be given leave while the ship was repaired."

"Damaged . . . then Rafe could be . . ."

"Wounded? Possibly. That's why I didn't want to tell Beth."

Lanna bent over her portmanteau, removing the folded underwear slowly. She did not want to question Damon further about the message Rafe had left for her. She remembered only too well Rafe's surreptitious visit to her room on the day before he left to join the Navy. Rafe must have told Damon of his intentions then . . . no wonder Damon had changed so abruptly.

She straightened up and looked across the room to her husband. "Damon . . . I'll admit I believed myself to be in love with Rafe. I even tried to take him away from Beth when we first arrived here, but he was too much of a gentleman. I would have gone away with him, then. But after he married Beth, my feelings began to change . . . I care about her, Damon, I've never cared this much about another woman. I would never hurt Beth . . . I understand now what you meant about her, she is so good, so pure in heart and mind and spirit."

"Well, cheer up, my pet," Damon said, pulling on a clean shirt. "Perhaps she'll die in childbirth and then you'll have clear sailing with her husband."

Lanna felt a wave of pure horror sweep over her and she could not speak. She stared as Damon tucked his shirt into his breeches, reached for his jacket and left the room without another word.

That afternoon Grandfather Grenville drew Lanna aside. "Come to my study, Lanna," he whispered. "I want to talk to you for a moment."

They sat before a crackling fire and he poured two glasses of wine. "I'm worried about her, Lanna," he said.

Lanna nodded sympathetically. "What does the doctor say?"

"What they always say. She's too delicate, her hips are too narrow," Grandfather Grenville growled, picking up a poker to jab at the spitting log. "Worry about her husband hasn't helped. And she does two people's work

164

around here. I thought when she maried young Danvers it would ease our burdens, but they've doubled since he ran off to the Navy. His father is drinking himself to death at Clearview and his mother spends her time and money foolishly. It's my little Beth who does most of the work and worrying."

"It's a pity Beth didn't stay in Charleston," Lanna said, "away from the work of the plantations."

"Will you talk to her, Lanna? Try to get her to rest more?"

"Of course. I'll do my best, but she always puts other people's welfare ahead of her own. You know that, Mr. Grenville."

He nodded gloomily. "Mine most of all, I suppose. She was never built for bearing children, and it breaks my heart to see her . . ." He stopped and pulled his handkerchief from his pocket, blowing his nose loudly.

Lanna patted his hand gently, not knowing what to say and fearful that she would convey to him her own anxiety about Beth.

"I wish she had your strength and stamina. Trouble is, she thinks because you survived having your child in the swamp . . . oh, I'm sorry, Lanna, I didn't mean . . ."

"Please, it's all right. I know what you mean. I'll do my best to get her to rest more."

That evening Lanna insisted that the supervision of dinner and the party arrangements be left to her while Beth joined the guests, pointing out wryly that Beth would actually be doing her a favor, since Lanna was dreading meeting Kathleen Danvers again.

"I'm sure she has quite forgotten your last meeting, Lanna. Such a dreadful misunderstanding. I often wonder what became of Lucas Bassey and Indigo." Beth sat down weakly, her hand straying to her side as she winced with pain.

Lanna looked at her sharply. "Do you have a pain?"

Beth's eyes betrayed her, even as she assured Lanna that she felt perfectly wonderful.

"You're about six months along now, aren't you?"

Beth nodded. "I shall rest as soon as Christmas is over, like the doctor . . ." She stopped and winced again.

"No, not after Christmas. Now. Come on, you're going to bed," Lanna said firmly. "And you're going to stay there even if I have to sit on you to keep you down."

"Not yet, Lanna dear. I must attend to the Christmas

165

gifts for the Negroes. You know they are like children at Christmas and Grandfather has no idea . . ."

"Tell me what to do. I'll attend to it," Lanna said.

"Well, we usually give the field hands each twelve quarts of rice and one quart of molasses. Then the men get two pipes and three hands of tobacco and a new hat. The women get handkerchiefs. The house servants . . ." Beth's head drooped wearily.

"Come on, I'm going to take you up to your room," Lanna said.

"But the guests . . . the party tomorrow . . . Christmas . . ." Beth protested.

Christmas and the guests and the party were forgotten the next day, however. Instead, Lanna and Zenobia sat in a darkened room, mopping Beth's fevered brow as she twisted and writhed in her blood-soaked sheets.

The long and harrowing day was almost over before Doctor Crawford arrived. He sent Lanna and Zenobia downstairs to wait with the others around the ashes of a burnt out fire.

Kathleen Danvers looked at Lanna silently. She had attempted to go to her daughter-in-law's bedside but had been restrained by Grandfather Grenville.

"Let Lanna stay with her. She's just been through childbirth herself and Beth won't feel she has to put on such a brave front for her," he said.

He was right, of course, but Kathleen knew that all of their bad luck had begun with the arrival of the Sassenach, and it galled her to have the Englishwoman care for Rafe's wife.

Grandfather Grenville took Lanna's hand in his and his skin felt as dry as an autumn leaf. Gazing into the greyness of his face, Lanna realized how very old and tired he looked.

"How is she?" he whispered, his voice breaking with the strain.

"She'll be all right now that Doctor Crawford is here," Lanna replied with more conviction than she felt. Beth had been in constant pain throughout the long night and day, and she had lost consciousness several times. "Please don't worry. Didn't Doctor Crawford pull me through the fever after Richard was born?"

Behind her, Zenobia began to cry softly and Lanna whirled around. "Go and get some sleep, Zenobia," she ordered. "And if you will all excuse me, I must go and see

166

to my son. I shall be in the nursery if Doctor Crawford needs me."

She saw Damon rise from a chair in the corner of the room and follow her, but she was too weary and worried about Beth to turn and acknowledge his presence. She was bending over the baby, removing his wet wrapper, when Damon spoke from behind her.

"How is she . . . really?" he asked, his voice low.

Lanna turned to face him, eyes blazing. "What do you care? You selfish, coldhearted . . . beast . . . didn't you suggest it would be convenient for her to die? You devil . . . you wished this upon her . . ." She bit her lip to choke back the angry torrent of words, afraid someone would hear.

Damon's face was ashen. His lips parted but no sound came. After a long minute he said stiffly, "I didn't realize what I was saying. I was crazy with . . . a feeling you wouldn't know anything about. I could never wish any harm to come to Beth."

"No, of course not. You only wish harm to come to me. But evil thoughts have a habit of spreading out and infecting the innocent as well as the guilty."

"So. You admit you are guilty?" Damon's jaw hardened. "Then let me tell you this, *Mrs.* St. Clair. You'd better wean that child because when you sail with me, he stays here."

The sound of their angry voices and the tension in the room made the baby cry. Lanna picked him up, held him close, and her lips pressed to his silky skin.

Damon was still standing in the nursery doorway when Zenobia came rushing along the landing. "Come quick, Mizz Lanna . . . the doctor . . ."

"Zenobia—stay with the baby," Lanna said. She brushed past her husband without a glance and ran to where Grandfather Grenville sat outside the sickroom, his tired face buried in his hands. At the top of the staircase Kathleen Danvers was crying against her husband's shoulder. Doctor Crawford, his face grave, stood waiting for Lanna.

"I'm going to need your help, Mrs. St. Clair," he said. "And Mrs. Danvers too, as soon as she's calmed down. Miss Beth has begun premature labor and I'm going to try to bring the baby to save her life. The child is in a breech position."

Kathleen Danvers lifted a tear-stained face and looked

167

at the doctor. "You mean you are going to kill my grand-child?" she asked.

"A six months' baby, Mrs. Danvers, doesn't stand a chance. But perhaps we can save Miss Beth."

"You shall not murder my grandchild. Our religion forbids it," Kathleen Danvers said. "You must try to save them both."

"Where is the husband? Can he be reached?" Doctor Crawford directed the question to Lanna.

"He is on his way home, but we don't know which port his ship will put into, or how long it will take him to get here."

Lanna felt Kathleen Danvers' eyes flash accusingly in her direction as she delivered this news. No doubt wondering how I know what they do not, Lanna thought.

"Then we will do the best we can . . . come on, both of you," Doctor Crawford said.

Stepping back into the room, Lanna looked at Beth's fragile form lying on the bed. She looked like a broken china doll.

Beth and her stillborn son died twelve hours later. Lanna fell into an exhausted sleep haunted by nightmares in which she and Kathleen and the doctor were torturing the poor broken body of Beth, causing her more pain and suffering than if they had not been present at all. Lanna would awaken for brief moments and remember that the reality had been as bad as the dream, the awful vision of the forceps, the knife . . . and blood, so much blood. Then the tiny blue creature plucked from his shrieking mother.

Lanna sat up in her sweat-soaked bed and screamed, a strange high-pitched wail that had no end. And in the darkness strong arms went around her, stroking her hair, holding her close, whispering her name . . . and she slipped away at last to dreamless sleep.

Rafe Danvers did not arrive in time for the funeral, nor had he returned when the *Wayward Woman* set sail. They did not know that their information had been incorrect, and that the *Constitution* was off the coast of Brazil, engaged in a fierce battle with the H.M.S. *Java*.

Nor had Rafe had time to let them know that he was sailing on what might be an extended voyage. Having missed the sailing of the *Constitution* while recovering from a leg wound, he was assigned to the smallest vessel of the American Navy. The *Essex* was a heavily armed frigate under the command of Captain David Dixon Porter.

While his wife and son were being laid to rest, the *Essex*, with Rafe aboard, was sailing southward, pursued by British warships. Rafe was soon to learn firsthand about the terrible storms he and Captain McLeod had discussed so long ago on the old *Sarah Jane*.

"Papa Porter," as the captain was affectionately known to his crew, gave praise when a job was well done. Although he often threatened to lay open a man's back with the "cat," he always returned to the theory that slashing a man's hide to ribbons had less effect than reasoning with him. The *Essex* was, therefore, a happy ship, and Rafe Danvers was glad to be aboard.

The crew of the *Essex* prided themselves on being able to prepare for battle in ten minutes even if surprised in the middle of the night. When the marine drummer beat general quarters during the day, every man could reach his station in fifteen seconds, cutlass in hand.

Putting into the Portuguese island of St. Catherine's for water, Rafe had news of his last ship, *Old Ironsides*. The *Constitution* had been victorious in a fierce battle with the *Java*. The crew of the *Essex* also learned that a British sixty-gun ship and several smaller enemy warships were on their way to the coast of South America. A blockade of St. Catherine's was possible.

Captain Porter made a momentous decision. He would take the *Essex* into the Pacific whaling grounds where British whalers moved sluggishly, waiting to be picked off like upturned turtles.

Captain Porter took quill in hand and wrote a letter to his crew:

Sailors and marines,

A large increase in the enemy's force compels us to abandon a coast that will not afford us security or supplies. We will, therefore, proceed to annoy them where we are least expected. We will attempt what was never before performed by a single ship. The Pacific ocean affords us many friendly ports. The unprotected British commerce on the coasts of Chile, Peru, and Mexico will give you an abundant supply of wealth;

169

*and the girls of the Sandwich Islands shall reward
you for your suffering during the passage around Cape
Horn.*

When the lookout first saw the stark shadow of Cape
Horn on the sunny horizon, Rafe and every other man
aboard thought that reports about the treacherous gales
and cruel currents around the Horn must surely be exaggerated.

Captain Porter had made elaborate preparations for the
perilous passage, and now he regretted all the extra work
his crew had performed, especially as they were on half
rations. He had lowered the center of gravity of his ship
by bringing down the royal masts and rigging, as well as
the light sails and all heavy items that were not absolutely
essential.

But suddenly the clouds hovering over the land began to
race toward them, and land and sunlight abruptly disappeared. Orders to reef the foresail and close-reef the main-
topsail had barely been carried out when the first shrieking gust of wind hit the ship, throwing her over on her
port beam. If they had not prepared, the *Essex* would
have foundered as soon as they sighted the Horn.

For the next two weeks every man aboard spent his
days and nights in soaking wet clothing. Icy seas swept
over the decks, screaming gales tore through the rigging.
The ship was plucked back and forth by the irregular
motion of two mighty oceans coming together in a terrify-
ing battle of surging currents and clashing winds.

There was no pattern to either the currents or the wind.
The pumps were manned constantly and still water rose
in the hold of the violently rocking ship.

Sleeping men were flung from their hammocks to splash
into bone-chilling water. Despite double lashings, guns
strained to be free, spars rattled about the deck like skit-
tles and anything that could float was tossed about the
ship upon a torrent of freezing water.

Fresh squalls sprang up from every direction, with racing
black clouds and bombarding hailstones. There was no
opportunity to make lunar observations because of the
clouds and, not trusting the chronometer, Captain Porter
sailed by dead reckoning.

The men were bruised and battered from falling, lacerated from handling wet rigging, hungry despite double

170

rations of the weevil-infested bread. But worst of all was the fierce, burning, mind-destroying, never-ending cold.

At last a steady gale-force wind set in from the northwest and the *Essex* reached eighty degrees west longitude. The order was given to set course northward again and the crew gave three shivering cheers. They were sailing into the Pacific and would soon make port where their rum would at last be replaced.

The *Essex* would capture a dozen British whalers and several merchantmen in the months that followed. For Rafe Danvers the two weeks he had lived through were a metamorphosis. He had met the sea in mortal combat and mastered her. She was his vanquished foe, his refuge, his immortality. Everything that had gone before was a blurred memory.

Lanna stood on the deck of the *Wayward Woman* as they cast off, looking at the city bathed in the soft light of the new year.

Lovely old city, she had not realized how much she had grown to love it and the gracious hospitality and charm of its people. She recalled spellbound evenings at the Dock Street Theatre, and the music and laughter of congenial friends gathering in elegant homes. Most of all she remembered Beth.

Below decks, Zenobia, wild with excitement at returning to her native island, was caring for the baby. Grandfather Grenville had insisted upon giving Zenobia to Lanna when he heard Damon was taking her to the Indies. The girl had been prostrate with grief over losing her mistress and was useless to him, Grandfather Grenville had said.

In the awful gloom that had descended upon everyone following the tragic loss of Beth and her baby, the announcement that Lanna was sailing with her husband created no more than a ripple of surprise. Lanna herself had moved through the days like a sleepwalker, refusing food, gazing vacant-eyed at anyone who addressed her, until at last Damon had come to her and told her she could take the baby with her to the Indies. They could remain there fairly safely until spring, at which time the Atlantic crossing would be less hazardous.

Alain had built a special crib, deep-sided and well padded, for the baby aboard ship. Strips of canvas were fastened across the top, to keep the child secure. Lanna need have no fear of injury even if they should run into heavy seas.

As always, Alain was the buffer between Lanna and Damon, carrying on the conversations they could not make between themselves.

Lanna had been numb since that cold dawn when she had watched Beth die. No emotion penetrated the dazed sense of shock and loss. Damon steered clear of her and even the baby had been of little solace. Deep inside, Lanna felt guilty. She had coveted Beth's husband. Was it possible that her desire had contributed to Beth's death?

The first days at sea passed uneventfully. Lulled by the soothing roll of the ocean, Lanna began to relax. She would soon see the Indies . . . Jamaica perhaps, or further south . . . Trinidad. Sir Jared owned property there. His ship was plying the Caribbean too. Zenobia told her of the lush beauty of the spice islands, of the exotic fruits and colorful birds, and Lanna began to look forward to their landfall, not knowing they would never reach their destination.

Later the crew would say bitterly that the English frigate had been waiting for them just off the coast and that the voyage had been doomed from the start. They pointed to all the evil omens that preceded their departure . . . the black cat that chased a rat along one of the lines, the man who fell between the ship and the dock wall when a sudden swell hit the *Woman,* crushing him to death. Worst of all, they said, were the women on board.

Lanna was in her cabin when she heard the shouts and running feet and, within seconds, the first explosion of gunfire. Wrenching open the cabin door, she looked into Damon's eyes and fear clutched at her heart.

"It's a British frigate. We shall try to run, but she's bearing down fast. Stay here with the child and don't come aloft for any reason until I send for you, understand?"

Lanna nodded and went back into the cabin, slamming the porthole hatch in place. She sat down beside Richie's crib, her body tense, waiting for the next explosion.

"Hush, hush," she whispered as he began to stir. She reached for Alain's music box, which stood on the sea chest, lifting the lid so the sweet sad music drifted out. *"On yonder hill there stands a lady . . .*

". . . who she is, I do not know. I'll go and woo her for her beauty, she must answer yes or no . . ." Lanna sang softly to her baby as the cabin reverberated with thunder-

172

ous roars and, from above, came the unmistakable sound of splintering masts and falling rigging.

Almost instantly, the cabin was filled with the acrid smell of smoke.

CHAPTER 19

Because of Lanna and the baby, Alain had struck his colors as soon as he realized they could not get away. But the British gun crews, having missed with the first broadside, could not resist firing a second time, disabling the *Wayward Woman*. Alain quickly dispatched a sailor to bring the women up from below so that they could board the first of the British longboats that were being launched from the frigate.

Damon's eyes were fixed on the bridge of the English ship. He could not see the captain's face, but the proud stance of the shoulders, the haughtily raised chin were chillingly familiar.

Sir Jared Malford spoke to his first officer. "Order the gunners to finish her off as soon as the boarding party returns with her crew. If St. Clair is aboard, leave him on deck to see his ship burn." The frigate *Grey Wren* had indeed been lying in wait for this particular ship, and had no intention of capturing her as a prize.

Sir Jared's eyebrow lifted in surprise when he saw that the *Wayward Woman* had women on board. A white woman with a child in her arms and a black woman at her side. Then he saw the pale gold hair and proudly held head and his index finger tapped thoughtfully against his thin lips as he recognized his adopted daughter.

"Take her to my cabin," he ordered.

"And the crew? In irons, sir?"

"All except the one called St. Clair. He is actually a

British subject and for the time being I am impressing him as part of my crew. Later I shall hang him for desertion, but we're short-handed and we can use him for now. Needless to say, we shall clap him in irons before we reach port."

"Aye, sir." The first officer's expression was properly blank, but he felt a twinge of pity for the one called St. Clair. He would have done better to perish with his ship than at the hands of the master of the *Grey Wren.*

Lanna was astonished when she came face to face with her guardian. "Father . . ." she said, force of habit making her forget he had told her he was not, in fact, her father.

"Sit down, Leona. This, I assume, is your son?"

Lanna nodded, her arms unconsciously tightening about the baby.

"Where were you bound when we intercepted you?"

"The Indies . . . the Leeward Isles, I believe. Damon . . . they were taking me there so that I might board an English ship."

"I see. Your husband has tired of you already?"

Lanna glanced away from Sir Jared's steely gaze and did not answer.

"Well, never fear. Your lost honor will be well avenged by the time I have finished with your husband. He did marry you legally, did he not? Or is that a bastard you carry?"

"We were married by Captain L'Herreaux. I believe it was entered in the ship's log . . . and there were witnesses. But please, father . . . I just want to go home, I don't want vengeance. The marriage was as much my doing as his."

"Your true father is dead, Leona. You may call me Sir Jared. It's more appropriate."

"Yes, Sir Jared. May I know who my real father was?"

"A rake and libertine who sired more than one bastard such as yourself. In your case it amused him to provide you with a surrogate parent, myself. He was, I believe, bewitched by your mother until the day he died."

"And my mother?"

"The less you know of her, the better. A woman of low morals. A notorious harlot. Your ancestry, Leona, is best left buried. Now I must see to the interrogation of the prisoners. A cabin will be prepared for you. You will have to share it with your maid and the child."

Disappointed that she was not to learn more about her

175

parents, Lanna turned to leave. She now felt very much afraid of what was going to happen to Damon and the other prisoners.

"We shall make a brief stop at an island where we maintain a transit compound for prisoners," Sir Jared called after her. "Then we shall take you to Jamaica. Meantime, try to keep out of the way of my crew."

This proved an easy order to follow because the next day the seas rose in huge swells, and the ship was in the midst of a squall. Lanna and Zenobia had to cling to the bunk and hold the baby to prevent him from being thrown about the cabin.

The young midshipman who brought their meals could not tell them much about the fate of the crew of the *Wayward Woman* except that they were below decks, in irons. They were prisoners of war, he said, and he'd heard that it was possible for ships' crews to be exchanged. There was no point in telling the pretty young mother that he'd heard they were all to be hanged as pirates. When Lanna asked specifically about Damon St. Clair, the midshipman was astute enough not to tell her that Damon was in the forecastle under the watchful eye of the boatswain, Lucas Bassey.

"Perhaps when the weather blows over, Sir Jared will allow me to visit them," Lanna said to Zenobia after the boy had left.

Zenobia's eyes were wide with fear and she was beginning to feel seasick, so she did not say what she was thinking—that the thin-lipped captain of the *Grey Wren* would not be likely to grant favors to anyone, not even his daughter.

When the ship sailed at last into calmer seas, Lanna approached her father for news of the prisoners and was curtly sent back to her cabin with orders to stay there until the prisoners had been put ashore. Making her way back across the deck, she glanced upward to the small figures high above, crawling like ants up the mizzenmast. Through some trick of the sunlight and swaying of the ship, she thought for a moment that one of the tiny silhouettes was Damon. Something about the way the long legs braced against the wind . . . but of course she was mistaken.

She was not permitted to see Damon or any of the prisoners, and no amount of pleading moved Sir Jared. She must learn to make a decision and stay with it, he said.

176

She had told him she wished to be released from her husband and returned to England, therefore there was no point in her seeing Damon again. After her second visit to Sir Jared's cabin, she found herself locked in her own cabin for the remainder of the voyage.

"What will become of him . . . and the others?" she had asked fearfully.

Sir Jared's eyes narrowed. "They will be put ashore on an island we are using as a prison, where it will be determined which of them were aboard the ship when she attacked peaceful English merchantmen, before the war started. Those crew members will be hanged. The rest may be lucky, they may be exchanged for captured English crews being held by the Americans."

"Damon . . . will be hanged?" Lanna asked, her eyes wide with horror.

"This interview is at an end, Leona. Please return to your cabin."

Three days later Lanna awoke to find the ship at anchor in a palm-fringed lagoon. Through her porthole she could see a boatload of bedraggled and chained sailors being sent ashore.

"Look . . . missy . . . he done forgot to lock the door," Zenobia was whispering to her, as their cabin door swung slightly ajar.

Lanna began to dress quickly, hoping to get up on deck in time to catch a glimpse of Damon before he was put ashore. He was not in the longboat that was already moving toward the island. She had to speak to him . . . to tell him . . .

That she loved him! She paused, her shoe slipping from her hand as she realized she did indeed love her husband.

How had it happened? When? But there was no use fighting to suppress the feeling any longer. She was overwhelmed by love and longing for him. It did not matter that everything had started out so badly. She had seen glimpses of another Damon, kind, considerate, loving . . . caring about his child, perhaps even about his wife. That he was driven by hatred and a need for revenge had tainted their relationship, but surely they could replace that terrible destructive need with a nobler purpose. Perhaps, one day, she could even make Damon love her in return?

With feverish fingers she picked up her shoe and pushed her foot into it. She must speak with him . . . she must plead with Sir Jared. She had to save Damon from the hangman's rope.

On deck the last of the prisoners were being herded into the longboat. She saw Alain, heard the stream of French invectives he flung at the marines who prodded him with muskets. There was no sign of Damon. But providence was with her. A small group of seamen from the *Grey Wren,* under the command of a young lieutenant, was going ashore for water and fresh provisions.

"May I go with you?" she asked the lieutenant breathlessly. "My . . . Sir Jared said I could, if you don't mind."

The lieutenant cast an uneasy glance toward the bridge, but did not see his skipper there. If he were to question the captain's orders, he would suffer the consequences, especially since it amounted to calling the captain's daughter a liar.

"Of course, miss. Here, let me help you," he said politely. "Though there isn't much on the island . . . a marketplace, a church and a few taverns."

"And the prison, of course," Lanna said, giving him her hand.

"Well, yes. More of a compound really, where they await the transports. Will you be able to get down the ladder to the boat all right? Perhaps if I stay at your side?"

How very tall the ship seemed, Lanna thought, as she stepped gingerly onto the first rung of the rope ladder slung over the side.

The lieutenant climbed to her side on the swaying ropes and the men in the boat below watched with interest as her skirts billowed out in the wind.

The ship was anchored almost a mile from shore, outside the coral reef that encircled the island. By the time Lanna was lifted to a quay, there was no sign of the prisoners who had preceded them.

"I'm afraid I can't spare a man to accompany you, Miss Malford," the lieutenant said, "but you'll be safe enough if you stay on the main street. You'll find some native traders, and there's a tea shop of sorts. When you've finished shopping, you can wait there. I'll come and get you as soon as I've got the provisions in the longboat."

The lieutenant watched her walk along the bustling street. It was some time before he remembered there was a thriving brothel above the tea shop.

The island was about eighty miles long. The Atlantic

pounded against it on one side, and the calm waters of the Caribbean lapped it gently on the other. The largest village, and best harbor, were at the southern tip. Beaches of a pinkish colored sand stretched around the small bay which protected the settlement.

Chickens wandered on the dirt road, pecking at dusty debris. Lanna wandered up the road, careful not to hurry lest she arouse the suspicions of the watching lieutenant. Directly ahead was a handsome church, complete with bell tower, that stood on a rise overlooking the village.

The beggars sprawled about the open air marketplace quickly came to attention at Lanna's approach. She was soon the center of a buzzing throng of beggars and vendors who spoke melodic English and smiled ingratiatingly. Beside the heaps of fruit and vegetables there were shells of all sizes and beautifully carved wooden pieces, from small statuettes to massive table tops.

Lanna brought a five shilling piece out of her purse, the last of her English coins. "I'll give this to anyone who will take me to the prison compound," she said.

There was a momentary pause in the hawkers' cries. Then one young boy, quicker than the rest, reached for the coin. The next moment he was flung violently aside by a tattooed forearm. Lanna followed the arm up to look into a leering face.

A white man, with a carrot-colored beard and a shock of hair to match. Two of his front teeth were missing and his lip had evidently been badly cut at one time, so that it curled upward over the missing teeth in an evil-looking grin.

"Nah . . . wot's a nice looking wench like you wanting to go there for?" he asked, removing the five shilling piece from her trembling fingers and sticking it between his remaining teeth to test its validity. The beggars and vendors withdrew silently.

"Are you a sailor, sir? Possibly you know of my father," Lanna said, feeling her knees wobble beneath her skirts. "He is the captain of the frigate *Grey Wren.*"

"That a fact?" He pocketed the five shilling piece. "And he sent you to look for the compound, did he?"

The crafty expression on his face told Lanna that instead of impressing him with her identity, she had unwittingly provided him with a reason to anticipate greater profit.

"Please . . . it's my husband. He's with the prisoners. He . . . he would pay you a great deal if you would take

179

me to see him. For just a moment?" Lanna said, fighting for composure. She must not let him know how afraid she was.

The mangled lips spread in an even wider grin. "Right you are then," he said. "Name's Murdoch. Bloody Murdoch they call me."

Lanna managed to keep from shivering. "Is it far, Mr. Murdoch?" she asked.

"Far enough so's you'll be sorry you're walking in them slippers," Bloody Murdoch said.

Lanna soon discovered the reason for his remark. They had to travel over two miles of stony beach and the sharp pointed rocks and broken shells jabbed painfully through the thin soles of her slippers as she tried to keep up with Bloody Murdoch's lumbering strides.

"Mr. Murdoch . . ." Lanna panted, "will they let me see him? Will I be able to talk to him?"

He leered down at her. "They will if you let 'em think you're my woman, come to spend the night with me."

"I don't understand . . . you are spending the night in the prison compound?"

"Usually do, girlie. I'm a guard there."

"Oh . . ." What am I going to do? she thought frantically. If I can't help Damon escape, I shall be at the mercy of this man. And Damon won't have the money I promised him . . .

The prison compound was smaller than Lanna had expected. It consisted of a few bamboo huts beside a wooden stockade. Because of the slow progress they made on the rocky beach, it had also taken considerably longer to reach their destination than she had anticipated.

Because of the acute shortage of men in all branches of English service, there were only two marines on duty at the compound. They were assisted by several islanders. Since there had been an influx of captured Americans within the past weeks, and also because of the casual approach of the islanders to their duties, it had been necessary for the marines to keep their prisoners in chains while they awaited the return of their commanding officer, who was arranging the exchange of prisoners.

Bloody Murdoch had been recruited from the beach and pressed into service as a guard. Because of his murderous temper and enormous strength, he set about his duties with relish, and the marines no longer worried about escaping prisoners. Unfortunately, Bloody Murdoch also

180

came and went as he pleased. He refused to take orders or conform to any set of rules.

Lanna's breath stopped as they came upon the compound. She was repelled by the stench of the tightly packed bodies. Many of the men had festering sores beneath their chains, moans of wounded men came from one of the huts, and swarms of flies hovered over all. But she held her head high and ignored the smirk of the young marine as Bloody Murdoch ushered her to one of the bamboo huts.

Behind the stockade the sea of faces blurred and ran together. The sounds were not those of individual voices; there was rather the anguished groan of a single writhing animal. But as she stumbled into the gloom of the hut, she thought she heard one voice cry out—a deep, resonant cry of shock and horror . . . *"Lanna! Mon Dieu! Non!"*

"Nah then," Bloody Murdoch was saying. "You can wait here and I'll fetch him. Make y'self comfortable."

Lanna looked about awkwardly, aware that there was no place to sit other than a narrow bed covered with a filthy blanket. An iron-bound sea chest stood beside the bed, and there was a pile of empty bottles and dirty clothes on the floor. She had no doubt that she was in Bloody Murdoch's sleeping quarters.

"St. Clair . . . Damon St. Clair is his name. His ship was the *Wayward Woman*," she whispered.

This brought a guffaw from Bloody Murdoch. "Named his ship after you, did he then?"

"Will you bring him here . . . please?" Lanna said. The sun had been high in the sky when they arrived, but she had no idea of the present time. She wondered anxiously how long the *Grey Wren* would stay at anchor. Her baby was on the ship. Well, if worst came to worst, the young lieutenant who brought her ashore would tell Sir Jared what had happened, and a search party would be sent to look for her.

Bloody Murdoch still lingered, looking at her with a glint in his eyes that made her flinch. She opened her purse. "Look . . . I have American money . . . you can have it, all of it. And my husband will give you more . . ."

Bloody Murdoch pulled back his misshapen lip, and a rumbling laugh sputtered from that hideous mouth. "American, is it . . . so you're a prize of war yerself, are you, me beauty? Thought you was the woman of an English deserter, I did."

181

His hand reached for her in a leisurely movement. The other hand closed around a full bottle of rum and raised it to place the cork in the convenient gap between his teeth.

Lanna screamed as she was pulled against his sweat-stained shirt. Her fists flailed, but she was otherwise powerless to move in his bone-crushing embrace. Almost apologetically, Bloody Murdoch tapped her smartly on the mouth with his rum bottle.

"Shut up. Don't like screaming wenches." He spat the cork across the floor and drank deeply from the bottle, the golden liquid running into his beard and trickling down onto the bodice of Lanna's dress.

She could taste blood on her lip and the bamboo walls of the hut swam hazily. A fly buzzed and landed on her eyelid.

"Damon!" She screamed his name. "Damon—help me!"

Then there was a hand in her hair and her face was being forced toward that scarred mouth. She heard the ripping of the material of her dress, felt the moist hand close over her breast, squeezing, kneading impatiently.

Oh, God, she prayed, don't let him kiss me! Anything but that . . .

CHAPTER 20

Britain was the only nation that had fought the massive power of France consistently from the beginning of the war in 1793, with only a short breathing spell in 1802. Britain was a small island, her manpower limited, and her need for men for her army and navy was never satisfied. It was that need that had brought the war with America, through the impressment of American sailors into the Royal Navy. That need had also produced circumstances in which officers unfit for command were given charge of ships and men. Officers like Sir Jared Malford.

The captain of a frigate in the Royal Navy had the power of life and death over his crew. Indeed, he wielded more power than did an English king over his subjects. Because of the sweeping thirty-sixth Article of War, known as the "Captain's Cloak," he was prosecutor, judge and jury, besides being the codifier of the laws at sea. For the most part, his crews were made up of simple and uneducated men. They were ruled by a handful of officers who carried out the captain's orders, backed by a detachment of His Majesty's marines.

The young lieutenant knew he would surely be flogged for having taken the captain's daughter ashore and allowed her to disappear. She had walked into the marketplace and vanished into thin air, and no amount of threats or promises would induce any of the islanders to even admit they had seen her. Ships' officers would come and go, but the terrible-tempered Bloody Murdoch stayed permanently.

183

They had searched everywhere, even among the grimy pallets in rooms above the tea shop, where the pathetic prostitutes plied their trade. Knowing that the ship was to sail with the afternoon tide, the lieutenant had returned to report to Sir Jared.

"Shall I send another party ashore to search?" the first officer asked Sir Jared after the shaking lieutenant had been dismissed.

Sir Jared's thin lips compressed slightly. "No. It's time my adopted daughter learned a little about the harsh life I have shielded her from all these years. I'll wait until morning. If she has not returned of her own volition by then, so be it. We shall be back here with more prisoners before long, I have no doubt. By then I'm sure she will be ready to leave."

"Aye, sir. And the black woman and the child?"

"We'll drop them off in Jamaica as planned. I believe I shall send them to England."

"And the lieutenant?"

"A dozen lashes should suffice."

Damon spent the brief time the ship was at anchor below decks, in irons, alone with his thoughts. Oddly, it was not his own peril that concerned him, but rather the realization that he might never see his wife and son again.

What a deadly trap he had forged for himself, and how inevitably it had been sprung. Throughout his life women had been there when he needed them. Claudine, to make a home and care for him when his parents were killed. Indigo, the calm anchorage to which he returned when he was sated with the excitement of the gaming tables and the easy women who hovered around them. There had never been a woman who represented more to him than a pair of parted thighs, or a warm meal on his table.

Nor had there ever been a woman he had wanted and could not have. Until now. Was it, he wondered, because he had possessed only that one small part of her? And, knowing that part, had wanted to explore her mind and heart and soul, to open all the doors she kept locked to him? Had those doors been opened for Rafe Danvers?

The rage he felt over her love for Rafe Danvers burst anew. That Rafe Danvers had possessed her body he knew for a certainty—her fear of possible pregnancy had been her sole reason for marriage.

184

Yet there had been moments in that disastrous union . . . moments when he believed the wall between them might crumble and they would come together in a unity that transcended bodily hunger. There had been something more than the simple fulfillment of passion the first time she had responded to him sexually. There had been the calm days after the child was born . . . the anguished nights after Beth died when in tortured sleep Lanna had reached out to him.

Ah, but with Beth dead, Rafe Danvers was free. Damon smashed his chains against the deck in a gesture of futility and despair.

A blade of light cut the darkness and Sir Jared stood looking down at him.

"You owe me a great deal, young man. How do you suppose you are going to repay me?"

Damon raised his head, leaned back against the bulkhead and glared defiantly at the captain.

"When your country is beaten to its knees, perhaps I will look into whatever assets you may have left in the Carolinas. Your miserable ship, as you saw, was not worthy to be claimed as a prize. The pound of flesh I shall extract from you hardly compensates me for my losses either. I shall have to give the matter careful consideration."

Damon knew better than to inquire about Lanna and the baby. He remained silent, poker faced. On no account must Sir Jared even suspect that Lanna and the baby were important to him, or the hawk-faced master of the *Grey Wren* would know exactly how to extract payment for Damon's misdeeds.

"Your seamanship is adequate, my boatswain tells me," Sir Jared continued. "Therefore, we shall have you work off part of your debt. Your wife, of course, would like to see you hanged immediately . . . but yes, I believe I shall deny her that pleasure while I'm short-handed. Rest well, Seaman St. Clair, we sail on the morning tide."

Damon let out a long sigh when the darkness closed around him again. So she wanted him dead, and soon, for then she could fly to Rafe Danvers' arms. And yet, how could he blame her? Rafe Danvers had no doubt been able to tell her all the things that Damon had not. Not just that she was breathtakingly beautiful, or that she carried herself with a proud dignity that was curiously vulnerable

185

. . . like a child bravely facing a world of bewildering adult values.

He thought of her sudden laughter as she romped with the baby, her delight in the surprises the world offered: the bright flowers of the Charleston gardens, the food that was exotic and different to her. He thought of the courage she had given to the old woman on that first voyage when they had almost foundered in the storms of Biscay, of her devotion to Beth.

Damon sweltered in the humidity below decks. He saw no one but the shadowy figure who brought him bread and water. Then at last there was movement and a faint breeze from somewhere—and they were under sail again.

There was no sign of land when he returned to the forecastle and his duties as able-bodied seaman. Damon quickly learned there were at least two other Americans on board. They had been impressed from American ships before the war had started. It was to these men he turned to see if he could learn their destination, and to speak of escape.

"Don't try it," Jeb Haney, one of the Americans, told him. "The cap'n goes hard on deserters . . . had one of his own officers flogged 'round the fleet for trying to jump ship. Think what he'd do to one of us. Besides, they lock us up when we're in port."

Flogging around the fleet was a sentence of three hundred lashes of the cat o' nine tails, administered in batches aboard different ships. The victim was taken from one ship to another until the sentence was complete, or he was dead. Usually it was the latter.

"You mean you've never been ashore since you were 'pressed?" Damon asked incredulously.

"Over a year I've been on this stinking scow now, and never seen land. Wait till you spend a month below decks in the heat of summer, lad."

Damon went to his task of swabbing the deck, thinking that Sir Jared could well afford to bide his time before exacting punishment. No doubt the longer Damon had to wait to find out what plans were made for him, the more fearful the anticipation would become. He did not speak with Sir Jared again in private, nor did the captain even glance in Damon's direction when they came within eyeshot of each other on deck.

Lucas Bassey, the boatswain, did not keep his distance, however.

"Slow, mate . . . that's how you'll go," he told Damon. "But not to worry about the pretty little mulatto. Indigo. She's safe in the islands and well satisfied with her lot, she is."

His elbow nudged Damon viciously, sending him teetering into the bulkhead. "She tells me you were never man enough for her. Hot-blooded little doxie, ain't she? You wouldn't believe some of the games we play. I shall have to tell you all about it." Bassey grinned, showing stained teeth. "But you, mate, you don't know what a treat old Luke has in store for you. See, old Luke is a lefty . . . left-handed I am. So when the bosun's mate is finished with you, I can lay the cat across your back in the opposite direction. Makes a nice criss-cross pattern, it does."

Damon wielded mop and holystone silently, not looking up at the boatswain. There was no point in worrying about Bassey's sadistic promises, nor about Indigo's treachery. Damon needed his wits about him to plan an escape. He had heard that they were bound for Jamaica, to put the women ashore, but he did not dare show too much interest in this for fear someone would report to the captain that he was inquiring about Lanna.

As it happened, the *Grey Wren* was so busy during the ensuing days that no one gave much thought to Damon. There were two encounters with American ships. The first was a sloop which was heavily out-gunned by the *Grey Wren*. It sank quickly. The second was a rich merchant-man that Sir Jared decided to take as a prize.

From the stern of the *Grey Wren*, Damon watched the American vessel as her crew was put into boats for transfer to the frigate. A prize crew would be put aboard her. If Damon could get on that ship, conceal himself in one of the longboats . . . it might be possible to hide somewhere until they reached port. He would be reunited with Lanna and the child in Jamaica, and they could pass as an English family in order to escape to a neutral port.

A lieutenant and several men had already been sent over to the merchant ship, and now several other seamen were being selected to join the prize crew.

"You'll never get away with it, you'll be missed," Jeb Haney whispered at his side.

"You could tell them I went mad and jumped overboard," Damon said without moving his lips. "If you could cover my absence until that ship is out of sight . . ."

There was no time to wait for Haney's response, the

187

moment would be lost. Damon inched along the deck, stopping when anyone glanced at him for more than a second.

The confusion of crew and marines milling about diverted attention as he worked his way into the center of the group. As the last American clambered aboard, the English sailors who were to man the prize climbed over the side and down into the longboat. Head down, Damon joined them.

Mustn't hurry. He was barely aware of the roughness of the ropes, the leaping planks beneath his feet as the longboat rode corklike upon the water. *Don't look up, don't call attention to yourself, sit down, pick up an oar.*

"You there . . . who ordered you aboard?" a voice asked. The midshipman was peering at him in a puzzled way.

Damon swung his oar, catching the midshipman under the knees and knocking him into the sea. Immediately the cry "Man overboard!" rang out and, as hands were stretched to the struggling man in the water, Damon kicked the boat away from the side of the ship.

They did not get far. As soon as the midshipman was back in the boat Damon was seized by two pairs of brawny arms, and the longboat returned to the ship.

As he went back up the ropes, prodded by a cutlass from behind, Damon looked up into the cold blue eyes of Sir Jared. The captain stood on the deck from which Damon had briefly escaped, a faint smile hovering about his thin lips.

The shrill calls came from the hatchways. "All hands to witness punishment! D'ye hear . . . all hands aft to witness punishment." Echoing throughout the ship, the shouts of the boatswain's mates were accompanied by piping.

Before the sound faded, men were running across the deck, gathering near the capstan just forward of the wheel. Marines came up the ladders, bayonets on their muskets, while the ship's doctor stood with the officers on the starboard side.

Damon and two other prisoners were brought on deck by the Master-at-Arms and an armed marine who was sweating in his red coat. Captain Malford, in full uniform of dark blue edged with gold, ordered the men to be lashed to the capstan, arms tied to the spoke-like bars which extended from the capstan drum.

There was a long silence as Sir Jared looked into Damon's eyes, ignoring the other two prisoners who staggered, bleary-eyed and uncomprehending, from the wretched results of the drunken binge for which they were to be punished. In his flat, precise voice, Sir Jared read off the name of Henry Stewart. The man on Damon's left shuffled forward.

"You are accused of being drunk and disorderly and of showing contempt for a superior officer. Do you have anything to say?"

Henry Stewart's mumbled reply was unintelligible.

Captain Sir Jared Malford, judge, jury, prosecutor and defense counsel, pronounced the man guilty and ordered him to strip. With his shirt removed, he was lashed to the bars, arms and legs outstretched. While his wrists were being secured, Sir Jared began reading from the Articles of War.

". . . all other crimes not capital, committed by any man in the Fleet, not mentioned in this act, shall be punished according to the laws and customs of such cases at sea."

Assembled officers and crew removed their hats as the captain pronounced a sentence of two dozen lashes. From a baize bag a boatswain's mate removed the cat o' nine tails.

Every twenty seconds the cat fell as the Master-at-Arms counted. Sir Jared's eyes never left Damon's face, even when the captain admonished the boatswain's mate to use more strength. When the two dozen lashes were completed, Sir Jared surveyed the man's back, his glance dragging Damon's eyes in the same direction. The lacerated flesh resembled partially roasted meat. The victim was barely conscious as he was cut free and half carried, half dragged below to await the ministerings of the surgeon.

The man to Damon's right was punished next. His crime: drunkenness and uncleanliness; his sentence a dozen lashes. A second boatswain's mate was ordered to take over, the first having used most of his strength in wielding the cat across the back of the first man.

Damon's eyes locked with Malford's again, and the two men's hatred was almost a bond between them. Damon was aware of his own sentence being pronounced . . . two dozen lashes for attempted desertion and another two dozen for striking an officer, to be administered consecu-

189

tively. Damon felt the tropical sun sear his scalp, felt the sweat run down his back as the shirt was ripped away. Then he was spread-eagled on the capstan wheel and he heard Sir Jared's voice.

"Boatswain, do your duty."

Damon heard the sound of the cat the second before it fell across his back and shoulders. He saw his own sweat and blood drip to the deck beneath him. For a moment he felt no pain other than an unbearable bursting sensation in his lungs. Again the cat fell, and Damon bit through his lip to keep from crying out. He tasted the blood as his teeth tore into his own flesh. He felt as though he were choking, as though his spine and rib cage were rupturing.

"Five . . ." came the count of the Master-at-Arms.

Damon tried to time his groans to the calling of the number, tried to keep from biting through his tongue, tried to slip away to unconsciousness. He kept the face of Sir Jared fixed in his mind, saw himself turn the cat on the captain . . . saw the captain's face at the end of a long dark tunnel through which the wind shrieked, taking away breath and life . . . He passed out as the Master-at-Arms counted thirty-two. At almost the same moment the cry came from the masthead.

"Sail ho!"

The strange sail that hove up on the horizon was flying a broad pennant from the maintopmast. It was a commodore's ship of war, almost certainly American, bearing down swiftly.

In the suffocating heat below decks, Damon lay on what felt like a bed of coals, hovering between consciousness and oblivion, only vaguely aware of the movement of the ship and the sound of barked orders above the roar of guns. There had been no time for the doctor to treat his back, or even force water between his lips, because the ship was preparing for battle.

Above decks men were reducing sail as Sir Jared brought his ship to windward and ran out his guns. Damon stirred and moaned as the first broadside shook the ship, the sound penetrating his pain-wracked senses.

He did not witness the skill of the two captains, who handled their ships as though they were foils in a fencing match, as they inflicted damage on each other's vessels. The American gunnery was accurate and clearly superior, but the British ship was faster. As the battle proceeded, the firing of the guns became less frequent. They were becoming red hot, and the crews were depleted by injury and death.

Despite the American's better marksmanship, she was no match for the English frigate. However, when the maintopmast of the American fell, followed by the mizzenmast, and yellow flame leapt from the trailing rigging, Sir Jared's ship was almost as severely damaged. It was finally necessary for the *Grey Wren* to limp into the nearest port for repairs—by the time Damon's senses returned, the ship was at anchor.

He did not know that he still lay in the sick bay by order of the sympathetic young ship's surgeon, who was on his first voyage and was sickened by the brutality of the "cat." Casualties had been heavy in their last encounter, and it appeared the captain had for the moment forgotten that Damon was one of the mangled men feebly moaning on blood-soaked pallets in the sick bay.

Still lying face downward, Damon's attention was caught by a brightly colored object fluttering at the edge of his vision. The effort to move his head caused the tattered flesh of his shoulders and back to contract agonizingly, and for a minute his senses swam again.

A butterfly. A brightly colored tropical butterfly, caught in a spider's web, struggling feebly. They were near land! He must escape now, before they realized he was conscious and clapped him back in irons.

He lay very still, listening to the sounds around him. Labored breathing, groans—the buzzing of flies. Yes, land was close by, very close. They must be tied to a dock. Some of the men mumbled incoherently; their wounds were infected, and fevers ravaged their shattered bodies. Lying on the next pallet was a man Damon recognized. Jeb Haney, the American, his arm and shoulder covered by a bloody bandage.

"Jeb . . ." Damon's lips were cracked and dry, and he was not sure he had made a sound until Jeb's head turned slowly in his direction.

"I'd advise you to lay low, mate," Jeb whispered out of the corner of his mouth. "The bo'sun Bassey was here looking at you not more than an hour ago to see if you'd come to your senses yet."

"Are we at anchor . . . or in a dock?"

191

"I felt her nudge something solid, reckon we're in a dock."

"Are you going to jump?"

"Reckon I'd rather not take the chance. But you might make it if you wait until after dark. You might get on deck without being seen."

Yes, Damon thought. Wait until after dark. Have to find Lanna and the child and take them with me. They must be locked up somewhere . . . the captain's cabin, perhaps? No, probably one of the officers had been deprived of his. They would be alone at night . . . oh, God, I hope she didn't see the flogging . . . hope she didn't hear me scream.

Damon closed his eyes and lay still. When footsteps came his way, he babbled deliriously.

For the rest of the long hot day he suffered tormenting thirst rather than asking for water. When the pain in his back grew unbearable, he watched from beneath half-closed lids as the exotic tropical butterfly was slowly devoured by the spider.

CHAPTER 21

Lanna lay perfectly still, eyes tightly closed, the pain in her lower back and sides competing for attention with the soreness between her legs. She was naked, and several fat flies crawled lazily over her breasts and meandered over the darkening bruises on her stomach and thighs. She could hear Bloody Murdoch humming to himself nearby, then the slurp of yet another drag on a bottle of rum.

Her throat was dry. She had screamed herself hoarse, but no one had come to her aid. Once, she had managed to pull away and kick at that gross appendage that ravaged her body. Her reward had been a teeth-rattling slap across her face and a further onslaught of the battering-ram of flesh that slammed her down against the hard bed and left her, finally, torn and bleeding, too weak to utter a sound.

How much time had passed? How could she know . . . there had been periods of merciful oblivion. It was dark now, the long white-hot afternoon had passed into aching night and her misery knew no end. Had the *Grey Wren* sailed without her? Why did no one come looking for her? Oh, my poor baby . . . my darling, where are you? Do you look for me and cry because I am not there? Damon, Damon . . . I tried to help you . . . will you believe that . . . will you think I gave myself willingly to this monstrous man? How shall I ever be able to give

193

myself to you, now, after what he has done to me? Oh, Damon . . . how shall I face you again?

A crash from the other side of the hut. Another bottle had been emptied and dropped to the dirt floor. A grunt as Bloody Murdoch struggled to his feet. Lanna tensed, hearing the sound of a whimpering animal, not realizing that it was coming from her own lips.

There were muttered curses as he crashed into the sea chest. Then his hand found her and separated her legs again. Fingernails bit into the bruised flesh and her body was wracked with sobs of pain and humiliation and despair. But the final degradation was yet to be.

"No!" she screamed, finding the strength to scream again as she felt the foul rum-sodden tongue forcing itself into her bleeding flesh.

God, help me, please help me . . .

Her prayers were echoed by a grim-faced Alain L'Herreaux as he listened to her screams rend the night air. Dragging his chains, he struggled through the sprawling prisoners to where the young marine sleepily maintained his watch.

"In the name of God and your mother's honor . . . help her! *Mon Dieu* . . . how can you let this happen to one of your own women . . ." He broke off, a stream of French dying on his lips as Lanna's screams stopped abruptly.

The young marine looked uneasily in the direction of Murdoch's hut. He wished his sergeant would awaken from his drunken slumber, wished the officer would return. The woman had not looked like one of the prostitutes that Murdoch occasionally dragged up here from the village. There were several white prostitutes, but he didn't remember seeing one with pale gold hair. And there had never been one who screamed in that heart-rending way.

"Her father is the skipper of an English frigate . . ." Alain did not know what Lanna was doing here. Surely she had not come to try to help him, and Damon was still on board the *Grey Wren*. Alain shook his chains in an agony of fear for her. The screaming had been chilling, but the silence was worse.

"If that's so," the young marine mumbled, "what's she doing here? No decent woman would come to the stockade with Bloody Murdoch."

"*M'sieur* . . . please . . . think of your mother, your sisters . . . help her," Alain pleaded. In the darkness a tear was sliding down his cheek.

194

The young marine hesitated, then nudged the sleeping native guard with his boot. "Keep an eye on 'em while I go see what Murdoch is doing to that woman."

He had no wish to tangle with Murdoch, and no love of the French. But no Frenchman was going to show more compassion for a woman than an Englishman. Besides, the girl's screams had been twisting his insides like a knife all afternoon, and the prisoners were in a constant turmoil. Silently he approached Murdoch's hut.

Murdoch was down on his knees beside the bed. The mop of hair was fiery in the glow of a single candle, and his great bare back glistened with sweat. In a single movement, the young marine stepped into the circle of light and smashed his musket barrel down onto the back of Murdoch's neck. He sprawled forward across the girl, who blinked once and then fainted.

Turning, the young marine saw that the native guard had followed him. "Throw something on that girl and get her back to the village . . . quick as you can . . . before he comes to. We'll let him think she did it to him . . . God knows she would have if she'd had the strength."

Indigo's heart was beating audibly beneath the silk dress and the dark area of her nipples showed clearly through the thin material as her chest rose and fell. He was here . . . Damon was on the ship.

She had tucked a fragrant hibiscus into her hair, and the centerpiece of the dining table was a mound of fruit and flowers. The house was small but immaculate, and two small lizards helped keep the insect population at bay.

Lucas was bringing his captain to dinner. She had never met the dreaded Sir Jared Malford and, since Lucas exaggerated his importance on board ship to her, she did not know that the captain did not socialize with the boatswain. When she had urged Lucas to bring Sir Jared to their home while the *Grey Wren* was in port, Lucas had merely laughed at the suggestion. But she had been insistent. Lucas, still amazed at the good fortune of having the beautiful Indigo with him, decided to ask the old man to dinner. After all, there were things Lucas knew about Sir Jared that no one else in the fleet knew. Sir Jared owed him more than one favor.

Damon had tried to escape the night before, but he had stumbled into the officers' quarters. He had been caught and thrown in irons. Indigo did not know more than this.

195

Lucas had not told her that Lanna and the child had been on the *Wayward Woman* when they had captured the ship.

Indigo sliced papaya and thought of Damon. She would help him escape from the English ship, and he would realize how much he loved and needed her. She licked the juice from slim brown fingers and tried to still the pounding of her heart when she heard Lucas' voice outside.

They were in shadow and she was in filtered sunlight as introductions were made, but Indigo felt the unmistakable surge of male interest that emanated from the very correct captain of the frigate. She extended her hand to him and smiled, looking up from beneath half-closed eyelids.

"Welcome to my house, Sir Jared. We are so happy you could come." She knew from the slight movement of his fingers as he raised her hand to his lips that her voice and accent were a surprise to him too.

A grey-haired man, but trim and lean and still at the peak of his manhood. The face was cruel. He would care nothing for others' pain, this one.

Lucas was pouring wine and talking loudly about the laziness and lack of skill of the native workmen. What a job it would be for their own ship's carpenters to make the *Grey Wren* seaworthy! Sir Jared and Indigo were silent. Their eyes met, held and stayed locked throughout the meal and the evening that followed.

When Lucas' head began to nod from a surfeit of wine and rum, Indigo murmured huskily, "How I should love to see a warship, Sir Jared. We came here on a battered old fishing boat . . . Lucas tells me the *Grey Wren* is one of the finest frigates of the line."

Sir Jared's thin lips parted slightly. "And so you shall. I will conduct you on a tour of the ship myself."

Indigo smiled and let her fingers stray across the tablecloth to touch Sir Jared's hand.

There had been many times after she ran away with Lucas Bassey that Indigo had considered leaving him. She had cursed her impulsiveness and wished she had made her way back to Charleston alone to wait for Alain. Alain would have protected her.

But during the weeks she and Bassey hid in the wild and isolated regions of the interior, living like Indians, she had

196

needed him to provide food and protection from human and animal marauders.

Greater than her fear of capture, however, was her dread of being returned to slavery on a white man's plantation. So she cooked for Lucas Bassey and washed his clothes in the river and lived like a squaw.

Bassey did not beat her, although she was often bruised during his lovemaking, which was brutal and frequent. It quickly became clear to Indigo that the way to avoid the bruising was to bring Lucas quickly to a climax. Her nightmare hours with Michael Danvers came to her aid. From him she had discovered there were certain things a woman could do that would dispatch a man rapidly. With Michael Danvers, his own tortured mind had held him back from the brink, but Lucas Bassey could be coaxed over the edge speedily.

When at last Bassey had enough of living like a savage in the wilderness, he decided to travel north in an effort to reach British lines. And so they began a long and arduous journey.

From friendly Indians they learned that the Americans had attempted to invade Canada. General Hull and two thousand men had reached the British post at Malden only to find British control of Lake Erie cut them off from their base in Ohio. His rear was under attack by the British and their Indian allies, and Hull quickly surrendered. The day before, Fort Dearborn in Chicago had been surrendered, and Indians massacred the men of the garrison as they tried to evacuate. The entire Northwest Territory was in British hands.

Bassey became bolder now. They often stayed in town if he had the money to pay for a room. Bassey supported them by robbing unwary travelers or isolated farmhouses. When Indigo protested, he said roughly that this was war and it was his duty to get to his own lines in any way possible.

Although Indigo never witnessed his plundering of the farmhouses or robbing of travelers, she always dreaded his return after such an episode. Lucas Bassey always came back not only with money and booty, but with a savage appetite for sex. Whatever he did to his victims, it stirred in him a primitive lust that took days to abate. In these periods of savagery Indigo used all of her skill merely to survive. It did not seem possible to her that what she did with Bassey she had once done with Damon, that what she now endured she had once enjoyed.

Strangely, it was not Bassey's sexual demands that she resented most, however. It was living like a savage with no permanent shelter. She remembered longingly Damon's fine house with its elegant furniture, its slaves to do her bidding. The gracious city of Charleston and her life there were in sharp contrast to camping out on a trail, sleeping on the hard ground. Even when Bassey had the money and they spent the night in town, it was not the same. She was grateful for a soft bed so that when Bassey's huge bulk pressed upon her body she was not being stabbed by the hard ground; but she wanted more than a room with a bed.

"Never satisfied, you ain't," Bassey complained one night. "I get us a room and it still isn't enough for my high and mighty half-white."

"Please don't call me that," Indigo said. "It's just that I'm so tired of traveling. Couldn't we stay somewhere for a while? Perhaps here in this town?"

"I keep telling you. We're going to get to British lines and then I'm going to find a ship for the Indies. Going back to my own skipper, Sir Jared, I am. And you are going with me."

"And what will I do while you are at sea?" Indigo said, rising from the bed and picking up a hairbrush, one of her few possessions. The bristles sank into the gleaming mass of her hair, dark as a raven's wing.

"You'll come with me, of course. Plenty of women go to sea with their men. I'm a boatswain and the captain will let me take you along." He rolled over and lay on his back, pale glassy eyes drinking in her beauty as the candlelight flickered over the taut hips and the sinuous lines of her back.

"I don't know if I would like it at sea . . . living in a small cabin. Oh, Lucas, I want a home of my own so much. I believe I would do anything just to have a little house of my own."

"Anything?" Bassey asked with a grunt of humor.

She went to his side, dropping to her knees beside the bed and running her slim brown fingers over the mass of his chest, which was as hairless as his head. "A little house of my own, Lucas. With no other woman to tell me what to do. A door I could lock against the world."

One thick arm wrapped about her body and lifted her effortlessly so that she lay upon the mountain of his flesh.

198

"You know I won't move a white wife in on you like your last master," he said, his voice growing thick with passion and his breathing becoming more rapid as he caressed the honey-colored skin.

"Got me a wife back in Bristol," he said, "and I'll never live with another. Old shrew she was. But if it'll make my pretty little mulatto happy, a house she shall have. In the Indies somewhere. We'll see when we get there." He pushed her long hair back from her face, keeping his fingers entwined as he pulled her head toward him. He mistook Indigo's shiver of distaste for the trembling of passion.

When at last they reached British forces and Bassey found a ship to take them to the Caribbean, he kept his word about the house.

Life was easier while he was at sea. When he returned to port, however, Bassey's presence in the house irritated her. His physical size dominated the tiny rooms, and his uncouth personal habits created a shambles in her well-ordered abode. He seemed to crush, mutilate and stain everything he touched. His physical size and strength had been an advantage on the long journey through the wild American continent.

In their tiny house, however, he was a caged bull elephant. Indigo held her breath every time he moved, waiting for another of her treasures to go crashing to the floor.

Then Sir Jared Malford came to dinner at his boatswain's house and Indigo looked at him, and also at his ship, at the way his men cowered in his presence. She noted the difference in his table manners, his grooming, his bearing. She saw the product of upper class British education, power and money. She learned that Sir Jared was a widower with extensive holdings both in Trinidad and in England.

All of this she registered but then ignored, because her only reason for wanting to meet Sir Jared had been her desire to help Damon escape. There was still only one man in the world as far as Indigo was concerned.

Lanna awoke to find a dust-filled beam of sunlight striking her face. She blinked at the drifting golden specks and tried to roll into the shade. She found she could not move her left leg without extreme pain. The entire leg throbbed, from the hip to the twisted ankle. Almost as soon as she

199

was aware of the sunlight and pain, her nostrils were assailed by the stench of her surroundings. Dimly she could make out the walls of a small room, a crude washstand against one wall, a chair beside the bed. Her hand shook as she reached downward and pulled a rough towel from between her legs. It was soaked with blood. Despite her soreness, she breathed a long sigh of relief. Her monthly cycle . . . it would cleanse her body. She rejoiced in the cramps that gripped her, wanting the torment that would make her forget her bruised and abused flesh.

Sounds of a door opening and bare feet padding across the floor. Lanna's neck was stiff as she swiveled her head slowly in the direction of her visitor.

A girl . . . white . . . with a short mop of chestnut curls and an impish face, very young. "You all right, duckie? Fair done in, you was, when they brought you 'ere. Said old Bloody Murdoch got 'is 'ands on you. Bloody swine 'e is. Won't 'ave nothing to do wiv 'im, meself. Not for all the tea in China. What's your name, ducks?"

"Lanna . . ." Could that croak be her voice?

"Well, 'ere you are, Lanna. Brung you a nice cup of tea. That'll put you right. And 'ere's a fresh rag for you, gimme that one, it's soaked."

The hot sweet tea was laced with rum and the warmth coursed through her veins. "M-m-murdoch . . . where . . . ?"

"Don't worry, Lanna. He won't get you again. They'll be busy for a while . . . searching the island for a prisoner who escaped last night. Must 'ave got away about the time the guard was bringing you 'ere . . . 'e thought you was one of us, Lanna. 'Course, we could see you weren't, from the state of you."

"A prisoner escaped?" Lanna's heart leaped.

"A Frenchman, they said. 'E would surely 'ave been 'anged today . . . a Frenchie."

Lanna handed the chipped cup back to the girl. Alain . . . at least he was free.

"He won't get far, o'course. In chains and all. Me name is Peggy. Can I get you something to eat now Lanna?" She wore black stockings under a torn wrapper, nothing else.

"No . . . thank you. But I must get back to the ship . . . my clothes, where are my clothes?" She struggled to sit up, waves of nausea overcoming her. How would she get back to the frigate . . . the longboat would surely have returned? Why were they not searching for her? Richard

. . . the baby . . . the room spun dizzily and she felt cool hands pushing her down against the foul-smelling pillow.

"There, there now . . . 'old on a minute. What ship?"

"*Grey Wren* . . . frigate . . . at anchor . . ."

"Oh, lor', ducks, it's gone . . . it was gone when I woke up this morning."

Gone . . . sailed without her . . . Peggy's face and the fly-specked room crumpled and dissolved before Lanna's horrified gaze as her senses left her.

Alain crouched motionless in the bamboo thicket. He breathed slowly, his eyes fixed on the rear window of the ramshackle building that backed on the encroaching jungle. He could see movement across the window and hear women's voices, and he wondered if Lanna had been brought here by the native guard. The sun had risen . . . it had taken a long time to drag his chained body this far.

The moment the young English marine had started for Murdoch's hut, Alain had quickly pointed out to the native guard that he should follow to help the young man, who would surely be no match for the huge Murdoch. "The prisoners mostly sleep . . . and we are all chained. Go help him," he urged, and the guard had rolled his eyes once and then obeyed.

In the instant the two of them disappeared into Murdoch's hut, Alain had flung his wrist chain over the top of the bamboo stockade, his long arms sliding over the sharply tipped poles. With most of his strength in arms and shoulders, his chained feet had followed easily. He fell with a crash of chains on the other side of the stockade and hopped, kangaroo-style, to the sheltering bamboo.

He remained hidden as the native guard carried Lanna's inert body from the hut and set off down a pathway that led toward the sea. The young marine returned to his post, more intent on keeping an eye on Murdoch's hut than on paying attention to the shadowy figures of the chained prisoners.

Alain began to inch his way slowly in the direction the native guard had taken, fearful that the rattling chains would give him away. He stopped frequently, taking short shuffling steps over the sharp coral beach until at last he had reached the thick growth of bamboo.

There was a burst of laughter from the window he was watching. A woman's voice screamed out, "No! I tell yer, it's time to go back to your ship. I've got to get me beauty

201

sleep, I 'ave." The next moment a sailor lurched out of the back door, and a young girl, naked except for a pair of black stockings, gave the sailor a good natured shove. She stood in the doorway, watching the man stagger away.

Alain decided to take a chance. After all, Lanna's safety was more important than his own. "Mam'selle . . ." he called as the girl was about to close the door.

"My God!" she exclaimed as he approached. "You'll catch it when they get you. Nobody escapes from the compound."

"Please . . . there is a golden-haired woman. I think they brought her back to the village . . . I must know where she is," Alain said, hobbling up to her.

"Lanna . . ." the girl said. "Yes . . . they brung 'er 'ere, but she's not 'ere now. We sent for the Reverend Weskins and 'e took 'er up to the church. Come on, I'll help you inside. I 'ear they're going to 'ang your lot today. Can't let a friend of Lanna's get 'ung, can I?" When he spoke of Lanna, the little man had anguish written on his handsome face. The young prostitute had forgotten there were men who cared enough to risk their lives for a woman. It was a side of men's nature that she rarely saw in her business.

"Merci, mam'selle . . . I thank you from the bottom of my heart," Alain said, as he hopped into the small hallway leading to the stairs. If she would get him a file . . . how long would it take to saw through the chains . . . and, in the meantime, would Lanna be safe at the church? He and Damon had allowed the beautiful Indigo to be snatched away from them. But while Alain lived and breathed, no further harm would come to Lanna.

She had been dreaming, of course—a terrible, disjointed dream. First she had been in a filthy room with a kind young girl. Before that . . . before that there had been something so awful . . . surely a nightmare.

There had been voices . . . a woman's voice, sing-song English, not the young girl's voice.

"Can't keep her here . . . need the room and the bed. Another ship coming in . . . Go and fetch the vicar, Peggy."

Someone had placed a cool cloth over her head and her eyes, blotting out the violent red images behind the lids. The sounds had penetrated . . . the creakings and gasps that seemed to fill the night. Then her pain-wracked body

202

was being lifted. She was in a carriage . . . or perhaps a cart . . . she was not sure. She was enveloped in a blanket that scratched and chafed.

Later there was moonlight flooding through a handsome stained glass window, illuminating an altar in its pale glow . . . pews . . . she was lying on the hard wooden bench. She closed her eyes and slept.

Sunlight and the soft touch of a warm hand awakened her. She looked into a deeply wrinkled face above the white collar of a minister. She was in a church.

"I'm sorry I had to leave you here, my dear, but I have only small bachelor quarters and they were already occupied by someone. Besides, I was unable to awaken and move you. How do you feel this morning? I am Reverend Weskins, Anglican minister here. Do you think you could walk, if I help you? I have some food ready. My quarters are behind the church. It isn't far."

Someone had dressed her in a voluminous gown of a coarse cotton material, she realized gratefully as she sat up, groaning as her stiff left leg touched the floor.

"My other guest," the Reverend Weskins was saying as she leaned her weight on his arm and inched her feet forward, "is Gideon Lacey . . . perhaps you know he is related to the archbishop? Naturally, I gave up my bed for the unhappy young man . . ."

A thin stream of warm liquid ran down her leg and she gritted her teeth against the pain of walking. Gideon Lacey . . . was that name supposed to mean something to her? If the young man was unhappy, she hoped he had as good a reason as her own for being so. In a few short hours she had lost everything she loved and cared about in the world and had been so disgraced that even if she were able to find Damon and somehow help him escape, he would be revolted by her.

She dragged her feet alongside Rev. Weskins, remembering what Sir Jared had told her. Your father was a rake and libertine . . . your mother a harlot. Now she was worse than either of them could possibly have been. She had not dreamed the foul-smelling room and the girl, Peggy . . . she had been in that dreadful place.

"Reverend . . . my father . . . my baby . . . are on the *Grey Wren*. Do you know where the ship is bound?"

"I'm sorry, my dear, the ship was only here briefly and in these times sailors are secretive about their voyages."

"My husband . . . Damon St. Clair . . . he is imprisoned

here on the island. Would it be possible for you to take a message to him?"

The Reverend Weskins' hands tightened under her arm. He did not tell her that with the exception of the Frenchman, who had somehow made good his escape, most of the prisoners from the *Wayward Woman* were being hanged at this moment.

"Of course, my dear. I shall do everything I can to help you." Silently Rev. Weskins reflected that he would prefer to place the young woman on board the ship that would be bearing Gideon Lacey back to England within the week. Despite her condition, it was obvious that the girl was from a good family.

He had been unable to help Gideon and he resented the archbishop for suggesting that the young man stop off at the island to see him. No one could help Gideon. Rev. Weskins knew only too well the hopelessness of the affliction. The family would have been able to keep the malady hidden had Gideon been just another ordinary young man. But Gideon Lacey was extraordinary. He was the most gifted portrait artist in Europe, and fame had placed him under public scrutiny. After the last unfortunate episode with a poet in London, Gideon had been sent on a long voyage.

The Reverend Weskins led Lanna into a small sun-filled room where bread and fruit and a pot of tea awaited her.

"I shall have to leave you alone for a while, I'm afraid. I have to go to the prison compound." He did not tell her the reason. "While I am there, I shall inquire about your husband. The girl who takes care of me will be along in a moment to see what she can prepare for your breakfast. Meantime, have some tea and try not to worry about anything. I shall be back shortly."

Lanna eased herself down into a chair and reached for the teapot, giving her host a wan smile as he departed. She was glad to be alone. As soon as the serving girl appeared she must inquire about taking a bath.

"Who are you?" a voice asked from the doorway.

Turning, Lanna saw a man wearing an artist's smock. His sandy hair was streaked with paint where he had brushed it from his brow. Of medium height and fine-boned, he had high cheekbones and a delicately curved chin. And under lustrous lashes he had the saddest eyes Lanna had ever seen. With longer hair and feminine attire, the man would surely have been as beautiful as any woman.

"Lanna St. Clair . . . you must be Gideon Lacey?"

"Must I, indeed? I take it we are acquainted, or that you know me from somewhere?"

"Only from the Reverend Weskins. He told me he had another guest staying with him."

"I see. Have you been in an accident?" He came to the breakfast table and picked up a piece of fruit.

Lanna flushed, acutely aware of the bloodstains on her skirt, and the bruises on her arms. Gideon Lacey's gray, tired eyes registered sympathy.

"No," Lanna said slowly. "I was raped . . ." and she began to cry, the tears rushing in a torrent down her cheeks.

CHAPTER 22

Indigo slowly slid the captain's arm from her shoulder, holding her breath as he stirred in his sleep. The edge of the bunk was hard under her thigh. Cautiously her foot searched for and found the floor. She stood up, looking down at the shadowy outline of the sleeping man who had surprised her with his stamina.

She fumbled in the darkness for her clothes. Sir Jared had been an improvement over Lucas Bassey, but neither gave her the fulfillment she found with Damon. It was only the instinct for self-preservation that allowed her to detach herself from men's assaults on her body and pretend an ardor that she did not feel.

Now, as the captain of the *Grey Wren* slept, Indigo left his cabin and moved cat-like through the silent ship in the direction of the brig. There was no one to challenge her progress until she encountered the guard who sleepily watched over the half-dozen prisoners. His back was turned and he didn't see the raised axe handle that smashed into his skull the moment before he crumpled to the deck. Panting, Indigo groped for the key ring at the guard's belt.

Damon was alone in the first cabin. There were chains around his ankles and wrists. A look of pure amazement passed over his face as he recognized his liberator. Then she was in his arms, her hair smothering his face, the chains cold and hard between their bodies.

"Indigo . . . Indigo . . . how in the name of . . ."

"Shhh! We must go. Quickly, before he comes to. Can you walk without rattling the chains?"

"Wait . . . wait a minute. What about Lanna and the child? Where are they? Have they been put ashore yet?"

Indigo froze, jerking away from him as though he had struck her.

"I can't leave them behind," Damon whispered hoarsely. "Can we get to them . . . take them with us? Indigo, in the name of God, help me . . . you must know where they are."

Indigo stared at him through the darkness but he did not see the terrible rage in her eyes. "Damon," she said at last, "come with me now, you must."

"My wife and son . . . I must go to them first."

"Damon, if you don't come with me now, you will spend the rest of your life on this ship."

"Please, Indigo. At least tell me where they are."

"Damn you!" She spat the words. "You can rot here forever." She spun on bare feet and darted back through the open door, racing away from him as he stumbled after her, falling over the body of the guard and bringing the man abruptly back to his senses.

Five minutes later Damon was locked up again, dazed from the guard's blow, and Indigo, shivering, was easing herself back into the captain's bunk.

So Damon had been more concerned about his wife and son than about escaping. After all Indigo had done to get the captain to invite her to spend the night aboard his ship. She had had to tell the captain that Bassey abused her and that she was afraid of him. She had begged Sir Jared to help her to escape from the clutches of his boatswain. In sultry tones she had told him of Bassey's demands, describing in titillating detail what was expected of her during the lovemaking. She had looked at Sir Jared from beneath silky lashes, the suggestion of tears in the molten gold eyes.

"It isn't that I would mind doing these things with a man I cared about . . ." she said softly. "But he is a great lumbering buffalo with no refinement . . . brutal to me." She had pressed her face against Sir Jared's chest and felt his arms enclose her like steel springs.

In the morning, Sir Jared invited her to accompany him on his next voyage and she accepted. Damon was still locked in the brig.

207

Three sailors had to carry the drunken Bassey on board before they sailed.

Gideon Lacey was putting the finishing touches on an appealing portrait of a young girl with impish features and unruly chestnut curls. The girl was almost naked, and it was with some relief that Rev. Weskins observed that the model for the portrait had departed. He averted his eyes from the canvas.

"How is your patient, Weskins old fellow?" Gideon asked absently.

"Sleeping. I must admit, my dear boy, I am in a quandary. If she is, as she claims to be, the daughter of Sir Jared, then why did he sail without her? And should I keep her here for his return? I am afraid, you see, that when the hue and cry over the escaped Frenchman has died down Murdoch may come and inform me that the woman is, in actual fact, his."

Gideon's haunted eyes surveyed the minister pityingly. "If he comes looking for her, say she is ill. Cholera, fever, smallpox . . . Use your imagination, man."

"But if the *Grey Wren* does not return . . ."

"Would you like me to take her off your hands?" Gideon asked casually, his brush underlining the curve of Peggy's breast. His artistry had given the girl a gamin quality, turning her into a tragic waif.

"Why, whatever do you mean, Gideon?"

"I could take her back to England with me."

"You would do that?"

"Why not? I certainly want to paint her. I have never seen such cheekbones . . . and those eyes. It will be a challenge to try to capture her remote, misty beauty."

"Gideon, Gideon," Rev. Weskins murmured. "You surprise me when you speak so of the fair sex."

Gideon dropped his brush into a jar of turpentine and smiled. "Because I prefer men to women? Is that what you mean? I am an artist, Weskins, who can appreciate beauty for its own sake. Besides, if the lovely Lanna will accompany me to London, think what it will do for my standing with my family! Not to mention the Prince Regent and his motley collection of aging hags. The commissions will come pouring in and my scandalous escapade will be forgotten. Especially if I can persuade her to live with me whilst I paint her portrait."

208

"And what will you tell her about your . . . ah . . . personal life?"

"The truth, of course. I have never found it necessary to lie to women. They fall into two categories: those who try to save my soul by seducing me, and those who accept me for what I am. Lanna will be of the latter group, I'm sure."

"What makes you think so?"

"After what happened to her at the hands of your frightful beachcomber? She will welcome the protection of a man who makes no demands on her other than sitting for a portrait. We are sailing in a well armed convoy, so the journey will be safe, and by the time we reach England her bruises will have healed. I just hope that when our Navy arrives in port her father's ship is not part of the escort . . ."

"You really have given the matter some thought, haven't you, Gideon?" the Reverend asked wonderingly. "Have you thought about the fact that she claims to have a husband and a child? I was told at the stockade that the husband was not among the prisoners brought ashore, that he is serving on the *Grey Wren* also."

Gideon peeled off his smock. His tapered fingers gestured airily. "They deserted her, old boy. I believe the whole thing is kismet. She was meant to accompany me to England. Come, let's awaken her and tell her the good news."

Lanna, whose mind and memory demanded a rest from turmoil, was content to let Gideon Lacey take her back to England when he promised to make every effort to reunite her with her child as soon as possible. And even more so when Rev. Weskins gently explained that her husband, Damon St. Clair, had not been one of the prisoners, but was, in fact, serving aboard her father's ship. An Englishman who had returned to the fold.

"Tell me, Mr. St. Clair," the captain said, "do you fence?"

Damon stood stiffly at attention in the captain's cabin, his eyes carefully avoiding Indigo, who was reclining on the captain's bunk. She was dressed in a filmy gauze wrapper. A fine silver chain about her slim ankle flashed as she made lazy circles in the air with her foot.

"Now that we are at sea again, I find I miss the pastime," Sir Jared continued. "None of my officers are proficient in the sport." He had not explained Indigo's presence

209

on the ship, but it seemed obvious from Lucas Bassey's black rages and brutal treatment of the crew that Indigo had dropped him in favor of bigger game. There was a rumor that the *Grey Wren* was returning to England to be completely overhauled. This was borne out by their direction and the fact that the frigate had avoided engagement with other ships since leaving the islands.

"Yes. I've used the rapier once or twice. In my line of work it was necessary to be adequate in all forms of self-defense," Damon answered.

"Good. We shall see what you can do. I trust your back and shoulders are sufficiently healed and that we might begin today?"

There was nothing in the captain's tone or expression to cause Damon to assume that anything had changed between them. He wondered if Indigo had anything to do with this new approach, but it did not seem likely that Sir Jared would be influenced by anyone, least of all a woman.

"Today will be fine." Damon had never addressed the captain as "sir" and had not yet been rebuked for this omission.

The joust was short. Damon was no match for the captain and he experienced agony with each movement of his arm. Sir Jared played with him for a while, dancing daintily about the gently moving deck. Then with several rapid thrusts he slashed the untipped foil lightly across Damon's bare chest, leaving a network of cuts that slowly oozed blood. The captain then handed his foil to the nearest officer and turned his back on Damon to return to the bridge. Indigo started to follow Sir Jared and was curtly ordered away.

Briefly, Damon allowed himself to fantasize another situation. He saw his body healed, his movements swift and sure, and Sir Jared lying in a pool of his own blood.

It was a puzzle why Sir Jared kept him alive, kept him aboard the *Grey Wren*. A cat and mouse game, yes . . . but why, and for how long?

"Come below," the young surgeon whispered to Damon, "and I'll treat those cuts with some salt."

"Thanks . . . you're more of a sadist than the skipper," Damon said.

"It will prevent infection. In this climate the festering starts so quickly."

"We're sailing north though," Damon said to the doctor when they were out of earshot of the rest of the crew.

"Yes. We'll soon be in a more temperate clime."

"Doctor, what became of my wife and son, will you tell me? Another seaman told me my son and the black woman had been put ashore in Jamaica. But no one seems to know what happened to my wife."

The doctor glanced nervously over his shoulder.

"She left the ship on her own. I don't know the details, St. Clair, but she left before the black woman and the baby were put ashore at Jamaica."

Damon was silent. He could not believe that Lanna would have abandoned her son. Yet what did he really know about women, he reflected bitterly. Sometimes old memories stirred and troubled him. Elusive recollections of his beautiful half-French, half-English mother. As a small boy he had worshiped her but had never been able to reach her. She had moved on the remote boundaries of his life, separated from him by servants, by Claudine, by the boarding school he'd been sent to two years earlier than most English boys. And then his mother had been snatched from his life before she had ever really been a part of it, along with his father, who had shared the burden of loving her.

"Are we bound for England, as they say?" Damon asked the surgeon.

"Alas, no. Bermuda, I believe. There is to be a meeting of Naval officers there, about the unexpected developments with the American Navy. No one in the Admiralty expected they would put up such a fight at sea. They are being beaten miserably on land, of course . . . but they have proved a nuisance at sea, as you well know. I suppose I shouldn't be talking to you like this, St. Clair, with your divided loyalties . . ."

"My loyalties aren't divided," Damon said tersely.

". . . but there aren't many men aboard I can talk to. The maiming and killing of men offends my soul. After an engagement, I see those who are left callously shoveling parts of bodies over the side . . . and I spend hours amputating limbs. Thank God it will soon be over."

"Over? The war, you mean . . . or your tour of duty?"

"Napoleon will be vanquished this year. It's a certainty. He should not have invaded Russia. Once we are finished with the French, we can turn our attention to America and finish her off."

"Bermuda . . . there will be other ships of the line

211

there . . ." Damon said thoughtfully, wincing as the salt was rubbed into his torn flesh.

"Bermuda . . ." he told Jeb Haney later, "not England, thank God. This time I have a plan and you are going to help me. We will have to act before they clap us in irons for the stay in port. Pity, I would have liked to do it when we were tied up next to a couple of other ships of the line."

"Do what?" Jeb Haney asked nervously.

"Blow up the ship. I'm going to set the powder magazine afire as soon as we sight land."

"You'll be killing yourself too," Jeb Haney said in alarm.

"Not if we get over the side promptly. There'll be enough wreckage to float us to shore even if we can't get a boat." *Indigo,* he thought, *will I have time to get to you?* "Besides, I'd rather go to Davey Jones' locker than serve in His Majesty's Navy."

"Reckon you're right. I just kept hoping we'd get in a fight with an American ship and be captured by our own."

"Malford would never surrender. He'd go on fighting until he had a ship full of dead men and then he'd scuttle what was left before he'd strike his colors. Now listen, I've got a plan that will give us time to get clear."

They had gone over the plan several times by the time the ship sighted Bermuda, yet Damon had a nagging suspicion that he had overlooked something.

The shells and gunpowder were kept at a safe distance from enemy gunfire, well below the water-line. The captain's cabin was in the after part of the ship, two decks up. On the deck above the magazine were the surgeon's quarters and sick bay. Damon visited the surgeon whenever he could and practiced making a dash to the general vicinity of the captain's cabin. There was no way he could get to Indigo in less than six minutes. Jeb Haney, therefore, would set a diversionary fire in the forecastle, give the alarm, and hope that Indigo would be brought on deck in case the fire got out of hand. Damon had concealed a piece of tallow candle inside his shirt and had fashioned a fuse from strips of canvas. He had laboriously chewed and sucked out the salt, after his experiments proved that salt-water-soaked canvas did not always ignite.

They waited, breath tight in their lungs, as the misty sweep of land on the horizon drew closer.

"Now," Damon said, "if we wait any longer they'll have

us in irons." He made his way below decks without haste as Jeb prepared to set his hammock afire.

The crew had grown accustomed to his visits to the surgeon. A friendship had sprung up between the two and they frequently conversed. He was not stopped as he detoured by way of the provisions room and descended to the magazine. The pungent smells of sulphur, bilge-water and dead rats combined to produce a putrid odor and the marine guarding the magazine had positioned himself as far away as possible. He had been on watch for four hours and was expecting to be relieved, but looked up in surprise at the seaman who approached.

"Fire . . . in the forecastle," Damon said quickly. "You'd better get aloft fast. It looks as if we may have to abandon ship." The marine turned and climbed up to the surgeon's deck. Damon followed with alacrity. A silent blow struck from behind as the marine set foot on the surgeon's deck. He didn't remember anything more. Quickly Damon dragged him into the midst of the kegs of supplies in the storeroom.

On the magazine deck Damon swept together the loose gunpowder that sprinkled the floor to form a powder train leading to the magazine. At the end of the powder train he placed his fuse and lit it with the stub of tallow candle. Then he raced up on deck, stopping short of the rail when he realized there was no sign of Jeb Haney, Indigo . . . or the panic a fire should have been causing.

There was no time to go to the forecastle to see what had gone wrong. One officer tried to stop him as he reached the captain's cabin, and Damon sent him sprawling on the deck. Yelling "Fire!," the most dreaded cry of all at sea, Damon burst into the cabin to find Indigo down on her knees before the naked captain.

Damon flung her through the door. Cursing, Sir Jared stumbled after them as the first explosion ripped through the ship. Almost simultaneously, the forecastle burst into flames. A sheet of orange flame shot up the mainmast and the first yards crashed to the deck, burning fiercely.

Damon dragged Indigo to the rail, shouting for help in lowering the boat. Sir Jared, oblivious of his lack of clothing, began issuing orders to fight the fire.

"Damon! Come with me!" Indigo screamed, as the ship began to list heavily to starboard. He pushed her unceremoniously over the side to the waiting boat. But in the next second another explosion sent clouds of black smoke billowing on deck, and Damon was pinned against the side of the ship by a tangled snare of splintered masts. He hung over the rail, trapped by his lower legs, feeling the grinding of bone against shattered bone when he tried to pull free.

Through the choking pall of smoke he heard the crackle of burning canvas falling from above. Then a searing pain began, and he clutched futilely at the air as he felt his flesh sizzle.

"Sink! Blast you, sink!" he wanted to shout, "Carry me down to the merciful release of the water!" But his mouth was full of smoke. In the few moments of consciousness left to him he knew what he had overlooked. The *Grey Wren* had avoided recent engagements with other ships. They were low on powder and shells. The explosion had set the ship on fire but had not blown a hole in the hull large enough to sink her. Jeb Haney kicked the burning canvas away from Damon before plunging over the rail, but by then Damon no longer felt the pain anyway.

Sir Jared did not abandon his ship. He took the helm himself while his officers fought the flames and the crewmen leaped into the sea. The *Grey Wren* limped into port, mortally damaged. Although most of the lower decks of the stern had been blown away, the remaining bow and midships of the wooden vessel stayed afloat.

The wounded were taken ashore, including Damon St. Clair who had, ironically, saved the captain's life by removing him from the cabin that was devastated by the explosion in the powder magazine. Not that anyone expected Damon St. Clair to live. His legs were seared and broken, and everyone knew that men did not survive burns such as those.

Sir Jared was without a command, his ship beyond repair. He was to be sent back to England, and there would be an inquiry into the mysterious explosions that had disabled the frigate. Realizing that he could not take a mistress on a Navy transport ship, Sir Jared quickly married Indigo so that she could accompany him.

Shortly after his arrival in London, Sir Jared was informed that his daughter was living with the scandalous artist, Gideon Lacey. And it was during a stiff visit to Gideon's studio one autumn afternoon that he brought Lanna the news of what had happened to her husband and son.

"Your husband redeemed himself somewhat by giving the alarm when the ship caught fire," Sir Jared told her. "I regret that there is not much hope that he will recover from the burns he sustained. The surgeon would not allow him to be sent to England for treatment."

"Thank you for coming to tell me this, Sir Jared," Lanna said, fighting for composure.

"I regret I have news of another unfortunate occurrence," Sir Jared continued. "The ship bearing your son and his nurse to England from Jamaica was attacked by American privateers and taken captive. We have no way of knowing the fate of the passengers and crew."

Gideon moved quickly to Lanna's side and gently put his arms around her.

"By the way," Sir Jared added, "since you evidently prefer to live in London, I am going to Kingsburch for a while. My bride wants to take up residence there during my temporary leave from the Navy. For some reason she has a longing to live in that castle. But I'm sure after a few weeks at Kingsburch, she'll be happy to return to the Indies with me."

"Your bride, Sir Jared?" Gideon said. "Who is the fortunate lady?"

"Her name is Indigo."

Lanna gasped in surprise, but offered no other comment.

"He's gone, Lanna," Gideon whispered against her hair, after Sir Jared had taken his abrupt departure. "Come, sit down. You must try to be optimistic. I'm sure your child and his nurse will be safe. The Americans would not harm a woman and a baby. I will write the good Reverend Weskins. We shall find out what happened. And your husband . . . would it help to remember that you did not really want to see him again?"

Lanna released her hold on Gideon. "I didn't want Damon to be hurt. I wanted him to live and be happy. I did not want to see him again because of my shame."

"Lanna, dear one, how many times must I tell you that it is not your shame? We should only feel shame for the cruelties and abominations we commit against others . . . not for what is done to us."

Lanna bit her lip. "Sir Jared said Damon could not survive his burns . . . my husband is going to die. Nothing matters now except my son . . . but I wanted him to know his father, to grow up with his father."

215

"You will tell him his father was a hero, who saved the captain of his ship," Gideon said. "Come on now, Lanna, don't be sad. At Christmas, when I unveil your portrait, you will be the most famous woman in London."

CHAPTER 23

Slowly the news filtered back to London. The Royal Navy was being humiliated by the American Navy and privateers. Despite their lack of numbers the Americans had developed a force of dedicated fighting men that was challenging the undisputed ruler of the seas.

Word also came of fearful Indian massacres on the American continent and of American rabble armies led by incompetent cowards.

In the London taverns and clubs they discussed the news of the war and decided that many of the reports were greatly exaggerated. Another topic of conversation that season was Gideon Lacey's mysterious mistress. Gideon's apparent devotion to her was part of the reason for their fascination. Gideon Lacey . . . of all men. Who would have thought he would have succumbed to a woman's charm? And it seemed the beautiful Lanna was completely true to him. All of London society was waiting to meet the woman who was the subject of a portrait on which Gideon was working in great secrecy.

The studio was a large attic room in a house situated in the mile-square confines of the city. Now, in addition to the clutter of canvases, it held a sculptor's clay and tools. Previously Lanna had had her bedroom on the floor below, while Gideon slept on a cot in the studio. But when Gideon's sculptor friend, Llewellyn Davis, arrived, Gideon apologetically asked Lanna if she would mind sleep-

217

ing in the studio so that he and Llew could use the bedroom.

"I shall do better than that, Gideon," Lanna answered. "I shall return to Kingsburch. I've been thinking about it for some time. It will be mine next year and I should be seeing to things there. By now Sir Jared must have returned to the service. He hasn't been given another command since losing the *Grey Wren,* but I heard he was trying to get on Admiral Cochrane's staff."

"No, Lanna . . . please don't leave London. Stay with us. Llew and I will be very discreet, and he wants to do a bust of you. He likes you as much as I do."

Lanna glanced away, knowing that Gideon's friend Llew was one of those men who was able to find equal pleasure with both sexes.

"I really feel it would be better if I went home. I shall only stay for a short time, but I need to go there. You see, when the war ends I must return to America to find my son. I should see that the estate is in competent hands before I go."

"I'm sorry that Reverend Weskins had no news of your son, but at least we know that that frightful beachcomber has disappeared from the island. Let's hope Mr. Murdoch has gone to his just reward. I just wish there were something more I could do."

"You have been so kind to me, Gideon. I should have been lost without you. You are a dear, sweet person and I shall always love you."

Gideon reached out and ran his long white fingers through her hair. "Perhaps it will be different for us in our next life. Maybe next time we shall not be doomed to love as brother and sister. I'm sorry . . . about bringing Llew here . . . but—"

Lanna placed her finger to his lips. "Hush. It's all right. I shan't leave for Kingsburch until after your exhibition . . . in the new year. Could you wait until then for Llew to move in?"

Gideon nodded, his melancholy eyes dropping from hers. "I shall miss you, Lanna."

"We shall see each other, don't be sad. Now I must go. I promised to visit Teddie this afternoon."

Lanna's decision to leave was based on more than Llewellyn Davis having moved into their lives, with his insinuating remarks and hands that reached for her knee beneath the table. Although only Teddie knew of her plans, she was already quietly making arrangements to sail to Bermuda. She had to find out what had happened to Damon.

Her carriage rattled through the streets of London, followed by the shrill cries of street hawkers. Throngs of people, rich and poor, swarmed along narrow pavements, and pickpockets lounged in doorways watching for easy prey.

They passed Hyde Park, and Lanna saw young hussars strolling beneath the trees with fresh-cheeked maids. It seemed that everyone in the world was part of a pair, and Lanna felt a wave of loneliness and longing.

Teddie was making hot toddies. "To ward off the chill, dear, winter's coming on. Oh, dear, Lanna, I wish you wouldn't leave. Gideon's good to you, isn't he? I mean, why do you want to rush off?"

"There's no need to go over that again, Teddie. Now, did you hear anything about whether Sir Jared and his wife have left Kingsburch?"

Teddie tossed back her red curls angrily. "She's still there. That woman. He had no right to take her there . . . He went abroad again, back to Jamaica or somewhere. But she stayed on."

"I see," Lanna said quietly. "Well, before I leave for Bermuda, I shall have to go and see what's happening, whether she is there or not."

At that moment Teddie's friend Harry Holmes sidled around the door. He was a burly ex-stevedore who knew everyone on the docks. He had spent some years in the Australian penal colony before being reprieved and repatriated. Perhaps as a result of his experiences, he was continually glancing over his shoulder, and he had the disconcerting habit of jumping visibly when people spoke to him.

"No use your going to Bermuda," he said to Lanna. "Damon St. Clair ain't there any more." He looked back over his shoulder, then closed the door. " 'E must of got on a ship and gone back to America. I got the straight facts from a couple ᵕof tars. They said 'e recovered, but the minute 'is broken bones was mended, 'e was off."

Lanna let out her breath in a long sigh. "Well, at least I know that he's alive, even if he is lost to me."

"Now you must change your mind and stay with Gideon, pet," Teddie advised.

"No, I can't, Teddie. I shall go to Kingsburch," Lanna said. "In the new year . . . after Gideon's exhibition. Perhaps 1814 will bring peace to the world and to me."

The oars creaked and glistened wetly in the moonlight. In the boat the two figures huddled in oilskins and silently watched the dark sweep of the beach drawing closer. Another flash of light came from the shadowed cliffs as an invisible arm swung a lantern to guide their way.

"Easy now . . ." the oarsman said, "we're getting close and there's rocks all along . . . ah!" The hull of the boat scraped over rock, and icy water sprayed their faces.

They could see the cloaked figure on the beach now, swinging the lantern back and forth. The oars touched the rocky bottom and the tide carried them into the narrow beach.

"Now . . ." the oarsman said, shipping his oars. They went over the side and dragged the boat onto the beach.

The woman put down the lantern, splashed into the shallows and flung herself at the tall man who limped toward her.

"You're here . . . you're here," Indigo said, laughing and crying, trying to find a way to get inside the oilskin and touch his flesh so that she could assure herself she was not dreaming. His lips when they kissed her were dry and warm, but without passion.

"We must make our way up to the house, before the tide comes all the way in. Can you help Geordie with the boat? It has to be put in the cave."

A short while later the three of them were making their way on hands and knees through a dank, tortuous tunnel. They were all breathing heavily when at last they emerged in the castle's secret room.

Indigo placed the lantern on the table. "This is it, Damon. It's very cramped, but only Geordie and I know of the room. You will be safe here. Geordie, go and bring food and be careful none of the others see you."

Damon peeled off the oilskins as Indigo stirred a small coal fire with a poker. She pulled the leather armchair closer to the fitful flames and motioned for Damon to sit down.

"So you married him," Damon said stretching out his hands to the warmth of the fire. "Must I address you as Lady Indigo now?"

She went down on her knees beside him and he winced as she touched his aching leg.

"Oh, Damon . . . I only did it so he would bring me here, so that I could help you. After you saved me on the ship, I knew you truly loved me, as I love you. Damon, we can find out what happened all those years ago . . . to your father. Geordie, the man who rowed you over from the other side of the bay, was here before Sir Jared came to Kingsburch. He is the only one left. All the ghosts can be put to rest. You and I can be together, Damon. We shall be safe here. There are no slaves, no one to point a finger at me because of my color. They think I am white. Oh, Damon, Damon, I love you so."

His hands reached out and closed over hers. He looked down into her eyes and she felt a stab of dismay at what she saw in his gaze.

"Indigo . . . don't, please don't. Nothing has changed. I am an American, and I intend to fight for my country as soon as I am able. My legs won't hold me on the deck of a ship yet, but they will in time. I don't even know if I want to find out about my father's guilt or innocence any more. Nothing seems as important to me as the outcome of the war . . . and . . ."

"Your wife," Indigo finished for him, bitterly. She stood up and looked down at the fire. "Is that why you came here when I told you I could slip you into the house? You thought she would be here? Well, she isn't."

"Indigo, try to understand. We are none of us the same people we were a couple of years ago. I suppose it's true that we don't know what we have until we lose it. I wasn't exactly an upstanding citizen, but I loved my country. I would get a lump in my throat every time we sailed back into an American harbor. Things are going badly in the war and they'll go worse if Napoleon is defeated. I have a terrible fear for America. We can't go back to being an English colony, Indigo, we can't."

"Then why are you here, Damon?" Indigo asked in a small voice.

"There was no way for me to get out of Bermuda and return to America. It was easier to get on a ship coming here. Now I can either return to Canada or, if I'm lucky, get on an a ship for the Indies. With your help . . . I shall need papers."

"And what about me?"

"Does Sir Jared mistreat you?"

"No."

"Then what do you want to do . . . do you want to go home?"

"Home! I have no home. I was born into slavery."

"I thought Kingsburch was intended for my wife. Does Sir Jared have another home?"

"He has a villa in Trinidad. He does not care to live in England."

"Then why don't you go to Trinidad? The climate would be more to your liking."

Geordie, the servant, came into the room through the false revolving cupboard. He was bearing a basket. They were silent as he placed a loaf of bread, a wedge of cheese and a bottle of wine on the small table.

"No one saw you, Geordie?" Indigo asked.

"No, milady, they be all abed."

"There is only a small staff of servants," she said to Damon. "Geordie's father was caretaker here years ago when Geordie was a boy."

"He is a simple man," Indigo said after Geordie had left. "His mind is not quick, but he is not an idiot, even though the other servants treat him as one. Since I've been kind to him it's natural that he should want to serve and please me. There are secrets locked in his simple mind, I'm sure of it, if we can find a way to reach them."

"Indigo . . ." Damon took a long swallow of wine. "You haven't told me about my wife. If she isn't here, where is she?"

Indigo looked at him with malice in her eyes. "She is living with an artist in London. She is his mistress," she said triumphantly.

The new year began with the hardest frost London had endured in centuries. The Thames between London Bridge and Blackfriars was frozen, and the frost was followed by a heavy snowfall. It was impossible for Lanna to travel to Kingsburch, and so she went to Teddie to ask if she might stay with her until the weather improved.

Inexplicably, Teddie's eyes filled with tears. "Oh, Lanna, love . . . I'd love to 'ave you, dear, but it wouldn't be right, you see. It wouldn't be good for you."

"Why ever not? Teddie, what do you mean?"

"Your reputation, Lanna. It would be ruined if you lived here with me."

"Reputation! Surely I don't have one after months of

222

living with Gideon. Only you and I know the truth of the relationship. Everyone else believes I am his mistress, and he has taken care to confirm everyone's suspicions. I didn't mind, really . . . it was protection for me too."

"No . . . lovey, it isn't the same thing. Living with one man—even if you was his mistress—and the way I live. I live with many men, Lanna . . . I mean, they share my bed. Even the Prince Regent when he's up to it. And everyone knows it. You'd be tarred with the same brush if you was to move in with me."

"I wouldn't care what other people said."

"But I would care, my precious. Listen, I'll get Harry to find you a nice little flat somewhere, all on your own. And you can have my girl come and do for you until we find you a maid."

Lanna sat down on the hassock in front of the fire and watched the snowflakes fly against the diamond panes of the window. Occasionally a flake would come drifting down the chimney and die in the coals with a faint hiss.

"Harry loves you, Teddie. Doesn't he?" It was a statement rather than a question and Teddie did not answer.

"Would you tell me about my parents, Teddie? Sir Jared told me my father was a rake and a libertine and my mother was a harlot. Is that true?"

"Oh, Gawd almighty . . ." Teddie said brokenly. "Let me tell you . . ." she composed herself with difficulty. "Your father was kind to your mother. He couldn't marry her, you see, because of the difference in their stations in life. But he was good to her while he lived. And he looked after you, didn't he? And your mother, Lanna, she wasn't a bad girl . . . you can't know what it's like to be poor. To be one of thirteen children and only half of them surviving while the others starve to death. Seeing your little brothers sold for three or four shillings to a chimney sweep . . . and being put in a flash house when you was thirteen." Teddie stared into the fire, seeing another world.

Lanna did not know what a flash house was, but from the horror in Teddie's voice when she spoke the words, it was easy to guess.

"Is that where you met my mother, Teddie . . . in the flash house?" Lanna asked gently.

Teddie nodded. "The men who go to the flash houses . . . they're beasts, Lanna. They hate women. They want to hurt and use women, but it's easier to do it to little girls . . .

223

like they was showing their contempt for all of us by abusing little girls. Well . . . your mum was lucky. Luckier than most. She ran away . . . oh, lots of times. But one time she nearly run under the wheel of this fancy carriage . . . coats of arms on the sides and everything. Next thing she knew, this man was carrying her into the biggest room she'd ever seen in her life. Big four-poster bed and a maid with a warming pan. They put her in a hip bath and washed all the muck off her and put her to bed in the big bed."

Lanna listened, fascinated, seeing the image of the frightened little girl warm and secure at last.

"He was my father . . . the man in the fancy carriage?"

"Yes. He saw to it your mum never went back to the flash house. And he didn't touch her himself, for a long time. He had a wife and family, you see . . . daughters, all daughters. I expect he was sorry for her at first."

"What became of her, Teddie? Is she still alive?"

"No, lovey. She died when he died. He was good to her while he was alive, but he didn't leave her nothing when he died. She found herself all alone again and she'd never been one to put anything aside for a rainy day. That was just the end of her."

"But she wasn't a harlot, Teddie, was she?"

"Try to understand, Lanna . . . he had duties, things he had to do. She was left alone, and men had always pestered her. It was hard for her to be good, Lanna. There were some other men, even while he was alive. She got a reputation . . . worse than she deserved, but she got one. That's why I don't want you to get one."

"Oh, Teddie, after what happened to me . . . I don't think I can ever lie with a man again. I believe I should kill myself first."

"No, Lanna, don't talk like that. You'll be able to love someone again, in time. Just because you've eaten moldy bread and the taste was foul doesn't mean you can never enjoy food again."

"I try, Teddie . . . I try. But they haunt me, every moment of every day."

"Who haunts you, Lanna?"

"My baby, and my husband . . . and the American girl who died, Beth. I loved them all so."

"Then be glad you loved them, Lanna . . . don't make yourself sad. If we just love someone for a little while, we shouldn't be sad. We never lose them, do we, they're always with us, in a way. Come on, lovey, I'll make us

224

some nice hot toddies and as soon as Harry gets here we'll talk to him about finding you a nice flat. Gawd, this perishin' weather is going to rot my bones if it keeps on. My poor chest fair aches with it."

"Gideon said he would come from the gallery and pick me up. You don't mind, do you, Teddie?"

" 'Course not, love. I don't care what anybody says about that young man, I like him," Teddie said firmly.

"The pictures are selling well. And he has commissions from the royal family again. I'm so happy for him."

"I hope he doesn't mind the gypsies in the kitchen," Teddie said. Teddie's home was well-known as a place to go if one needed a meal or a helping hand. Lanna had grown accustomed to the strange and exotic people who passed through.

"He won't mind. He'll probably want to steal a couple of them and paint their portraits."

"Sounds like he's here now," Teddie said as footsteps pounded up the stairs. Gideon burst into the room and smiled joyfully at Lanna.

"News! Lanna, dear heart, good news! A letter from our old friend Reverend Weskins. He has news of your son. The girl Zenobia and the child were taken by privateers to an American port. They are safe and well . . . New Orleans, Lanna, they are in New Orleans."

The *Essex* had been away from home for almost a year when she dropped anchor in the tranquil bay which the islanders called Nuku Hiva. Captain Porter named it Madison's Island and ignored earlier Spanish and English claims to the archipelago.

Standing on deck with the other officers, their glasses trained on the lush profusion of breadfruit groves and coconut palms, Rafe Danvers thought fleetingly of the dismal world of black slaves and plantation woes he had left behind forever.

The girls swimming toward the ship ranged in coloration from very light tan to deep bronze. Their lithe limbs and slim torsos sliced through the water with effortless grace. As they drew closer, they smiled and giggled, showing astonishingly white teeth. Behind them their long lustrous hair floated gracefully over the surface of the sparkling sea.

Rafe sighed in mock horror. "Temptation, gentlemen," he said, "is about to engulf us."

The warriors of Nuku Hiva had welcomed the ship the previous day, and Captain Porter had been surprised to find two white men in their midst. One was an Englishman named Wilson who had lived with the natives for four years. He was fluent in the Marquesan language and well versed in the people's customs.

"Wilson said that in their culture sex is considered a normal and natural part of life, not to be specifically confined to marriage," the oldest of the midshipmen said excitedly.

Marriage . . . Rafe thought. Beth's frail countenance and ethereal presence had faded into the misty recesses of his memory. Some day he would return to find a steward to run the plantation . . . explain to Beth and his parents that he could never again live ashore. The sea fever was a part of his blood forever, and a man did, after all, have only one life to live.

The Polynesian girls were swarming up the anchor cables now, the sun making their bodies glisten. They wore only neck ornaments above rounded breasts, and flowers were pinned in their hair.

Captain Porter reasoned, "If an allowance can be made for a departure from prudential measures, it is when a handsome and sprightly girl—whose every charm is exposed to view—invites a man to follow the dictates of nature." He was nevertheless proud of the restraint shown by his officers in the first mad scramble on the decks.

Soon the gundeck, the berth deck and the forecastle were covered with couples locked in each other's arms. Sighs and whispers of ecstasy rippled through the ship.

Petty officers who had keys to the storerooms used their special privilege to secure privacy, and some brawny topmen carried their consorts aloft to make love on the small platforms at the mastheads.

The orgy seared the night. Captain Porter locked his cabin door and closed his ears to the squeals of rapture coming through the bulkhead. After all, the men had endured a year of celibacy.

Rafe watched, bemused, for a while. There were not enough girls for all of the crew, and besides, an officer had to maintain some dignity. Then his glass found the beach again and he saw her.

She was standing watching the ship, her head held quizzically. Her body was as beautiful as that of any statue, and there was something about the way she held herself

226

that reminded him of another woman . . . long ago . . . She had the aristocratic bearing of Lanna. But Lanna was lost to him and, oddly enough, he no longer felt pain when he remembered her. It must be that she was a part of that other life, that confining world of the plantation that he had so gladly escaped. The girl standing on the beach was as wild and as free as the trade winds that caressed her lovely island.

The following day he learned that she was the granddaughter of the tribal chief and that her name was Piteenee. She lived with her grandfather in a thatched-roof house surrounded by a small grove of plantains. When Captain Porter and his officers went ashore to meet the chief, his granddaughter smiled bewitchingly at Rafe and her slender brown fingers reached out to touch his bronze hair wonderingly.

She wore a garment of spotlessly white paper-cloth, with a flowing cloak knotted modestly about her neck. As the evening progressed, however, the cloak began to slip flirtatiously over one shoulder, exposing a pert breast as she hovered hopefully near Rafe.

At last Rafe arose and, with a beaming nod of approval from the chief, took Piteenee's hand and led her through the rustling plantains toward the cool seclusion of the beach. Fragrant flowers decorated her hair and a whale's tooth hung between her breasts. It was a symbol of her high birth, for whale's teeth were more precious to the islanders than jewels. Everything was relative, Rafe thought languidly. Whale's teeth or diamonds. Servitude or freedom.

Gathering Piteenee into his arms to draw her down to the sand, Rafe caught a glimpse of his ship, silhouetted against the tropical night. Sailors were lost at sea . . . perhaps he would simply never return . . . He looked down into the promise of limpid eyes and the invitation of parted lips, then untied her cloak and laid it aside.

He sighed deeply, contentedly, as his body enveloped hers. The landlubber in whose form the sailor had been trapped was left forever on the far side of Cape Horn. In a different ocean, a different life.

CHAPTER 24

Everyone told Lanna it would be impossible for her to travel to New Orleans. Teddie, Harry, Gideon, all of them were adamant. Even apart from the war, the gulf ports, particularly New Orleans, were swarming with pirates. One of Teddie's friends, who had connections in the Admiralty, told Lanna confidentially that England might try to recruit the pirates to help in an invasion of the American continent. There was a man named Laffite, who led the lawless band, and on whose head the Governor of Louisiana had put a price. New Orleans was the last place in the world to go to in such times.

Still, Lanna was determined. The problem was that she needed money. Money to buy her way to America, money to take care of her son when she found him. It was time to visit the solicitors and find out what her resources were.

The news was disappointing. Kingsburch and its holdings would pass to her on her twenty-first birthday, still months away. Until then her expenses would be met by the trust, and they would not allow her to borrow money against her future inheritance. Legally, Sir Jared was custodian of the estate until her birthday. And his instructions had been to only take care of Lanna's normal living expenses.

At last, not knowing where else to turn, she approached Gideon. Without telling him the reason, she asked him to lend her a large sum.

"Well, dear heart . . ." Gideon said thoughtfully, "my

portraits are not making me rich, and my allowance was cut off years ago. We are mostly a church family, you know . . . not wealthy in our own right. My most valuable asset at the moment is your picture. Ironic, isn't it? I shall have to sell it so that you can have the money. What on earth do you need it for?"

"Please, Gideon . . . don't ask. I shall pay you back, I promise. And you can always paint another portrait . . . I'll sit for you . . . even the way you want me to, if you like. It doesn't matter to me any more, nothing matters except . . . well . . ." she broke off.

"Nude, Lanna? You mean it? You'll pose nude for me? Oh, my love, would you?"

"But first the portrait you've finished . . . you will sell it and get as much as you can for it?"

Gideon paced back and forth in front of the fireplace, lost in thought for a few minutes. Lanna waited expectantly.

"I believe . . ." he said at length, "that we shall get the best price if we indulge in a little showmanship."

"What do you mean?"

"A party—the biggest party of the season. We shall take over Almack's for the night perhaps . . . invite everyone to come and, as a climax to the evening, we shall auction the portrait."

Lanna's eyes fell. "Must we, Gideon? I shall be so . . . uncomfortable, as if it were me they were bidding for. I know it's ridiculous, but . . ."

"Then you shall go incognito, my lovely. We shall have a costume ball. What do you think of that? With masks and wigs . . . we shall tell them that the lovely Lanna will be present and they will have to guess who she is. Then we shall be sure to have at least a dozen young women wearing the same costume as you. Perhaps as a reward you will dance with whoever buys your portrait . . . then you can leave as soon as your identity is known.

"And you will start sitting for me again, soon? When I give you all the money I'm afraid you are going to be less eager. It will take me a few weeks to make all the arrangements . . . we could get the first sketches done by then."

"All right, Gideon. But be sure you have a good supply of coal and logs in the studio, or I shall freeze to death."

The jaded matrons and gullible young girls of London were agog over the mysterious stranger who had appeared so suddenly and caused such a stir. He had coolly cut a swath through the gambling houses and clubs of London, and had relieved many of their patrons of considerable amounts of money. Who was he, and where had he come from? He was a gentleman, obviously. He walked with a limp and chose his words carefully, as though he had lived among foreigners and was using English again after a long time. There were rumors that he had been wounded fighting the French, others that he was a gallant Naval officer, on leave while his wounds healed. It was known that he spent hours practicing with the finest fencing masters in London. In a world of perfumed dandies, the ladies found him refreshingly masculine and they vied with one another for his attention. From time to time he would disappear. But sooner or later he would be back, gambling with a calm professionalism.

Inevitably, he made enemies. Twice he was called out and the second time was forced to fight a duel. His opponent was badly wounded but he sustained only a grazed arm. He called himself, simply, Devlin.

A pseudonym, of course. Perhaps he had a price on his head somewhere, or was the bastard son of a well known family. Everyone tried to guess who Devlin really was, and only the forthcoming party and auction Gideon Lacey was planning could stir up the same excited interest.

Lanna had paid little attention to the gossip about London's newest mystery man. She posed for Gideon and studied maps of the Gulf of Mexico. It was no wonder Laffite's pirates were such a problem in the area. So many inlets and waterways. Sometimes her hands would press against the map and her eyes would brim with tears. If only she could will herself to be there . . . to fly like a bird and land on that tiny dot.

Zenobia would care for her son. She would not allow any harm to come to him. But how would she support them in a strange city? Lanna worried and counted the minutes until her portrait was sold and she could be on a ship. She had decided to say that she had to go to her father, Sir Jared Malford. A ship to the Indies . . . from there she would find a way to get to the American coast, or perhaps the Bahamas and then America. But no explanations were necessary for now. Not until after the auction.

"Dear heart, you are fidgeting again, do you want to take a rest?" Gideon asked from behind his easel.

"No. I'm sorry. Please go on, Gideon."

"Your legs, my dear, are a work of art in themselves. This picture is going to be even better than the portrait. I feel it in my blood. I believe I have been able to capture your sorrow more effectively this time."

"Am I sorrowful, Gideon? I try not to be."

"You still pine for your American, don't you, dear? No, don't deny it. Don't you think that perhaps it wouldn't be quite so magical as you remember if you were reunited with him? There is really no such thing as true love, you know. Yours has lasted because it is nurtured in your mind. Without diversion. Why do you not indulge in *les amourettes,* as the French call them? Some little loves, Lanna. Keep your grand passion in your mind, if you must, but feed your starving body."

"Gideon, you are outrageous," Lanna said, smiling.

"Hello in there . . . may I come in . . ." Llewellyn Davis pushed open the studio door too quickly for Lanna to cover herself completely.

"Llew, I asked you not to return until tea time," Gideon said in a pained tone.

"And sorry I am about it, old chap. But there was a devil of an argument going on at the club and you know I hate violence." He squeezed Gideon's shoulder as he went by and sprawled on the narrow bed.

Lanna did not look at him as she pulled on her wrapper and slipped her feet into mules, but she felt his eyes upon her.

"Your beautiful friend hates me, Gideon," Llew said, kicking off his boots. He was a darkly handsome man, taller and sturdier than Gideon, and several years older. As a sculptor he enjoyed only moderate success.

"I hate you too, you interrupt my work," Gideon said darkly.

"She will not sit for me and I need her to finish the bust, Gideon. Plead my case, there's a good fellow. As it is I have worked solely from your blasted portrait. Just one sitting, so I can put on the finishing touches and bring it to life."

"Gideon . . . no," Lanna said quickly.

"She thinks you are going to suggest I work on my bust at the same time you work on the current masterpiece, Gideon," Llew said, laughing. "Unfortunately, Lanna, I have recreated you only from the neck up. And I do need you, desperately. I'm afraid I lost a little money at cards. That Devlin fellow. I should have known better, but I didn't believe he was as good as they said. I learned to my cost that he was."

"Lanna, dear heart . . . won't you sit for him, to please me?" Gideon asked. "I shall be present if you wish."

"So you don't trust me, Gideon. I am devastated," Llew said mockingly.

Lanna was saddened to see the pain in Gideon's eyes, and she spoke quickly, "Very well, Llew . . . how about tomorrow afternoon? Gideon is going to be busy with the arrangements for the auction on Saturday."

Lanna felt uneasy as she met Llew's eyes on her way out. They mocked her in much the same way Damon's had when they first met. It was a glance that held a thinly disguised challenge.

Teddie had warned her that bets were being placed in the clubs and gaming houses on who would be the first to melt the defenses of the "ice maiden." Now that she no longer lived with Gideon she was considered fair game. Since by his own admission Llew had gambling debts, he had even more reason to pursue her. How foolish she had been to agree to come to the studio when Gideon would be gone. Teddie, she thought, I shall ask Teddie to come along with me.

Stewards and servants did not remain long at Kingsburch. The house itself was isolated and had few visitors. Even when he was in residence, Sir Jared did not entertain. And the exotic Lady Indigo had been content to remain a recluse after Sir Jared had left. Old Geordie, the half-witted caretaker, was often confused by the changing faces of stewards and servants, and he rarely remembered their names. Lately, they noticed, he was acting more strangely than ever, shuffling about the halls of Kingsburch with a covered basket over his arm and appearing and disappearing out of thin air. The young kitchen maids were convinced that old Geordie was not flesh and blood but merely one of the spirits that haunted the king's fortress.

In the grip of winter, the house was as cold and damp as a subterranean cavern, and Indigo shivered in spite of being enveloped in petticoats and shawls. She was waiting in the secret room when Geordie returned with his passenger.

"You are foolish to stay in London so long," she said after dismissing Geordie. "Someone will find out who you are."

Damon stretched his arms and flexed his shoulders. "I swear that passage through the cliff gets smaller each time I crawl through it," he said reaching out to pull her into a friendly embrace. Instantly Indigo's arms went around his neck. She tried to kiss his lips but Damon turned his head so that she kissed his cold and unshaven cheek instead.

"Why are you so cold?" she demanded.

"Because, my sweet, it's freezing out there . . ."

"You know what I mean."

"Indigo, you're beautiful and desirable and you know I'd welcome the opportunity to cuckold Sir Jared. But perhaps I'm learning a little compassion at last. I know it would be wrong to make love to you."

"But why, Damon, why?"

"Because of what it would do to you emotionally. Women need to love with their minds as well as their bodies."

"You want me, Damon. I know you do."

"Indigo, why do you stay here? Why don't you move to London, meet some people, have some fun?"

"I stay here to wait for you. Why else?"

"I won't be coming back again. I've enough money now to buy passage back to the Bahamas and my flesh is healing."

"I believe that your manhood may have been burned along with your legs, Damon St. Clair. Why else would you not take what is offered to you?"

Damon laughed softly and settled down into the leather armchair. "I'll take you with me, if you want to go. But think carefully about it. Being Lady Malford could have many advantages. Especially after I make you a widow."

Indigo flung herself onto his lap, her fingers tracing the outline of his face, dropping to the buttons of his shirt and finding their way to bare flesh. He disengaged her hands gently and planted a kiss on the end of her nose.

"Let's be friends, Indigo. I am having Geordie take me back to the village in the morning. I only returned because I promised I would and I wanted to say goodbye."

"When will you leave the country?" she asked dully.

"A week or two. I have struck up an acquaintance with a man who may be able to tell me a little more about what happened to my father. He worked the press gangs years ago when my father was an Admiralty clerk. This man knew every captain and thug on the waterfront and I'm told if anyone knows what happened to my father, it is he.

It seems that right after my father was imprisoned, this man was sent to the penal colony in Australia. I'm told his sentence had some connection with the Admiralty scandal. Of course, he doesn't know who I am yet."

Indigo squirmed closer, letting her hand drop to Damon's breeches.

"You're not listening to me, Indigo. Come on now, get off my poor burned legs."

Her fingers had found their target and she laughed with triumph as she realized she had awakened the sleeping prince. "Let me see your scars, Damon . . . I've never seen your scars," she whispered huskily. "Is that why you won't make love to me, because you are afraid I shall be horrified at the sight of your scars?"

She slid from his lap to the floor, her fingers busy with his belt. At last, with a sigh, he stood up and allowed her to lay bare his scars.

The firelight flickered over the scar tissue that extended from halfway down his thighs to his feet.

She drew in her breath sharply, running her hands over the taut skin. "Ah, Damon . . . but the best part of you is not touched . . ." she said softly, and her fingers closed about his erect member as her lips parted and moved closer.

Harry Holmes furtively glanced down the rainswept street as he admitted Lanna. "She's not feeling well," he said. He jerked his head upward as he took her redingote. "In bed with the grippe, she is. I've sent 'er maid down to the apothecary to fetch 'er a draught."

"Oh dear, I'll go right up," Lanna said.

Harry twitched visibly. "She's asleep now. So don't wake 'er up. But you can stay with 'er until the maid comes back, if you will. I've got to meet a bloke. I was going to bring 'im back here, but what with Teddie not feeling well and all, maybe I'd better not. She'll be disappointed, she's been wanting to meet 'im. That Devlin they're all talking about."

"I have to go to Gideon's studio this afternoon, but I'll stay with her until then."

"She got your costume for you, for Saturday night," Harry said, his eyes racing about the hallway. "In the parlor it is, if you want to go and see it. Said to tell you Gideon made sure it was exactly the same as all the others."

"Yes, thank you, Harry."

"Right. I'll be off then. Tell 'er I'll be back tonight to look in on 'er."

In the parlor Lanna regarded her costume with dismay. She had suggested a gypsy costume, with yards of printed calico and a black wig to cover her hair . . . instead Gideon had chosen something from the Arabian Nights. Only the small veil which would cover the lower part of her face, and which was attached to an elaborate beaded helmet, was opaque. Her breasts would barely be covered by gold brocade. Floating veils would clearly reveal her bare midriff and the pantaloons, caught at the ankle with gold bands, would certainly show all of her legs. Even in an age of exhibitionism, the costume was daring in the extreme. No wonder Gideon had waited until the last minute to reveal it to her. The party would be held in two days, hardly enough time to devise another costume. "A slave girl," Lanna thought. "Oh, Gideon, this is unworthy of you."

Teddie was still asleep when the maid returned, and Lanna made her way to Gideon's studio and her appointment with Llewellyn Davis.

He had a huge fire roaring in the fireplace and the studio had been tidied up. Gideon's canvases were stacked neatly against the wall, except for the nude painting of Lanna, which stood on the easel. The bust Llew was working on stood on a table in the center of the room. He had placed a chair near the fireplace.

"You could have a glass of wine while I work, if you like," he said. A small smile hovered about his sensual lips, and there was a familiar gleam in his eyes. "Perhaps it will warm you and help you to relax."

"Thank you, but I'm perfectly relaxed. I can only stay a short time, so I suggest you get to work. I must hurry back to the bedside of a friend who is ill."

"Of course," Llew said, his smile widening.

Lanna sat beside the fire and he worked in silence. The only sounds in the room were the ticking of the clock and the splash of raindrops against the skylight.

Lanna sat motionless, staring into the fire. Neither of them knew exactly when Gideon would return, and for this reason Lanna did not worry too much about Llew making any unwelcome overtures. She was fairly certain that Llewellyn Davis lived on Gideon's charity and would not, therefore, do anything to jeopardize his status. She would have preferred to have Teddie along as a chaperone as she had planned, but it now seemed as if that precaution was unnecessary.

She jumped when she felt his hand on her shoulder and turned to see him standing beside her chair, eyes hooded, lips smiling. "You'd better stand up for a moment, Lanna my lovely, or your neck will become stiff," he said. She obeyed, uncomfortably aware of his nearness.

If only he didn't remind her so disturbingly of Damon. He was not quite as tall, but he had the same dark hair and eyes. Even his voice, sometimes caressing, sometimes vicious, was similar.

She stood mesmerized as he slowly reached for her and pulled her toward him. The throbbing kiss evoked memories of the past. His face blurred, became Damon's face. It was Damon sliding his hands over her body, finding her breasts, resurrecting forgotten feelings, bringing her body to life. He was pulling her down on the rug before the fireplace and she was yielding to his searching hands. Her eyes were closed when she heard the voice. "May God damn you both," Gideon said brokenly.

CHAPTER 25

"It was Teddie who got me the reprieve," Harry Holmes said. "I'd still be rotting down under if it weren't for 'er."

Damon pushed another tankard of ale across the table.

" 'Er friend the duke, it was actually. But she was the one who asked 'im. Not that I was above bending the law a bit, mind you. Got sick of bashing 'eads in and slinging poor buggers in longboats, I did. No one knew the river like old 'Arry though . . . or the men who came and went on it. In them days the French were thick, back and forth across the channel, what with their bloody revolution and all."

Harry blew the top from his ale and licked his lips. "So when this toff asks me who would be interested in buying some information . . . well, what did I care? Only then I finds out that some poor bastard is in the bleedin' Tower and I knows for a fact that the real culprit is still at large, 'cos I'd seen 'im 'anging around the docks. So I presents meself to the Admiralty, I does. I can't abide a man that lets another take 'is blame. Now, I was just going to warn 'im that 'e'd best do something about the fellow in the Tower, see. But next things I knows, I was on a boat with an 'atchful of convicts."

Harry Holmes slurped noisily on his tankard of ale, glanced furtively about the bar and drew his head deeper into his overcoat. "How did you 'ear of me anyway, guv?"

"I inquired among some of the older members of the

237

seamen's clubs. They told me that you know everything that's happened to sailors or ships in the last twenty years. I hadn't dared hope you would have firsthand knowledge of Sir Jared Malford and Richard Trelayne."

"Are you related to 'im, then?"

"Yes."

"Well, I don't want to know more than that. And I won't testify for you, guv. But I will tell you this . . . Teddie found out the whole story, after it was all over. Trelayne and his missus were dead and I was in Australia. See, it was all the woman's fault. It's always the woman, ain't it, guv?"

Damon felt a chill deep in his bones. "The woman?" he repeated.

"Trelayne's wife. Malford wanted Trelayne's wife. It weren't that 'e wanted to make money selling secrets . . . it was all a plot to get Trelayne out of the way so's Malford could have 'is wife. They was both clerks at the Admiralty, see. So Malford planned the whole thing so as Trelayne would be blamed. Only 'e didn't reckon on me. Thought when 'e paid me to keep me mouth shut, I'd do it. And I would of, too. If it had just been information 'e was selling. Only it was a man's life. 'Course, as it turned out, 'e killed both of them. I reckon 'e hadn't bargained on Trelayne's wife going to the Tower to 'elp 'er 'usband escape. So the whole thing was for nothing."

Harry's eyes probed the recesses of the inn and did not look into the stricken face of the man who sat across the table from him. Damon wanted him to stop speaking, but could not utter the word to stem the awful narrative. His mother . . . it had all been his mother's fault. Damn women, damn their treacherous, soulless bodies . . .

Damon began to drink, and continued drinking until Harry Holmes' Cockney voice no longer penetrated the fog of Damon's mind. But somewhere in his befuddled senses a question formed. Had Sir Jared Malford really loved Damon's mother . . . enough so that he could not bring himself to destroy the son of the woman he had loved? Was that why he was still alive? No matter. Malford had lusted after Trelayne's wife . . . now Trelayne's son was going to take Malford's wife away from him. Malford had not cared about losing an adopted daughter . . . Indigo would be a different matter. Damon knew only too well the persuasiveness of Indigo's embrace.

With his decision made, why then did Damon St. Clair's

238

drunken thoughts turn again and again to the party that would be held the next day?

Lanna shivered in the flimsy costume and avoided glancing at herself in the mirror as she wrapped her heaviest cloak about her shoulders. Gideon would hardly be likely to call for her, so she would have to go to the party by herself. She did not want to remember how he had looked when he had discovered her in Llew's arms, or the fawning excuses Llew had made, blaming Lanna for the incident. How could she have allowed Llewellyn Davis to kiss her that way . . . perhaps it was a blessing that Gideon had arrived at that moment, in time to stop something worse from taking place. Surely she would not have permitted it . . . ? It was that unexpected kiss, so disturbingly like Damon's.

When her maid announced the arrival of Mr. Gideon Lacey, Lanna was surprised. She hurried into the sitting room to meet him. His melancholy eyes regarded her without malice.

"I see you are ready, Lanna. Good. The carriage is waiting. I would like to be the first to arrive."

"Gideon . . ." Lanna began, but he silenced her with a quick gesture of his hand.

"Lanna . . . there is no need. I love you both too much not to forgive and forget a moment's temptation. Come now, and before you chastise me about that costume, let me tell you that I decided *all* of the ladies present will be so attired. The lights will be dimmed, so that it will be difficult to distinguish the color of your eyes above your veil . . . and speaking of lights, did you know they are installing the new gaslights?"

Grateful for his easy conversation, Lanna did not notice the tension in his delicate features, or the trembling of his hand as he took her arm.

The banquet room had been cleared for dancing and small tables encircled the perimeter of the floor. A dais had been set up for the orchestra at one end of the room. The portrait, covered by a white cloth, stood on a second platform at the other end.

Lanna was whirled onto the dance floor as soon as the orchestra began to play the first waltz. That dance was now sweeping England, despite the protestations of the dancing masters, who had kept the waltz out of England until 1811. Lanna had eaten little all day and the wine from

239

numerous festive toasts had quickly gone to her head. Her partner asked her playfully whether she could possibly be the mysterious model for the portrait, and whether she knew that Gideon proposed to wait until the stroke of midnight to uncover both picture and model.

Midnight . . . it seemed so far away . . . and in between there was more wine. Warm hands pressed against the bare skin of her back. Then all at once her mind was playing tricks on her and she was taken back to that night so long ago at Clearview plantation . . . Damon, appearing from nowhere to claim her . . . the dancing, and then the lovemaking. She had fought him and yet she had wanted him. The dark gods of the loins . . . who had said that? Why had the past become the present?

Just before midnight the lights were dimmed and the musicians played a fanfare as Gideon rose to stand before the portrait. There was a hush in the crowd, and several of the men surged toward the circle of light in which Gideon stood. Friends of Gideon had seen the portrait during its creation and the word had spread that it was his masterpiece. Everyone held their breath as he reached for the cord to release the covering cloth.

A sigh escaped as the portrait was revealed. The rumors had been correct. It was a masterpiece. The bone structure was exquisite, the lips were both sensual and vulnerable. It was the eyes, however, that were most arresting. They were the blue of a bottomless ocean and expressed both sorrow and hope. Pale gold hair streamed about the creamy shoulders and, except for the eyes, the picture had a delicate misty quality that suggested the model had been conjured up out of the artist's dreams.

An excited murmur broke out among the crowd as it pressed closer to the dais. Over and over again it was whispered that Gideon had to be in love with his model to paint such a portrait.

Lanna sat in a corner, behind the portrait. She closed her eyes and listened as the professional auctioneer called for an opening bid. The wine and dancing had made her head spin and she was limp from the strain of the last twenty-four hours. It was Gideon's triumph, she thought. She was not a part of it at all.

"Five hundred pounds . . ." the auctioneer was saying, "I have five hundred pounds . . ."

"One thousand pounds," a voice said and Lanna's heart stopped. She strained her eyes into the crowd. She must be mistaken. It was merely the shock of someone doubling the bid . . . one thousand pounds was a princely sum.

"Devlin," a voice whispered nearby. "That has to be Devlin. I'd know that voice anywhere. But what would he do with the portrait if he gets it? They say he lives in inns and rooming houses."

"Oh, I wish I were the model for that portrait," a girl sighed, "and that Devlin would buy it and sweep me off my feet." There was laughter and a chorus of agreement from ladies nearby.

Lanna cringed in her chair. She would be expected to dance with the purchaser of the portrait. In a moment it would be sold and she would be as much on display as her image on the canvas.

A sudden cheer went up. The picture was sold, and Gideon was calling to her to come forward.

A circle was cleared on the crowded floor and Gideon placed her hand into that of her partner.

"Mr. Devlin has bought your portrait, Lanna," Gideon said, and his voice sounded hollow. "Please be gentle, my friend."

Did Gideon ask him to be gentle with the portrait, or with me? Lanna thought as the hand drew her out onto the floor. He held her too tightly, pulled her too close. His costume was makeshift. A crude caricature of a pirate, red silk scarf tied buccaneer-style over his head, the black patch over one eye . . . tight leather breeches . . . and, oh, how dare he! She tried to pull away from the certain evidence that he was aroused by her.

"Sir . . ." she began.

"I picked you out of the crowd hours ago, Lanna," he said softly. "I'd know those breasts anywhere, and the way your lower back dimples . . . right here . . ."

She felt her knees buckle. He caught her to his chest and she knew from the churning of her blood and the sudden sharpening of her senses that it could only be he . . . the scent of him, the feel of him, the way their bodies melted together and became one.

There was a roar of approval from the watching crowd, and glasses were raised in a toast before the other couples moved out onto the floor to join them.

"Damon . . . where did you come from? How did you get here? Is it really you?" The words came in tight little gasps. She wanted to say that she had longed for this moment, prayed for it, been sick with fear and worry about his safety . . . been only half-alive all these months . . . that she loved him, desperately, wantonly . . . but the words did not come.

"Your lover painted you well," he was saying in an off-hand manner. "I hear that his future as a painter of royal portraits is assured because of this picture of you."

Her mind would not function, the shock of seeing him again, feeling him near her . . . and knowing he wanted her, no matter how cold his voice. He was waltzing her toward the doors. They were out of the banquet room now and he slipped his arm about her waist and led her down the corridor, up a flight of stairs to the darkened floor above. At the third door he stopped and produced a key.

"You wouldn't believe how much I paid for the use of this room," he said, holding the door for her.

"Am I dreaming?" she wondered as she stepped inside and turned to face him. "How did you get to England? Oh, Damon, won't you be caught and hanged as an enemy?"

"Don't get your hopes up yet," he said carelessly, unhooking the veil from her headdress and removing the patch from his eye.

"You must be cold in that costume." His eyes raked her body and he began to unbutton his own shirt.

"Damon . . . we must talk . . ." she began, but his arms went around her and his lips smothered the words while his hands caressed her in the old way, the new way.

They were naked upon the bed in the darkness. His mouth devoured her as she thrust herself toward him, wanting him to be inside her, never wanting him to be anywhere else. He buried his face in her breasts and she placed her hands on taut buttocks to draw him into her, running her fingers lightly around the flesh of his hips, touching his hardened member wonderingly. Then her whole being exploded with delight as they became one.

Time had no meaning. It ebbed and flowed in the rhythms of desire and fulfillment, of leisurely exploration and fevered demands. It was as though no one in the world had ever done these things before, felt these feelings, known this ecstasy. It could never end . . . and yet, it did.

She lay on the bed, not feeling the chill of the unheated room, but only the loss of his warmth as he suddenly arose. She could hear him fumbling in the darkness, stumbling against the bed and his boots.

242

"Damon . . ." she murmured, the warmth and scent of him still lingering within her.

"There is business to attend to before I sleep, my love," he said lightly.

"Damon . . . please don't go . . . can't it wait until morning?"

"My dear, you overestimate my capabilities. Even in your experienced hands, the well doth run dry eventually. I shall be back shortly, but I must go and see to the safety of my extravagant purchase. I paid a great deal of money for your portrait and I've left it untended long enough."

Lanna pulled the coverlet up over her nakedness. She heard the door close behind him and curled up to await his return. He was back, he had been returned to her . . . together they could go and find their son and all of her prayers would be answered. Her heart sang for joy and her eyelids drooped heavily as the first rays of dawn spread their cold light over the rooftops outside the window. She slept, contentedly, happily. Damon was back in her life where he belonged.

The hand that awakened her shook with urgency and fear. "Lanna, Lanna . . . wake up. Lanna—"

She opened her eyes and stared unbelievingly into the dark eyes of Llewellyn Davis.

"What—Llew! What are you doing here . . . where is Damon?" In her confused state, between sleep and wakefulness, she thought for one disoriented second that she had dreamed Damon's return.

"Devlin—the man called Devlin, who bought the portrait. He's going to kill Gideon. You must save him."

"Damon—Gideon? But why . . ." She was fighting to get free of the blanket, heedless of her nakedness, as Llewellyn's terror enveloped her.

"Here, I have your cloak. Come quickly, I must show you what happened."

"Llew . . . were you here all evening? . . . What happened? Why would Damon want to kill Gideon? . . ."

Her feet went into her slippers, the cloak was wrapped around her. "Where is Damon?"

Llew was opening the door to a deserted corridor. Icy drafts swept around them as they hurried toward the stairs.

"Gone. They're all gone . . . asked to leave after what happened . . . everyone was shouting and screaming. Those

243

who were left, anyway. Not many were. Most had gone home when he came bursting into the room. Before anyone realized what he had in mind . . ." Llew breathed heavily as he dragged her down the stairs and back to the empty banquet room.

The room looked stark in the grey light. Unwashed glasses stood on soiled tablecloths. Some chairs were overturned. Pieces of litter lay about the floor. Lanna's eyes swept the room.

"Gideon challenged him to a duel. *Gideon!* And gave him his choice of weapons . . . and he chose *foils*. It's well known that Devlin has been taking fencing lessons ever since he first appeared in London. It will be murder, Lanna. You must stop it. Gideon has never held a rapier in his life."

"But why . . . why?" Lanna asked numbly.

Llew turned her around and pointed. At the far end of the room the easel still stood on the dais, but Lanna's portrait had been slashed viciously until it was unrecognizable.

CHAPTER 26

He had been a fool to lose control, he knew that. She wasn't worth it. No woman was. Women were chattel . . . just as the law said. Would a man plunge himself into such a rage over his horse . . . his chair? A woman was worth no more. They were on the earth to give pleasure and to breed. Not to get inside a man's thoughts and mind.

He had wanted the portrait. It had not mattered then that the artist had obviously known her even better than he had known her himself. Indigo had not lied about them. She had lived with him, the artist. Lanna, his beautiful wife. She was just as faithless as his mother had been, as fickle as Indigo.

The artist and a few of his friends were still in the banquet room, discussing the portrait, when Damon had returned to claim it. They had been unaware of his presence as he had paused in the shadows to look again on what was without a doubt the most breathtaking picture he had ever seen.

"I still don't know how you can bear to part with it, old man," one of men had been saying. "Despite the large sum of money the Devlin fellow paid. I mean, good Lord, you surely don't need the money, do you? Isn't it true that you've more commissions from the royal family than you can handle?"

"Yes," the artist answered, walking slowly to the portrait

245

and looking up at it. "But I shall paint her again . . . another portrait like this. After I have finished the full-length work."

Damon could taste her on his lips. His blood still raced with need for her.

"Full length . . . clothed, I take it?"

"No. Nude," the artist said calmly, and Damon sprang toward him with a hoarse cry on his lips. The knife that had been added to the belt of the pirate's costume for effect was suddenly in his hand. And it was not the pale features of the artist with their great haunted eyes that Damon saw as he raised the knife. It was the dark blue eyes of his wife. Sad, innocent, alluring, mocking . . . He was slashing at her composure, purging his need of her with each thrust of the knife.

The rest was a blur. The artist, sagging in the arms of his companions, had called him out. He was to duel with that milksop at dawn tomorrow. They were to leave London because the Prince Regent frowned on duels, particularly those involving rapiers. In a moment of caustic wit, Damon had suggested that Kingsburch would be an ideal place for the duel. The ancestral home of the woman who had caused all the trouble.

He had not returned to the room where Lanna waited. She had gone there willingly, given herself freely, as she would have given herself to any man who had bought her portrait. That was what the auction was really about. The highest bidder owned not only the portrait, but the woman herself, at least for one night. Before she returned to Gideon to be painted in her nakedness.

As soon as it was light he was journeying back to Kingsburch. This time he would ride in boldly through the main entrance. It did not matter who saw him. If Sir Jared Malford had returned, that was even better. He would kill the artist and then kill Sir Jared. Then he would go back to war and kill as many Englishmen as he could. He had been hard put to keep silent all these weeks, when they talked about the war. They dismissed the Americans lightly. The war with the French was all that mattered. Napoleon Bonaparte. Many Englishmen did not even know the name of the American president. An unimportant skirmish, they said, forced on England dishonorably by the hotheads in the American government, not by the American people.

246

Damon's lust to kill grew stronger as he journeyed toward his wife's home.

The bitter winter was coming to an end. The promise of spring was in the sunshine that warmed the grey walls of Kingsburch and in the tiny white crocuses that pushed through the softening earth. Indigo was beginning to feel that it belonged to her, that it had always belonged to her. She had never had this feeling before, not in the house that Lucas Bassey had given her nor in the tiny house she had shared with Damon, Alain and Claudine. At times she would think to herself, "I must remember to show this to Alain . . ." before she remembered he was far away.

She loved to walk through the wide corridors, to stand in the great hall and imagine the feasting and merriment that had once taken place there. She could never hear enough of Geordie's stories of the old days. Although the royal family had never lived here, a favored subject was given tenancy from time to time and then the great hall had been used for banquets and balls. Sometimes Geordie would become vague, and forget what he was saying, but Indigo's imagination filled in his lapses of memory.

"When they thought of putting in the secret room," he said, "they thought they was making a hiding place . . . and a way for the Royalists to run away. Made the passage down to the beach, they did, so they could sneak out and be rowed to a boat in the harbor." The fishing village of Cromwell's day was rapidly growing into a seaport on the other side of the rocky bay, and ships of all sizes lay at anchor.

"They didn't realize that where you can get out, you can get in. The royal yacht came . . . long ago. Just like Mr. Devlin came." Geordie chuckled to himself. "Even *he* had to get down on his belly and crawl through. That was when he brought the master here." Georgie's eyes clouded.

"Sir Jared?" Indigo prompted. She was happy, knowing instinctively that Damon would return today. They had made love before he went to London, and although he had not been the exciting lover of her memory, she had known the joy of serving her own needs instead of those of a man she cared nothing about.

"Yes. Then soon they brought the baby girl. So pretty she was, like a little angel with a golden halo."

"You may go and bring more wood for the fire now, Geordie. And I shall take a bath this morning," Indigo said. "Tell the girl to heat water when you get back to the kitchen. Then you'd better get over to the village. I expect Mr. Devlin will be needing you to row him across as soon as it's dark."

"Yes, milady."

Indigo wondered fleetingly if it would be warm enough to wear one of her gauze gowns. She had heard the maids gossiping about the women in London who dampened their clothes before wearing them, in order to make them cling more cunningly to their curves.

Her glance drifted to the large oil painting that hung above the mantelpiece. It was a picture of a woman wearing sixteenth-century dress, a small child at her side. In the background were the towers of Kingsburch. The shadows cast by the fire seemed to bring the figures to life, giving the impression that they were walking along the cliffs. The woman had dark hair, almost as dark as Indigo's.

Indigo enjoyed seeing herself as mistress of Kingsburch. She loved the feeling of protection that the stout walls and the rocky cliffs gave her, and she dreaded having to leave. She hoped the war with America would last forever, since Sir Jared had agreed that she could stay in England until it was over.

A change had come over him since the loss of his ship. And Indigo wondered if the change had been brought about by their marriage. Before the ceremony he had been an ardent lover, even though his public manner was cold and disapproving. The moment they were married he began to have problems with impotence, and for a time Indigo feared she would have to deal with the same kind of horror Michael Danvers had inflicted upon her. But Sir Jared was too proud for failure of any sort. Rather than fail, he simply did not approach her. She wondered if he were secretly glad to leave her behind when he was ordered back to the Indies.

For all their physical strength, men worried about failure and rejection and how they compared to other men. Sir Jared had questioned her in detail not only about Lucas Bassey's prowess, but also about Damon's.

Damon . . . Indigo frowned suddenly. He was still able to excite her, fulfill her physically, but he was no longer the careless, arrogant, ruthless man she had loved. She wondered if it had been his coldness and ruthlessness that had captivated her. The old Damon had cared for no one but himself. But that man was gone forever. Even his love-

248

making had become gentler. And there were times when she wanted him to take her brutally, as in the old days. Preoccupied, she picked up a copper urn that stood on the mantelpiece, burnishing it with her fingers. She was still lost in thought when Geordie returned, breathless with excitement and fearful anticipation. "He's back, milady . . . he's coming in through the front entrance as bold as you please. Handing his hat to the butler . . . and the new steward's down there too. They've all seen him now, they have. They'll send word to the master and you'll be done for. Oh, milady, you must run away." Geordie rubbed his hands together in anguish. Indigo had been kind to him, almost as kind as the golden-haired lady used to be before she went away.

"What are you talking about? Calm down." She felt a little thrill of fear pass through her body. Surely Damon would not be so reckless as to come to Kingsburch in broad daylight? How could he be so foolish . . . after all the care they had taken to keep him hidden from everyone? What if someone did indeed send word to Sir Jared . . . what would happen to her? Suddenly she knew what she wanted. She wanted Kingsburch. It was the only thing in her life that had ever really mattered. Ancient stones and weathered wood could never betray her, could never point the finger of scorn and say she was not good enough . . . Damon was only a man and the world was full of men. There was only one Kingsburch.

He burst in through her bedroom door and she spun around to face him, eyes blazing with fury.

"You fool! You've spoiled everything!" she shrieked.

Teddie's eyes were tired, and it was difficult to see Lanna through the fog. The pain that had tormented her for so many days had left her weakened, and now she no longer tried to writhe away from it. The draught from the apothecary had helped. She was drinking more and more of it, and it had almost the same effect as her hot toddies. Only it made her mind play tricks on her. She was young again and the prettiest girl in all of London. The king himself had sent for her and warned her that she must not let the duke forget his obligations . . . Poor mad king, but he had not been mad then . . . She had been fond of the duke, of course, he had been kind to her. But now in the twilight she remembered her true love . . . the brave young hussar who had given her a child and ridden off to die in battle.

249

"Wait for me, Teddie, and we'll be married when I return . . ." he had said. She had known at the very instant it happened that she would bear his child. Ah, he was so young, so dashing in his uniform . . . golden hair shining . . . deep blue eyes alight with love.

"Teddie, can you hear me . . . are you asleep?" Lanna whispered. "I have to go away for a time . . . to Kingsburch. But I'll be back in a few days, I promise. Please try to get well, Teddie . . . please. Harry has promised he will stay with you. Can you drink some more of your medicine? Teddie, I've sent for a physician. He'll be here soon. So many people were ill this year, because the winter has been so hard. Sleep now, Teddie . . ."

Teddie smiled. She saw the golden hair and blue eyes of her hussar. He was waiting for her, somewhere in the mist.

Lanna patted Teddie's limp hand, biting her lip to keep her tears in check. Teddie looked so frighteningly ill, reminding Lanna of Beth when she had been in the throes of death. She hated to leave, but she had to stop Gideon from committing suicide. He and Llew were already on their way to Kingsburch, and Lanna had lost precious time by stopping to see Teddie.

Lost in despair, Lanna went silently down to the waiting carriage. First Beth . . . now Teddie. Would it be Gideon tomorrow? No, she must think of other things. She turned her attention to the scene outside the carriage window. Was it her own desolation that made the streets of London seem ominous today? Had the faces regarding the barefoot beggar children always been so unconcerned?

She was glad when the city streets were left behind. She feasted her eyes on the beautiful English countryside. There were huge elms, great oaks, ash, chestnut trees . . . standing in meadows that would soon be yellow with buttercups. Even the great landscape artists Gideon so admired did not do full justice to its magnificence. Gainsborough, Morland, Farington, Turner . . . what was happening to Gideon?

The fragile sunlight was gone by the time she reached Kingsburch, and the house was as menacingly grey as she remembered it. Shivering, Lanna alighted from the carriage, remembering the warmth of Charleston. She had been more at home there than she had ever felt in this great house.

Indigo was waiting in the hall herself when the butler took Lanna's redingote and hat. Geordie was hovering in the background, wringing his hands and muttering to himself. Lanna smiled at him as she went forward to meet Indigo.

"Welcome home, Lanna," Indigo said. Her voice was timid, less assured than Lanna remembered. There was a difference in her eyes too.

"You've done wonders here, Indigo," Lanna said, glancing about. "The house has never looked warmer or more inviting." It was true, she realized, as she followed Indigo to the drawing room. Indigo had crackling fires burning brightly in all the grates, and vases had been filled with evergreens. Every piece of brass and metal in the house glowed, and the wooden floor of the drawing room had been recently treated to a coat of beeswax.

"Are they here?" Lanna asked as Indigo closed the drawing room door.

"Yes. I gave them rooms in different parts of the house. They have not met since they arrived. What are we going to do?"

Lanna sat down near the fire. We, she thought. Yes, it would be up to her and Indigo to stop this madness. How strange that they should have a common goal. She glanced toward the woman Damon had preferred over her and tried to quell her jealousy.

"I don't know. I tried to talk to Gideon, but he wouldn't listen." Lanna did not add that she had not been able to talk to Damon at all.

"Perhaps," Indigo said, "the man Davis, who came with your Gideon, will be able to stop it? He told me to keep them apart, that if we were able to keep them apart long enough, he might have a plan."

"Llew? Yes, I suppose in his own way it matters a great deal to him what happens to Gideon."

"Shall I send for wine or food . . . ?" Indigo asked. Lanna shook her head, and Indigo went on quickly. "I know I shouldn't have stayed on here, Lanna . . . Sir Jared told me that this spring the estate would become yours. I hope you don't mind . . ."

"No, I don't mind," Lanna said. *Keep the house, give me back my husband*, she thought miserably.

"What arrangements have been made . . . about the duel?"

"Tomorrow at dawn. Davis and the steward and two of the footmen are to act as seconds," Indigo said. "After it's over . . . do you want me to leave the house?"

Lanna glanced at her sharply. Surely she was not more

concerned about the house than the possible murder of a man she was supposed to care about? She drew a deep breath and said, "I would like to go to my husband's room now." *Damon, I am going to fight for you. Somewhere the man who came to me in the swamp and delivered his son is still waiting . . .*

Indigo stared at her for a long moment, but Lanna's dark blue eyes did not waver. "Yes," Indigo said, "of course."

Following Geordie up the wide oak staircase, Lanna tried to think what she would say to Damon, tried to imagine what it would be like to confront him in this setting. She had always faced him on his ground . . . aboard his ship, in his house in Charleston . . . even the plantations were more his milieu than hers. And yes . . . the party when her portrait was auctioned, even there, Damon had dominated the scene. No doubt his raw masculine power would control here as well.

He was standing at the window, looking out over the sea, when she entered. Black clouds were racing in over the horizon, and white caps were forming in the bay waters. As he watched, raindrops started spattering against the glass.

"Damon . . ." Lanna said. He turned to face her, dark eyes opaque.

"So we meet at last under your roof, my lady wife," he said. "You will forgive me if I don't sweep you into my arms and . . . allow my passion to carry us away. I'm afraid I'm not feeling very romantic."

"Please, Damon. Don't . . ."

"If you came to plead with me to spare your lover, you can save your breath," he said, turning back to the window.

"He wasn't my lover, Damon."

"Oh, for God's sake . . . don't lie, Lanna. There have already been enough lies between us."

She went to his side and laid her hand on his arm, hoping the touch would convey to him what her words did not. "I'm not lying. Gideon is a dear friend and I don't want to see him hurt, but he was never my lover."

"I am to believe that you lived with him, but he was never your lover. And that you came here merely to save the life of an old friend. You must think me very gullible."

"I came here because it's your life I'm worried about, Damon, even more than Gideon's. You are in danger every

252

moment you are in this country, you know that. No matter what happens tomorrow, you are calling attention to yourself. Someone is going to wonder about you and ask questions . . . what if someone finds out you are actually an American prisoner of war?"

He turned and looked at her for a moment, his eyes probing hers. Then he shook his arm free of her grip. "You're wasting your time, Lanna. I will make a concession, if you wish. Your friend may use pistols instead of foils if you think that will give him a better chance. I took the precaution of bringing a pair along. But since we have this moment together, there is something you can tell me."

"Yes—anything, what is it?" Lanna asked eagerly.

"Where have you hidden our son?"

"He and Zenobia are in New Orleans. The ship they were on was captured by privateers."

"Good. I shall be heading in that direction as soon as my business here is finished. One of the prisoners I met in Bermuda told me Alain was aboard a ship in Gulf waters."

"Then he made good his escape? Oh, I'm so glad."

"You knew he had escaped?"

For an instant a picture of the stockade flashed into her mind and in it was the grinning face of Bloody Murdoch. She shuddered, and her hand went to the hollow of her throat in a protective gesture.

"Tell me, have you visited your artist and apprised him of your presence yet? Please don't let me detain you here. I shan't want for company during the long night, you know. Just as you have your artist, I have Sir Jared's wife to warm my bed."

Her composure cracked. Anger and sorrow battled briefly in her breast. Then she was beating on his chest with her fists, screaming the curses she remembered from the waterfront.

Then all at once she was not trying to hit and scratch and hurt. Her arms went around his neck. His were hard about her back and their mouths were meeting hungrily.

"Damn you . . ." he whispered savagely, but he could not stop kissing her, and she had learned only too well where and how to caress him. He had taught her about the dark gods of the loins. He picked her up and carried her to the bed.

When the maid knocked at their door to announce she had a tray with their dinner, they sent her away. Once he whispered to her, "This isn't solving anything . . . isn't

253

changing anything. You know that . . . this is a spell you cast, and I'll find a way to break it."

But she closed his mouth with her lips and said the words wonderingly, "Damon, I love you." He ached to believe it was so, even though he knew it could not be.

She had fallen asleep in his arms and the fire's embers were dying when their door burst open. Indigo came running into the room.

"Damon—Damon . . . get up, you must go. Now, this minute," she cried.

"What is it? What's happened?" He placed Lanna's head gently on the pillow and swung his legs over the side of the bed.

"Runners . . . they came for you. They think you are a Frenchman—they believe you are a spy. They are downstairs waiting. Oh, Damon, Damon . . . I pretended to be shocked and said I would get you, so your wife wouldn't be frightened."

Damon was pulling on his breeches and Lanna stirred, reaching out for him in the bed. He looked down at her and gave a short laugh. "Congratulations, my lady wife. Another round goes to you . . . perhaps. But you haven't won yet."

"Damon, hurry. Geordie is waiting in the secret room. The sea is rough, but he says he can get you to a ship in the harbor. But we have only minutes . . . I will go down and tell them you are dressing, keep them as long as I can."

She flung his coat about his shoulders and then pulled his face to hers to kiss him before turning to race from the room.

Lanna sat up, not believing what she saw. Indigo and Damon . . . a nightmare, surely. She did not have time to call his name before he plunged through the door and disappeared.

CHAPTER 27

In France, the British cavalry was riding to Boulogne and Calais, quaffing champagne and feasting their eyes on countryside unravaged by war. The infantry marched to Bordeaux to await transportation to England . . . or to America. The small matter of the American war had still to be settled, but for the moment the English soldier could luxuriate in victory and peace. Europe was no longer under the heel of the tyrant, and Frenchmen as well as Englishmen rejoiced. But it would be weeks before news of the victory reached the remote house on the rocky English cliffs.

On the morning the duel was to have taken place, two men and two women met for breakfast.

"You are sure he reached a ship?" Lanna asked for the third time.

"Geordie saw him climb into a ship that sailed today for Portugal. He's safe," Indigo said again.

"You understand why I had to do it, Lanna . . . I had to save Gideon," Llewellyn Davis said. "Nothing else mattered." His dark eyes sought Gideon's ʾvacant stare, wanting approval. "I tried to get the Watch in London to stop him. In desperation I sent word to the village that a spy had forced his way in here." He looked about the small group, as though expecting congratulations on his cleverness. "Told them he was a Frenchman. Lanna, I had no idea he meant anything at all to you. I simply wanted to save Gideon. Gideon is . . ."

255

"Llew," Gideon said tiredly, "please let the matter rest. Lanna, what are you going to do now?"

"I shall return to London first. Teddie is so ill. After that . . ." *After that I shall find my way to New Orleans and my son*—that was all that mattered now. Damon believed she had betrayed him. Even the most selfless love could not survive such mistrust. Lanna reached across the table and touched Gideon's hand. It was ice cold.

"I'm sorry about the portrait, Gideon. I must have made him angry. We seem to do that to each other every time we meet. I suppose I am lucky it was not my flesh he was cutting. Oddly enough, I know how he felt. I have felt the same about him. I've wanted to tear his heart from his living flesh . . . I love him and yet I hate him. A strange madness overcomes both of us, as though we were two incompatible elements."

Indigo watched closely the expressions on the faces of the others, but she did not speak. She was wondering if she should have told Damon who betrayed him. If she had, perhaps he would have taken his wife with him, and Kingsburch would have been hers again. But then, it would only have been her domain briefly. Soon it would belong to Damon's wife. As Damon belonged to her.

"A love-hate relationship is not uncommon, Lanna, dear heart," Gideon was saying with a ghost of a smile as his mournful glance touched Llew briefly.

Llewellyn smiled back at Gideon, relieved to be back in his good graces. Then he turned his attention to the woman with the magnificent mane of blue-black hair. She was a bird of rare and exotic plumage. And her husband abroad somewhere. There was a faint scent of musk about her, and she had a way of looking at him from beneath half-closed eyes.

"Have you noticed, Gideon," Llew said, "that the light here is extraordinary? Perhaps the closeness of the sea . . . and I was just thinking, . . . perhaps we should not be too hasty in returning to London. For one thing, everyone is expecting you to have fought Devlin. And then too, think of Lanna . . . if you return with word that Devlin was her husband and an American prisoner of war . . . well, you won't be doing anyone any good. If Lanna . . . and Lady Indigo . . . don't mind, we could stay here for a while. Perhaps you could even do some painting. I would certainly like to make some sketches for a bust of Lady Indigo." His face was a study of bland innocence.

256

"You are certainly welcome to stay as far as I'm concerned," Indigo said. "But of course, the house belongs to Lanna."

"Yes, stay, Gideon. I believe it would be a good idea," Lanna said. "And Indigo, you can certainly remain here as long as you wish. I shall not be coming back to Kingsburch. I'm afraid I was never very happy here. Perhaps when it becomes mine I could appoint you as steward, Indigo . . . if you want me to. At least until you rejoin Sir Jared."

Indigo's heart leaped, and for an instant she wanted to embrace the Englishwoman. Llewellyn Davis saw the glow in her amber eyes and his moist lips parted. Gideon looked from one to the other with stricken eyes.

It was June and the people of London were exulting in their hardwon victory. The British army was invincible. All that had gone before—defeats, betrayals, the collaboration of allies with the enemy—all was forgotten in this glorious moment of triumph. And now the Russian Czar was coming to London . . . and the King of Prussia . . . surely London was the most exciting city in the world on this day.

Lanna washed Teddie's sunken, emaciated face and gently pushed back the wisps of greying hair. The physician had exhausted his skills. His potions and leeches no longer helped. He had finally announced that she was simply dying of old age. Teddie was forty-two.

"She's asleep, is she, Lanna?" Harry Holmes' hoarse whisper came from behind the screen Lanna had placed around the bed to ensure privacy when she bathed Teddie's wasted body.

Lanna pulled the sheet over the inert figure and went around the screen.

"Yes, she's sleeping again. She isn't in any pain now . . . at least I don't think so. Sometimes she speaks to me, but I don't think she knows me any more. Oh, Harry, I want to stay and take care of her, but the time is slipping away from me. I'm afraid I shall lose my son forever if I don't go to find him soon."

"Nah . . . Lanna, you can't go back to America now. But don't you worry, the war is over. Good as, anyway, now Boney's finished."

"What will happen . . . to the Americans? I heard the

257

French are just as overjoyed as we are that the war is over. Will it be the same with the Americans?"

" 'Course it will. Cor', you should see the crowds in the streets today. Been pouring in since dawn, they 'ave. There's coaches and carts all the way to St. James' and wooden stands on the street corners. Everyone waiting for the Czar and all the royalty to arrive."

"Yes. The maid was telling me she couldn't get through the crowds to the apothecary. She said every coach from Kent is being set upon by happy mobs, that the people plan to unhorse the royal coaches and drag them in triumph over London Bridge."

"The Prince Regent sent 'is postilions, but they didn't do no good. Londoners ain't going to be done out of this celebration. They've waited for it too long. Shouldn't wonder if they even gave the Regent a cheer instead of an 'iss today†"

"I thought perhaps Gideon and Llew would return for the celebrations. I haven't heard from Kingsburch for weeks. Of course, it's a tiresome journey. Do the crowds really hiss the Regent? I thought that was one of Byron's wild stories."

"Oh, they 'iss 'im all right. Every chance they get. Fat bastard. I 'eard a funny rhyme made up by Charles Lamb the other day:

> "By 'is bulk and by 'is size,
> By 'is oily qualities,
> This (or else my eyesight fails)
> This should be the Prince of *Whales*."

Lanna smiled. The Prince Regent's great backside was becoming legendary.

"Will you stay and dine with me, Harry? Or do you want to join the throngs in the street?" She did not add that she had a feeling of dread, and did not want to be alone today.

As their lust for one another grew, Llew and Indigo had not bothered to conceal their affair from Gideon. Gideon, his haunted eyes fixed on the easel he'd set up on the cliff, doggedly painted a seascape that he knew was bad. But it kept him out of the house, away from their hot glances and the reek of their lovemaking.

258

When Gideon pressed Llew to return to London, he said lightly, "Why don't you go back, old boy? Things will have blown over by now and you can finish the nude of Lanna."

"Come with me, Llew . . . please come with me."

"Not now, Gideon. I'm not ready to leave yet."

"What if her husband returns, Llew? You saved me from Lanna's husband . . . let me save you from Sir Jared. Come back to London, you can stay at the studio with me again. I will support you. Llew, please. She is destroying you. You haven't worked since we came here."

"And you, Gideon . . . you call that work? I'm tired of you, Gideon. Go back to London and leave me alone." His dark eyes moved over Gideon's shoulder as Indigo came silently upon them.

She frowned slightly when she saw Gideon, then tossed her curtain of hair back over her shoulder as she looked at Llewellyn Davis. As always, she was struck with his resemblance to Damon . . . the old Damon, before he became civilized. Llew Davis was as selfish and arrogant as Damon had once been, and there was a cunning and trickery about him that appealed to her. Indigo knew only too well the necessity for cunning and trickery in an unfair world. With Llew Davis, Indigo did not feel unworthy. If she was the devil's handmaiden, then he was the devil. As Damon had once been. The hungry dark eyes, the black hair, the kiss with its vital force . . . and his hands, those sculptor's hands. Firm, strong, demanding . . .

She felt a quickening of the senses and a familiar ache began inside her. She moved to Llew's side and pressed herself against him. Almost casually, Llew's hand slid around her waist and upward to cup her breast. He stood there, fondling her, as Gideon watched miserably.

"Gideon is leaving us, Indigo," Llew said. "He's decided to go back to London and Lanna." His fingers hooked the thin material of her bodice and slid it downward to reveal a dark nipple that was already hard to his touch.

"We must have a farewell dinner for him, then," Indigo said, breathing rapidly. How she loathed the white-faced painter. He had corrupted Llew, she knew that. The night Lanna had left Kingsburch, Indigo had paused outside Gideon's door and heard a little of what was taking place inside. It had been a pleasure to save Llew from the clutches of such a man . . .

259

"Yes," Llew said lazily, "that would be nice. Shall we go and discuss it now?"

Gideon did not move or speak. He stared at Llew in mute appeal as Indigo let her hand drop to the tightly fitted breeches that clearly revealed Llew's arousal.

Gideon remained where he was until they left, clinging to each other and whispering huskily. Then he moved heavily to the door and along the stone-flagged hall.

The summer sunlight spilled into the great hall as he pushed open the doors and crossed the courtyard. He walked slowly, feeling the warmth of the sun, hearing the distant cry of wheeling gulls. The turf along the clifftop was springy beneath his feet, and it smelled sweetly of rebirth. At the top of the cliff he stood before the panorama of the deep blue sea and mirror-still sky. Far below, the water cascaded against the rocks and splashed into glittering fountains. For a moment he looked down at the moving, beckoning spires of water. Then he stepped over the edge and entered the glass cathedral of water and hewn rock.

Teddie had roused herself early, refused the physician's draught and asked fretfully for Lanna. Harry and the maid had tried to soothe her, but Teddie had been adamant. She wanted Lanna. She must talk with Lanna. They were to go and bring her, otherwise she would not eat or drink or speak to them again.

At last Harry motioned for the maid to step out of the sickroom. "I'll go and see if she'll come," he whispered, flinging a glance over his shoulder. "You stay with 'er."

It had been three days since Lanna had seen Teddie, three days since she had received word of Gideon's death. For seventy-two hours she had sat in her room with the curtains drawn, and her maid's efforts to get her to eat or drink had mostly been in vain.

Harry tore down the curtains in his haste to bring light into the room. Then his eyes rested on Lanna, who was lying motionless on her bed.

"Now you listen to me, milady. You're going to get up and go to Teddie. She needs you." He stood beside her bed, glaring at her.

"Oh, Harry . . . if I go to her she'll die. Everyone I love dies," Lanna said, turning her face from him.

"Sooner or later, everybody dies. Now get up, Lanna."

"I can't, Harry. I can't go to her. If Teddie dies I won't

260

be able to bear it. I killed Beth and I killed Gideon. I'm afraid my husband and my son may be dead too. My mother and my father . . . everyone is dead."

Recognizing the rising hysteria in her voice, Harry bent down and pulled her roughly into a sitting position.

"Your mother is still alive, girl. And you'd better bloody well go to 'er or I'm going to break your neck." She shook her head, trying to recover her senses.

"Wh-wh-what do you mean?" she gasped.

"Teddie is your mother, that's what I mean."

"Teddie . . . but . . . but . . ."

"She never wanted you to know. She thought she weren't good enough for you. Well, let me tell you, nobody in the world is better than my Teddie . . . she never 'ad a wicked thought in 'er 'ead for nobody, not even them that 'urt 'er. She'd 'ave been rich . . . years ago . . . if she 'adn't given away every farthing she 'ad. Every beggar and thief knew where to go for a soft 'eart and a fast shilling. Broke 'er 'eart it did, to give you up. But she wanted you to be a lady . . . a lady . . . there ain't nobody more of a lady than my Teddie . . ."

Lanna looked up in disbelief as Harry's burly shoulders began to shake and his voice dissolved into deep wracking sobs.

She stood up awkwardly and reached out toward him.

He rubbed his fist over his eyes and nose furiously, shriveling her with his glare. "And you . . . you . . . with all your talk of death. Maybe it's your own death that frightens you. You ever stop to think that? That it reminds you that you're going to die yourself some day? Well, Teddie ain't afraid to die, because she weren't afraid to live. And that artist friend of yours killed 'isself, so 'is death don't count. But my Teddie is going to die 'appy, and you'd better get dressed and come with me."

Lanna splashed water over her eyes and her fingers shook as she replaced the pitcher on the marble wash stand. She went to the wardrobe and reached for a dress. Was he right? Was it only self-pity she felt? Was it fear of her own mortality that made her withdraw into herself? And was it really true that Teddie was her mother?

Teddie's maid was crying softly in the hall when they returned. Lanna ran up the stairs with Harry at her heels, not wanting to lose another moment. The physician was at the bedside. Harry shoved him aside and pushed Lanna toward Teddie's searching eyes and barely moving lips.

"Lanna . . . promise me . . . you won't be sad." Lanna's hand closed over limp fingers and squeezed gently. She did not dare speak. She bent her head closer and with great effort Teddie raised her hand to touch the pale gold hair.

"Find . . . the man you love . . . tell him . . . you love him. Love makes everything all right . . . Even the bad things that went before . . ."

"Mother . . . Mother . . ." Lanna whispered the word.

"Oh, no, lovey . . . your Mum was a lady . . . not a common baggage . . . like me." Teddie sighed and a small frothy bubble appeared at the corner of her mouth. Her eyes gazed vacantly at a point somewhere over Lanna's head.

"He was so brave . . . so young and so brave . . ." A slow smile spread over her face and in the instant that was left to her, Teddie Digby's face was transformed into radiant beauty. A royal duke had defied his family for her and a young hussar had ridden into battle, his heart bursting with love for her.

It was all over. Gideon's body had been recovered and claimed by his family. Indigo looked at the sobbing Llewellyn Davis as if seeing him for the first time. He was not like Damon at all, she thought in amazement. How could she ever have imagined a resemblance?

If he had not announced immediately that he was returning to London, Indigo would have ordered him from Kingsburch. Indigo knew that he didn't feel any real sadness for what had happened to his friend. What Llew Davis feared was some kind of divine retribution. Over and over he had screamed that she was a witch, a temptress who had bewitched him and come between him and the man who was everything to him.

Indigo looked at him coldly and realized for the first time that she had indeed been using him. She had used him as a substitute for Damon. She did not even particularly like Llewellyn Davis. His physical resemblance to Damon and his skillful lovemaking had attracted her. The only words they spoke were words of passion. They shared nothing of each other's thoughts or dreams.

As Indigo pondered this knowledge, she thought that the same had been true of Damon . . . and even Sir Jared and Lucas Bassey. There had been only one man in Indigo's life who had provided companionship, friendship, one man with whom she had been able to talk and live simply and naturally. It had been so long ago. While she waited fearfully to hear whether Lanna St. Clair would send her away from Kingsburch because of Gideon's death, Indigo wished that she could place her head on Alain L'Herreaux's broad and comforting shoulder.

After Llewellyn Davis departed, a letter came from Lanna St. Clair, saying again that Indigo was to consider Kingsburch her home for as long as she pleased. Lanna made it very clear that she would never return to live there herself. Indeed, if Sir Jared and Indigo wished, she would sign any necessary documents transferring the estate to them.

Lanna St. Clair intended to make her home in the land of her husband and son. She intended to let no one come between her and the man, child and country she loved. Indigo read the letter and accepted it as a statement of fact. She understood. In a way she and Lanna were very much alike.

Indigo allowed her imagination to run away with her for a moment. She contemplated a future without Damon, but within the safe stout walls of Kingsburch. Yes, Indigo would settle for that gladly . . . and some day she would find a way to have Alain L'Herreaux join her there. Damon . . . Sir Jared . . . Lucas . . . Llew . . . they represented the union of the flesh only, but Alain . . . ah, sad sweet Alain, with the face of a saint and the gentle sensitivity that had meant more to her than any passionate embrace, had she only been wise enough to see it. Besides . . . it was possible that Alain might surpass all of them when it came to lovemaking. He was, after all, a Frenchman. Indigo smiled. Like Lanna St. Clair, she knew which man and which country she wanted. Now all she had to do was decide how this could be brought about.

For three weeks the Czar and his companions toured London, riding the ancient streets of Westminster, stopping at the Tower where the strange English exhibited their king's jewels, visiting the British Museum beside the Bloosbury fields, pausing at shop windows filled with silver and glassware and silks and china.

The citizens of London caught glimpses of the Muscovite threading his way along their cobblestoned streets. He had a smile for the men in tall hats and neat broadcloth, for the elegantly gowned women carrying their shopping baskets, the workmen in aprons and leather jackets, and the children bowling their hoops.

By the time the Czar's visit came to an end, Teddie had been laid to rest, and Lanna was on her way to New Orleans by way of the Indies.

At the same time representatives were being chosen to mediate the American conflict. Diplomats from both countries were to meet and decide upon terms for peace at a place in Belgium called Ghent.

Ghent was a vast distance from New Orleans and word of the peace made there would not reach New Orleans in time.

CHAPTER 28

In Bermuda her ship stopped briefly amid a fleet of troopships at anchor. They were awaiting orders to invade the American continent, she was told. These were bad times for a young woman to be traveling alone. The warnings were politely received with a slight squaring of the shoulders and a calm glance from deep blue eyes. Admonishment about danger only served to make her more determined to continue her journey.

Lanna was on the high seas when British troops marched into Washington and put the torch to all of the public buildings, as well as many private ones. Panic and desperation swept the streets before the advancing redcoats.

In the south, however, a general named Andrew Jackson was wreaking havoc with England's Indian allies, despite lack of orders or supplies from Washington. Meanwhile, in New Orleans two old friends were meeting again.

Alain's eyes misted with tears as his long arms embraced Damon in a bonecrushing greeting.

"Ah, *mon frère*, I thought never to see you again." The sob in his voice was unashamed, and he pushed Damon away to search his friend's face for signs of change.

"Alain, you old pirate, I'd given you up for lost too. Thought by now you'd be hanged at least, drawn and quartered too, probably." They both roared with laughter to hide their emotion and, pounding each other on the back, elbowed their way to the bar. Alain thumped the wet wood until every tankard rattled, and the barman moved quickly to fill their glasses.

"How did you find me? Where have you been? Ah, *mon frère, mon frère* . . . I have missed you."

"As soon as I heard of the Baratarians, I knew you'd be one of them. Although they kept directing me to Dominique You . . . who, I understand, is about your height but wider and more villainous looking than you are."

Alain grinned. "Alexandre . . . the one who goes by the name Dominique You . . . he has powder burns on his face and the nose of a hawk. He look ferocious, not handsome like me!"

"The younger brother is your leader though—Jean Laffite?"

Alain's face lit up with unabashed admiration. "Ah, *mon ami,* that Jean Laffite is a rare one. You would not believe some of the things I could tell you. And not just his exploits with the ladies . . . although, *mon Dieu* . . . in that regard . . ." Alain coughed suggestively and then added, "Did you know that the Governor of Louisiana offered a five-hundred-dollar reward for Laffite, and the next day Laffite offered a five-*thousand*-dollar reward for the governor?" Alain laughed, slapping the bar with glee.

Damon laughed with him. There were many such stories about the buccaneer whose men ruled the bayous from their headquarters on Barataria Bay. They plundered vessels at will, marketing their booty in New Orleans. That Laffite was a flamboyant character, an expert duelist, and had a wry sense of humor Damon already knew. He also knew that the buccaneers' most profitable cargoes were human. Slaves for the plantations were in short supply since legal importation had been abolished.

"What is he really like, Alain? And how many men does he have?"

"*Mon ami,* first you had better tell me why you ask these questions. I am one of his men, do not ask me to be disloyal for the sake of our friendship. Did you seek me out for friendship's sake . . . or to ask me to betray my leader? Forgive me, but I must ask you this. You are an American, Damon. And here in New Orleans the Americans and the Creoles are in different camps."

"But your leader, Jean Laffite, professes to want to save New Orleans from the English?"

"And the American governor refuses his help and tries to drive us out of Barataria. And would succeed were it

266

not for all the friends we have in New Orleans. Jean's brother, Pierre, is slowly dying in chains in an American jail. *Non, mon ami,* not even for our boyhood together will I tell you anything that might harm Jean Laffite."

"Alain, I came to New Orleans to find my son. That's my main interest in Laffite. The child and his nurse were on a ship Laffite took as a prize. After I find my son, I will offer my services to your pirate chief. I understand his men grow more wealthy every day, and that the treasure now comes from British ships as well as Spanish. You know I have experience as a privateer . . . and a liking for easy money."

Alain regarded his friend for a moment. A small voice in the back of his mind warned him that Damon was not being entirely truthful. "Damon, most of Laffite's men are French. Sometimes the crews of ships we take will join us. But the elite . . . the men closest to Jean are French. I don't know . . . maybe you were always a buccaneer at heart, but, *mon ami,* you are not the kind of man who likes to take orders. I fear you would find it hard to be less than you were on the *Woman.*"

Damon picked up a bottle of whiskey and motioned for Alain to follow him to a secluded corner of the tavern. "Alain, old friend," he said as they were seated. "I have served as an ordinary seaman . . . been tied to the capstan wheel and flogged . . . chained in the brig . . . I no longer act from pride or arrogance." Briefly he told Alain of his life aboard the *Grey Wren.*

Alain watched Damon's face closely throughout the recital and at last he nodded, satisfied. "Besides, I have French blood," Damon said. "My mother was half-French. And I still use Claudine's name . . . St. Clair. Let me at least have a chance to prove my worth to Laffite. You're right that I don't want to serve aboard a Navy ship, and we don't have a ship of our own any more. But I'll take orders, Alain, I promise. At least help me find out what became of Zenobia and my son. I learned they were on a ship called the *Jamaica Star.*"

Alain shifted uncomfortably in his seat. "Damon . . . the woman, Zenobia . . . she was black, a slave. I do not know exactly what happened to her, but I can guess. There is a never ending market for slaves, indeed it is Jean's most profitable cargo. He has a *chênière* he calls the Temple, where slave auctions are held. He announces them in New Orleans and the planters come to bid. If the wom-

267

an Zenobia was on a captured ship, that is probably where she would have been taken."

"A *chênière?*"

"On an island . . . in the swamp. Built, I think, by Indians years ago. I can take you there, the location is no secret. Perhaps we can learn something about the woman."

"But the child . . . what would have become of the child?"

Alain's hands closed reassuringly over Damon's. "Do not worry, old friend, Laffite is not a monster who eats little babies. The ship *Jamaica Star* was taken before I joined him . . . I do not know. But tomorrow we go to the Temple and maybe . . . maybe I take you to Grande Terre."

Damon's eyes gleamed. He did not have to be told that Grande Terre was the island home of Jean Laffite.

The young prostitute had been sent to the seedy waterfront hotel with instructions to go to the room of an Englishman registered under the name of Mr. Lane. The young gentleman in question had requested an English whore and there were not too many of those in Cartagena. This one had been left behind by a sailor who had smuggled her aboard his ship but had forgotten her one night in the Colombian port.

There was no response when she tapped hesitantly on Mr. Lane's door, but after a moment the lock was drawn and the door creaked open. A shadowy figure beckoned for her to enter, and she peered about the room. A stub of candle did little to illuminate the narrow bed and gaping wardrobe that contained a single traveling bag. The young prostitute removed her cloak and coughed nervously.

"What would you like tonight, guv'nor?" she asked, her voice a little shrill as she began to unbutton her dress.

"No—don't disrobe." The voice was a low whisper, and the prostitute noted with some alarm that the figure had moved between her and the door. "Please . . . listen to me," the voice continued. "And I beg of you not to give me away. I promise I will pay you your usual fee."

The voice . . . it was a woman's voice!

" 'Ere . . . I don't do no tricks for women," the prostitute said haughtily.

"Nothing like that. I need help to get to the American port of New Orleans. I thought you would be able to tell me which ships belong to the buccaneer Laffite. He has letters of marque from Cartagena, which is why I came here. Please, don't run away . . . I am desperate. My son is in New Orleans and I must get to him. He is just a baby."

The woman stepped closer to the candlelight. She was dressed as a man and her pale gold hair was cut short, but she could never pass for a man on close inspection.

"Cor' . . . you must be mad. Why would you want to get on a ship with that pack of cutthroats?"

"I told you . . . my son. I came from England, as you did. England and America are at war . . . I must get to New Orleans. Please, I will pay you to help me get onto a ship, as a stowaway. I thought perhaps you would know some of the sailors on Laffite's ships. When they come into port you could help me bribe someone to smuggle me aboard."

"Got a little boy, 'ave you? I 'ad a child once . . ." A tear slid down her grimy cheek. "You 'aven't got any rum, 'ave you, dearie?"

"We can send downstairs for some."

"It was a good idea to dress as a boy. Maybe we could get you on a ship going to that place you want to get to," the prostitute said, sitting down on the bed and staring at her client appraisingly. "But you'd 'ave to bind your breasts, and rub dirt on your face and Lawd knows what we'll do to them long eyelashes. You might still get spotted."

"I took the precaution of purchasing this before I left Jamaica," Lanna said. The slim blade of the stiletto shone in the candlelight.

The young prostitute smiled. There was something preposterously brave about the slim girl who faced her holding a dagger in much the way a lady would hold a fork. Wouldn't be too hard to stow her away on a ship. Probably the worst that would happen to her would be that the sailor who helped her would try to take his pleasure with her. The young prostitute could tell her a way to avoid that. It would be a lark, really. And she'd be paid for it. It would be easier money than some she earned.

"I'll 'elp you, dearie. 'Ad a little tyke of me own once, I did."

"My men, m'sieur, are corsairs. Not pirates," Jean Laffite said quietly. "Since you are a friend of L'Herreaux, I will forgive the slip of the tongue this time." He filled Damon's glass with sparkling wine. The silverware and crystal gleamed on the expensive damask tablecloth and the large house was opulently but tastefully furnished.

"My apologies. I did not intend to offend you. I am grateful for this opportunity to meet you," Damon said, regarding Laffite over the rim of his glass as he raised it to his lips. Laffite was handsome, despite the bold nose. About five foot ten, Damon guessed, with the lithe body of a fencer, and flashing eyes. There were some who claimed Dominique You was actually his older brother, Alexandre, but there was no family resemblance. Dominique You was short with massive shoulders and a hot temper. The "ruffled eagle," as he was called, had shown the reason for his nickname many times in New Orleans. Luckily, he was not present on Grande Terre tonight.

Damon lowered his eyes to avoid Laffite's appraising stare. "You have some news for me regarding my son, Alain tells me."

"Yes . . . but first tell me what you heard in New Orleans. Have you any news about my brother, Pierre? Do you hear what Claiborne plans for him? Is Pierre still chained?"

"I'm sorry. I know only that Pierre is not as ill as he was during the summer."

The forty-mile journey from New Orleans to the buccaneers' stronghold had been a tortuous one. They had traversed the narrow waterways of the bayous in a pirogue, a slender skiff. More than once they had skimmed by the horny snout of an alligator, and seen deadly moccasins swimming in the misty blue-green swamp. They had been forced to take shelter when a sudden storm came shrieking in from the Gulf, blackening the sky, bending the trees and piercing the air with lightning and earsplitting crashes of thunder. The "land" where they had crawled for shelter was a shifting mass of quicksand, but fortunately it was familiar to Alain and the other oarsmen.

Now they were dining graciously, waited on by silent black servants. They lingered over the meal for some time until all but Jean Laffite and Damon drifted away.

"There was a woman with a child who could have been white," Jean Laffite said, "although he had black hair and we thought perhaps it was the woman's own child by a white planter. She said she had been trained as a ladies' maid, so she was sold to a plantation as a house servant. It is not far from here. She was allowed to keep the child

270

with her, because of his age. We can arrange for you to be taken to the the plantation."

"I am most grateful to you, sir," Damon said. "And after I have taken care of my son? Alain has told you I would like to serve on one of your ships?"

"It will be necessary for you to prove yourself first, my friend."

"You have something in mind?"

"Yes. You may have the honor and privilege of getting my brother Pierre out of Governor Claiborne's jail. When Pierre is free, we shall talk again. Now come, we must join my other guests. I have a female companion who awaits me, and if I drink any more of this wine I fear I shall disappoint her by not remaining awake for nobler activities."

Damon smiled as he stood up, but his heart sank at the enormity of Laffite's request. Governor Claiborne would never let Pierre out of jail, not even if Andrew Jackson himself requested it. And not even the best of Laffite's men had been able to break in and effect an escape, although many had tried.

Some of Laffite's henchmen lounged about the elegant drawing room, drinking and flirting with bold-eyed wenches, while others had wandered back to their own quarters. Behind Jean Laffite's house was a large warehouse, bulging with booty, and scattered about the island were the palmetto-thatched huts of his closest lieutenants: René Beluche; Nez Coupé—so-called because he had lost part of his nose in a saber duel; the villainous Gamble, who had brought most of Claiborne and the other Americans' wrath down on the heads of the buccaneers because he refused to follow orders and stop sinking American ships; and Alain L'Herreaux, the most recent follower to graduate to the honored position of living on Grande Terre.

Alain sprawled comfortably on a settee in Laffite's drawing room, glass in hand, one long arm about a young Creole wench who whispered invitingly that it was time to retire. "Alain . . . *gros animal* . . ." Her lips formed the words against his ruffled shirt. The tightness of his breeches in the region of his groin confirmed this, but he lingered, waiting for Jean Laffite and Damon St. Clair to rejoin the group.

Damon had changed. Alain knew that it was more than just the hideous scars on his friend's back, or the angry

271

burns on his legs. But the gambler's mask remained and it was difficult to read the emotions that seethed below the surface of those chiseled features. Damon had always been reckless and hotheaded, acting first and thinking afterward, but his rages—and passions—had always been short-lived. Now Alain sensed something that had not been there before . . . hatred, or burning need, something that would be with Damon St. Clair forever.

The desire to find his son and to join the buccaneers was reason enough for his being here, Alain told himself again. Still, he sensed that Damon had not given all his reasons for wanting to come to Laffite's stronghold. During their journey Alain had tried several times to learn what had become of Damon's beautiful wife, but seeing the pain at the mention of her name Alain had quickly retreated from the questions. He considered telling Damon that Lanna was safe in England and how he came to know it, but he decided the time was not right. Alain had still not recovered from the news that Indigo had become the wife of Sir Jared Malford, and he was pondering the varied ways fate had of punishing a man.

Damon's main concern seemed to be that Laffite was not considering an alliance with the English. He had asked the question over and over again, in different ways, as their pirogue had glided through the bayous.

"But the British . . . have they been in touch with the Laffites, do you know?"

"*Mon ami*, no! I keep telling you. Not to my knowledge."

"They plan to invade, Alain. The Creeks will fight with them, and they'll free the plantation slaves as they go. Andrew Jackson has marched into Spanish territory to recapture Pensacola from the British. He and his men may not arrive in time to defend New Orleans. Alain, no matter what Governor Claiborne does, do you believe Laffite will fight on the side of America?"

"*Mon ami*, I *know* it. Jean said it would be his lifetime work to fight the Spanish . . . but now he makes England his enemy too. He will not let them take New Orleans."

Now, recalling their conversation, whispered back and forth in the pirogue, Alain thought again that Damon must be concealing something.

As Jean Laffite and Damon entered the drawing room, Alain searched their faces anxiously. Jean was smiling broadly, as though at a joke, but Damon's mask was in place. They were quickly surrounded by eager female companions. Alain would not learn tonight what had transpired during their conversation.

The Creole wench had slid up onto Alain's lap. Her arms were entwined around his neck, and her thighs were positioned precisely over the bulge in his breeches. It was time to retire. Jean Laffite expected his men to behave like gentlemen while in his house.

"The British have not contacted him," Damon told the young major. "I believe if they do, he will refuse to help them."

"No one saw you come here?" the major asked.

"No, sir. I was careful. I have just come from visiting the plantation where my son and the woman Zenobia are living. I am arranging to buy them and send them back to Charleston, if possible. If Laffite's men are watching me they will believe that is the reason for my coming here. I believe he will allow me to sail with him."

"Good. We have made the necessary arrangements with the Navy. You are relieved from duty aboard your ship, and a contact has been arranged for you here in New Orleans. I shall be returning to General Jackson immediately. Your son is well, I trust?"

"Yes, sir." Damon smiled. The child with his dark hair and eyes was already tottering about defiantly.

"I have received a communique from General Jackson's headquarters," the major continued. "He is desperately in need of flints for his muskets, and no supplies are coming to us from Washington. Do you think your buccaneers will be able to supply the flints?"

"I'm sure of it . . . cannon too, probably. There doesn't seem to be anything Laffite has not plundered from somewhere. Did Old Hickory tell you when he would be coming to New Orleans?"

The major frowned at Damon's use of Andrew Jackson's nickname. A nickname the major knew Jackson hated.

"Your contact will be in touch with you. He is the son of a local planter whose plantation lies between New Orleans and Grande Terre. Report to him any unusual activity on the island . . . any ships you are unable to identify. Above all, any Englishmen who arrive. Your contact's name is Charles Gervais. That will be all, St. Clair."

Charles Gervais was waiting in Damon's room when he returned to his lodgings. He was a handsome, blonde young man with reckless eyes and a rangy frame. He was impeccably groomed, except for spattered boots.

"I am to give you directions on how to get to our plantation," Gervais said. "And if the British contact Laffite, you can bring word there immediately. I, in turn, will relay the message to the army." He had already drawn a map and spread it across Damon's bed as he explained the route from Grande Terre.

"The army—not Claiborne?" Damon asked.

Gervais smiled. "Our governor already wastes too much energy worrying about Laffite instead of our real enemy. We will deal directly with Andrew Jackson's men."

"The major asked about flints," Damon said as he concealed the map. "Are they to be sent to your plantation also?"

Gervais laughed. "No need for secrecy there. Send the flints into New Orleans, to the militia. You're new here, St. Clair, so I suppose you aren't aware that most of the city's supplies come by way of Barataria, Governor Claiborne notwithstanding. The Laffites have always been well-known and well-liked in New Orleans. They ran a blacksmith's shop for years, on St. Phillip and Bourbon Street, before privateering became profitable for them."

"Laffite's brother, Pierre. He is still in jail?"

"Since early this year, poor devil. He had a stroke of apoplexy—in 1810, I believe it was. That was when Jean took over. I hear Pierre's been ill most of the time he has been in jail . . . and swearing all the time that the Laffites are loyal Americans."

"Look . . ." Damon said slowly. "I didn't mention this to the major, but the price for my joining Laffite is his brother's freedom. Can you help me get Pierre out of jail?"

Gervais whistled. "That will be a tough proposition. Pierre is chained to the wall and under heavy guard. It will take more than you and I to get him out."

"Other prisoners? Is he alone?"

"Three or four Negroes, I believe."

"The guards and the jailor . . . could they be bribed?"

"Everyone can be bribed. Even me, my friend," Gervais laughed. "But, having gained entry to his cell, what about the chains?"

"I have a friend who was able to saw through his own chains and escape from a British stockade. He assures me that if we can get in, the chains can be severed."

"Then we shall bribe the guard and get in. I have some friends who will help us. But you do realize this is slightly more than I bargained for when I offered to help the major?"

"So?"

"So, I shall expect something in return. Will you use your influence to buy me something from Jean Laffite's Temple?"

"The slave auction? I understand he boldly announces the auctions in New Orleans. Why not just attend one and buy what you want?"

"This choice morsel won't be put on the block, from what I hear. Laffite has her hidden away while he tries to find out who she is and if she is part of a trap set up by Governor Claiborne. Or it may be that Laffite is holding her for himself, awaiting his own pleasure. But if we free Pierre Laffite . . . surely Jean's gratitude will know no bounds? Perhaps I may be able to purchase at least a little of her time?"

"What is so special about this particular slave? Have you seen her?"

"No. But I've heard whispers ever since the ship arrived. It seems she was a stowaway . . . from Cartagena, but not a Colombian. The woman, they say, has pale gold hair and large blue eyes. Luckily, she wasn't discovered until they reached Barataria, so I understand she isn't damaged in any way. Blonde beauties are a rarity in Creole New Orleans . . . and I've never had a woman with coloring the same as my own. I've always wondered . . ."

Damon's head was pounding. Surely . . . surely it could not be she.

"Long gold hair, you say?" he asked in a faraway voice.

"Not long. Short, like a shining golden halo, was what I heard. She speaks English. I am intrigued."

"So am I," Damon said. "I'll look into the matter."

CHAPTER 29

The roar of a cannon, coming from the direction of the Gulf, awoke Damon. Stumbling over Alain, he stepped out of the hut they shared and was caught up in a throng of Baratarians who were running to see what had happened.

A British sloop was anchored at the entrance to the Pass and one of the Baratarians' ships was aground, no doubt having been fired upon.

Damon arrived in time to see Jean Laffite and four of his men row out to meet the tender that was flying British colors and a flag of truce. A moment later, Alain pushed his way to Damon's side.

"So," Damon said, "Laffite does not deal with the British?"

"This will be the first time," Alain answered grimly. "And the last, if we can judge by the mood of the men."

Angry growls and curses were spewing from the watching buccaneers, along with shouts of "Make them prisoners." Many brandished knives and pistols as Jean Laffite and the Englishmen came into the harbor.

"What about the golden-haired stowaway? Has she anything to do with this? What did you find out about her?"

"I do not know who she is. She is not in the barracoon with the other slaves. The men say she has a private room and a guard. They say she is English. Damon, if it is Lanna, she comes for the same reason as you. To find her child."

"Or to help her countrymen," Damon said, watching the British sailors step ashore behind Jean Laffite.

"What do you mean?"

"Nothing. Quiet. Here they come."

The glowering Baratarians were watching every move. "I am Captain Lockyer," one of the Englishmen said. "Is Jean Laffite at home in the bay? I have an important communication for him." It had amused Jean Laffite not to tell them who he was until this moment.

"I am Jean Laffite," he said. He took the package of documents from the surprised captain's hand. They were addressed simply to: "Mr. Laffite—Barataria."

The crowd was pushing closer and someone shouted. "They're spies . . . come to invade and plunder. Seize them, make them prisoners and send them to the Americans in New Orleans."

Jean Laffite silenced the men quickly. "These men come under a flag of truce. We must respect it." He turned to the Englishmen. "You had better come to the house."

For a moment it seemed the mob would not break to let them through, but then Jean smiled at the nearest man and pushed him aside. "Keep a guard on the sloop while I see what is in the papers they bring. These men will be my guests. Come, we will eat and drink together and see what is written in your letters."

Several hours passed before Alain returned to their hut. Damon waited impatiently as Alain relayed the British proposal.

"Britain threatens to destroy Barataria unless we help her invade the United States. If we do help them, they promise rewards. We will be made British subjects, and the men will receive lands taken from the United States. Jean Laffite will be made a captain in the British service and be given $30,000. Also . . . his brother Pierre will be set free. The bribe, of course, is paltry when one thinks what we have in the warehouse . . ."

"But Pierre's freedom," Damon said carefully, "that is a different matter?"

Alain's eyes blazed. "Not even for his brother's freedom will Jean betray his country! In the morning, the men will make an angry demonstration around the house. Jean will ask for time to think over the proposition, and we will send the Englishmen back to their ship. Then we will send word to New Orleans."

Damon let out a long breath. "Your Jean Laffite is an honorable man. I begin to see why you are so loyal."

Alain stiffened suddenly, noticing that Damon had changed clothes and was now wearing leather breeches and a dark shirt. "Damon . . ." Alain said slowly, "you look like a man who is dressed to travel . . . secretly. I see also that you have a pistol in your belt. *Mon ami,* you would not be planning to go to New Orleans yourself, would you? There would be no reason . . . would there, *mon ami?*" He advanced toward Damon slowly, his hands forming into fists.

"Alain—" There was no time to argue. Alain flung himself upon Damon with a great cry of rage. Damon crashed into the wall. He staggered back under an avalanche of blows, regained his balance and swung at Alain's livid face in order to defend himself. Alain went down and Damon fell on top of him. He shouted to make himself heard over the stream of accusations.

"Listen to me . . . will you listen? It's true I came here to spy . . . no, damn you, listen! But not for Claiborne . . . for Jackson. Andrew Jackson is coming to New Orleans, and he wants to meet Laffite . . . but we had to be sure of his loyalty. Alain, God damn it . . . I believe in him too."

Alain stopped struggling and looked up at his friend. "Then prove it . . . let him send word to New Orleans about the British."

Damon stood up and extended his hand to Alain, pulling him to his feet. "All right, I'll give him time to do that. But I can't hang around the island too long . . . if Dominique You returns, I'll be a dead man anyway. He was in New Orleans when I first arrived and I learned later he had been imprisoned too . . . and interrogated by a certain major with whom he'd seen me. It was only for a minute, but he may remember me."

"Damon . . . you, a spy." Alain rubbed his jaw. "I should lock you up."

"No need now, old friend. *We're* on the same side, even if the rest of the Americans and Creoles haven't yet realized that the British are the enemy."

Lanna had managed to keep the dagger concealed inside her boot when the grinning black girl had brought her water to bathe and a change of clothing.

She had heard the cannon and excitement that morning

278

but could not see what was happening from the narrow slit of window in her room. As dusk fell, she lay on the bed. Despite the agony of waiting to be summoned to the dreaded pirate's presence, she smiled as she remembered her arrival in Barataria.

The voyage from Cartagena had been a nightmare of hiding in the cramped space between decks and fighting nausea from the stench of bilge water. After they were safely at sea, Lanna had followed the young prostitute's advice on how to handle the sailor who smuggled her aboard. The first time he brought food and then reached for her, she'd used the words and made the gestures the girl had taught her. The sailor had recoiled as though he had touched a raw flame. According to the prostitute, the words and gestures would convey that Lanna was in the terminal stages of a disease he would fear greatly. Unfortunately, he feared it so greatly that he did not return again with food, and so Lanna had been forced to prowl the ship at night for what few scraps she could find.

By the time she heard the sounds that heralded the approach of land, Lanna's hunger was greater than her fear of facing the privateers. She staggered up on deck on weak legs and made straight for the villainous-looking officer who was barking orders at the men who were climbing the shrouds. In the flurry of activity, few men gave the slim boy in the filthy clothes more than a passing glance.

Lanna tugged at the officer's sleeve and said, "I am a stowaway. I wish to be taken to Jean Laffite."

He looked down at her uncomprehendingly, responding only to his leader's name. Then, looking more closely, he reached over and pulled the battered hat from her head. The sunlight caught her hair, which stood up all over her head in uneven tufts. She had hacked it off with the dagger that now lay coldly against her body. Her hand strayed inside her coat, groping for the hilt of the knife. Those privateers who were close enough to see what was happening fell into an astonished silence.

"I have important business with Jean Laffite," she said. "Do you understand English? M'sieur Laffite will be well pleased with the man who delivers me to him."

The officer looked at the skinny, grimy youth who reeked of bilge water, but who stood straight as an arrow with head held high. Then the officer roared with laughter. *"M'sieur,"* he said gravely, in English, "I shall be happy to present you to Jean Laffite . . . after you have washed the

279

stench of the bilges from your body." He turned and shouted in French to one of the men, and Lanna looked up to see a grinning sailor approaching her with a bucket of water.

"No!" Lanna screamed a second before the cold water doused her from head to toe. Gasping and choking, she felt the dripping coat being pulled from her shoulders. She clutched at her side to keep the dagger from slipping into her wet breeches, then realized that her breasts had burst free of their bonds and were clearly outlined under the sodden shirt. Slowly her eyes met the alert gaze of the officer.

"So . . ." he started to say, but Lanna read his eyes and thoughts and, before anyone realized what she was about, she leaped to the rail and jumped overboard.

It had been a short but difficult swim to the shore, because of her weakened condition and because she was hampered by her clothes and boots. The men who finally dragged her from the water were not as starved for female companionship as those on board the ship, and they had taken her to the Temple, where Jean Laffite kept the slaves that were to be sold. Her captors ordered a black slave to scrub her and dress her in women's clothes. After that she had been fed, and left in a room by herself. Several days had passed, and no one had come to her except the black slave who brought food. Now it was dusk again.

There was a sudden commotion outside her door. Lanna leaped to her feet. The slave stepped into the room, followed by a buccaneer in an outlandish costume. He was short, with massive shoulders, and on his face were fearful black stains that looked like smoke. He gaped at her in the same amazed way she stared at him.

"Forgive me . . ." he said at last in a French accent, "for this intrusion. Had I realized I would confront a lady of such beauty, I would have taken time to change from my seafaring clothes."

"Are you Jean Laffite?" Lanna asked.

"Now why do all the ladies seek Jean?" he asked ruefully. "Because he is taller than I? No, my lady, I am Dominique You. I come to ask you to join Jean and some guests in his house. He would have come himself, but he has a matter of some importance to discuss." The short man continued to stare and Lanna felt that he could see right through her clothes.

"Of course, I shall be happy to meet Mr. Laffite and his

280

guests," she said. "May I have just a moment to prepare?" She ran her hand through her jagged locks.

"Certainly, mademoiselle. I shall wait for you outside." He lingered another moment, dark eyes scrutinizing her with frank admiration. Then he stepped outside and closed the door.

The dagger, Lanna thought, what shall I do with it? It would be too risky to try to go to Laffite with it concealed under her dress, but she did not want to leave it behind. So far, she had been treated well by the privateers, but the awful memory of Bloody Murdoch was never far from her mind and she did not ever intend to allow a man to degrade her again.

In the wardrobe were the dresses she had been given, as well as the hessian boots she had worn with the man's clothing.

When Dominique You conducted her to Jean Laffite's drawing room, the assembled men were too busy staring at her face to notice what all of the women saw immediately. The strange golden-haired woman was wearing a magnificent gown of pale silk, the color of ice beneath a blue sky. Her waist was tiny, breasts full, hair extraordinary. The gown set off all of her attributes, but called special attention to the ugly pair of men's boots beneath the hem.

Lanna noticed the English uniforms at once. Even as Dominique You was presenting her to Laffite, her startled gaze found the young lieutenant who had taken her ashore on the prison island and left her there when the *Grey Wren* sailed away.

"Mademoiselle, I would have come to welcome you sooner had I known we had a fair princess in our midst . . ." Jean Laffite was kissing her hand, but his flashing eyes had managed to intercept the glance she had exchanged with the lieutenant.

"Madame. I am Madame St. Clair," Lanna said. "Mr. Laffite, I came here because I believe you may know where my son is. He was in the care of a nurse on the *Jamaica Star*."

"Curious," Laffite said, taking her by the hand to lead her to the Englishmen. "We have another by that name in our midst. However, first I must introduce you to Captain Lockyer and his men . . . unless, of course, you are already acquainted with them?"

"Damon . . . Damon is here?" Lanna asked, her heart leaping.

"We shall send for him. You did not answer my question as to whether it is necessary to introduce the Englishmen."

"Miss Malford and I have already met," the young lieutenant said stiffly. The scars on his back reminded him very well who the woman was.

"Miss Malford . . . Madame St. Clair?" Laffite expressed mild surprise.

"You'd better explain yourself, lieutenant," Captain Lockyer said. "We do not want Mr. Laffite to misunderstand why we are here."

"The lady is the adopted daughter of Sir Jared Malford. He was my captain on the frigate *Grey Wren*," the lieutenant answered. "He is now with Admiral Cochrane."

"Ah, so the father of the young lady is not far away, out in the Gulf?" Laffite said.

"It's no secret," Captain Lockyer said. "But we had no idea this young woman was here. She has no connection with our mission."

"Please, Mr. Laffite," Lanna said, "I came only to find my son. I beg of you to tell me where he is."

"Gentlemen, excuse me please," Laffite said, and Lanna found herself being propelled away from the group. After seating her in an alcove, Laffite conversed rapidly in French with the fearsome Dominique You. She caught the name "St. Clair," and felt the tension in the room. Despite the appearance that they were friends enjoying a meal together, she could tell from the way the privateers watched the Englishmen that they were actually prisoners.

Laffite gave instructions to one of the men. He disappeared through the door and a few minutes later reappeared with Damon at his side. Everyone turned to stare at the man in the dark shirt and leather breeches, particularly Dominique You, who clutched Laffite's arm with a muttered curse.

Laffite smiled blandly and turned to Lanna. "The gentleman is your husband, madame?"

"Yes. Oh, yes," Lanna breathed, her eyes fixed on Damon. He saw her but did not show surprise. She wanted to shout his name, fling herself into his arms.

"Your son is safe, madame," Laffite said. "Your husband will tell you all about him in a more private place."

The room where they were taken was a great deal less comfortable than the one in which she had spent her first days. It was, in fact, a bare hut, without windows or furniture. The door closed behind them and a wooden bolt was drawn.

Lanna clutched Damon's arm. "The baby . . . Richard, have you seen him?"

"He and Zenobia are well. They're on a plantation not far from here. I shall send them to Charleston as soon as I am able. So you can stop worrying about them and get on with your other business."

Lanna's hands flew to cover her mouth and her eyes closed briefly as she murmured a silent prayer of thanks. Then she looked up at Damon and said, "What do you mean, other business?"

"You want me to believe you are not either working for the English, or for the privateers of Laffite? I had thought surely you were an English spy . . . but since Laffite locked you up with me, I now wonder if he feels you could learn more than his men."

"Damon . . . no, I don't know what you are talking about. I'm so afraid. I went to Cartagena by way of Jamaica. It seemed Negril Bay was filled with sail . . . the water was so packed it looked like a giant wash tub. English ships are gathering there in force, and they must mean to invade soon. We have to get the baby away from here."

"Your acting does you credit, Lanna. You almost make me believe Richard is your only concern."

"He is. I'm so tired of your war . . . I want my baby. I want to make a home for him, a real home."

"Where—in England? He's an American."

"No, I had not planned to take him to England. I'd really rather stay here . . . I thought perhaps Charleston." *Your home, Damon, to be near you.* She did not say it aloud.

"I see. You've grown tired of England and your artist lover?"

"Gideon was never my lover, but even if he were . . he's dead. An accident, he fell from the cliff at Kingsburch."

"An accident, or did he kill himself because of you, Lanna?"

"Oh, no, Damon," Lanna snapped, "you can't make me feel guilty again. I was not responsible for Gideon's death."

"Nor was it my fault that Beth died. But you took pleasure in making me feel guilty about it."

283

"Damon, what does it matter now? Can't we stop torturing each other?"

Damon didn't answer, but rather moved to the walls of the hut, pressing here and there, testing the strength.

"What are you doing? Are we prisoners?" Lanna asked.

"Yes, because Dominique You recognized me. Now I worry that Alain will be in trouble for bringing me here. You . . . well, if you're speaking the truth, either they are giving us some last minutes together before we both go to meet our Maker, or I am to be treated to the spectacle of you being given to the men."

"Oh, Damon, no . . . Damon, listen to me, there is something I must tell you . . . in case we are going to die. It was not I who betrayed you in England. It was Llewellyn Davis. I want you to know that . . . he did it to save Gideon. And I wouldn't have left our son aboard Sir Jared's ship, not for anything in the world . . . but I thought you were a prisoner on the island and I went ashore to see if I could help you escape. Damon, I'm not lying . . . there is a minister there who would tell you . . . oh . . ." She covered her face with her hands, remembering that there was more the minister could tell.

She felt his arms go around her and he was whispering close to her ear. "Lanna, don't. We've got to keep our wits about us. All that matters now is getting out of here. There's bound to be a guard outside the door, but I don't think they will do anything tonight. Alain told me the Englishmen will remain until morning."

"Then we will overpower the guard," Lanna whispered back.

"I've been thinking about that. If there's only one of them, we could get him in here. With you along I'm sure Alain would help us, especially since he's going to be in trouble for bringing in a spy. Lanna, would you call to the guard . . . tell him I'm hurting you, anything, to get him in here? But don't scream so loud you bring others. I'll have my hands full taking care of one man with a pistol."

Lanna nodded and went to the door, pressing her lips close to the crack, *"M'sieur . . . m'sieur, s'il vous plaît . . .* oh, please help me . . . please, he's hurting me."

She tapped against the wood and gasped loudly, while Damon stood on the other side of the door, tensed, ready to spring.

Knocking his pistol from his hand, Damon brought down the first man who entered the room. But a second guard was hard on his heels and he felled Damon with a blow to the back of the neck. On his knees, Damon stared into the muzzle of a pistol inches from his nose. In the same second Lanna was fumbling with her boot. There was a flash of steel as she ripped open the guard's arm. Yelping with pain, he dropped the pistol to the floor.

Damon grabbed both pistols while Lanna stared in horrified fascination at the dripping dagger in her hand. One guard was still unconscious and the other pressed his fingers to the superficial wound, regarding Lanna with disbelief.

"Lanna . . . we must tie them," Damon said urgently. "Take my belt. Tear off a piece of your dress for a gag. Hurry, we haven't much time."

The pirogue slid into the black water, the dipping oars making a faint splash. *Mon Dieu,* " Alain said again. "What am I doing? Jean will kill me for this."

"Not after we get Pierre out of jail, he won't. Can't we go any faster?"

"In the darkness, we must be careful . . . and there are only two of us to row."

"Give me an oar, I can help," Lanna said.

"We have to get to the Gervais plantation, Alain. We can leave Lanna there. We will put our plan into action tonight. Gervais has been collecting money for the bribes. If we get Pierre out of jail tonight, not only will we redeem ourselves in Laffite's eyes, but he will have no reason to accept the British offer."

"He would not accept anyway, *sacré bleu!* If I were not in love with your wife, I would take you back to him."

"When we take Pierre back, I'll tell Jean everything, I promise. Andrew Jackson will accept Jean's help, once he meets him. I'm sure of it. And Jean will understand about Lanna . . . I had to take my wife out of danger. He's a Frenchman, he understands *l'amour.*"

"Ah, but will he? I do not know if I understand it," Alain sighed. "Not with you two."

"Shut up and row," Damon growled.

CHAPTER 30

Jean Laffite sent all of the British documents to Jean Blanque, owner of many of the Baratarians' ships and a member of the Legislature with considerable influence in New Orleans. Laffite also sent his own letter to Blanque, who immediately took everything to Governor Claiborne. A quickly convened committee meeting agreed the whole thing was probably a ruse to free Pierre Laffite, and demands were made to clear out the pirate stronghold. Only one voice spoke in defense of Laffite.

"I know them," Major Villère said. "They are not pirates, they are privateers with letters of marque from Cartagena. They cannot bring their prizes into our ports legally. Their only crime is that they dispose of prize goods illegally. The United States is their adopted country and they see it threatened with an enemy they hate. These documents are genuine. We must believe the Baratarians."

Governor Claiborne ignored the Major's plea. Although Claiborne himself did not vote, he allowed the rest of the committee to make the decision. Commodore Patterson was ordered to go to Grande Terre and destroy the Baratarian establishment.

The next day a notice appeared in the newspapers, and posters were displayed throughout New Orleans. The notice read:

ONE THOUSAND DOLLARS' REWARD

Will be paid to whoever apprehends Pierre Laffite, who last night broke from the parish prison and escaped. The said Pierre Laffite is five feet ten inches tall, of robust stature, light complexioned and somewhat cross-eyed. It is believed that a more complete description of the said Laffite is useless as he is so well known in this city.

Shortly thereafter Governor Claiborne received a letter directly from Jean Laffite, dated 10 September 1814. It was addressed to *Son Excellence*, Monsieur Wm. C. C. Claiborne, *Gouverneur de l'Etat de la Louisiane*. The message was flowery, but sincere. It read, in part, *"I tender my services to defend Louisiana . . . I am the stray sheep wishing to return to the flock . . . I have never sailed under any flag but that of the Republic of Cartagena . . . if I could have brought my lawful prizes into the ports of this State, I should not have employed the illicit means that have caused me to be proscribed."* The letter was signed, *"J'ai l'honneur d'être, M. le Gouverneur,* Jean Laffite."

Nevertheless, six gunboats, one launch and the *Carolina*, equipped for battle and carrying part of the 44th Regiment, were dispatched down the Mississippi to Grande Terre.

On the Gervais plantation, Lanna waited anxiously for Damon to return. He had promised that she would be reunited with the baby and Zenobia as soon as he could return to purchase them from their owners. They were safe for the present, and there was a greater urgency to ensure that Jean Laffite was not won over to the British side. Alain had protested, but Damon told him that he would only stop worrying when Pierre was out of jail and Andrew Jackson had had a chance to meet Laffite.

Charles Gervais, the fair-haired son of the plantation owner, returned the following day and told Lanna that Damon and Alain were on their way back to Grande Terre with Pierre. Since no one had explained to Charles that the pirates' golden-haired captive was Damon's wife, he lost no time in beginning a flirtation with his beautiful guest.

Lanna was unsure how to handle the situation. She had

been told curtly to say nothing. Damon was obviously playing some kind of deadly double game involving both the Americans in New Orleans and the buccaneers of Barataria. Since Damon had not seen fit to tell Charles who she was, she decided not to discuss either herself or her child until he returned.

"I shall, of course, offer marriage if necessary," Charles Gervais told her in a stage whisper at dinner as he leaned across the table.

Lanna had drawn her knees as far away as possible, in order to avoid Charles' leg, which seemed to be straying in her direction.

"Can you imagine the children we would have?" he went on, to her acute embarrassment. "All golden-haired, like us."

"You are an outrageous flirt," Lanna whispered back. Despite Damon's instructions, she would have to put a stop to this. "And I must tell you at once that I am a married woman."

"Who has run away from her husband to visit a pirate stronghold! That is even better. An adventuress. Instead of marriage and children, I shall offer you a blazing, passionate affair. Excitement. Intrigue."

"Believe me, I've had all the excitement and intrigue I need for some time," Lanna murmured, with a vague smile in the direction of Charles' parents, who did not speak English nearly so well as their son. His grandparents and several other guests, including the son of Major Villère, were also at the table. The young Villère was gallant, but not so bold as Charles Gervais.

Charles nibbled slowly on a piece of bread as his hand slid beneath the tablecloth and found Lanna's knee. His eyes locked with Lanna's and there was no mistaking his thoughts as his mouth encircled the bread caressingly.

Lanna dropped her glance to her plate, thinking with some dismay that if Damon were suddenly to return, he would immediately assume she had been encouraging Charles Gervais. A sudden image of Teddie flashed into her mind. *"It was hard for her to be good."* Yes, Lanna thought, it is easy not to get into trouble if one is never tempted. She put her hand down under the table to disengage Charles, whose fingers were creeping up her thigh.

The black butler entered the room, announcing a guest. As if in answer to Lanna's thought, Damon arrived. His dark eyes swept the table and found Lanna immediately.

288

"What news?" Charles asked at once. His hand promptly left her leg.

"Our blasted United States Navy attacked the stronghold," Damon replied stonily. "They captured Dominique You and about eighty Baratarians . . . loaded all the loot they could carry into their ships, and burned the warehouse."

"And the Laffites?"

"They left before the attack . . . Dominique You was left in charge. Pierre was ill; we didn't think he'd live to see his brother again. Jean removed some of their most valuable possessions and maps . . . and left orders that his men were not to resist the American attack. They didn't fire a single shot in their own defense." There was some awe in his voice.

"What of Alain, is he all right?" Lanna asked.

"Yes. At least five hundred Baratarians escaped before the Navy arrived. God damn them . . ." Damon sank to the nearest chair, his face livid.

"Why, M'sieur . . ." Charles said in surprise. "Surely you should be glad. Your mission is accomplished. The Baratarians are routed and will not be able to guide the British through the bayous to New Orleans. Yet it sounds as though you damn your own Navy, rather than the pirates."

"I do," Damon said. "They may have just given New Orleans—and the country—to the British."

There was a long silence. At length Madame Gervais asked in her halting English if Damon had dined.

"Thank you, yes. I would like to ask for your hospitality for the night, however. I haven't slept for a couple of days."

"Of course. We shall prepare a room."

"No need. My wife and I are old-fashioned. We share a room," Damon said with a gleam in his eye. Lanna stared at him and he returned her look as she explained quickly that she and Damon were indeed married. The disappointment on Charles' face was obvious.

While Damon conversed briefly with Gervais, Lanna went upstairs to make preparations. A few minutes later Damon came into the room and found her sitting on the bed.

"I suppose you weren't able to go to the baby . . . in view of the attack on Grande Terre?"

"No. I'll take you to them tomorrow. If it's not too late, I'll get you all out of here before the British invade."

289

"No, Damon, I think not."

"What are you talking about? An invasion is a certainty."

"I don't mean that. I mean I shan't leave. Unless you are leaving too."

He looked at her guardedly. "What do you mean?"

"I would like to stay with you, Damon. Take care of our son, make a home for both of you. I won't make any demands, I promise. But . . . well, because of me you lost your former housekeeper. Indigo is going to stay at Kingsburch until the war is over, and I suppose then she will join Sir Jared in the Indies. I ask only that you let me keep house for you. You once told me that I could be an asset in that respect."

He stared at her for a long moment and then said quietly, "You realize there will be danger for you and the boy, if you stay here."

"Damon, he was born in danger. In his short life he's already come through more danger than some men are ever called on to face. He is going to be one of the men who build this vast country, Damon, I feel it . . ." She broke off, as though the words were not her own but had come to her from some unseen intelligence.

Damon came to the side of the bed, kicked off his boots, and unbuckled his belt as he stood staring down at her. She was wearing a silk nightgown. The material draped softly over her breasts and his hand touched her, tracing the outline of the nipple beneath the silk.

"Your haircut is atrocious," he said. "Why did you do it?"

"In order to pass as a man. To get onto one of Laffite's ships. I stowed away."

Damon bent closer to her breast, sliding the nightgown aside so that his lips could find their mark. "A man . . ." he said softly, "with breasts like these . . ."

The next instant he felt a sharp point under his chin and looked in amazement at the stiletto in his wife's hand.

"No, Damon," she said in a voice of deadly seriousness. "Tonight we don't serve the dark gods of the loins. Tonight we talk, even if I have to cut off your manhood to make you listen to me . . . talk to me."

He stared, his mouth open in disbelief. Then he threw back his head and roared with laughter. He did not, however, continue to caress her. He sat up, very properly, and folded his arms.

290

"There is one thing I have to say about you, Lanna my lady wife," he said, still grinning. "You have never bored me. I never know what to expect from you next. I hadn't realized you still had that knife."

"Damon, I want to tell you everything that happened to me after Sir Jared captured the *Wayward Woman,*" she said, not smiling back at him, "and I want to tell you about Gideon. And I don't want you to say a single word until I have finished. I won't beg you to let me stay with you, but I won't give up my son either. Either we can arrive at some kind of amicable arrangement, or we can waste our time and efforts battling one another. I want Richard to have his birthright. I want him to grow up as an American, not a colonial Englishman. A woman cares little about political loyalties, Damon, but she understands their importance to men. I understand how Richard will feel one day . . . that's why I want him to stay here."

She told him briefly and dispassionately all that he did not know, working backwards from the night Llewellyn had betrayed his presence at Kingsburch. Damon listened silently. He'd had a nagging suspicion about the artist ever since the night he'd destroyed the portrait. The small group of men with Gideon . . . there had been no women present . . .

"And so I shall never go back to Kingsburch. I hated it before, but now Gideon would haunt me. As a child, I used to think I had been locked away there because of some dreadful thing I'd done but couldn't remember. Something so awful my parents didn't want to see me. I thought Sir Jared only came out of a sense of duty and he always looked at me with such distaste . . . I can't let that happen to our son, Damon. We must make him a real home and always let him know we love him. No matter how we feel about each other."

Damon glanced down at the dagger lying on the bed between them.

"Damon, there is something else I have to tell you. There was a man . . . on the island, who had carnal knowledge of me. Not with my consent. But I want you to know about it . . . I can't tell you more than that because I find it painful."

Damon looked into her tormented eyes and his hands formed fists against the sheet. "There is only one thing I would ask you, Lanna. What about Rafe Danvers?"

"So . . ." Lanna said. "It has always been Rafe between

291

us. Is that what you are telling me?" She ran her fingers through her sheared hair despairingly. "Yes, I loved him once. He was my first love . . . the prince who came to rescue me from my gloomy castle. But it was a love built on no more than that, and it faded as quickly as it blossomed."

"Have you heard from him?"

"No. Not since he sailed away on his ship and . . . I fear, forgot both poor Beth and me."

"I'll find a house in New Orleans for you and the child. I shall be returning to my duties soon, but I'll provide for you. Now that I no longer have a job to do in Barataria, I expect I'll be assigned to a ship somewhere. I may not be here to protect you if there is an invasion. Are you sure you want to stay here? There's still time to leave."

"I want to stay," Lanna said.

A long time later, after he had undressed and lain beside her, he touched her gently. A questioning caress that found her breasts, then moved to her thighs. She turned to him and pulled him close and they met on that plane that had always been theirs. But even then, Lanna remembered that Damon had never told her that he loved her.

Southern and Western newspapers clamored in vain about the aid the Spanish governor of Pensacola was giving to the British. And Andrew Jackson did not have the men to drive them from Florida. He would have to wait two months for men to come from Tennessee and Kentucky and the Mississippi Territory. Meanwhile, the British decided to attack Mobile without waiting to see if Jean Laffite and his buccaneers would aid them.

The fort held. The British were turned back and they decided to bypass Mobile. They had been ordered to occupy the province of Louisiana by advancing directly on New Orleans, or by moving into the friendly Indian territory of Georgia. They chose the direct approach to New Orleans.

Jean Laffite, despite the American attack on his men, refused to guide the British through the bayous of Barataria. So instead they decided to sail up the Mississippi to New Orleans.

Andrew Jackson fretted and fumed while waiting for the volunteers from Kentucky and Tennessee. He self-righteously ignored the "hellish banditti," as he called Laffite's men. At last his volunteers arrived and Jackson pre-

292

pared to march on Pensacola. Pensacola surrendered; the British retreated, leaving behind their disillusioned Spanish and Indian allies.

Old Hickory, doubled up with dysentery, his body wasted to skin and bone, prepared to depart for New Orleans.

Damon found a small house in New Orleans for Lanna and his son. Zenobia shared their home more as a member of the family than as a servant. The city was more foreign and exotic to Lanna than even Charleston had been. She worried because their house opened directly onto the street, and Richard was an energetic infant, forever wanting to run and explore. She and Zenobia kept a constant watch on the front door and the lacy iron balcony on the second floor onto which the bedroom windows opened.

Damon stayed with them for a few days, awaiting his orders. He played with the child and was considerate and polite to Lanna. Their lovemaking still thrilled her, and yet, when he left to arrange the meeting between Jean Laffite and Andrew Jackson, Lanna felt more keenly disappointed than ever. Perversely, she wished he would return to the old cruel, mocking Damon. There had been more emotion in that fiend than this stranger showed.

She told herself that either he had decided to accept her on the terms she had offered and wanted no more than a housekeeper with bedroom privileges . . . or he could not accept as a wife in the true sense a woman who admitted she had been used by another man. Once again Bloody Murdoch's evil leer began to haunt her nightmares.

Toward the end of November, Alain L'Herreaux came calling. Lanna was swept into his long arms and given a warm kiss full on the mouth.

"*La belle Anglaise* . . . Madame St. Clair, you make it hard for me to hate your countrymen," Alain said, picking up Richard and tossing him into the air. The child screamed with delight.

"Americans are my countrymen now, Alain. Damon and Richard are Americans . . . and I . . ." She broke off wonderingly, feeling a surge of concern that was close to patriotism.

"Alas, we Creoles fear Americans are our enemies also," Alain said, handing the child to Zenobia.

"Oh, you men," Lanna said, exasperated. "Will you

never be able to forget all of your ancient feuds? Tell me, have you seen my husband?"

"Lanna, that is why I come to see you." Alain took her hand and she jumped in alarm at his suddenly grave expression. "Ah, no, Lanna, he is all right. I did not mean to frighten you. But he will not be able to return to you now. He has been assigned to a ship."

Lanna turned away, her eyes misting with tears. "And he sent you to tell me, he could not even come to tell me himself?" The gulf between Damon and herself was as wide as ever. She had been a fool to think otherwise. Enemy . . . it was the favorite word of men . . . she was Damon's enemy just as she had always been. Enemy was a word that aroused their passion more than any other . . . more than lover, or even friend.

"There was not time, Lanna. But he is not too far from here. He may be able to get back to see you. The Navy has a small gunboat flotilla on Lake Borgne. Damon was sent to replace a man who was stricken with fever. Lanna, please do not look so sad, I cannot bear it."

"I'm sorry, Alain. It's just that I love him so much and he doesn't love me. He has never loved me and now . . . how could any man love a woman who had been used by a man like B-b-bloody Murdoch . . ." She buried her face in her handkerchief.

Understanding flashed into Alain's eyes as he drew Lanna back into his embrace. That fool Damon St. Clair . . . that stupid fool. And he, Alain L'Herreaux, was just as stupid. Why had he not forced Damon to listen when he tried to tell him what had happened on the island? Lanna was right, men spoke more of wars and feuds than of love and family.

Alain's mind went back to the island, to the days of hiding in different rooms in the brothel, the girls shuffling him from one cupboard to another, while he painstakingly filed through his chains.

Peggy, with the impish face, had taken him under her personal wing in more ways than one, and had also brought him news of Lanna. A relative of the minister, an artist, had seen Peggy in the marketplace and asked to paint her portrait. She went up to the church to sit for him. The minister and the artist were taking care of Lanna. No one would tell Murdoch where she was. Alain had to leave the island soon, however, because they could not hide him

294

indefinitely. Certainly he could not approach Lanna, who seemed to be dazed and unaware of the world around her.

Peggy reported to Alain that the artist was "one of those," not interested in women's bodies except to put them on canvas. When Peggy told him that Lanna was returning to England with the artist, Alain had also been on the point of leaving. A fisherman would take him to the nearby deserted island where privateers sometimes stopped to discipline their men and divide booty.

Mon Dieu, Alain thought as he gently stroked Lanna's hair and comforted her, that fool Damon did not realize what she had gone through in her futile effort to save her husband from the British.

"Lanna, hush, *chérie,* it will be all right. In time everything will be all right."

"I'm sorry, Alain. I didn't mean to act like a fool. I'm so glad to see you. It's always such a relief to be able to talk to you . . . We shall have a special dinner tonight. I've been learning to make gumbo."

Watching her place the dishes upon the table, occasionally looking up at him to speak or smile, Alain felt an old pain stab at his heart. What would have happened, he wondered, if he had been able to free himself from his chains before she sailed away from the island with her artist? Would he have dared to ask her to come with him?

Long ago, in this very city, a young Creole girl had laughed at his love. Called him "monkey" . . . "gorilla" . . . told him clearly that he had no right to love like a man. Since that time he had contented himself with the kind of love that could be bought. Yet Lanna had grown fond of him, he knew that. She turned to him for affection and companionship, just as long ago the lovely and wild Indigo had. Neither of them had ever looked at him with pitying eyes, or worse, averted their gaze when he stood up on his short legs.

Yes, back on that godless island there had been a moment when the fates might have brought him and Lanna together. There had been a hopeless abyss between Damon and his wife then. He was sending her away, and she showed no emotion when she looked at the father of her child. Had Alain had the body of a normal man, he would not have hesitated to tell her then of his love for her.

He had taken savage pleasure in killing Bloody Murdoch before he escaped from the island. Murdoch had come to the brothel where Alain was hiding, had forced his way in to look for Lanna. When Murdoch was told the golden-haired woman had already left the island, he had gone crashing into Peggy's room, flinging aside her terrified client.

Stepping into the room after him, Alain had said softly, "M'sieur . . . I have something for you."

Turning, Murdoch had looked down on the stunted little man whose powerful arm wielded the cutlass swiftly and cleanly.

The women of the brothel had been more than happy to help him carry away Murdoch's body and bury it in the dense jungle of bamboo. The island would later breathe a sigh of relief that the terrible tempered Murdoch had found other beaches to comb.

If Lanna had not already sailed away . . . but the moment had been lost forever. Now she and Damon were together again, and her eyes were filled with a love that her husband was too blind to see.

Alain sometimes wondered what it was that caused him to love the women who loved Damon. Indigo . . . Lanna. But Damon could not have both of them, they would not allow it. If Damon made a choice, then perhaps the one who was left . . .

Meanwhile, on Lake Borgne, the six gunboats that had been used against the Baratarians were stationed under the command of Lieutenant Thomas Ap Catesby Jones. The gunboats were to give warning of enemy approach. Tac Jones received his orders shortly after Damon reported for duty. The orders read:

Proceed to Pass Christian for reconnaissance. If the enemy forces try to cut off the gunboats, retreat to the Rigolets. There, with the protection and help of Fort Petites Coquilles, *sink the enemy . . . or be sunk.*

CHAPTER 31

Old Hickory had arrived. General Andrew Jackson, gaunt, cadaverous, was in New Orleans. Royal Street thronged with people, and Lanna and Zenobia took Richard to see the famous old warrior who had come to save the city.

Lanna held her son in her arms as the general came out onto the second story gallery of number 106 Royal Street. His words were translated into French for the crowds below:

"I have come to protect the city. I will drive our enemies into the sea or perish in the effort. Good citizens, you must all rally around me in this emergency. We must resolve to save this city from the dishonor and disaster which a presumptuous enemy threatens to inflict upon it."

The city, so divided by opposing factions, at last had a leader everyone could trust.

Jackson proclaimed the city under martial law. Every boat in the harbor was restricted; none would be allowed to sail. Every militiaman must report for duty. And Old Hickory, reluctantly, would meet with Jean Laffite and his hellish banditti. To his surprise, Jackson liked the buccaneer immediately and directed him to man the defenses south of the city.

A large fleet of British ships under the command of Admiral Cochrane was sailing toward Lake Borgne. Sir Edward Packenham, brother-in-law of the victorious Duke of Wellington, commanded eight thousand redcoats, sailors and marines.

In their path, five gunboats under the command of Lieutenant Tac Jones patrolled the shallow waters of Lake Borgne.

Captain Lockyer, who had led the unsuccessful British mission to recruit Laffite's privateers, was given a flotilla of forty-five barges, forty-three cannon and twelve hundred sailors and marines. They were sent in pursuit of the American gunboats, who were scurrying before the wind to try to reach Fort Petites Coquilles. On the morning of December 14, Jones and his gunboats had bad luck. The wind died completely.

Jones stationed the gunboats in a line across the channel and waited. An hour later when the enemy hove into view, the gunboats deliberately opened fire.

Lanna and Zenobia stood in the window. Richard jumped up and down excitedly on the seat of the chair as he saw the men marching into New Orleans.

They appeared by the hundreds, coming out of the swamps . . . American, French, Slavic . . . slim youths who were the sons of planters, swarthy men with cutlasses and swords . . . fierce men, smiling men, grim men, determined men. Lanna felt her heart beat with unexpected pride. These men would defend their homes. They would not let the invaders pass.

Oddly, Lanna no longer thought of the invaders as Englishmen. She thought fleetingly of the day in London when the Czar had arrived to celebrate the victory over Napoleon. The happy throngs in the street then had been elated over victory in a war that had never touched their land directly. How different to have a foreign invader on one's own shores.

"Daddy . . . Daddy!" Richard shouted when a tall man with black hair would appear among the crowd, and for a moment Lanna's heart would leap. But Damon was on a gunboat on a lake called Borgne and there had been no word from him.

"Dominique You has been released from prison," Zenobia said, "and they say Jean Laffite spends much time with General Jackson. Oh, Miss Lanna, what's going to happen?"

"They won't take the city," Lanna said firmly. She did not add that she was concerned that some of the citizens still did not seem to realize the gravity of the situation. She had grown impatient with more than one Creole woman who shrugged off the whole affair as "American business."

"We are all Americans," Lanna retorted. "We have to stand together."

Lanna stared out of the window, praying for the hundredth time that day that she would have some word of Damon. Alain had stopped by briefly to tell her he was returning to Grande Terre. Jean Laffite was defending the very spot where he had held his great auctions.

Among the crowds in the street, she caught a glimpse of blonde hair among the dark heads. She rushed to the door in time to call to Charles Gervais, who quickly broke ranks to come to her.

"The beautiful stowaway who stole my heart," he lamented, catching her hands in his to kiss them. "I should never have sent Damon St. Clair looking for you had I known he would claim you as his bride."

"Charles . . . can you stop for a moment, some wine perhaps?" Lanna asked, laughing. She stopped abruptly as he followed her into the house. "You say you sent Damon to me?"

Charles gave her a crafty glance and placed his musket against the wall to free his arms for an embrace. "Of course. Didn't he tell you it was I who told him you were a captive of the villainous pirates and must be rescued at all costs? I told him as soon as I heard they had a golden-haired captive. Lanna, *ma petite*, there are so few of us golden-haired ones left!"

Lanna allowed him to peck her lightly on the cheek. "I see. I thought Damon had other orders. Zenobia, some wine, please, for M'sieur Gervais."

"Where is your husband, madame? Is he not here to defend you? And the city swarming with men? Foolish husband!"

"He had orders to report to Lieutenant Jones and is on Lake Borgne," Lanna said.

Charles Gervais' mildly flirtatious expression was quickly replaced by a look of dismay that was not lost on Lanna.

"What is it? Charles, tell me."

"Lanna, I'm sorry. I had no idea. I would not have joked about him had I known."

"Known what, in the name of God?"

"Villère's son managed to escape from their plantation to bring word. The British put seven thousand men ashore at his father's plantation . . . it's only nine miles from New Orleans, Lanna."

"Yes, but . . . what of Damon? Please, tell me."

"Lanna," Charles said heavily, "the gunboats on Lake Borgne put up a gallant battle—I hear they lasted three hours."

"Lasted . . . Charles, what are you saying?"

"They were defeated, Lanna, but they fought against incredible odds. They were between the British and the Villère plantation . . . they are all either dead or in enemy hands."

General Andrew Jackson ordered a night march and clashed with the British in foggy darkness, fighting in biting cold.

The next day word reached the city that Old Hickory had been defeated. His men were in complete rout.

Now panic swept the city. The British were at the gates, nothing could stop them. Lanna and Zenobia watched from their window the frightened, hurrying crowds. Zenobia sobbed that they should run away too. At last, Lanna suggested that Zenobia should go to her room.

"Just go there and lock your door. I promise I won't let the British have you," Lanna said. She could not leave. Damon was a prisoner. If he were wounded . . . he would need her.

"No, no . . . we must run away . . . take the baby," Zenobia wailed hysterically.

Lanna raised her hand and brought it across Zenobia's cheek with a resounding slap that startled both women and made Richard howl in fright. The next moment the three of them were in each other's arms and Lanna was trying to murmur soothing words. "Zenobia, we must keep calm. I'm sorry I slapped you." She stopped, a sudden thought striking her. "You know what I just remembered? I had completely forgotten what day this is . . . do you know what day this is?"

Still sobbing, Zenobia shook her head.

"It's New Year's Eve. Tomorrow is the first day of the new year of 1815. Come, we will have a glass of wine, and a tiny sip for you, young man," she added to Richard.

At that moment Andrew Jackson was regrouping his forces and making plans. The Rodrigues Canal, flanked by cypress swamps on the west bank of the Mississippi: a thousand yard battle line consisting of regular infantrymen, dragoons, artillerymen and cannons, sharpshooters from Tennessee and Kentucky armed with Kentucky rifles. Jean Laffite and his privateers, sailors from the Indies, Frenchmen, New Orleans militia and some Choctaw Indians. They were all ready for the last battle.

Sir Jared Malford, on Admiral Cochrane's staff, was impressed with the audacity of the small group of American gunboats that challenged their flotilla on Lake Borgne.

Captain Lockyer was in command of the landing barges, and Sir Jared resented accompanying him as a subordinate. Still, Sir Jared was anxious to set foot on American soil with the first sailors. He desperately needed to bring glory on himself in order to regain his lost command.

The inquiry had, after a lengthy investigation, decided that the *Grey Wren* had been lost due to sabotage. And the captain of one of His Majesty's frigates who allowed someone to sabotage his vessel would wait a long time for another command. Damon St. Clair, of course. Who else? Sir Jared had often wondered about the fortuitous warning he and Indigo had received minutes before the explosion.

The air was absolutely still; the day would be hot. The British tars had rowed steadily for thirty-six hours. They were tired, hungry and grimy. They could see the boarding nets up on the American gunboats, the cannon at the ready. A small sloop to the southeast was attempting to join the other Americans, despite the lack of wind.

Captain Lockyer ordered Captain Roberts of the *Meteor* to take several barges and cut off the American sloop, whose little four-pounder threw a couple of harmless balls at the attackers. Meanwhile, the rest of the British barges would stop and have breakfast, allowing time for strength to return to aching muscles.

The American sloop with its crew of eight surrendered. Captain Roberts sent a crew aboard and guided his barges back to the main attack.

Across the water, Lieutenant Jones' tiny force stood at their guns and looked at the mass of barges. The British ate a leisurely breakfast and then the oars began to move again. The current had swept two of the gunboats, one of them Jones', ahead of the other three, so the line was no longer solid. Jones ordered his men to open fire. The cannon roared and a spout of water shot up well ahead of the oncoming barges. The other gunboats began to fire, all of them off the mark.

301

The barges made small targets and the British tars pulled hard as shells exploded about them. Now the barges began to fire back, balls and grape whistling through the hot still air. The water churned and a pall of smoke hung languidly over the gunboats. The Americans feverishly loaded and fired, seeing the barges close in around them. Shots were hitting the decks now. Men screamed and scrambled over slippery blood as they were hit.

Three of the barges forged ahead of the rest, and the cannoneers found the target, silencing the British guns aboard. One barge rowed away but the other two began to sink slowly. The Americans did not have time to stop and congratulate themselves, because four more barges had already taken the place of the three that had been turned back.

Captain Lockyer had already received a minor wound and now he was struck a second time, but he followed his men as they clambered aboard the gunboats, cutting their way through the boarding nets.

Lieutenant Jones fell, blood gushing from a deep shoulder wound. He crawled from the deck as his men grappled with the British who were pouring over the bulwark. Within minutes both Jones' gunboat and a second boat that had drifted out with the tides were in British hands. Now British sailors manned the cannon and fired on the three remaining gunboats. The barges pressed closer and two more gunboats were captured.

The British cannon were now turned on the last American gunboat. Resistance was useless. The captain surrendered to save the few men who were not already dead or wounded.

Through the smoke and over the moaning of the wounded, Damon St. Clair became aware that the roar of cannon had stopped. The engagement was over. His clothes were spattered with blood and his hands were burned from the red-hot guns. He had been knocked unconscious for a few minutes by flying debris, and there was a throbbing swelling on his scalp. He was luckier than many of his shipmates. The Americans had lost one-third of their men.

Captain Lockyer, despite his two wounds, was grimly satisfied. Those American gunboats could have harassed invading troops, and the British warships could not have approached the shallow waters of the lake. Lockyer's men had rowed for forty hours, had fought a hard battle, and now, in the noon day heat, they would have to row back up the channel to the anchorage. The American prisoners would be put aboard a storeship for transport to Cat Island.

It was Lucas Bassey who told Sir Jared that Damon St. Clair was among the prisoners.

Bassey had been Sir Jared's unwelcome shadow ever since the loss of the *Grey Wren*. Their former relationship had ended when Indigo had left Bassey. The captain now walked warily and never turned his back on the boatswain. It had angered Sir Jared that this uncouth bully had once possessed his beautiful wife, and he took every opportunity to punish Bassey, who was too stupid, or too wrapped up in plans of his own, to place himself outside of the captain's jurisdiction.

"You are sure it is St. Clair?" Sir Jared asked, his eyes gleaming with anticipation. "Is he wounded?"

"A lump on his head, that's all. Hit by a splinter, I reckon." Sooner or later, Bassey thought, the pretty little mulatto will put in an appearance. Maybe St. Clair knew where she was. If they could get a chance to question him . . .

"Thought maybe you'd want me to fetch him to you."

"I'll let you know if I need you further, bo'sun. You are dismissed," Sir Jared said.

Providence had been too kind. Sir Jared made haste to speak with Captain Lockyer about the information that could be obtained from a certain defeated enemy.

Captain Lockyer agreed absently as the surgeon bandaged his wounds. Lake Borgne was crucial to the British landing. Now that it was theirs the task of putting large numbers of men and equipment ashore had to be begun. It would be helpful to know how many men Andrew Jackson had to defend New Orleans.

"However, I can't spare any marines at the moment," Lockyer added.

"I shan't need them. My former boatswain is aboard the storeship *Gorgon* with the prisoners," Sir Jared replied.

Damon was startled when the young English marine called him by name. Damon's senses were slowly clearing. Vaguely he remembered picking up a badly wounded man and abandoning ship . . . the deck was slippery with blood, the air black with smoke and powder. At the time it seemed that if he gave all of his attention to taking care of the wounded man, who was unable to walk, Damon

303

would have direction and purpose for a mind that was strangely empty and a body that was curiously not his own.

Perhaps I'm dreaming, he thought, as he followed the English marine. Dreaming I'm on an English ship surrounded by redcoats and guns and stores . . .

He was shoved inside a cabin and the door closed behind him. Facing him was Sir Jared Malford, in full uniform, a sword at his side. In the shadows he could make out the bulk of the boatswain, Lucas Bassey, his face surly and his shirt streaked with blood.

"So. Mr. St. Clair. We meet on American soil." The thin lips pursed. "You are about to see your country's final humiliation."

Damon blinked and shook his head slightly, trying to clear the fog that clouded his mind.

"How many men does Jackson have defending New Orleans?" Malford asked. His voice seemed to be coming from a long way away.

It was absurd, Damon thought, that all he could think of at this moment was Lanna . . . and that other woman long ago.

"Were you my mother's lover?" he asked, as surprised by the question as Malford was. The weakness that clutched at arms and legs had somehow extended to his brain. What the hell did it matter what had happened twenty years ago? What had that to do with now . . . with the country about to be enslaved?

"I see," Sir Jared said, still in that distant, muted voice. "It was your mother's honor that concerned you more than your father's. You know, St. Clair, I could have forgiven your sinking of my poor merchantmen, could certainly have overlooked your taking my adopted daughter. Your Indigo was a fair exchange. Oh, yes, I knew she had belonged to you. Our friend Bassey here told me he had not been the first, did you not, Lucas?"

Bassey did not meet his captain's cold stare. He had followed orders since Indigo had left him for the captain, but he held a profound grudge. It was not only that he regretted losing the beautiful mulatto. The captain unreasonably resented the fact that she had first belonged to the boatswain, and his attitude toward him had changed abruptly. Telling the captain that they had both stolen her from St. Clair had not helped.

"You see, Mr. St. Clair," Sir Jared continued, "what I cannot forgive is that you cost me my command. I will answer your question about your late mother when you have told me how many men Jackson has and where they are deployed."

"Fifty thousand. And more coming from Kentucky," Damon said. A rough calculation of Jackson's actual forces would have been five hundred militia and a couple of regiments.

Bassey snorted. "Want me to 'ave a go at him?" he asked.

Damon swayed slightly on his feet. Sir Jared's face had gone out of focus. Something flashed before his eyes and registered on his mind a moment later. Sunlight reflecting on something lying across the sea chest just to the right of Sir Jared. A fencing foil, tip safely attached. He put his hand to his head, running his fingers over the raised bump on his scalp. Then he staggered as though about to lose consciousness.

"What about my mother?" He had to know . . . somehow it would make a difference to him and Lanna.

"I suppose it makes little difference now. Yes, she was my mistress. I tried to get her to leave your father. My own wife was dying. I would have married your mother, despite what the scandal of a divorce would have meant to my career. I believed she stayed with him out of a false sense of duty. But in the end she chose to run away with him."

"And die with him . . ." Damon blinked, rolled his eyes and pitched forward on the deck. His hand closed around the hilt of the rapier.

At the same instant Sir Jared said, "Stay where you are, bo'sun. I'll handle this." He withdrew his sword, without haste.

Damon was back on his feet, the tip removed from the rapier.

In the shadows Bassey laughed and moved backward.

"Wouldn't you say that both your mother and I paid dearly for our sins?" Malford asked, as though nothing had happened. His sword flashed and barely touched Damon's skin as it ripped through his shirt. Damon deflected it with the rapier.

Malford parried, then thrust. The sword sliced the underside of Damon's arm as he sidestepped to defend himself.

"Do you know what our footsoldiers call you Americans?" Malford asked. His sword brushed the rapier aside,

305

almost playfully. "Dirty shirts. No sense of honor. Refusing to fight in the time-honored traditions. Sneaking about the swamps under cover of darkness. Shooting from ambush. Hiding in the trees like pirates and thieves while the British soldier marches in formation." The sword displaced the air and connected briefly with the rapier blade, which rippled under the impact. The light rapier was no match for the heavy sword, and the cramped quarters offered little room to move out of range.

Damon suddenly saw an opening and lunged. The sword crashed down on the rapier, slicing the blade cleanly from the hilt. Damon was down on one knee, looking up into the cold steel and the colder blue eyes. He flung his arms about Malford's legs, sending him sprawling, grappling for the handle of the sword as they struggled. There was a clatter of steel as the sword slipped to the deck, and Damon smashed his fist into flesh and bone. He was unaware of the blows that were exchanged as he strove to reach Malford's throat. All the time he was thinking: Fencing lessons . . . all those hours of fencing lessons and I'm going to kill him with my bare hands.

Then Sir Jared jerked backward. A spasm passed through his entire body as his lips opened in surprise.

Behind him, Lucas Bassey held the bloody sword and watched his captain slip to the deck. Bassey gestured to Damon with the sword.

"See, it's like this, mate. Now they're going to think you killed him. Bloody swine. Stole me woman and then turned on me because I'd had her first. No need for you to worry, though. It's against regulations to duel with prisoners, see."

A nightmare, Damon thought. It doesn't make sense.

The citizens were united at last, on a cold grey dawn of the new year. Lanna stood on the balcony and watched the cannon rumble through the streets, followed by bearded, swarthy men. Dominique You and Beluche . . . even Gambie and his men in their odd and colorful costumes. The people sang . . . the *Marseillaise* and *Yankee Doodle Dandy.*

Women passed food to the men as they marched by. White men and black men, men in finely tailored clothes and men in rags, carrying rifles, muskets, swords, pistols, cutlasses. Old men, boys, masters, servants—the women cheered as they went by. Andrew Jackson sat on his horse and watched the ragtag force of two thousand who were to defend the city against twelve thousand highly trained and seasoned troops.

Outside the city they came upon signs placed there by the British:

LOUISIANANS, REMAIN QUIET IN YOUR HOMES. YOUR SLAVES SHALL BE PRESERVED TO YOU, AND YOUR PROPERTY RESPECTED. WE MAKE WAR ONLY AGAINST AMERICANS.

The British did not know that the citizens of Louisiana were all Americans, every last one of them.

CHAPTER 32

Lanna and Zenobia spent every waking minute turning blankets into shirts and pantaloons to send to the men in the encampment. The weather was miserably cold and wet. Men on both sides slept in the mud, eating cold food. They were surrounded by swamps as deadly as their human enemies. Alligators were a constant menace, feared by the British soldier more than the unseen sharpshooters who picked off their sentries. Some men simply disappeared, sucked beneath the quicksand.

Bent over their sewing, the two women jumped as the sound of cannon fire rattled through the air.

"Zenobia," Lanna said, "when the battle is over, we shall be returning to Charleston. Would you like to come with us?" Damon was all right, he had to be. Wounded perhaps, but surely not seriously.

Zenobia nodded, her eyes darting to the window as the cannon rumbled again. The shutters were closed, the door locked against the eerily deserted street. Richard was taking his morning nap, unconcerned.

"I'm not sure how it's done," Lanna continued, "but we will legally give you your freedom as soon as we can. So you can go wherever you please. I mean, if you feel Charleston would bring back unhappy memories . . . of Miss Beth."

"Oh, no, Miss Lanna. I want to stay with you. It wouldn't bring back no bad memories. Life's for the living, Miss Lanna, not the dead."

Lanna pricked her finger and she licked the tiny drop of blood. Zenobia's simple wisdom somehow shamed her. Brushing back her hair, which had begun to grow again and was hanging in her eyes, she reflected that she had prided herself on being the strong one, on keeping the frightened Zenobia from losing her wits. Yet in a single remark, the girl had shown her the answer to much of what had plagued her . . . and Damon.

A week had passed since the men had marched out to the encampment. Before the cannon shattered the peace, there had been that peculiar silence that comes before a great battle.

A British Congreve rocket went up, blazing a trail of flame across the sky. It was answered by a burst of American fire. Then slowly, sixty abreast, the redcoats began to march. Some carried scaling ladders, hastily hammered together. They cheered as they came, sunlight glinting on the scarlet coats, drums beating. In the minutes before they were enveloped in a solid sheet of American fire, they were a stirring sight.

"Give it to them, boys. Let's finish this business today," Jackson yelled to his men.

Instantly the American line was ablaze with cannon fire. Grape and cannister ploughed into the British column. The redcoats advanced, stepping over fallen comrades. They were soon within musket range and a constant rolling fire echoed through the forests. The vibration from cannonade and musketry shook the earth as flashes of fire illuminated the marching, falling men. A bloodied mass of scarlet and tartan lay in the mud.

On the right the second brigade rushed the canal. They scrambled into the ditch and attempted to bayonet their way up the ramparts, but they fell back under withering fire.

One British regiment broke into the crescent redan held by the Kentuckians but was cut to pieces before anyone came to exploit their success.

The pipers of the 93rd began to play "Monymusk," their regimental charge, and the tartan-trousered Highlanders broke into a run. Murderous fire hit them from an invisible enemy, and seconds before they reached the ditch they were ordered to halt. The officers and men were mowed down. Lacking orders, they stood their ground, neither advancing nor retreating.

309

Within an hour, over two thousand Englishmen lay dead or dying. They had faced a new type of war and been beaten by it. In the cruel Napoleonic wars they had advanced in their neat formations, their blood racing with the glory of battle. They had met the enemy on similar terms and crushed him.

Now they were beaten by a smaller force, an untrained mob of pirates and dirty shirts who hid behind barricades and blew apart their ranks. The American casualties would be one-tenth of the British losses.

By noon riders galloped into New Orleans to spread the word that the British had been thrown back and were in complete retreat.

That evening, the wounded, both American and British, began to reach New Orleans. The women put aside their sewing to care for the broken bodies. Everywhere there was the stench of blood and mutilated flesh. Some of the casualties were lodged in the barracks and the rest were taken into private homes.

Lanna bandaged, and forced water between parched lips. She did not have time to think about anything but caring for the wounded men.

A few evenings later, as she stood on the balcony where she could briefly escape the smell of death, she saw a familiar figure come loping up the street. She hurried downstairs to greet Alain. He was bearded, dirty and elated. He hugged her fiercely.

"Alain! Oh, Alain, I'm so glad to see you," she cried, flinging her arms about him.

"Damon?" he asked.

She shook her head. "I don't know. There's been no word."

He followed her into the kitchen, tiptoeing past the wounded men, who slept fitfully. She began to prepare food for him as he sat wearily at the table.

"What will you do, Alain?" she asked later when he had finished the meal. "When it's all over, I mean. Will you stay with Laffite?"

"I don't know, Lanna. Sometimes . . . I feel I would like a home. I feel I would like to take a wife."

"Yes, Alain. You should marry. What a wonderful husband and father you would be."

He looked at her in surprise, to see if she mocked him, but those large, expressive blue eyes were completely sincere.

310

"Eh, Lanna, you think a woman would marry me?"

"And be fortunate to be chosen to be your wife, Alain."
She looked away shyly. "I shouldn't be so bold . . . but I
believe I've always been a little in love with you myself."
The color rose in her cheeks and she added quickly,
"Damon and I . . . I believe, in spite of everything, we
were meant for each other. But how I wish sometimes he
had been blessed with your capacity for caring . . . had
been given your insight. Alain, there were many times I
believe I would have gone mad if you had not been my
friend."

"Ah, Lanna . . ." He did not trust himself to speak.

That night, despite his weariness, he lay awake for a
long time, thinking of what she had said. Perhaps, he
thought just before he fell into a deep and dreamless sleep,
it was time to leave the Baratarians. Perhaps he would
sail for England when the war ended, and find the lonely
castle where Indigo lived. And if not Indigo, then there
would be another woman, somewhere, one who would
look at him in the way Lanna had for a moment . . . when
she confessed that she had been "a little in love with
him." After all, many marriages were built on less than
that. Including the marriage of Damon St. Clair.

On the morning of the 23rd of January, they were
awakened by salvos of artillery. Zenobia screamed that the
city was again under attack.

Lanna ran to the windows, throwing open the shutters
and calling to the nearest passerby, "What is it? What is
happening? Have the British come back?"

"No, ma'am . . . Old Hickory's going to the cathedral
and we're going to pay tribute to him and his men for saving the city," came the yelled reply.

Lanna had been up all night with a boy who had in-
ternal wounds. He babbled incoherently in French and
clutched her hands, staring at her with glazed eyes. She
was still wearing the bloodstained gown she had worn for
the past two days. She thought tiredly that she must bathe
and change her clothes.

"Why don't you go and watch the celebrations," Lanna
said to Zenobia. "And take Richard. It will be a moment
to live in his memory . . . and if he's too young to remember I shall be able to tell him about the day that he
saw the great general. I shall stay here and take care of
the men."

311

Zenobia went gladly, an excited child dragging her by the hand. Lanna promised herself a bath as soon as the wounded men had been given food and water.

She was bending over the young Creole when the front door opened, sending a stream of sunlight across the blood-stained carpet.

"Zenobia . . . is that you? Is it over already?" she called over her shoulder.

"It was over nearly a month ago, Lanna," Damon said.

She whirled around, her hands clutching at her dirty gown. "Damon! Thank God you're all right."

She stood awkwardly, wanting to fling herself into his arms but overcome with shyness. He was a silhouette against the bright light from the street. She could not see his eyes or the expression on his face. A stranger, she thought, as I am a stranger to him . . . from different worlds, how could we ever have understood each other? And yet I love him . . . I'll always love him.

"You look like you've been busy," he commented with a glance at the sleeping men. Then he dropped heavily into the nearest chair.

"Can I get you something? Food . . . something to drink?"

"No. Where is Richard? He's all right?"

"Yes. Zenobia took him to watch Jackson's pageant. Are you wounded . . . your shirt . . ."

He glanced down at his torn and stained shirt and shook his head. "Nothing . . . a few cuts. Lanna, Sir Jared is dead."

"You saw him?"

"Yes. While I was a prisoner. I have to tell you that he interrogated me and there was a fight . . . of sorts."

"You killed him?"

"No. Bassey killed him. God knows why. But I would have killed him, if Bassey hadn't stepped in."

"What a terrible way to die," Lanna whispered, almost to herself. "Killed by one of his own men . . . I am sure he would have preferred to die in battle . . . or at sea. I knew he was with Admiral Cochrane . . . the lieutenant who was with Captain Lockyer at Jean Laffite's house told me. Indigo . . . we must let Indigo know." She looked at Damon, and a terrible pain knotted her throat. The words she wanted to say to him would not come. She was afraid that in a moment he would explain that he had merely come to tell her of Sir Jared's death.

312

"Indigo is still in England?" he asked.

"Yes. She won't need my help, of course, she'll be heir to Sir Jared's estate. But I believe I shall write and tell her she may stay at Kingsburch, if she wishes. She loves the place as much as I hated it."

"Love and hate," Damon repeated softly. "You use the words, but I wonder if you truly know what they mean."

"I know what they mean, Damon. I suppose with Sir Jared dead your quest for vengeance is over. Where will you direct your hatred and need for revenge now?"

There was a long pause and Lanna wished his face were not in the shadow, so that she could see if there was any feeling there. A sense of desolation was sweeping over her. His indifference was far worse than his hatred.

"I believe . . ." he said at last, "I'd already begun to see that my quest was useless, even before he died. We can't go back . . . there's no way to go back into the past and put things right again. We just disturb the order of the present. Have I destroyed the present, Lanna? Have I destroyed two lives for the sake of two others that can never be brought back?"

Lanna felt the tears sting her eyes and she sat down limply, her face turned from him. Her legs were a dead weight and her hands were trembling. "I don't know, Damon," she whispered.

"I loved a woman once, Lanna," he said. "I reached out for her and could never make her a part of my love or my life. I'm not excusing the way I've behaved to you—and to other women, but I'm telling you this so perhaps you'll understand. I spent my life avoiding love, guarding against offering love and not receiving it in return."

"The woman . . . who was she?"

"Some day I'll tell you all about her. She's in the distant past and I don't want to live in the past any longer. I want to live in the present and future. Lanna, I love you. I've been slowly learning to love you for a long time, only I didn't know it. I was blinded by hate and vengeance and jealousy . . . feelings that were too strong to allow tender thoughts into my mind. But now, I believe my love for you is strong enough to blot out all those useless passions from my mind."

He came slowly to his feet. "I'd been walking for some time . . . I was afraid I'd fall over. Lanna, I treated you badly. If you've changed your mind . . . about wanting to live with me . . ."

313

She was on her feet too, tears streaming down her cheeks. "Damon, I've loved you for a long time . . . oh, Damon, I never told you this, but I have a beautiful wedding dress . . . with a fourteen-yard train and a little pearl headdress. I left it in Charleston . . . I believe I left it there deliberately. Could we get married again, Damon, really married . . . in a church . . . and mean the vows we make?"

He grinned as he stepped into the sunlight, the lines of weariness lifting from his face. "Of course, if you wish. People might think it strange that our son attends our wedding, but I've never let convention get in my way before, no reason to start now." He reached for her and drew her into his arms. "You know, Lanna, you and I . . . and the war between America and England, how very much alike the endings have been."

"What do you mean—the endings?" Lanna asked, as her body pressed gratefully against his.

"Our glorious battle of New Orleans . . . was fought two weeks after they signed the Peace Treaty in Ghent. The war has been over since last Christmas Eve. That is why I am home—the British released me as soon as they heard. They were stunned . . . their casualties were so heavy compared to ours . . . they just simply turned us loose."

Lanna ran her hands over the muscles of his back. "Later, perhaps, I'll think of something profound to say," she whispered. "For now I'd rather talk about you and me."

"Well, we kept fighting our battles also, even when the outcome had been settled long ago." Damon smiled down at her, smoothing her hair from her forehead.

As always, in his arms with his mouth close to hers, war and battle and every other frailty of man receded far away. Lanna thought fleetingly that war and misery were the true dark gods . . . not the joyous surging of spirit and mind that carried two bodies away to heights of unsurpassed glory.